SEASON'S MEETINGS

Praise for *Secret Lies*

"I'm impressed at how well Dunne balances the darker story lines against the burgeoning romance between the two main characters to produce a remarkably good first novel...Dunne captures the intensity of first love, weaving in all the overwhelming wonder and joy as well as the doubts and fears of coming out. Dunne has created characters that feel real and easy for the reader to connect with."
—*C-Spot Reviews*

"When a book makes me laugh with intensity and can also bring me to tears, I stand up and take notice!"—*Rainbow Book Reviews*

"This is Amy Dunne's debut book and she is off to a flying start in the world of lesbian fiction. She's shown she can pen a good book on extremely difficult topics. Abuse, self-harm, homophobia and two inexperienced young women embarking on their first lesbian romance together, comprises just a small part of this well written and researched story."—*Terry's Lesfic Reviews*

"This is an excellent and enthralling first novel. Amy Dunne has caught the mood of 17-year-old emotions and experience brilliantly. On the one hand it is a tale of young adults emerging and exploring, with all the angst and melodrama that entails. On the other it is a serious exploration of both abuse and self-harm and the impact they have on these girls' internal and public lives."
—*Lesbian Reading Room*

"*Secret Lies* by Amy Dunne is a lesbian romance where you will find all the ingredients that make a wonderful story. Characters with whom you can relate on, difficult situations which are real and moving, and the promise of a happy ending for those who are courageous enough to fight for what they want...Amy Dunne surprised me with her characters, the perfect balance between dark and light scenes and the beautiful message based on self-respect, courage and how love can save you from the deeper abysms only if you're willing to take risks. Thanks for a wonderful journey!"
—*Lesbian Fiction Reviews*

By the Author

Secret Lies

Season's Meetings

SEASON'S MEETINGS

by

Amy Dunne

2014

SEASON'S MEETINGS

© 2014 By Amy Dunne. All Rights Reserved.

ISBN 13: 978-1-62639-227-4

This Trade Paperback Original Is Published By
Bold Strokes Books, Inc.
P.O. Box 249
Valley Falls, NY 12185

First Edition: December 2014

Credits
Editors: Lynda Sandoval and Cindy Cresap
Production Design: Stacia Seaman
Cover Design by Sheri (graphicartist2020@hotmail.com)

Acknowledgments

First and foremost, I wish to thank everyone at BSB for their hard work, support, and guidance. Radclyffe, you remain a constant inspiration. Sandy Lowe, thank you for always being there to answer my never-ending list of questions and offer support. Sheri, I can't express how much I love this cover—you're incredible. Lynda Sandoval, thank you for showing infinite patience with me. I truly appreciate all of your hard work, time, sense of humour, and guidance. Cindy Cresap, thank you for helping me improve my writing—I only sighed and shook my head a few times. Ruth Sternglantz, thank you for always being there to offer advice, answer my questions, and make me laugh. Thank you to Connie Ward, Toni Whitaker, and everyone else who works tirelessly behind the scenes.

I'd like to thank my family and friends for their unwavering love and support. I'm very blessed to have you all in my life. I'm fortunate that Christmas has always been a family affair. I look forward to the love, laughter, cheer, and closeness that we share every year, which is where the inspiration for this story came from. I love you all.

The world is now a better place thanks to the birth of beautiful Charlotte Mary Redfern Carroll in 2014. Charlotte, I hope you and your family have a wonderful time celebrating your very first Christmas.

I especially want to thank my mum, for listening to all of my mini meltdowns, believing in me, and supporting me during the whole writing process. I love you millions.

Chrissie Baxter, thank you so much for your wonderful support. It means so much to me.

Elizabeth Fisher, thank you for being a wonderful friend. I really appreciate your support, love, and laughter. You're a star.

And to the readers, thank you for your overwhelming support of my debut novel, *Secret Lies*. The response has been incredibly positive. Thank you for taking the time to write reviews, contact me directly, and share your thoughts. I hope you enjoy reading *Season's Meetings* as much as I enjoyed writing it.

Lou, thank you for being my wife, best friend, and soul mate. There isn't a day that goes by that I don't appreciate everything you do for me and our little family. You're the kindest, most selfless, and funniest person I've ever met. I love you with my heart, body, mind, and soul. For always.

Finally, I have to thank our very own little cairn terrier, Kimmy. She's the star of the cover and also features in this story. Thank you for all the doggy kisses, cuddles, slobbery toys, stubbornness, and the unconditional love you show us every day. Please try to not let the fame go to your little grey head, because you're already a diva. Your mummies love you very much.

Lou, I love you.
Thank you for making all of my dreams come true.

CHAPTER ONE

Catherine Birch handed over a crisp note to the taxi driver. "Keep the change." She climbed out of the warm car and was immediately chilled by the icy evening air. She made her way up the stone steps to the apartment doors, pulling her coat up close to protect her face from the bitter wind. She hated the cold.

Jeff the night porter opened the door and gave a nod. "Evening, Miss Birch. Not another late night at the office?" he asked.

Catherine gave a tired sigh. "I'm starting to think fifteen-hour working days are normal."

His expression showed he was concerned. "You need to take it easy sometimes or else you'll burn out."

"Night, Jeff. I'll see you tomorrow." She walked into the elevator and pressed the twentieth button. The circle lit up.

"Good night, Miss Birch," he said, as the elevator doors closed.

She'd lived in the apartment for seven years, and Jeff had worked as night porter for the entire time. He'd known her from when she was fresh out of university brimming with potential and eager to go out into the world and make herself a success. He'd seen the five years Paula and she had spent living together in the apartment. Three years of happiness followed by two of hell. He'd also witnessed the last year and a half after Paula had left. Catherine had thrown herself into work to avoid being alone in the apartment.

The elevator reached her floor. She took out her keys and opened the door to her apartment. Darkness greeted her and invoked the usual feeling of despair. It had been this way since Paula left.

She locked the door, dropped her keys onto the dresser, and

switched on the hallway lights. Her apartment remained mostly empty. Paula had taken all of her belongings, and Catherine hadn't gotten around to replacing them.

Every room in the apartment had white walls that she'd once considered light and refreshing. Now they were void of any sort of decoration and made the space feel large and cold.

The mirror Granny Birch had given her as a present hung on the wall above the dresser. It had a vibrant rainbow mosaic border and remained the only thing in the hallway with colour. Catherine studied her reflection carefully. Her hair remained tied up in a professional bun without a single wisp being out of place. She scrutinized her hair carefully, searching for any of the stray grey strands that seemed to have appeared overnight a few months ago. She found none.

Her eyes appeared larger through the lenses of her slim-framed designer glasses, but there was little sparkle in them. Her eyelashes were coated in black mascara that maximised their length and curl. Her eyebrows remained as she liked them, thin and perfectly styled. As she assessed the crow's feet around her eyes and the rest of her face for any signs of future wrinkles, she nibbled on her lower lip. They didn't look any worse, but they were still there. She promised herself as soon as they got noticeably worse she'd deal with them.

"Botox," she whispered under her breath. She cringed at the thought of having a needle inject her face. "Shit."

Her complexion still looked pale even with the additional colouring from the variety of makeup she wore. She'd lost a hell of a lot of weight since Paula had left. In fact, she couldn't remember a time when she'd been this skinny.

At work, her personal assistant, Eve, had been badgering her for months about her poor eating habits, but she'd dismissed them as interfering ramblings from the old woman. In truth, she had little interest in eating. Everything tasted bland and she got no enjoyment from the mundane task. Be that as it may, she made a silent promise to herself to try eating substantial food more often.

She turned her attention away from the mirror and walked into the living room. The room consisted of a single brown leather chair, which had originally come as a pair. A large flat screen TV stood on a stand in a corner but had been unused since Paula's departure. Three large bookshelves covered the back wall of the otherwise bare room, their shelves groaning beneath the volume of books filling them. An iPod and its docking station stood beside the phone and answering machine on a small table. Those were the few things that made up her living room—in which not much living was done.

The answering machine's red flashing light blinked at her from across the room. She didn't usually get many calls, but recently she'd come home to a new voicemail every night from the same irritating person. She crossed the room and reluctantly pressed play.

"Hi, Cat. It's Beth, again. If I didn't know you better, I'd think you were ignoring me...but you wouldn't do that, would you? Especially not to one of the mothers of your only goddaughter."

Catherine rubbed her face with her hands, feeling guilty. She'd received all of the messages but had felt too exhausted and been too busy to reply. "Give me a break, Beth," she said. The bedroom offered no respite for Catherine as she got changed; Beth's voice was as relentless as she was in person and followed her.

"I know the excuse is you're busy at work and haven't had a chance to reply."

Catherine pulled her shirt over her head. "I haven't."

"That's fine, but I want you to know one thing. I'm not going to give in and I'm not going away. Eventually, you'll have to speak to me if only to get some peace. Florence is five now. You haven't seen her since she was three."

Catherine pulled up her pyjama bottoms. "It hasn't been two years!"

"Two years, Cat. She's started preschool. She can write her own name and tie her own laces. She never shuts up. And you're missing out on it all. At this rate she'll be going on eighteen before you next see her. Can you remember what she looks like?"

Catherine made her way to the kitchen. "Yes, I remember what she looks like," she said, annoyed at being harassed in her own home. "This is why I don't return your calls."

"We want you to come and stay with us for Christmas and New Year celebrations."

Catherine froze, her heart began to pound, and her mouth went dry. *You didn't just say that!* She grabbed a glass off the draining board and poured the dregs from the already opened bottle of red wine. She lifted the glass to her lips and gulped the liquid down.

"This is your first Christmas without Granny Birch. I know you probably want to hide, pretend Christmas doesn't exist, spend the time drinking it away and reading books, but we're not going to let that happen."

Catherine placed the empty glass on the counter and wiped her mouth. "Why not? It sounds perfect." She opened a cupboard, took out a new bottle of red, and with trembling hands began opening it.

"You're coming to spend it with us in our home, which you also haven't seen since we moved in. There's going to be us three and a few other close friends. You'll get to see Florence open her presents. You'll get to eat a proper Christmas dinner instead of a nasty frozen microwave meal for one. Please, Cat? Please say yes? For Katie, Florence, and me, please? Have a think about it and I'll phone you tomorrow evening so we can talk. We love you."

Catherine poured another large glass of wine, not bothered that it hadn't had time to breathe. She picked up the glass and hesitated before picking up the bottle and carrying them both into the living room. She sat in her chair, listening to the silence and drinking.

She loved Beth, Katie, and Florence, but she couldn't spend Christmas and New Year's with them. It'd be unbearable.

She'd always been forced to spend the holidays with Granny Birch. Family responsibility, tied with the ongoing threat this was probably her last Christmas on earth, had meant Catherine had been unable to refuse. When Paula and she were together, it'd been pleasant enough.

The last two years had been quiet affairs shared with only Granny Birch and herself. She'd stayed over at Granny Birch's house in the room she'd inhabited since she was nine. They'd spent their time eating, drinking, playing cards, and reading lots of books. Which were the same things they'd spent the last twenty-two years doing. As much as Catherine complained about it, she'd secretly always enjoyed going back home and spending time with Granny Birch.

Six months ago, Granny Birch had passed away, leaving Catherine all alone. She'd gone back to her house only once, to choose some mementos to keep. They were now stowed in two large boxes in the unused dining room. She hadn't been sure what to do with the house. It'd been her home for some years, but primarily it'd been Granny

Birch's home, and when she'd last visited it'd been a different place. It'd been empty, with only haunting memories for company. In the end, she decided to sell the house. She'd never return to live there, and the house and garden, which had been Granny Birch's pride and joy, deserved to be maintained and appreciated.

The house was snapped up by a young family wanting to escape the city. Catherine felt sure Granny Birch would've approved of them. The money from the sale of the house, Granny Birch's inheritance, and her parent's inheritance all sat in her savings account growing with interest. With the exception of university fees and the purchase of the apartment, the majority of the money in her savings account remained untouched. She earned far more each month from her salary than she could spend and so a large percentage of her wages also went into the account.

"I miss you, Granny Birch. I can't believe you've left me here all alone." She poured another glass of wine and sipped it. "How the hell am I going to get out of Christmas? Beth's plain evil when she sets her mind to something."

For the next two hours, she tried to come up with a decent excuse to get out of spending Christmas with her only best friend and her lovely family. The more she thought about the sickly sweet celebrations, the presents, the tree, the colourful decorations, the holiday spirit, and the good cheer she'd have to fake, the more she drank to console herself. She decided to continue ignoring Beth's calls for the time being. There were four weeks until Christmas, and if she tried hard enough, she might succeed in avoiding speaking to her altogether.

"Bah, humbug." She scowled at the empty wine bottle on the floor. "I love you, Beth, but I'm not spending Christmas with you. No way." She sliced the air dramatically with one hand. "And another thing—" Her trail of thought was interrupted. She felt unwell and knew she'd made the fatal mistake of consuming the entire bottle of wine on an empty stomach. "I need to go to bed."

She sluggishly crawled off her seat, returned the glass to the sink, and discarded the wine bottle in the recycling bin. After stumbling into her bedroom, she collapsed on the bed and quickly fell asleep.

❖

Catherine glared menacingly at the staff team seated silently around the conjoined rectangular tables. The latest regional sale figures were in, and Catherine's inept supervisor had demanded she talk to the team and resolve the issues immediately. She'd spent the last forty minutes ranting, motivating, strategizing, and basically being a royal bitch to them.

Catherine loathed Jonathon Bowler-Hays and resented he'd been promoted two years ago to the position of Executive Regional Director of Sales over her. The professional rejection still smarted and often flared up in situations like this one when she was left to do all the hard and dirty work while he was nowhere to be seen.

Jonathon was the grandchild of the organization's founder, and that prestige had gotten him everything. He had no concept of what was involved or how to fulfil his current role. It was Catherine who ended up doing all the hard work, enforcing policies, and formulating intricate sale strategies, while Jonathon kept the title and reaped all the rewards.

Catherine straightened her shirt with both hands. She disliked this part of her job but also happened to be rather good at it. "So, if we don't dramatically increase our sales before the Christmas break, January's going to be a bleak month. With the current economic situation I'm sure I don't need to emphasise how difficult finding a new job is. If you want to still have a job in the New Year, you've got to sell more in the next two and a half weeks than you did for the whole of last month."

Tom, a lanky man with thinning blond hair, raised his hand. Catherine nodded curtly, giving him permission to speak.

"Isn't that basically a threat, Catherine?"

Catherine folded her arms and regarded him coolly. "No, Tom. It's an honest prediction of what's likely to happen. I'm not here to be nice, to be liked, or to tell you comforting little lies. I'm here to get results."

"But it's so close to Christmas," Alice said in an infuriatingly nasally whiney tone. She was plump with grey hair and a bright red nose from her incessant nose blowing. Large novelty Christmas tree earrings hung from both earlobes. "What you're asking is practically impossible."

"What I'm asking is difficult, but not impossible," Catherine said. Exasperated by the attitude and glares she was receiving, she tried to boost their morale. "If we follow the strategies and give our all, we can achieve our targets. We've a distinct advantage. While all the other departments and sale companies dramatically slow down and take their eye off the prize in the lead-up to Christmas, we can reap the benefits. Unfortunately, there are going to be some restrictions. From this moment on, no more annual leave requested before Christmas will be authorised—"

"Just because you have no family or friends doesn't mean you can take it out on us. We should be getting ready to celebrate Christmas, not being threatened with redundancy and certainly not being given an impossible task to complete. My daughter's Christmas play is coming up, and there's no way in hell I'm missing it because you won't authorise my leave. I'll go to HR," Alice said, slamming one of her hands on the table. Murmurs of agreement were voiced until Catherine's glare cut them off.

"Tell me where exactly in your contract it states leading up to Christmas you can be lazy and forgo your responsibilities?" She paused, staring each person down in turn. "That's right. It doesn't." Catherine began to pace up and down, daring someone to interrupt or argue with her. Her temper seethed beneath the surface, and it wouldn't take much to send her over the edge. *Spoilt, selfish, lazy idiots.* "Feel free to speak to HR, Alice. They'll tell you, as stated in your contract, all annual leave must be requested with one month's prior notice. Any requests previously granted within a shorter period were done so at my discretion." The expression on Alice's face gave Catherine tremendous satisfaction, but the dangling earrings, which blatantly contradicted the strict formal dress policy, only fuelled her anger. "And as for the comment regarding my personal life, from this moment onward, you're—"

A loud knock was followed by the door bursting open. Eve, Catherine's personal assistant, barged straight in. She paid no attention to the staff and focused solely on Catherine. Her brown face looked drawn, and her usual bossy disposition seemed quelled."My apologies for interrupting, but I've been made aware of a serious personal situation. There's a phone call waiting."

Catherine's seething temper calmed to mild annoyance. "Okay. Whoever the call is for may be excused from the remainder of the meeting."

Eve grimaced and looked at the floor. Her tone remained soft, but with an edge of urgency. "The phone call is for you, Catherine."

Catherine opened her mouth to speak but couldn't find the words. *For me? There isn't anyone to call me.* The last time she'd received a message like this from Eve was when the hospital had phoned to tell her about Granny Birch's passing. She had no family left.

"Catherine? Shall we go?" Eve asked.

Catherine swallowed hard and nodded. She started toward the door and then hesitated to glance back. "Meeting's over."

She followed Eve out into the hallway and in the direction of her own office, struggling to keep up with the quick pace. For an oldie who frequently moaned about arthritis, Eve could sure move when she wanted to.

"I don't have any family, Eve," Catherine said. "There's no one who'd call me."

Eve didn't slow down. "Beth's on the phone. She says it's urgent."

Fear and guilt crashed down over Catherine. "Beth? Is she okay?" Fear suddenly rendered her paralysed to the spot. "Is Florence okay? Nothing's happened to her, has it?"

Eve walked the last few steps past her own festively decorated desk and opened the door to Catherine's office. "As far as I'm aware, Florence is fine."

Catherine's relief was short-lived as another thought struck her. "Is Katie okay? What's happened?"

Eve shook her head. "You need to speak to her, Catherine. I don't know anything."

Catherine took a deep breath and nodded. Not daring to ask any more questions, she entered her office. Eve closed the door behind her. Catherine tentatively walked over to her desk. The red light was flashing on her phone.

Feeling weak, she sat in her leather chair and picked up the handset. She tried her hardest to ignore the disturbing thoughts churning over in her head. *Whatever it is, I need to find out instead of torturing myself.*

She drew a deep breath, held it, and slowly released it as she pressed the button next to the red light. "Hello?"

"Cat?" a familiar voice asked calmly.

"Is Florence okay? What's happened?" Catherine asked. She covered her eyes with her spare hand, bracing herself for the answer. The line remained silent for a few long seconds as if Beth was hesitating. *Oh, shit! If she can't say it, then it's got to be bad.*

"Please don't be too angry with me?" Beth asked sheepishly.

Catherine's tense shoulders slumped; her hand lowered from her eyes and clenched into a fist on the table. "There's no emergency, is there?"

"Well, it depends on how you look at it. I've called you every night for over a month. I was beginning to think you were dead in your apartment and nobody had realised. That, in my opinion, is classed as an emergency—"

"I was ignoring you, Beth. If I was dead in my apartment don't you think Eve would've noticed?" Catherine glanced up. The floor-to-ceiling glass walls of her office normally had blinds drawn to give her privacy. She'd not had time to close them this morning, and from her desk she had the perfect vantage point to spot Eve, watching her from behind her desk. In a flash, Eve's face disappeared behind her computer screen, but her grey hair bobbed above the red tinsel framing the screen. "I should've known she was in on it, too. I'm going to make her suffer for this."

"Eve had nothing to do with it—"

"Yeah, and I'm Santa Claus," Catherine said. Her temper was rising again because she'd been made to look a fool.

"I'm glad you brought up the subject of Christmas. That's why I'm calling."

Catherine bit a fingernail. How could she have been stupid enough to use Santa as an example?

"Please agree to come and spend the holidays with us? I promise it won't be anywhere near as bad as you think it will."

"Thank you for the offer, but I've already got plans."

"No you haven't, Cat."

"Actually, I have."

"What are your plans and who are they with?" Beth asked in her *I know you're lying to me* tone that Catherine hated.

"It's going to be a quiet affair and you don't know these friends. I'm spending it with Chris and his friend." Catherine nibbled her bottom lip, waiting to see if Beth believed her blatant lie.

"Would that be Kris Kringle and one of his little helpers?"

"Beth, I love you. There's no way I'm coming to stay with you, though. Nothing you can do or say is going to change my mind. I'm adamant. Seriously, you need to accept it."

After what felt like a lifetime of silence, Beth finally spoke. "Okay, I understand. I accept there's nothing I can say that will change your mind."

Catherine sat back in her chair, startled. *This was too easy.* She began to grow suspicious. "Good."

"I'm sorry, Cat."

"For what?" Catherine asked. Her palms grew sweaty and she blotted them on her trousers.

"I've tried to be reasonable with you. I've given it my best shot, but you're right. I can't change your mind. You've left me no choice." Beth sighed dramatically. "I've got to use my secret weapon. I'm sorry."

Catherine felt a chill slither down her spine. *Secret weapon?* The realisation dawned on her a split second too late for her to react. "Beth—"

"Hello, Aunty Cat. I miss you lots. I got your Christmas present today from Tim the postman, but Mummy Beth and Katie won't let me open it. It looks big. What is it? Is it a puppy?" Florence asked without pausing to take a single breath.

Catherine could hear Beth's whispered voice in the background. *The conniving witch!*

"I've been such a good girl this year. Mummy Beth says you *and* Santa are both coming to see me. It's going to be the bestest Christmas ever—'specially if I get a puppy from Santa. I'd call him Bob. Are you coming to visit, Aunty Cat? Please? I miss you."

It was over. Catherine's steel resolve melted into a gooey mess. "Yes, I'm coming to visit, Florence. I miss you, too."

Damn you, Beth!

Twelve minutes later, Catherine placed the handset down and buried her head in her hands. *I'm screwed.* Beth had refused to let her off the phone until she'd promised Florence she would spend Christmas with them.

A gentle rapping sounded on her office door, but Catherine chose to ignore it. She wasn't finished wallowing in self-pity yet.

The door creaked open and someone came inside the room. Catherine knew only one person would dare to venture inside without her granting permission. Peering through her hands, Catherine asked, "Why would you do this to me? You've ruined everything."

Eve gave a loud tut as she walked over to the desk and placed down a steaming cup of fragrant coffee and a small dish. "Stop being so dramatic."

Catherine glared ferociously at the cup, the delicious looking muffin, and finally at Eve. "Bribery? Or are you feeling guilty? Which you should feel, by the way."

Eve sucked her teeth in annoyance and sat opposite. "Neither. I happen to know what's best for you."

Catherine sat back in her chair and folded her arms defiantly. "I'm thirty-one, Eve. I'm more than capable of deciding what's best for myself. You're my assistant at work. In no way does that give you permission to interfere or meddle in my life."

Eve raised an eyebrow. "I made the pumpkin muffins last night. Eat it and then we'll talk. You're always cranky when you haven't eaten—"

"I'm not cranky," Catherine said, scowling. "And I'm not hungry either." A loud, ravenous growl sounded from her stomach. Embarrassed, she tightened her folded arms.

A twitch of a smile touched the corners of Eve's mouth. "How did the meeting go?"

"Awful. They're lazy and workshy," Catherine said. She reached across the table and drew both the coffee and muffin closer. She deliberately didn't look at Eve as she bit into the muffin. It tasted delicious and she had to physically restrain herself from gorging on it.

"Well, it certainly looked intense in there," Eve said. She absentmindedly began tapping her glittery red fingernails on the desk. "So am I booking you a flight for Beth's or not?"

Catherine wiped her mouth with the back of her hand. "Yeah. There's no way I can get out of it unless I'm lucky enough to break my leg or something."

Eve gave a loud tut. "Here you go." She pushed some papers across the desk.

Catherine scanned the text from the first page quickly. "You've already booked the tickets. I should've known."

"You wouldn't have wanted them to be sold out now, would you?" Eve smiled sweetly.

Catherine skimmed the rest of the pages, making mental notes. A taxi was booked for Friday evening after the office Christmas party and would take her to the airport. The flight was two hours, and thankfully, she was seated in first class. Beth had already promised to pick her up from the airport and drive her to their house, which was situated in the middle of bloody nowhere. "What about presents and things?"

"They've already been purchased, wrapped, and posted. Beth and Katie have some decorative candle holders and Florence has a SpongeBob SquarePants pirate ship."

Catherine looked up. "A pirate ship?"

Eve smiled. "Yes, I've had it on good authority she wants one."

"Not as much as she wants Bob the puppy," Catherine said dryly. "If I make a list can you get me a few things and ship them up to Beth's, please?"

"I'll have to send them before tomorrow afternoon or they won't get there on time." Eve frowned and sat back in the chair. "What things are you after?"

Catherine scribbled a quick list of items and handed over the sheet. Eve started reading and Catherine waited for her response. The first few items were fairly mundane, but the more Eve read, the higher one of her eyebrows arched.

"A drum kit and a crate of red wine?"

"Don't worry. The wine's for me," Catherine said. "Make a note the drum kit is a New Year's Day present for Florence and can't be opened before."

"What on earth are you up to?" Eve asked.

"I want to make sure my lovely goddaughter starts her New Year with a fun hobby. What child doesn't want to learn to play the drums?" *And Beth's New Year starts with a bang.*

"You're wicked," Eve said as she continued to read. Suddenly, she snapped her gaze from the paper to Catherine. "I'm not getting Florence a puppy called Bob, Catherine. That's not going to happen, and you should be ashamed of yourself for suggesting it," she said, her Jamaican accent becoming more pronounced with her irritation.

"It was worth a shot." Catherine shrugged. In her mind she could picture the expression on Beth's face. *That would ensure this was the last invite I ever get for Christmas.* "You're a spoilsport."

CHAPTER TWO

Catherine rushed down the busy pavement, nimbly weaving in and out of the herd of people charging against her. Although it was after four in the afternoon, the sky was growing dark and the chilly temperature was plummeting. When she reached the familiar heavyset doors, she took a moment to blow out a deep breath that formed a rolling cloud of steaming fog.

Cool and collected, she pushed open one of the doors and made her way into the building. The public library was welcoming thanks to the lights and warmth. As Catherine walked toward the Homework Room, she felt a sense of calm wash over her.

She loved this place, but then she'd yet to find a library she didn't love. There was something comforting in the quietness. The rows upon rows of shelves holding books gave protection.

She'd only been volunteering here for a little over a year, but it had made a huge difference to her life. It meant two nights a week she'd something that didn't revolve around work or spending time in her depressing apartment.

As she approached the closed door, she could hear the muffled lively chattering of children's voices. With a smile, she turned the handle and went inside.

"Hi, Catherine," Rose said. She passed by busily setting up the tables and chairs.

"Hello. Sorry I'm late."

Rose stopped, looked up pointedly at her, and smiled. "Don't worry. It means the world you're here as often as you are. I don't know how we'd cope without you."

Catherine shuffled her feet, uncomfortable with the gratitude.

Rose was the coordinator, and two other single parents, James and Veronica, volunteered on the same days Catherine did. They were both busy watching over the children, but they'd smiled in greeting when she'd entered.

She glanced around the room and took in the usual faces, noting one in particular was missing. Twelve children were scattered around the room. The seven younger children's ages varied from five to nine, and they were either rushing around or playing on the carpet, their happy high-pitched voices bellowing out. The five older children were aged up to thirteen and sat away from the younger children talking about something important, if their serious expressions were anything to go by.

She knew all of them—their names, personalities, likes, and dislikes, although the older they got the more frequently the last two aspects changed. Their reasons for coming to Homework Club varied. Some parents didn't finish work until later, and this was a safe educational place where their children could come after school. Some children came because they wanted to. Others came because their parents or teachers felt some additional help might benefit their educational development.

"Should I help set up?" Catherine asked. She was eager to get started.

Rose walked over to her. In a whispered voice she said, "I was hoping maybe you could do some one-to-one work today?"

Catherine nodded. "Of course. Who with?"

"Dominic," Rose said, lowering her voice so it was barely audible. "He's upset today but won't talk to anyone. He's hiding under the table in the far corner."

Catherine had noted Dominic was missing when she'd first glanced around the room, and looking again, found she still couldn't see him. "Okay, I'll see what I can do."

Rose thanked her before asking the children to pick up their homework folders and come sit at a table.

Catherine walked over to the deserted corner of the room where two rectangle tables had been placed together. The furniture in the room came in two different sizes. Half of the chairs and tables were smaller in stature, perfect for the younger children. The rest were average-sized.

Catherine pulled out one of the miniature chairs and blew out a breath, wishing she'd had the foresight to carry a decent-sized chair over with her. She always felt uncomfortable when using the tiny furniture.

She lowered herself into a sitting position, hoping the chair would hold her weight. Her muscles and back immediately complained in protest. Managing to perch half of one bottom cheek on the seat, she planted her feet firmly on the ground and reluctantly accepted her knees were going to remain up to her chin.

She knocked on the tabletop.

"Go away. I'm not talking to nobody," a tiny voice said.

We're off to a great start!

"We don't have to talk, but I was here first so I'm not going anywhere," Catherine said. She was trying to unbutton her coat and simultaneously prevent herself from falling off the chair.

"You wasn't. I've been here for ages."

"Not as long as I have, I'm afraid," Catherine said. The chair legs groaned beneath her weight.

"You just got here. I've been under here forever."

"I thought you weren't talking to anyone?" Catherine asked good-naturedly. Her coat was going to have to stay on for the foreseeable future. After a few moments of silence, she got a reply.

"You tricked me."

Catherine smiled. "Maybe I did. Is it okay if I sit here for a bit? I've had a horrible day."

After some shuffling, Dominic looked up at her from beneath the table. His handsome face showcased well-chiselled features, unblemished brown skin, and vibrant hazel eyes that sparkled with innocent curiosity. His forehead was creased with a deep frown and his eyebrows were narrowed.

"You had a bad day?" he asked, his voice quiet and expression solemn.

Catherine nodded. "Yes. I had to tell some people off at work and they didn't like it."

Dominic chewed on his bottom lip and then shifted from kneeling to sitting down crossed-legged. "Were they naughty?"

"No, not naughty. They need to try a bit harder before Christmas."

Dominic nodded and then seemed to think hard about something. He rubbed his nose on his sleeve. "I had a bad day, too."

Catherine leaned forward. "You did?" she whispered. He nodded dramatically. "What happened?"

His tiny shoulders shrugged. "We had to read our lines out loud for the Christmas play. I'm the head shepherd." A flicker of pride transformed his face before quickly disappearing. "But I didn't do it good. I kept messing it up."

Catherine felt her throat tighten. "Maybe it wasn't that bad—"

"It took me ages to read them and I got loads of words wrong. Everybody was laughing at me, and I got really mad and ran away. Mrs. Baxtor shouted at me and writ a note in my diary for my mum. I'm so stupid," Dominic said. He folded his arms.

"No, you're not. You're clever," Catherine said. Anger swelled in her chest. Dominic struggled with reading and writing, and there was a strong possibility he was going to be diagnosed with dyslexia. They were waiting on further tests to confirm it. Both his self-esteem and confidence had suffered because of his struggle and he attended Homework Club for additional support with his literacy. His teacher should've done something to help him instead of letting him go through such an embarrassing ordeal.

She remembered the embarrassment and humiliation from her own past. An involuntary shudder swept through her body. It all felt a little bit too familiar. Memories and emotions she'd kept hidden deep inside were awakened. Clenching her jaws and grinding her teeth, she forced herself to swallow the bitter memories down.

She took a shaky deep breath and then said, "In fact, you're one of the most intelligent seven-year-olds I know." With each word she felt her heart race and her stomach lurch. Thankfully, she hadn't stuttered.

"Really?" Dominic asked. He perked up a little.

"Yes," Catherine said in a matter-of-fact tone. Her legs and lower back were aching from being perilously perched on the chair. Accepting defeat, she got off the chair and sat on the worn green carpet instead. "Did I ever tell you about my stutter?"

Dominic's eyes widened. He wriggled closer and shook his head.

"Do you know what a stutter is?" Catherine asked.

Dominic nodded. "My friend at school called Oscar has a stutter. He can't talk right sometimes, but I don't mind 'cause I can tell what he means. He's a sheep in the Christmas play. He has no lines."

Catherine gave a weak smile and wrapped her arms around herself, warding off a chill. "Well, when I was a child I had a stutter like your friend Oscar. I struggled to get my words out. It always made me sad because I couldn't say what I wanted to. I hated having to speak or read out loud in front of people because I felt silly and stupid. It got so bad I used to keep quiet and only speak when I had to."

"I hate having to read out loud as well," Dominic said. His expression looked thoughtful. "Why don't you stutter no more?"

"My granny could see how much it was upsetting me. She told me to be proud of myself and to not let other people bother me. Every night she'd help me practice reading out loud, and with time I got better at it. When I got a little bit older than you are, I started having classes after school to help me."

"Like I come here after school and practice my reading and writing?" Dominic smiled brightly, showing his cute dimples.

"Exactly," Catherine said and then lowered her voice. "But it wasn't easy. It took a lot of hard work and sometimes on rare occasions I still stutter a little bit, but it's okay."

"Maybe if I work hard I won't mess up my lines no more."

"That's a great idea," Catherine said. "How about you read your lines to me and we practice them lots and lots so they stick in your brain so you remember them? Then you won't have to read them out again because you'll know them by heart."

Dominic sat up and jiggled excitedly on the spot. "Okay." He scampered off to bring back his homework folder. Catherine took the opportunity to stand and shake off the pins and needles prickling up her left foot.

Rose appeared carrying an average-sized chair, which she placed in front of Catherine. "Great job, Catherine. Here you go. This might make life a bit more comfortable."

Catherine opened her mouth to say thanks, but Dominic appeared beside her in a flash brandishing some ruffled sheets of paper. Rose shot her a wink before leaving.

"Right, let's get started," Catherine said. She sat, scooting her chair closer to the table. While she was scanning the lines of text for the head shepherd's lines, Dominic pulled up a chair next to hers. He sat and splayed his arms across the table.

"Miss Birch? I'm a bit scared."

Catherine dropped the sheets and turned to face him. He looked so small and vulnerable it made her heart ache. "Of reading out loud?"

Dominic shook his head. "I'll be okay when I learn my lines by heart. I'm scared 'cause…" His bottom lip began to quiver slightly and tears threatened to puddle in his eyes.

"Because of what?" Catherine whispered. She gently tapped the back of one of his hands.

"My mum's gonna be so mad at me about running off, and Mrs. Baxtor says she knows Santa and tells him when we're good or bad. She's gonna tell him about me being bad and I'm gonna get no toys on Christmas Day."

Catherine watched helplessly as tears began to roll down his cheeks and snotty sniffles were quieted by the disgustingly grubby sleeve of his jumper.

"Your mum might be a little bit angry, but only because she loves you. Running away from the teacher isn't something you should do because it could be very dangerous. You know that, don't you?"

Dominic nodded. His head bowed in shame as more quiet sobs escaped. "Yeah, I know."

"You have to tell her you're sorry and explain why you felt you had to run away. But you must also promise to never do it again, Dominic."

"I promise," he said. His bottom lip pouted and tears continued to fall. "I didn't mean to. And I didn't wanna upset my mum or make her mad at me."

"I suppose I could have a word with your mum when she comes to pick you up. Tell her how good you've been this evening and our plan about getting you to learn the lines, if you want?"

His head shot up. "Yes, please, that would be good," he said, wiping his tear-stained face with both hands. "What should I do about Santa Claus?"

Catherine took a breath and tried to think of her response. She was already seriously out of her depth in the uncharted seas of children's imagination, hopes, and dreams.

"Erm, well, let's see." She tapped her fingers on the table while desperately trying to think. "Am I correct in thinking Santa has a list?" Dominic nodded vigorously. "Excellent. So if you're good, I mean the best behaved little boy in the whole wide world, he'd see that, wouldn't he?"

Dominic broke out into a grin, revealing his white teeth and the gap at the front from a missing tooth. "Yeah, he'd see I was good and I'd be on the nice list again."

Catherine sat back in the chair. "Well, it seems to me everything's sorted. If you're incredibly well-behaved, polite, work hard at school, learn all of these lines, and never run away from Mrs. Baxtor or any other teacher again, you should be fine."

"Thank you, Miss Birch," Dominic said. He suddenly leapt forward, taking Catherine by surprise as he wrapped his arms around her neck, giving her a big hug. After getting over the initial shock, Catherine gave him a gentle pat on his back.

"Right, we'd better get started on these lines so we can show your mum," she said. Dominic released her from his embrace. He sat back down and looked up at her, his eyes sparkling and his lips curved in a big smile. His chest was notably puffed out with pride, his legs swung back and forth beneath the chair, and the rest of his body seemed to be surging with energy.

Reading through the lines of text, she said, "So you're shepherd number—"

"I'm the head shepherd."

"Of course you are," Catherine said. She found the correct lines for Shepherd Number One. "Do you think you can handle the responsibility of being head shepherd?"

Dominic's expression turned serious. "Yeah. I'm gonna be the bestest head shepherd there ever was."

Catherine gave a curt nod and placed the page between them. "I have no doubt you will be. This is your first line," she said underlining the sentence with a green pencil. "Take it nice and slow. Only I can hear you, and if you get stuck I'll help."

For the next half an hour, Dominic practiced all eight of his lines, and by the end of it he could reel them off confidently. Catherine congratulated him but also reminded him, although he knew them now, he had to keep practicing so he didn't forget them.

When his mum arrived Catherine had a quick chat with her. She explained why he'd been so upset, mentioned the note from Mrs. Baxtor, and praised his hard work this evening. As she watched them leave the library she couldn't help but smile. The warm fuzzy feeling stayed with her for the remainder of the night.

CHAPTER THREE

Catherine mustered her evilest look and aimed it at the back of Jonathon Bowler-Hays's bulbous head. She wished there was something hard and heavy at hand to throw at it. He'd left her office seconds ago, and now she watched as he playfully joked and high-fived some of the men and flirted with some of the women while making his way to the elevators.

"Bastard." She massaged her temples. Everything was going to shit, and once again, she was expected to be the bearer of bad news. She picked up her receiver and asked Eve to come into the office.

"It's such good news about the figures," Eve said. She closed the door behind her. "But you don't look happy. What's happened?"

Catherine let out a growl through clenched teeth. "Knob-head there—"

Eve let out a loud tut as she sat in the chair.

"Well, he is," Catherine said angrily. Eve must have sensed this wasn't the time to argue because she remained uncharacteristically quiet, allowing for Catherine to continue. "Jonathon was happy to tell everyone about the figures and take all the credit as usual. But what he didn't tell them is they've now got to complete all of their reports before they break up for the holidays. The deadline is tomorrow at midday."

"What on earth?" Eve's hand shot to her mouth. "He can't seriously expect that? They all break up today and the Christmas party is this evening."

"Apparently, it's what the great and powerful board of directors have ordered. He hasn't got the balls to tell everyone himself, so once again he's left it to me to do. He's probably known for days, if not weeks, and didn't mention it."

Eve continued to shake her head. "Oh, Catherine. What are you going to do?"

Catherine looked out at the staff communal office area. Her team buzzed happily. They'd achieved their targets and were clearly excited about the Christmas party and breaking up. How could she tell them their hard work wasn't over? That although they'd done exactly as she'd asked of them, the goalposts had been moved farther away? It wasn't fair. She might be the office bitch, but there was no way she was going to reward their hard work by demanding they try to meet unachievable targets—especially not today, of all days. Her stomach twisted with fiery anger. Her jaws bunched and her fists clenched tightly. She turned back to Eve and said, "I'm going to do them myself."

Eve's eyes widened. "It takes each of them hours to do their own. Doing them all by yourself isn't possible—"

"It has to be. There's no other way."

"Your flight is this evening."

Catherine bit her bottom lip and nodded. "I know. I'll have to try my hardest to get through them as quickly as possible. Can you arrange for the taxi to pick me up here instead of at the venue?"

"Of course. Is there anything else I can do?"

"Don't let me be disturbed, under any circumstances," Catherine said. She rolled her shoulders, tilted her head from side to side, and cracked her knuckles. She focused on the screen and opened up the first report.

❖

Catherine heard the distinct knock on her door, but ignored it. Her attention remained focused on the current report even when the door opened and the soft tread of footsteps made their way across the carpeted floor.

"Catherine, you need to stop for a while," Eve said, her concern palpable.

Catherine gave a quick shake of her head but didn't look away from the screen.

"With the upmost respect, if you don't stop and have a break right this minute, you'll give me no choice but to intervene."

"I asked not to be disturbed," Catherine said. The last thing she needed was Eve on some kind of mission. She wanted to power on through these reports until they were done.

"And up to now you haven't been disturbed, but if you don't stop I'll be forced to physically remove you from that desk of yours," Eve said, steel determination lacing her tone. "You've worked solidly for almost eight hours and it's not healthy."

From her peripheral vision Catherine watched as Eve took a determined step toward her. She pushed her chair back from the desk and glanced at her clock. Eve was correct in her estimation. She'd been sat at her desk working for over eight hours straight. No wonder her body was stiff, her eyes grainy, and brain sore.

Wincing, she stood and stretched out her arms, back, and shoulders. Pins and needles erupted up through her right leg, making her avoid putting her foot back down. After a few quick blinks, she finally took in her surroundings and noted the communal offices were deserted. Only Eve and she remained. The situation fully dawned on her. One thought in particular was a jolt.

Shit! The flight.

"I'm only halfway through. There's no way I'm going to make the flight and—"

"I cancelled both the taxi and the flight. I also spoke to Beth and told her what's going on, but I'll tell you about it in a little while."

Catherine rubbed her face. She did feel crappy, in body and mind. Her next thought was significantly less stressful but still unpleasant. The Christmas party. She'd had no desire whatsoever to attend it, but it seemed unfair Eve had missed out, too.

"Eve, why aren't you at the party? It started over two hours ago." Catherine looked directly at her, noticing how tired she looked. Her face was drawn and heavy bags hung beneath her eyes.

"I'm sixty-eight years of age. I've no interest in going to a party full of young 'uns who choose to parade around wearing practically nothing, hell-bent on getting drunk. I also can't abide the rubbish they listen to these days. It gets on my very last nerve."

Catherine smiled. "It's just music."

"It's loud and lacks rhythm and soul. That's not music. I'd rather wait until Christmas Day when our grandbabies come over to visit to experience the young. At least I'll be in the comfort of my own home, listening to real music and thoroughly enjoying threatening them that if they're not careful, I'll be buying them all clothes and a Bible next Christmas."

"Jeez. And there was me thinking I'm the only Christmas Grinch around here," Catherine said. "Also, correct me if I'm wrong, but didn't your shift end hours ago? Why are you still here?"

"What I choose to do is my own business. Now come on, follow me."

Guilt mixed with tiredness made Catherine grumpier than usual. "I didn't need you to stay. I'm fine by myself, and your interfering annoys me."

Eve chose to ignore her comments and headed out of the room. Too tired to argue, Catherine reluctantly hobbled after her, cursing each uncomfortable step.

She was surprised when Eve led her to the management conference room, but as soon as she walked through the door the tantalising smell of spicy food welcomed her. Her body immediately reacted; her mouth began to salivate and her stomach growled in anticipation.

Eve stepped aside and revealed an intimate setting for two. A gap broke up the large interlinked rectangle of tables. A single table had been moved over to the window. Cartons of steaming Mexican food had been placed in the centre of the table, and plates, cutlery, and a plastic cup were positioned at either end. The lights were dimmed, which drew all attention to the magnificent view outside of the window.

The sky was almost a translucent grey. Small snowflakes danced hypnotically on the rhythm set by the evening breeze. A few stray flakes momentarily stuck to the glass, showing their beautiful intricate design before changing into icy droplets. The panoramic view of London's skyline, which was impressive during daytime and summer, had now transformed into a winter wonderland. A dazzling kaleidoscope of colourful lights twinkled as far as the eye could see and stood out against the pristine whiteness of the snow. As if by magic, everything the snow coated looked clean, fresh, and slightly illuminated. It robbed the night of its usual cloak of darkness. The snow forming on the window ledge glittered with miniscule diamonds. Glistening, jagged icicles hung perilously from the top of the window.

"Come and eat before the food grows as cold as the snow outside," Eve said. She took a seat at the table and started plating up rice.

The room was warm, but Catherine rubbed a pleasant imaginary chill from her arms. She had to admit looking out on such a stunning view and watching the snow fall made her feel better. The rumbling of her stomach reminded her she was starving, so she rushed around the side of the table to take her place.

Eve presented her with a plate filled with huge portions of colourful rice, spicy grilled chicken, peppers, onions, bean chilli, the biggest tortilla Catherine had ever seen, and lashings of red salsa, sour cream, and bright green guacamole. She graciously accepted. They began to eat, and the silence formed between them was a comfortable one.

"This is the best Mexican takeaway I've ever had," Catherine said before quickly demolishing another mouthful.

Eve smiled. "Can I interest you in something chilled and bubbly to drink?"

Catherine frowned. "I'm only halfway through the reports, and I need a clear head to finish them. I don't think drinking alcohol would—"

"Who said anything about alcohol?" Eve asked. She held up a bottle of Coke.

Catherine smiled. "In that case, yes, please."

They continued their meal with light conversation and Catherine was surprised at how pleasant it was. Eve told her about her first experience of snow in 1963, when she and her husband had emigrated to the UK, and how she'd been fascinated by the stuff ever since.

As the meal drew to an end, Catherine wiped her mouth on a napkin and placed it on her plate. She couldn't put off asking any longer. "What did Beth say? Is she furious with me?"

"Not at all," Eve said. "She's worried about you. And disappointed, which is understandable."

"Maybe I could try and get a flight tomorrow—"

"I'm sorry, Catherine. I tried to book you another flight this afternoon, but every single one is fully booked. And with the horrendous weather forecast over the next few days, it's unlikely they'll be taking off anyway."

Catherine forced a weak smile and tried to swallow around the lump of disappointment stuck in her throat. Guilt weighed heavily on her conscience, but it was the disappointment that bothered her most.

She'd actually resigned herself to going to Beth's. Secretly, she'd even started to look forward to seeing Florence open her presents on Christmas morning. The whole situation left a bitter taste in her mouth. A painful ache flared in her chest, and she tried to convince herself it was only heartburn from the spicy food.

"Beth did suggest alternative travel arrangements for you to consider," Eve said a little too casually.

"Go on."

"One of Katie's cousins is driving up there from London tomorrow evening and then returning after—"

"You can't be serious! You both expect me to travel by car? With a stranger. In horrendous weather conditions." Catherine glared vehemently. "Not going to happen. I can't believe you even suggested—"

"Okay." Eve shifted in her seat and held up a placating hand. "I told her you wouldn't go for it. I think she knows it was a long shot. I'll call her back and tell her as soon as I've cleared all this away."

Catherine's heart was hammering in her chest. Her mouth was dry and her body was sweaty. *How could Beth and Eve even ask that of me?* They both knew about her parents.

"Catherine, it was an option, but I apologise for bringing it up. I should've told her no straight away—"

"Why didn't you?" Catherine asked, her tone harsher and more accusing than she'd meant it to be.

"Because I wanted you to go spend Christmas with Beth. I think it would've done you a world of good."

Catherine shook her head trying to ward off the whole host of emotions and thoughts. She wanted to go to Beth's. It pissed her off to admit it, but it was true. Five minutes ago, she would have considered anything if it meant she wasn't going to break her promise to Florence. But the thought of taking a car journey at this time of year filled her with full-blown fear.

She couldn't do it.

Could she?

Gnawing on a fingernail for the first time in years, she forced herself to consider the question. Could she do it? Surely it wasn't too different from the taxis she got to and from work every day? Plus the person driving obviously felt confident enough with her ability to make the journey regardless of the bad weather forecast. All she'd have to do was sit in a car for a few hours. That wasn't so hard. If she took music or a book she could probably distract herself.

And even more importantly, if she didn't face her fear now, she might as well give up on ever trying to. She hated being a victim held to ransom by her fears.

An image of Florence's smiling face flashed in her mind's eye, and it answered the question. She would make herself do it.

"Tell Beth I'll do it. Let me know the details before you leave." She felt some satisfaction when Eve's jaw dropped and her mouth gaped. For the first time in their working relationship, Eve was rendered speechless.

Catherine walked back to her office refusing to think about anything other than completing the rest of the reports. There would be plenty of time for freaking out tomorrow.

CHAPTER FOUR

Catherine didn't make it home until after seven in the morning. Eve left not long after their meal ended, but had first made the arrangements with Beth for the car journey.

Catherine and Katie's cousin would split the cost of petrol. Arrangements had also been made for them to have an overnight stay in a hotel part way. Why an overnight stay was needed was never explained. Catherine was simply told to be ready outside her apartment building at five o'clock in the evening, but infuriatingly, the vague details stopped there.

One positive aspect of missing the flight was her suitcase was already packed and in the hallway. She chose to forgo breakfast in the hope of catching up on some much needed sleep. She was emotionally, physically, and mentally drained. However, once in bed, she struggled to succumb to her tiredness. Her mind refused to stop racing and her anxiety about the upcoming journey plagued her. Eventually exhaustion won, but her dreams had been nightmarish.

At three o'clock she got up, showered, and dressed. She then spent the next hour pacing around her apartment trying to think up a reasonable excuse to cancel. By the time she had only fifteen minutes left, her nails were bitten down to their quicks.

She peered out of her window to the street below, her anxiety spiking. A snow shower had begun, and a light dusting covered everything. The clouds hung heavy and menacing. Her stomach squirmed at the prospect of journeying in these conditions.

At five to five, she dressed in her coat, scarf, and gloves. She pulled out the suitcase's extendable handle and dragged it to the door. In a fleeting moment of hesitation, she ran to the kitchen and grabbed three bottles of wine. Hugging the bottles to her body, she rushed back into the hallway and knelt down. Although it was fairly solidly packed, she managed to fit two of the bottles inside the suitcase. She would have to carry the third.

Unable to procrastinate any longer, she gripped the handle again and dragged the suitcase out onto the communal landing before locking her door. With quickened breaths, she forced herself into the elevator. As each descending floor number lit up, her fear physically manifested itself. Her heart pounded and the sound of blood rushed in her ears. Acid scorched the back of her throat as she fought against the need to be violently sick. She ground her jaws together and braced her legs from buckling when the metal doors opened.

With tentative steps, she walked out into the festively decorated reception area. The rhythmic rolling of her suitcase on the tiled floor was interrupted by an annoyingly high-pitched squeak from one of the wheels.

Catherine counted each laboured step in her head, and at thirty-six, she finally reached the door. The day porter, whom she didn't know, held the door open and wished her a good evening. The freezing air hit her and the shock caused her breath to catch in her throat. She hunched her shoulders and sought to bury herself deeper into her coat and scarf. The cold was bitter, and any bare flesh quickly began to sting from the nipping of its icy talons. Her ears got the brunt and she regretted not wearing a hat.

She rolled her suitcase down the stone steps, praying the wine bottles inside remained intact. She then stood on the pavement and waited.

She couldn't be sure if she shivered because of the cold or her fear. She tried to distract herself by breathing through the dense material of her scarf and watching the clouds of steam. Snow continued to fall, and although light, it soon began to gather on her coat and the material of her suitcase. With each car that drove by, she felt her stomach lurch and her pulse quicken.

At quarter past five, her fear was replaced by annoyance. She was freezing and pissed off. Tardiness was something she loathed at the best of times, but in this weather it was plain rude. As soon as this cousin pulled up, she was going to give him a piece of her mind.

Holding the bottle of wine beneath an arm, she rubbed both hands together, cupped them, and blew inside, but the heat was lost almost instantly. Her gaze fell on the latest car to be travelling down the road.

What a death trap! The rusting piece of junk looked like it was going to keel over or break into pieces at any moment. Blotches of hospital green were randomly splattered in its worn forest green paint, brown rust clearly visible, even from this distance.

Appalled someone was out driving such a vehicle in this weather, she looked away, then glanced at her watch. Twenty minutes late.

The crunching of tyres pulling to the curb drew her attention. The death trap car had pulled up in front of her. Figuring the driver probably needed directions, as they clearly didn't live in this well-to-do area, she cautiously walked up to the passenger window.

Through the misted glass she saw the driver lean over and start to roll down the window by hand. A lively Christmas song was blaring out on full blast, and Catherine groaned in irritation. As the frosted glass lowered a little more with each abrupt movement, Catherine finally laid eyes on the driver.

A young woman peered up at her. Her blond hair fell past her shoulders in tight curls. Blue eyes, rosy cheeks, pale, freckled skin. A glint of silver shone from the bar piercing in her right eyebrow. Dimples formed at the corners of her mouth and her smile was magnificent—full pink lips showcased perfect pearly white teeth. Her left ear was pierced four times, and novelty Christmas pudding earrings dangled from her lobes.

Slightly stunned by the beauty, Catherine felt the warm, unfamiliar feeling of arousal settle in the pit of her stomach. It took her a few seconds to regain her composure and ask uncertainly, "Can I help you?"

"I think it's the other way around," the woman said, having to shout over the music. Her smile intensified as she let out a hearty laugh. "I'm Holly Daniels. Katie's cousin. I'm your designated chauffeur. Catherine, right?"

Catherine almost dropped the bottle of wine as she stumbled backward a step.

This can't be happening. This has to be a mistake.

Holly turned off the engine, which cut the music. She clambered out of the car and came around to where Catherine was standing. She was wearing a large woollen jumper with penguins on it and a tight-fitting pair of jeans.

"We'll pop your suitcase on the backseat. The boot is pretty full, sorry," Holly said. She took hold of Catherine's suitcase and rolled it over to the car. The dented car door made an unhealthy clattering sound as its hinges were forced open.

Catherine could only watch in horrified silence as Holly put her suitcase in the back.

"Right, shall we go?" Holly asked, her tone incredibly cheery as she turned around.

"I think there's been a mistake," Catherine whispered.

Holly tilted her head slightly, her brow creased in what looked like confusion. "I don't think so. I was told to come here and pick you up at five. I'm sorry we couldn't leave earlier, but it was the last big day at work before the holidays."

Catherine gulped down a mouthful of icy air. She was in a worrying state of mind…well, actually two states of mind. Part of her wanted to run away from Holly and hide in her apartment, far away from the death trap car. The other part wanted to pull Holly in close and kiss her and perhaps never stop.

What the hell is going on with me?

Holly swept a stray curly strand of hair behind her ear before huddling into the large jumper. The snow was getting heavier.

"No offence, Catherine, but it's friggin' freezing out here. We've also got a four-hour journey ahead of us this evening and the weather's getting worse. Can we leave please?"

Catherine was taken aback by Holly's assertiveness. Although young in appearance she seemed confidently mature.

"Catherine?"

Catherine quickly weighed up her options. She either got in the car or she didn't. Everything about this situation went against her better judgment and seemed to be the epitome of everything she hated: death trap car, bad weather, sexy young stranger full of festive cheer who was dressed in a Christmas jumper, Christmas music blaring. And yet she felt inexplicably attracted to Holly and excited at the prospect of travelling with her.

Her fear was still at the forefront of her mind, but the ache of arousal propelled her body into motion. Acting on instinct, which was something that went against her nature, she gave a curt nod and climbed inside.

Holly rushed around the front of the car and got behind the wheel. With another gorgeous smile, she looked at Catherine and said, "Buckle up, partner. We're in for a festive ride."

Catherine opened her mouth to reply, but with the starting of the engine, the speakers came back to life, and the same Christmas song picked up from where it left off. As the car pulled away from her apartment building, a sudden thought struck Catherine: *I think I've made a terrible mistake. This is going to be the road trip from hell.*

Chapter Five

Catherine's heart continued to pound in her chest and her mouth had never felt so dry. She tried to calm down, telling herself she only had to endure a few hours in the car and then she'd be at the hotel. And tomorrow she'd do the same again and then she'd be at Beth's.

The main problem was the car. The interior left a lot to be desired and was only marginally better than the outside. It was rickety, old, and everything about it screamed to her inner panic that it was unsafe.

Her legs were crammed into an uncomfortably small space. The seat belt was far too lax, as if it had previously had all of its elasticity wrung from it, leaving it pathetically lifeless and limp. The car seat was lumpy and she struggled to find a position where her backside wasn't prodded by the camouflaged springs seeking escape. It was also uncomfortably hot thanks to the air blasting through the vents. She was also overly aware that the car had been manufactured in a prehistoric age before such safety advances as airbags had even been dreamt up.

As much as she tried, she couldn't shake the feeling she was sat inside a death trap whose dented shell would offer no protection whatsoever should something happen. Her body rattled up and down with every hurly-burly bump and dip of the road.

The only minuscule positive she could take from the experience so far was the warm, almost spicy fragrance of ginger and cinnamon laced with the earthy sweet aroma of chocolate lingering tantalizingly in the air. Although she'd looked around the car for the source of the smell, she couldn't spot it. There was no air freshener, and in the end she had to stop searching, as the things she was noticing instead only added to her anxiety.

The wing mirror on her side was actually taped on, which led to the conclusion something had taken it off aggressively in the first place and Holly hadn't seen fit to get it professionally repaired. One of the windscreen wipers was slower than the other. The clock taunted her by blinking neon green digits that told the wrong time. Dust and fluff had accumulated in the ventilation slits. The dashboard was chipped in random places, and the gearstick head didn't match the rest of the interior.

Sensing she was being watched, she looked up to find Holly looking at her and beaming a megawatt smile before turning her attention back to the road beyond the windscreen.

Catherine fidgeted in her seat, astounded and embarrassed by the fiery ache of arousal stoked inside her. From seemingly nowhere a question whispered in her mind: perhaps the source of the incredible fragrance was Holly…

A groan escaped from Catherine's mouth but was thankfully hidden by the recent irritating Christmas song blaring out. Perhaps her biggest problem wasn't the car and was actually Holly. This beautiful, cheery stranger was wreaking havoc on her life. For some unknown reason, Catherine's long-lost libido had returned in full force and gone straight into overdrive. She couldn't remember a time when she'd felt like this. Of course she'd felt attracted to Paula, but it had been a gradual, delicate thing. Whatever this was, it most definitely was not delicate or gradual.

Perhaps it was her first experience of lust?

Or maybe she was going crazy?

Regardless of the reason, it had to stop. One night, during their first week at university, Beth had opened up to Catherine about a recent upset in her personal life. They made a pact that they would never get romantically involved with family, each other's love interests, or close mutual friends. It hadn't been an issue at the time. Catherine had no family other than Granny Birch, no friends other than Beth, and was still a virgin whose sexuality was so far back in the closet, it may as well have been in Narnia. She'd never envisioned herself being romantically involved with anyone and was still a few years away from being seduced by Paula.

Holly was Katie's favourite cousin, and was therefore family to Beth. Plus, Catherine wasn't interested in a one-night stand, or capable of anything more than that. Her heart was irreparably damaged from everything that happened with Paula. But the biggest reason why nothing would or ever could happen was simple: Holly was obviously straight. Wasn't she?

She could feel the makings of a headache flaring behind her eyes. She needed to try to calm down and perhaps even sleep. The most important thing out of this whole sordid mess was, Holly felt confident in both the car and her ability to safely drive them to their destination. That was enough to instil some calmness.

After another half an hour of overanalysing everything and being subjected to one cheesy Christmas song after another, Catherine could take no more. She found the off button on the car's stereo and didn't hesitate in pressing it. The inside of the car plunged into silence.

"I take it you're not a fan of that song," Holly said, her tone clipped.

Feeling self-conscious, Catherine fidgeted in her seat, realising a little too late her actions could have beem construed as rude. "Sorry. I don't like Christmas songs. I had an incredibly late night at work last night and can feel a headache coming on. Do you mind if we drive without music?"

Holly flicked a glance at her and smiled. "That's fine. It'll give us time to get to know one another."

Catherine gulped. She'd planned to sleep, in the hope that when she awoke they'd be at their destination. The prospect of talking with Holly and getting to know her better simultaneously panicked and excited her in equal doses.

Now the obnoxious Christmas music was silenced, another problem became astoundingly clear. The loud desperate chugging from the car engine sounded as though it had developed a dire strain of emphysema, and the rhythmic thudding of tyres on the snowy road filled her with dread. Considering putting the music back on to drown it out, her plans were foiled when Holly spoke.

"I know you missed your flight and this was your last option, Catherine. But I've got to be honest with you. I'm so relieved you agreed to come on this journey. I've never driven to Scotland before, let alone in snow. I never normally venture out when the weather's bad, so this is also a first. At least if anything happens there's the two of us to deal with it."

Catherine wasn't sure if she wanted to laugh, cry, or throw up. She covered her mouth with a gloved hand and bent forward.

"Are you okay?" Holly asked. "Do you need me to pull over?"

Catherine shook her head, not daring to actually speak in case she said what was repeating over and over in her head: *We're going to die.*

"What made you decide to spend Christmas with Katie and Beth?" Holly asked.

The last thing Catherine felt like doing was partaking in small talk, but as the only alternative was to contemplate their untimely demise, she reluctantly answered. "Beth got Florence to guilt trip me."

Holly laughed and the sound was pleasantly musical. Catherine turned in her seat, wincing as another spring poked an already sensitive part of her backside. If they were going to die, she might as well make the most of the journey up to that point.

"Beth does tend to get what she wants," Holly said. She laughed again. "Although I bet you gave her a run for her money."

"Yes, she does, and yes, I did," Catherine said wryly. "She left me voicemails every night for over a month. Eventually, she resorted to phoning me at work under the pretence of there being a family emergency. Finally, she used her secret weapon: Florence."

"Whoa, that's some hardcore tactics. You never stood a chance." Holly smiled. "What do your family make of you spending Christmas in the Highlands of nowhere?"

"I don't have any family," Catherine said. "My gran died in July, so it's just me."

"Shit." Holly gave an apologetic grimace. "I'm sorry, Catherine."

Catherine shrugged and tried to mask her grief. "It's fine."

They drove in silence. Before Holly had asked Catherine about her family they'd been having a pleasant chat, but now it was ruined. Catherine supposed it was perfectly reasonable for Holly to ask about her situation. The subject was bound to have been broached at some point, but now the atmosphere between them was awkward and Catherine regretted it. If only she'd had the foresight to have thought up an acceptable answer, or had even stopped at having no family; there'd been no need to mention Granny Birch's death.

"So…you don't like Christmas songs?" Holly asked, her tone tentative.

Catherine raised her chin. "I don't like Christmas."

"Oh," Holly said. She seemed stuck for words. Her eyebrows arched and she blew out a long breath. Sweeping the unruly curly strand of hair behind her ear again, she said, "I know some religions don't celebrate—"

"I'm an atheist," Catherine said. She noted the frown on Holly's forehead. This conversation was quickly heading in the same direction as the last one. She didn't want to have to discuss the death of her parents, as it would only add to the macabre impression Holly undoubtedly had of her. In an attempt to prevent the inevitable, Catherine quickly said, "My reasons for disliking Christmas are personal. I'd rather not talk about them."

Holly shrunk away from her. "Of course." Shaking her head, she said, "This all sounded a lot better in my head. Why don't you ask me some questions instead? Go ahead. Ask me anything."

Catherine sat up straight, panic surging through her body. Her mind was blank. She kept trying to grasp at fleeting questions, but they were elusive, and each passing second added to her mounting stress. She didn't want to make herself sound like a complete arse by asking something inappropriate.

"Be gentle with me." Holly gave a playful wink.

Catherine said the first thing that came to mind. "Why are we staying in a hotel tonight?" *What the hell?* Seemingly unable to stop talking, the barrage of words kept coming, and with each one Catherine cringed a little more inside. "Surely it makes more sense to continue driving through the night, especially as the forecasts have predicted awful weather for tomorrow. We don't want to end up stranded somewhere."

Holly burst out laughing.

Confused, Catherine remained silent. As far as she was aware she hadn't said anything amusing.

Holly's face flushed with colour and her smile was as magnificent as ever. After a few deep, calming breaths, Holly glanced at her, eyes sparkling and cheeks pink. "Are you really that uninterested in me? You could've asked me anything, but you chose to ask about the journey instead."

Her face burned with embarrassment. "My mind went totally blank," Catherine said. "I'm such an idiot."

Holly laughed again. "Don't be silly. I think it's endearing. Anyway, in answer to your surprise question"—she gave a playful nudge with her elbow—"I've been up since three this morning for work, and I didn't finish until this afternoon. I'm usually in bed by nine, and I'm already tired. Eight hours is a long time in general, but in this weather, I don't think it would be safe to attempt to drive it all in one go. Whereas four hours today and then four tomorrow seems doable."

Happily reeling from having been called endearing and by the unexpected touch of Holly's elbow, Catherine nodded. "Always better to be safe than sorry. You're a competent driver and I respect your decision." She paused, then added, "If I came across as bossy or rude before, I apologise."

"Not at all," Holly said. "It's a shame you don't drive because we could've taken it in turns and continued through the night." She hesitated. "I was a little surprised, actually, when Katie told me you don't drive."

Catherine fought back a groan. She'd finally started to loosen up a little, despite having embarrassed herself, and the last thing she wanted to do was explain why she'd never learnt to drive. That would lead back to the death of her parents—something she didn't relish delving into.

"It never interested me." Before Holly could ask why, Catherine tried to change the subject. "I was hoping maybe you'd let me have another go at asking you a question. I might do better this time."

"I doubt you could do worse," Holly teased her. "Sure, go ahead. In fact, I'll give you five questions."

"Five?"

"Yes. You can ask me anything and I'll answer you honestly."

"You don't have much faith in my questioning abilities," Catherine said with a chuckle. "But I'll take all five." She couldn't be certain, but it looked as though Holly was blushing. "Ready?"

"Yes."

Catherine opened her mouth, but Holly spoke first.

"That was actually worse than your first question. Only four left, I sure hope they get better."

"That didn't count," Catherine said.

"Well, it sounded like a question to me."

"It was a question, but it wasn't one of my five."

Holly gave a dramatic shrug. "I suppose I'll let you off this once."

Catherine opened her mouth and hesitated, thinking through the next question carefully. "How old are you?"

"Marginally better. I'm going to turn twenty-six on Christmas Day." Holly wiped her steamy window with her gloved hand. "What about you?"

Catherine folded her arms. "I'm the one asking the questions." Holly gave a sheepish smile but didn't speak. It was enough to melt Catherine's resolve. "I'm thirty-one."

"I definitely thought you were older."

"What?"

"No, you look good. It's not that." Holly's gaze flickered from Catherine's legs and travelled up her body until their eyes met. A moment later, she turned her head and focused on the road.

Catherine slowly released a shuddery breath. Beth had always said she wouldn't recognise flirting if it slapped her in the face. She couldn't be certain, but she had an inkling perhaps straight Holly was flirting with her right now. She could be wrong. But the possibility was exhilarating.

"What job do you have?"

"I own a small bakery called Indulgence," Holly said. She sat up straighter and wet her lips. "I opened it in January, and I haven't looked back since. I love it. I even look forward to waking up at three every morning." Her eyes sparkled with passion. "There's nothing better than creating something beautiful with your bare hands. It's the most sensual job in the world. I get to immerse myself in incredible smells, tastes, and textures. Knowing what I've created isn't just aesthetically pleasing but also delicious, well, that's the proverbial cherry on top."

Catherine was a little stunned. She hadn't been expecting Holly to reveal she owned and ran her own business, especially at only twenty-five years of age. That was an incredible accomplishment. Holly was clearly a skilled and driven woman.

"Was it something you always wanted to do?"

Holly laughed. "Not really. Although I'll confess I've always been good with my hands." She shot another mischievous wink at Catherine before continuing. "I was never bothered about being an academic starlet and so left it to my older sisters to fight it out between themselves. When I left school I had no idea what I wanted to do, and

I happened across an advertisement for a catering school. It sounded interesting and so I enrolled. During those two years, I discovered my culinary skills were quite good. At eighteen, I'd given my parents heart failure when I told them I'd no interest in university and was planning to go travelling around Europe by myself. I worked two mundane jobs for over a year until I'd saved enough money, and then I made the best mistake of my life. I headed straight for Paris. I got a job working for a grumpy pastry chef who never spoke a word of English. My fate was sealed. I never ventured any farther than Paris because I'd found my calling. I stayed there for nearly three years and he taught me everything I know."

"Why did you leave?" Catherine asked.

"I could've happily stayed there forever, and that was what bothered me." Holly's shoulders slumped. "I was homesick. I missed my family and England in general. Plus my girlfriend and I had split up, so there were no ties."

Girlfriend was the word Catherine heard the loudest.

Holly nibbled her bottom lip for a few moments before continuing. "I suppose I wanted more. As much as I loved it, it was his dream. I wanted the opportunity to realise my own."

"Which is exactly what you've done," Catherine said. She was trying to hide her astonishment. Holly had said girlfriend. The connotation of that one word meant Holly was bisexual at the very least, and, in theory, Catherine might stand a chance.

Holly nodded. "Yes, but it wasn't easy. For starters I was forced to move back in with my parents, which was a huge shock to the system. It took a few months to settle down and get work. I ended up working for over two years at a full-time office job during weekdays. Five evenings a week I tended a bar, and my weekends were spent working in a café. It was soul destroying, and I almost gave up, but my parents persuaded me to persevere. They gave me the same amount of money both my sisters had been given for their university tuition. That, paired with my savings and a hefty bank loan, was about enough to cover the overheads for a gorgeous little bakery I'd seen and secretly set my heart on. The rest, I suppose, is history."

The incredible smell inside the car made sense.

"What job do you do?" Holly asked. Frowning, she peered out the windscreen. Catherine followed her line of sight. The snow was falling thicker and faster now, covering the windscreen in a light blanket of snow between each swoosh of the wipers.

"I'm a regional sales manager."

"Do you like it?" Holly asked. She flicked the lever beside the steering wheel, increasing the pace of the wipers.

Catherine felt the car slow down. "I'm good at it. It's full of challenges, and I happen to be excellent at developing strategies that enable us to meet our targets. It also pays well."

Holly leant forward, squinting at the road ahead. "I asked if you enjoy it, not if you're good at it, or if it pays well."

"It's the same thing."

"No, it isn't," Holly said reverently. "I was good at my office job, but I didn't enjoy it. It was monotonous and nearly bored me to death, so I left. It's going to take a while for the bakery to prove if it's viable and will pay me well, but at least I enjoy it."

Catherine was a little taken aback. Holly had made a valid point. If Catherine genuinely considered her question, the answer depressed her. She didn't enjoy her job. Yes, she was good at it, and perhaps for the first few years she did enjoy the challenge, but recently it'd become ever more stressful. The long hours, always being delegated the crappy and difficult stuff, while Jonathon stole her ideas and reaped all the credit. She wasn't even convinced she was appreciated by her staff team, let alone by the board of directors.

She didn't want to admit to Holly that she didn't like her job, so she told a barefaced lie. "I enjoy it. A lot."

Holly held her gaze for a few seconds before turning away. "Okay."

Catherine was certain Holly knew she'd lied, but at least she had the grace not to call her out. "What made you decide to spend Christmas in the Highlands of nowhere?"

Holly laughed. "My parents are spending the whole month in Canada with my oldest sister's family. Two of my mum's sisters and their families, including Katie's parents, also live out there, so it's a bit of a reunion. I couldn't afford to take the time off work or waste the money on travelling. They offered to pay for me, but I refused. When the business is making loads of cash and I'm rich, I'll go over then."

Catherine suspected money was a bigger issue than Holly was letting on but remained quiet.

"Anyway, news soon spread through the family grapevine, and

I got a call from Katie insisting I spend Christmas with them. I knew better than to argue with her."

Catherine had one question left, and she needed to build herself up to asking it. Even as she tried to think of the right words, her face grew warm. With fumbling hands she rolled down the window a few centimetres and silently rejoiced as the icy air cooled her face.

"Are you okay?" Holly asked.

"Yeah, just a bit warm," Catherine said. Bracing herself, she prepared to ask her final question. "So, do you have a partner?"

Holly raised an eyebrow. "You mean a business partner? No. The business is mine."

Catherine struggled to swallow. Her tongue felt too big for her mouth. A sudden fear of her stutter returning slammed into her chest, which was ridiculous because she'd not stuttered in a long time. Pushing the thought from the forefront of her mind, she took her time to carefully speak. "Actually, I meant do you live with someone?"

"A roommate?" Holly asked. The corners of her mouth twitched slightly. "No, I live alone, in the apartment above the shop. Although I'm seriously thinking about renting out the spare bedroom. The apartment is such a huge space for me, and I won't pretend the extra cash wouldn't help. Plus it'd be nice to have some company. This year's been a bit lonely. The early starts mean I've barely had a night out."

Catherine was growing increasingly frustrated. She wanted to discover if Holly was single but was failing miserably.

"We've made it," Holly said with relief.

Catherine looked out her window and saw the neon lights of the upcoming hotel's sign. Although she was relieved at their safe arrival, she was also disappointed the first part of their journey was over.

"Do you have a girlfriend?" Catherine blurted out without thinking.

"It took you long enough to ask. I was starting to give up hope," Holly said. She parked the car, put on the handbrake, and with the engine still running turned in her seat to face Catherine. "No, I'm single. Are you attached?"

Catherine replied in a croak, "No."

"Good," Holly said. She switched off the engine.

Catherine sat in stupefied silence as Holly climbed out of the car.

CHAPTER SIX

Catherine stumbled over the threshold and into the warm hotel lobby. Her arms ached and she bent forward with a groan and lowered the hefty suitcase to the floor. It turned out having a wheelie suitcase was great except when contending with a foot of fresh snow. At least by carrying the bloody thing, she'd ensured the contents remained dry. Glancing out of the glass door, she noted Holly was still hovering around the boot of her car.

Tapping her feet on the welcome mat loosened the encrusted snow and made a bit of a mess. The woman on reception was quiet but efficient, and within a few minutes Catherine had her room key card and had also booked a table for two in the restaurant for an evening meal.

The prospect of sharing an intimate meal with Holly, especially after the conversation they'd shared, stirred nervous butterflies in her stomach. She tried to unsuccessfully convince herself the meal would have no romantic connotation whatsoever. It was simply a nice change from eating alone.

She mentally went through the clothing she'd packed and tried to choose a suitable outfit. Having not considered she'd be in this position, most of her clothes were casual. Perhaps her fitted purple shirt and favourite pair of black trousers would suffice? She wanted to look good without appearing as if she'd tried to look good. Under no circumstances did she want to come across as presumptive or desperate.

"Shit," she whispered under her breath. What was she doing? After only a few hours in a car with Holly, she'd presumably lost her mind. She hadn't stressed about clothing in years. Plus she should surely be trying to instil some sort of barrier between Holly and herself, not thinking up ways to encourage something to happen.

The main doors opened and Holly appeared. Face flushed, she shrugged off her coat, spraying icy droplets everywhere. She glanced up and gave a dazzling smile, which nearly made Catherine's knees buckle.

As Holly checked in at reception, Catherine loitered to one side trying to act casual and failing miserably. Sitting in the car had hidden the shape of Holly's body. The cream woollen jumper was big and only hinted at the size of her chest. The incredibly tight-fitting jeans, however, left little to the imagination. The jeans were tucked into a pair of scuffed walking boots. The boots had no heel, so Holly was clearly comfortable with her height.

Try as she might, Catherine couldn't stop staring. Worse still was her gaze seemed glued to Holly's pert backside, which made her feel like a complete pervert. Antsy, she turned away and pretended to peruse the nearby display stand showcasing an array of leaflets for local attractions.

A gentle tap on her shoulder shot tingles across her skin.

"Ready?" Holly asked. She was brandishing her room key. "We're on the same corridor."

Catherine nodded mutely, her pulse still racing from the innocent touch. She reclaimed her suitcase and obediently followed Holly. Each corridor looked identical to Catherine, but they eventually found the one with their room numbers. As they approached Catherine's door, she finally managed to speak.

"I booked us a table in the restaurant for an evening meal," Catherine said, stumbling over her words.

Holly stopped abruptly and Catherine nearly walked into the back of her. Holly's hunching shoulders, the frown creasing her forehead, and the way her gaze shot to the floor made it clear to Catherine they weren't going to be sharing a meal.

Perplexed, Catherine instinctively tried to backtrack. "I should've checked with you first. Don't worry about—"

"It was sweet of you, Catherine," Holly said. She was hugging herself and looked uncomfortable. "I'm tired. The early start, paired with driving in the snow, has taken it out of me. I'm exhausted. I think maybe it's best I get an early night."

"Of course," Catherine said, internally chastising herself for being so presumptive. "It's fine, honestly."

"Thanks for understanding." Holly shuffled her feet, and after a few lingering seconds of awkwardness said, "I'll see you in the morning. Sleep well, Catherine."

"Sleep well, too," Catherine said. She tried to mask her hurt as she watched Holly walk down the corridor. "Holly?" When Holly looked back, Catherine felt a pang of bitter disappointment. "Thank you for today."

"It's been a pleasure," Holly said. An unreadable expression flickered across her face. She swiped her key and opened the door. With one last fleeting look she said, "Good night." The door closed behind her.

Catherine remained rooted to the floor staring at Holly's closed door. What had happened? Had she said or done something wrong? How had things changed so dramatically from parking the car to finding their rooms?

Self-conscious, Catherine fumbled in her pocket for the key card, swiped the lock, and rushed into the room. Once inside, she locked the door, placed the key card in the holder to activate the light switch, and wheeled the suitcase over to the bed. Hands on hips, she surveyed her surroundings.

The room was clean and although the colour scheme and furniture looked a little dated, she was impressed with the overall standard of the room. Eve had booked her reservation, but it was Holly who had mapped out the route and chosen this particular hotel for them. Travelling for work meant Catherine had stayed in many hotels, some of the finest in the UK, and she would previously never have entertained the thought of booking herself into this particular chain, simply because it was renowned for being cheap. In retrospect, she now felt a little ashamed of her snobbery. Although this hotel room was hardly five stars, it was clean, spacious, provided all of the essentials, and was an excellent value for money.

She called reception from the room phone and cancelled the restaurant reservation. After quickly scanning the menu she ordered a burger, fries, and a large beer. If she fancied some wine later she could always open one of the bottles from her suitcase, but she suspected the beer would suffice.

Unpacking took less than five minutes. All she needed were her pyjamas and toiletries. She decided, after she'd eaten, she'd relax in a hot bubble bath. She'd then spend the rest of the evening in bed reading one of the many books she'd been hoarding on her tablet. Hopefully, her mind would be distracted and all thoughts of Holly would be held at bay.

Twenty minutes later, her meal arrived, and once again she was pleasantly surprised by the quality. It was hot and tasty, and the icy beer accompanying it went down smoothly. It didn't take long for her to devour everything, and as she sat uncomfortably full, looking down in dismay at the crumb-littered plate, she realised her long-lost appetite was also apparently back. Unable to bring herself to move her podgy backside any farther than climbing on top of the bed, she lazily pointed the remote and flicked the TV on.

She found a relatively comfortable position, which entailed lying sprawled diagonally across the bed. After dozing for a while, her attention was drawn to the TV screen. The spritely weather forecast presenter was practically jumping up and down, while big red warnings flashed across the screen. Getting to her knees, Catherine edged closer, studying the map. An icy chill crawled down her spine and an overwhelming sense of foreboding settled over her. A horrendous-looking snowstorm was due to hit the UK tomorrow, and Scotland was going to get the brunt of it. The warnings were clear: prepare, stay indoors, and do not attempt to travel.

Her stomach lurched. The burger and fries had been a mistake.

What the hell were they going to do? She needed to tell Holly about the potential danger. Frustrated by her lack of driving knowledge, she considered potential alternatives. They could head back to London tomorrow. They could stay in the hotel for another night, although the forecast had said the storm could produce up to two feet of snow, so travelling afterward would be hindered.

A loud rapping on her door broke her trail of thought. She switched the TV off, discarded the remote, and looked through the peephole. Holly stood outside the door. Catherine wiped her face, ran her hands over her hair to smooth it, and straightened her rumpled clothes before opening the door.

"Hi," Catherine said. She was almost rendered speechless by how adorable Holly looked dressed in her matching pyjama top and bottoms. The white material was scattered with glittery pink and purple snowflakes. The top closed at the front with purple buttons. She'd rolled up her sleeves, but the length of the bottoms overhung her slippers. Though the pyjamas weren't particularly revealing, Holly looked snug and gorgeous.

"I'm sorry for bothering you, Catherine," Holly said. She moved half a step forward. "I watched the weather forecast for tomorrow."

"So did I," Catherine said weakly. She was overly aware of the close proximity between their bodies. The same spicy and earthy fragrance that had tantalised her senses in the car radiated off Holly.

"It's not looking good." Holly chewed on her lower lip and began to wring her hands.

"No, it's not," Catherine said, resting her back against the door to keep it ajar. "What are your thoughts?"

Holly shrugged. "I can only think of two. We could leave early and risk it, or we could turn back and head home."

Catherine met Holly's gaze and became captivated by her eyes. The rings of light blue had flecks of gold surrounding each iris. The blond eyelashes were long and curved, framing her eyes perfectly.

"Catherine?" Holly asked uncertainly.

Catherine blinked. "Uh, sorry?"

The corners of Holly's mouth twitched. "I was asking whether you want to risk it or go home?"

Catherine swallowed hard. They should turn back. There was no question. And yet, her heart and mind refused to accept it. Surprising as it was, she didn't want to go back to her apartment and spend Christmas alone. The thought was depressingly crippling and it wedged a lump in her throat. She wanted to journey with Holly and continue to get to know her better.

"You're the one driving," she said. "Ultimately, it's your decision."

Holly gave a weak nod. "I think I want to try. I know it could be dangerous, but if we leave early enough I think we could make it before the worst of the storm hits. We're only four hours away, and although there's bound to be additional time constraints because of the weather, I honestly think it's doable."

A spike of excitement coursed through Catherine's veins in response to her newfound recklessness. "Let's do it."

Holly's eyebrows shot up. "Seriously?"

Catherine nodded vehemently, even though her insides were squirming. "Yes. What time do you want to leave?"

Holly took a few seconds to consider her answer. "I think if we leave at six we'll make it without any problems. It means you'll have to skip having breakfast here, though. We can pick something up when we stop for petrol if you like. I'm going to need some strong coffee."

The thought of food made Catherine grimace. "That's fine with me."

"Okay. Shall I come and knock for you at six?"

"Yes, please."

"Well, I better go return Katie's calls. I think she and Beth are freaking out," Holly said. She took a step back and, balancing on the ball of her foot, seemed to hesitate. A moment later she leaned forward on tiptoes and placed a gentle kiss on Catherine's cheek. With a shy smile and blushing cheeks, she pulled away and practically ran back up the corridor. Opening her door, she called back over her shoulder, "See you at six."

Catherine stood flabbergasted, gently touching the spot on her cheek where Holly's lips had touched her skin. On wobbly legs, she pushed backward, opening her door and returning into the room. She engaged the lock and entered the bathroom with a spring in her step. As the bath filled with water and bubbles, she replayed the feel of Holly's kiss over in her mind. She wiped the condensation from her glasses and glimpsed her reflection in the mirror. She had to laugh at the stupid grin she wore.

What had originally been planned as a relaxing bath quickly escalated into an unexpected grooming session. Her teeth were brushed, her nails clipped, all types of body hair dealt with, and her skin scrubbed and moisturised within an inch of its life. Feeling chipper, Catherine dressed in her pyjamas and climbed beneath the duvet.

With a contented smile, she switched on her tablet and automatically went to delete the welcome message from the hotel's Wi-Fi, but then changed her mind and connected instead. She told herself she was innocently going to check social media. She signed in and perused some of her so-called friends' status updates, despairing at the dirty laundry they were happy to air in public. What was the world coming to? So much for the season of good will.

The only reason she had an account at all was because Beth had set it up for her under the false pretence of keeping in touch when they moved. The real reason quickly became apparent when Catherine started getting personal messages from random lesbians who coincidentally happened to be single. She'd been furious, but Beth had, of course, denied everything. After changing the password, the account's privacy settings, and her profile information, she'd successfully prevented any further contact from strangers and subsequently pissed Beth off at the same time. Success all round.

Thinking of Beth logically led Catherine to have a nosey at her profile, which was filled with recent photos of Florence. Guilt crashed down over her. She'd grown up. How many of Florence's important rites of passage had she already missed? Had Florence lost her first tooth yet? Beth had said she could write her name and tie her laces. What else had she missed out on?

When Florence was born, Catherine had become uncharacteristically smitten and broody. She'd visited Beth and Katie regularly, even though it'd caused even more problems between Paula and her. She'd been genuinely surprised when they'd asked her to be Florence's godmother, but hadn't hesitated in accepting, even though she was an atheist. It wasn't a position she had entered into lightly. She'd secretly sworn to herself and Florence she would do her best to uphold the responsibility bestowed upon her.

During the first two years, she'd been a constant part of Florence's life, but then the shit had hit the fan with Paula, and everything had fallen apart. The following year had passed by in a bit of a blur. Heartbroken and betrayed, she'd cut herself off from everyone. Her visits to see Florence became few and far between. Every time she visited, it became harder to act like she was fine, and as much as she loved Florence, her heart ached with grief for the destroyed family plans she'd secretly harboured for Paula and herself. A year later, Katie had been offered a job in the Highlands of Scotland, and they'd moved. Catherine had never made the journey to visit, using one excuse or another, or blatantly ignoring Beth's outright attempts to invite her. In part, her avoidance was guilt-driven. She'd broken her promise to Florence and was too ashamed to grant herself a reprieve. She'd also thrown herself into work after the split and genuinely hadn't allowed herself time for a break.

Determination swelled in her chest. The newly realised epiphany made things crystal clear. She needed to concentrate on the important people in her life. She would make the journey with Holly tomorrow, repair bridges with her friends, and even more importantly, make up for her absence with Florence. She would call them regularly and try to visit every couple of months. Money wasn't an issue, and she'd saved enough annual leave.

While looking through Katie's profile, she happened to accidentally purposely stumble across Holly's. For the next hour, she did something she genuinely wasn't proud of. She basically stalked Holly's profile, photos, timeline, and messages. She had no doubt whatsoever her actions were wrong, and she wasn't even sure how she'd be able to face Holly the following morning…but none of that provided enough motivation to make her stop.

Holly had over a hundred friends, unlike Catherine, who only had sixteen. There were over a thousand photos that tagged Holly, although most had been taken by other people at social gatherings. There were three albums Holly had uploaded, and these were particularly interesting.

The most recent was of her bakery, Indulgence, and included photos of the building work, decorating, sign unveiling, and grand opening. There was an older album with photos from a family wedding. Katie, Beth, and Florence were in them.

Katie and Holly's family were basically a huge close-knit clan. Catherine had been introduced to the mass of relatives on two separate occasions: Beth and Katie's wedding, and Florence's christening. Being an only child with no living relations other than Granny Birch, she'd found both occasions daunting and loud, but also fascinating. It'd been impossible to remember all the names, let alone how they were related to Katie.

A thought struck.

Had she been introduced to Holly either time? Try as she might, she'd no recollection of meeting Holly before this afternoon. Holly would only have been eighteen at the time. Drawing a blank, Catherine turned her attention back to the screen.

The final album was the largest. It was a collection of photos taken by Holly during the three years she'd spent living in Paris. Catherine was so enthralled by what she saw, she went through the album twice. Some photos were taken during the height of summer and others during snow-filled winters. A fair few were of the usual tourist traps and stunning Parisian architecture. The other photos gave a deep insight into Holly's personal life. One photo in particular showed her with a stern-looking man. They were both dressed in chef's whites and stood behind a glass counter that showcased row upon row of beautiful, intricately decorated cakes and pastries. Holly was smiling, her head held high. Pleasure and pride showing in equal measures.

There were also various photos of Holly with a tall, tanned, older woman whose name was tagged as Lacina. It didn't take a genius to work out that Lacina was Holly's ex. As Catherine scrolled through each photo, she felt blatant jealousy burn inside, intensified by each smile and every embrace the couple shared.

Having enough of snooping—especially because she didn't like what she'd found—Catherine logged off and tried reading before quickly giving up on that, too. She removed her glasses and switched off the bedside light, stifling a yawn as she rubbed her grainy eyes. In the dark, thoughts and feelings became interchangeable, leaving her in a constant state of flux.

"What the hell are you doing?" she asked herself.

She couldn't remember ever having felt so drawn to another person. It was as though Holly had bewitched her. Every time she thought about Holly's smile, laugh, or the feel of her soft lips pressed against her cheek, her heart bucked against her rib cage. Could Holly be playing a game with her? Flirting and then leaving her high and dry? Maybe she was only interested in a festive fling. Catherine's spirits sank. It would explain why Holly had suddenly changed when she'd mentioned the restaurant. Had the kiss been a cruel joke, dragging out the flirtation?

"She's not like that," Catherine whispered. From the short but intense time she'd spent with Holly, she instinctively knew Holly wasn't a player. Plus her photos and profile showed how important friends and family were to her. There hadn't been any horrible messages from disgruntled one-night stands—Catherine had thoroughly searched.

She'd never met Holly before—to her knowledge anyway—but there was an undeniable connection between them. Something had niggled in Catherine's subconscious from the moment she sat in the car. It hinted at déjà vu and warned of negative connotations. Still, she failed to grasp the hidden reason and had to give up trying. Holly was a lovely, bubbly, gorgeous, confident, and successful woman. But she was also Katie's favourite baby cousin and had a strong family tie to Beth. Reality came crashing over Catherine like a tidal wave, forcing her to face the past. The promise she'd made to Beth years ago forced a sharp shock of reality that burst all romantic thoughts.

"It's been years," she whispered to herself. Would Beth still hold her to that promise? Would she remember it? Her stomach squirmed in answer. It didn't matter whether Beth remembered; Catherine remembered, and that was all that mattered. She'd made the promise to her best friend and therefore should keep it. Nothing more could happen with Holly.

As she closed her eyes, she heard the familiar sound of Granny Birch's voice in her head. "If you play with fire, Catherine, you've got to expect to get burned."

CHAPTER SEVEN

Catherine had never been a morning person. After a miserable night's sleep and having to wake up at such an ungodly hour, today was proving to not be an exception to the rule. Even after allowing herself an entire hour in which to get ready, she was still aimlessly shuffling around like a zombie when Holly quietly knocked on the door.

With one last glance at her reflection, she had to admit defeat. The dark rings beneath her eyes were there to stay, as apparently no amount of makeup was going to cover them. Her left eye was bloodshot and bleary after she'd managed to poke herself twice with her mascara brush. Appling makeup was never an easy task, as without her glasses she was practically blind. But attempting it while half asleep had caused mess and pain.

She studied her reflection in the full-length mirror. Her hair was okay. Her face looked haggard, her makeup heavy-handed. It was too late to do anything about it now. The jeans were a little creased but comfortable. The red turtleneck jumper looked surprisingly festive, which hadn't been her intention. Her sneakers were the only shoes she had packed with decent grip, and so she had to wear them even though they didn't go with the outfit.

While buttoning up her coat, she peered through the peephole. Her breath caught in her throat.

Holly looked beautiful. Her glossy hair, including the troublesome wisp, was tied back in a bun. She was fresh faced, without so much as a hint of makeup or tiredness. She was wearing her coat but hadn't fastened it up, and beneath she wore a baggy grey hoodie. Catherine was disappointed. Thick black sweatpants had replaced the tight-fitting jeans from yesterday. A pleated purple scarf wrapped around her neck, and she'd donned the same raggedy boots.

"Jeez," Catherine whispered, embarrassed about being so overdressed. "Talk about bright-eyed and bushy-tailed."

Holly raised her hand to knock again, but Catherine quickly unlocked the door. "Morning," she said, wincing at the lame greeting. She became increasingly uncomfortable, knowing she'd spent last night purposefully invading Holly's privacy.

"Good morning," Holly said cheerily. "You look great."

"You look beautiful," Catherine said. She'd spoken without thinking again. Her face erupted into a fiery blush, and she begged herself to try engaging her brain before opening her mouth.

"I'm pretty sure I look like I'm homeless, but thank you." Holly smiled. She shifted the shoulder strap of her rucksack and asked, "Shall we go?"

Catherine nodded. She wheeled her suitcase out into the corridor and then attempted to quietly close the door. Still wallowing in humiliation and not trusting herself to speak again, she silently followed Holly.

They were met at reception by a male member of staff whose overbearing cheeriness irritated Catherine immediately.

"A very good morning to you, ladies," he said, brandishing a toothy grin.

Catherine ignored his sickly sweet greeting and tossed her key card onto the desk before turning her back to him.

Holly stepped up next and handed over her key card. "Good morning."

"Thank you," he said, placing the key card behind the desk. "Wanting to make an early start? I don't blame you. I had to walk to work today. With the snow that fell last night it was the safer option."

"You really walked?" Holly asked. "In this weather?"

"I did, indeed. Fortunately, I live nearby. In weather like this I always walk and leave the car at home."

"We're going to try to get to our destination before the big storm hits," Holly said.

He gave a nod. "The weather forecast said it's going to be a nasty one. I hope you don't have far to travel."

Holly shuffled her feet. "We're heading to Aviemore, in the

Cairngorms National Park." She shoved her hands into the hoodie's front pocket. "It's at least a four-hour drive."

The man's cheerful disposition changed. Now he looked worried. "No. I'm afraid it's four hours in good weather. With last night's snowfall and the warnings for the storm that's coming, well, I wouldn't even hazard a guess as to how long it'll take you."

Pretending not to listen, but hanging on his every word, Catherine's heart sank.

"That's why we're leaving so early," Holly said weakly. "I'm sure we'll be fine."

"Look, I know it's not my place to say it," he said, lowering his tone. "But I really don't recommend attempting to drive that distance today. The roads are dangerous already. But when that storm hits, they'll become lethal. I don't want to upset or worry you needlessly, but in the past we've heard of people getting stranded and freezing to death in their cars."

Holly gasped. "How awful."

The man shook his head sadly. "The weather we get can be unpredictable. I'd just hate to think of you trapped somewhere. Have you considered waiting it out? We've had some cancellations, so there are plenty of rooms available for tonight. I know it's not an exciting prospect, but it's safe."

Catherine turned, her gaze flicking between the man and Holly. Perhaps they should take his advice.

"Thank you for your concern. It's very kind of you," Holly said, rebuffing him politely. "But we've made important plans and we can't let our family down. I promise we'll be extra cautious."

"Well, if you're sure I can't persuade you?" he asked, pausing with expectation for a few seconds before shaking his head softly. "I'd better let you get on your way, then. I really do hope you get to Aviemore safely. Good-bye, ladies."

"Good-bye. Oh, and Merry Christmas," Holly said.

"You, too."

Turning to face Catherine, Holly blew out a deep breath. "Ready?"

Catherine nodded. They walked to the main doors, stopped, and stared in dismay. At least another foot of snow had fallen overnight. The flakes were still falling, dense and heavy. Catherine felt claustrophobic. The weather showed no signs of easing. The car park was eerily aglow from the brightness of the snow. Even the cloudy sky was surprisingly light, which only made everything seem all the more surreal. Under different circumstances, Catherine would have admitted the car park looked beautiful. Having lived down south for most of her life, she'd never seen so much snow. It became startlingly clear to her that, although stunning, the snow could easily become a formidable enemy. A chill broke out across her flesh as she remembered the reception man's warnings and horror story.

Holly glanced down at Catherine's sneakers and said, "Your feet are going to get soaked. I've got a spare pair of wellies in the car. I'll go fetch them for you."

Catherine had no choice other than to accept. She watched helplessly as Holly trudged her way through the fresh snow to her car. After dumping her rucksack in the boot, she started up the engine and rooted around in the boot before returning with a pair of bright pink wellies.

Catherine removed her sneakers and forced her feet inside the wellies, which was an uncomfortable squeeze. Holly's feet were at least a size smaller. They both picked up an end of her suitcase and plodded back to the car, where Holly shoved it onto the backseat.

Catherine clambered into the passenger seat. She hissed many swear words while pulling off the wellies so she could return to the comfort of her sneakers. As she tied her laces, she watched Holly scrape the snow from the windscreen.

The inside of the car was quickly warming up, and Catherine made the executive decision to remove her coat. Yesterday she'd gotten too hot and it had only added to her grumpiness. After dumping the wellies and her coat in the back, she successfully managed to move her seat backward. The additional two inches of leg room she garnered gave her immense satisfaction.

With all the windows now clear of snow, Holly got inside the car and removed her coat, flinging it into the back. She spent a few minutes faffing around before shoving a dog-eared map into Catherine's lap.

"Just in case," Holly said, a little too flippantly for Catherine's liking.

Slowly, they set off. Catherine felt surprisingly calm, especially considering she was once again a passenger seated inside the death trap car, facing a potentially hazardous journey and an impending snow storm from hell. She reminded herself in a few hours she'd be hugging Florence, and that would make this whole trip worthwhile.

❖

The plan was to stop at the nearest rest stop for petrol, snacks, and more importantly, coffee. After an hour of driving, they had yet to come across one. They made slow progress, as Holly was only comfortable driving at a sluggish speed. They'd also barely spoken. Catherine didn't want to interrupt Holly's intense concentration.

Holly sat bolt upright on the edge of her seat, with both hands tightly gripping the steering wheel. Her jaws locked as she rolled her shoulders. Catherine had always struggled with gauging other people's feelings, but she could feel Holly's fear. Real fear. Try as she might, she couldn't think of anything worthwhile to say to calm Holly. She was scared, too.

They'd been ludicrous to consider driving in such conditions. But voicing that opinion would only succeed in making Holly feel she didn't trust her driving abilities, which was only partly true. You wouldn't tell a knife thrower you doubted her ability to hit the apple on top of your head with her next throw. For better or worse, she was stuck on this ride until the end, and she only hoped their end would be safely arriving at Beth's house.

In the distance, she spotted lights. "Rest stop ahead."

Holly kept her eyes glued to the road, but gave a curt nod. Five minutes later, they pulled under the petrol station's canopy. In a flash, Catherine unbuckled herself, opened the door, and jumped out onto the concrete.

"I'm going to use the restroom. Fill her up. I'll pay on the way back," she said. She managed one stride before the blare of the car's horn made her nearly jump out of her skin. She turned in time to see Holly marching over to her.

"Why say that?" Holly asked.

Taken aback by Holly's gruff tone, Catherine took half a step back. "It makes sense to fill the tank up now that we're here."

Holly placed her hands on her hips. "Of course I'm going to fill the tank up."

"I don't understand what the problem is."

Holly huffed, and her breath formed a cloud of steam. Although they were out of the snow, the air was still freezing, and Catherine's teeth were starting to rattle.

"Have I done something wrong?" Catherine asked. She was tempted to fetch her coat, but suspected it wasn't a good idea. She didn't want to aggravate Holly further.

"What makes you think I can't afford to fill the tank up?" Holly shrunk farther into her hoodie, but her eyes pierced Catherine with their icy stare.

"I don't think that."

"Why offer to pay, then?"

Catherine hunched and turned away from an icy gust of wind. This was ridiculous. "I was told we were going to split the cost of the petrol." Her tone was harsher than she intended, but her irritation was growing with every second of freezing her arse off. "Was it agreed or not?"

Holly's eyes opened a little wider. "Yeah, that was agreed."

"Then what exactly is the problem?"

Holly looked at the floor. "I'm sorry—"

"Am I paying for the petrol or not?" Catherine was close to losing her temper.

"Yes," Holly said sheepishly. "Thank you."

Catherine stalked away, her annoyance momentarily taking precedence over the bitter cold. After using the restroom, she studied her reflection while washing her hands. She looked tired and her left eye was still bloodshot. Dark smudges of mascara had smeared beneath her eyes. She wiped them away and then hovered near the hand dryer, allowing the stream of hot air to thaw out her numb hands.

What the hell had gotten into Holly? She'd been so feisty and argumentative for no reason. Her eyes had shone so brightly and her face was flushed in the cold. If it hadn't been for the fact Catherine was now likely to develop hypothermia, she might have found the physiological responses of Holly's outburst sexy.

"You're a mess," she said to herself. Feeling fed up, she headed back to the petrol station's store.

Holly sat in the car, so Catherine picked up a basket and quickly scanned the shelves looking for nothing in particular. She threw in a couple of packets of sweets, four large bottles of water, and a large bag of crisps. She queued up and tried to ignore the Christmas song playing over the radio system. When she reached the counter, she told the cashier the pump number and watched as he rung through the items in her basket.

"Emergency snow kit?" the cashier asked in an emotionless tone.

Catherine looked at the display he was pointing to. After a moment of hesitation she said, "I'll take a torch, batteries, a pair of gloves, and one of the hats."

The cashier added the items to her bag and updated the total, while Catherine read an advertisement for snow chains for car tyres. "I'll take four snow chains, too." They were expensive, but Catherine wasn't about to put a price on their safety.

"Sold out."

"Do you have anything similar?" Catherine asked, trying not to get annoyed at the pimpled-face brat, who seemed incapable of stringing together a sentence.

"Nah."

Biting her tongue to keep back an unsavoury retort, Catherine paid on her card. She gathered the bag by its handles and left. She sprinted to the car, put the bag in the footwell of the backseat, then dove into the front passenger seat.

As she drew the seat belt across, Holly said, "I'm going to park by the main terminal."

Catherine gave a nod. Holly started the engine and carefully drove them. Unlike the relatively deserted petrol station, this car park was brightly lit and held many cars. Lots of people were braving the weather to scurry inside the building.

Holly pulled on her coat, and then turned to Catherine. "Fancy getting a coffee and something to eat? It's my treat."

"Shouldn't we continue driving?"

"I think we should eat something substantial, and I need a coffee. Just half an hour and then we'll get back on the road."

Catherine was about to protest when her stomach growled loudly. Holly laughed and so Catherine gave up being stubborn. What was the point? She could sit sulking in the car while Holly went inside, but that'd only waste petrol. Plus she was ravenous.

"Okay. Half an hour and then we leave. I'm worried about the storm."

"Me too." Holly grimaced. "Come on. The sooner we get in there, the sooner we can get back on the road."

The fragrance of strong coffee welcomed them as they stepped into the lively, warm entrance. They quickly found a coffee shop and ordered their drinks and a bacon sandwich each. True to her word, Holly insisted on paying. Not spoiling for another fight, Catherine graciously accepted and found them a table. A few minutes later, Holly presented their food and drinks. They settled into a slightly awkward silence. The nourishment seemed to perk them both up.

Holly wiped her mouth on a napkin and tossed it onto her empty plate. "I'm sorry about before."

Catherine drained the dregs of her coffee and waved a hand. "Let's forget about it."

Holly looked relieved. "I'm going to nip to the restroom and then we should probably go. It's starting to get light and I'd like to get as far as possible before we meet traffic."

Daylight eventually arrived but was kept hostage behind a sky full of thick, menacing clouds. Snow relentlessly fell, and a breeze picked up. Surprisingly, the roads were full of drivers who'd chosen not to heed the warnings.

Conversation had become stilted and so they drove for a while in silence. It was only when one of the large motorway signs warned of a hazard three junctions ahead that Catherine spoke."Should I put the radio on?"

"Yeah," Holly said, her face etched with worry.

After a few attempts at retuning and avoiding yet more Christmas songs, Catherine settled on a local travel station. The news wasn't good. A pileup had occurred at the aforementioned junction, and traffic was at a total standstill. The presenter read a warning issued by the police and highway patrol. Drivers were advised to steer clear of the junction and find an alternative route. Although emergency services were reportedly at the scene, the scale of the pileup and the adverse weather conditions were creating more problems. It was unlikely the road would be clear before the worst of the storm hit.

"Shit," Holly said. She nervously drummed her fingers on the steering wheel. "What do we do?"

"Take the next exit." Catherine was fighting her own panic, but told herself it was vital Holly remain as calm as possible. She turned off the radio. "We'll find a safe place to pull up and we'll re-evaluate everything."

It seemed to work. Holly steered the car into the queue of slow-moving traffic. After finally breaking away, she drove them to a nearby residential street and parked up. She left the engine running.

They watched a group of five children playing in a large front garden of one of the houses. Three of them were having a snowball fight and two others were rolling a large snowball for presumably the body of a snowman. Brandishing rosy cheeks and red noses, they looked cold and snotty, but happy. As far as they were concerned, the snow was a plaything.

Catherine recovered the map and began riffling through the pages.

"I don't know what we should do," Holly said, nibbling on a thumbnail.

"We're here," Catherine said. She pointed to an area of the map. Using her index finger, she led a trail upward and then stopped. "This is where Beth's house is."

It didn't look too far. But then the map didn't account for the motorway being closed, the imminent storm, and the already adverse driving conditions.

"Is there an alternative route we could take?" Holly asked. She was now clutching at the drawstrings of her hoodie.

Catherine retraced the trail backward, this time cutting out the motorway. "Yes. It'll add maybe another hour to the journey, but it takes us where we need to go."

"I don't know if we should risk it." Holly rubbed her face with her trembling hands. "But then what would we do instead? We've come so far and it's too late to turn back."

"We need to decide quickly," Catherine said. She noticed the breeze had turned into a blustery wind sweeping the snowflakes into a hypnotic swirling vortex.

Holly searched around the car, opening various compartments until she found what she was looking for. She held up a shiny coin.

"I say we toss this to decide. Heads we carry on. Tails we try to find a hotel or some other place to wait it out."

"You can't be serious?"

"Have a better idea?"

"It's so immature."

Holly pursed her lips and rolled her eyes defensively. "It's quick and it makes the decision for us. Right, here we go." She flipped the coin off her thumb and they both watched as it somersaulted in the air before landing safely in her palm. Glancing at Catherine, she asked, "Ready?"

Catherine's stomach was tied up in knots. Were they really leaving this mammoth decision, a decision that could lead to a matter of life and death, to the outcome of a coin toss? It was ridiculous.

The question must have been rhetorical because Holly slowly opened her fist. They both peered down. Heads.

"We carry on," Holly said in an emotionless tone. "Unless you want to do best out of three?"

Catherine swallowed down her growing nausea. "Let's go. We can't afford to waste any more time."

Holly shoved the coin into one of her pockets. She checked her mirrors and began doing a slow three-point turn. "I hope you're good with directions."

"So do I."

❖

For the next ninety minutes, the road conditions were surprisingly decent and they made good progress. The snowflakes fell thicker and faster, but neither of them chose to mention it.

Catherine was secretly impressed with how well they were working together. Having the job of navigating kept her mind occupied and her nerves at bay.

"We're on this road for quite a while," she said, placing the map in her lap, as Holly gave a grunt affirming she'd heard her. She looked out her window. There was no denying the Scottish countryside was stunning. She could make out rolling, snow-covered hillsides, the backdrop to the sparse white fields, hedgerow, and scattered trees.

It didn't take long for an increasing unease to creep over Catherine. The sky had grown unnaturally dark for daytime. The oppressing clouds descended like a fog, blanketing the distant and not-so-distant scenery with worrying speed. Where only a little while ago Catherine had seen the shapes of the hillsides, now her view was nothing but white.

As if sensing her distress, Holly slowed the car's speed. She hovered on the edge of her seat, her nose practically touching the glass of the windscreen. The loud howling from the wind sounded almost animalistic as it pelted the glass with thick snowflakes. The wipers speedily swiped, but to no avail. Visibility was minimal. It didn't help that the road was deserted. All the while they'd been travelling along it, they hadn't passed another vehicle, house, farm, or even sign.

"I can barely see," Holly said in high-pitched tone. Her panic was palpable.

Catherine opened her mouth to speak, but the car lurched and the back end skidded out.

"Shit!" Holly said. Her hands held onto the wheel fighting to keep control. The car slid to a stop at a diagonal angle splayed across both lanes.

Breathing hard and eyes wide, Holly turned to Catherine. "I don't know what to do. I can barely make out anything in front of us. This road is dangerous. I'm scared I'm going to lose control."

Terror clutched Catherine in an icy grip. She didn't have any answers or words to instil confidence. Her rationality was overwhelmed by her terror.

We're going to die. We're going to die.

"Catherine." Holly reached out, but Catherine flinched at her touch. "You're so pale. What can I do?"

Foreboding unlike anything Catherine had ever known weighed down on her, crushing her with its intensity. She sensed, no, knew instinctively something bad was going to happen. It went beyond feeling it in her gut. This was so strong and clear.

"Catherine?"

Fear reverberated down Catherine's spine as if each vertebra was being played like a glockenspiel. She could only manage to draw short, wheezy breaths, and with each gasped exhale, her own panic tightened its grip around her chest, crushing her ribcage and constricting the breath from her body.

"We can't stay in the middle of the road like this. It's not safe. I'm going to drive slowly, and the next town or house we come across, we'll seek shelter," Holly said. She found the gear she needed and slowly accelerated. "We're going to be okay."

Catherine opened her mouth to speak but couldn't find the words and didn't have the breath to verbalise her thoughts. Hot tears spilled down her cheeks as she helplessly waited for the inevitable.

The wind had worked itself up into a raging, roaring gale. It bore down on the car, hammering the battered shell and glass with snow and ice. A mixed array of unhealthy clattering and creaking sounds were forced from the car as the wind engulfed it, seemingly intent on finding some way to rip it apart.

The temperature had plummeted. The car's heat blasted out on full, but wisps of steamy breath materialised from both of them. Outside, the world was greyish white, as if the thickest fog imaginable had descended over the earth. Catherine couldn't make out anything, not a fleeting glance of the road ahead or surrounding countryside. They could be heading straight for a brick wall or another car and they wouldn't know until it was too late.

A violent gust of wind struck Catherine's side of the car with such force she was certain the car would flip over. Holly slammed on the brakes and pulled up the handbrake, but the car continued to blow across the road, inch by stinted inch.

"G-go," Catherine said, as soon as the gust died off a little. If Holly noticed the stutter she didn't show it. She was probably too distracted by the current situation—a tiny blessing.

Catherine clenched her fists and tried to drum up some self-control. Her mouth was dry, and she gently bit down on the tip of her tongue, subconsciously preventing any more stuttering.

It'd been years since she'd last stuttered, although she'd come close at Granny Birch's funeral. During times of intense stress or emotion, her stutter threatened to return—which was infuriating, because obviously whatever she was going through at the time was stressful enough, and the unwanted addition of her stutter only made things a million times worse.

Perhaps it was a one-off? A different thought snapped her attention back to her most pressing concern. *If you're about to die, then yeah, it probably was a one-off. Happy now?* That was enough of a jolt of reality to give her perspective. Stuttering was the least of her worries.

Holly had put the car in motion again, and Catherine tried to consider their options. It was paramount they stay in the car. The chances of them coming across a town, house, or farm, were slim, especially as visibility was so dire, but that was their only real chance of survival. They had to keep moving slowly, because if they stopped on the road, they would be a sitting duck, and the chances of a collision would be ridiculously high.

Catherine turned to tell Holly her thoughts but stalled. Whether psychological or not, she could feel the niggling compulsion that used to accompany her stutter. It had always been there balancing on the tip of her tongue, the infuriating whispered threat of possibly stalling, sticking, and splitting the simplest of words. In her mind she could see every syllable of the words she wanted to say, hear the sounds, and know the feel of them in her mouth, but somewhere between knowing and saying, the compulsion would take hold and wreak havoc.

Refusing to become a slave to her old rival, she took a deep breath, opened her mouth, and said, "Holly—"

The car gave a sudden violent jolt as the right front tyre struck something hard. Holly flattened the brake pedal but caused the back tyres to lock. As both Catherine's and Holly's screams conjoined in a eerie kind of harmony, the car lurched into a spin. With total loss of control Holly uselessly pawed at the wheel. Their momentum was predetermined, and as the car slid into a freewheel skid, they both braced themselves a little too late.

The front tyres hit something, and with an audible crack the bonnet raised high. Gravity came into play and brought the front of the car crashing down. Before Catherine fully clenched her eyes shut, she became aware of two things: firstly, they were descending, and secondly, for the first time since the whiteout had struck, she glimpsed something imminently ahead.

A deafening sound of screeching metal sounded before the car came to an abrupt stop. Momentum threw Catherine's and Holly's bodies forward. Catherine had been right: no airbags. The dashboard greeted them with a brutal smack. The car plunged into darkness as the power cut out.

Catherine's head painfully ricocheted off the dashboard before her body was flung back in the seat. With double vision swimming before her, she blindly felt her face for her glasses, which had wonkily slumped down the bridge of her nose. Pushing them back up into their rightful position did nothing to improve her vision. She started to roll her head to the side, but came to a wincing stop as a stab of pain shot from her neck down to her shoulder. Hissing mumbled swear words, she turned her head a little farther, grimacing against the pain. She needed to check on Holly.

Holly's limp body lay draped over the steering wheel with no signs of movement.

Catherine tried to move but was restricted by disorientating pain and weakness. As she reached a shaky hand toward Holly, a wave of vertigo assaulted her and she dropped her arm pathetically to her side. A barrage of jumbled thoughts and emotions streamed through her mind until she passed out.

CHAPTER EIGHT

The shaking of her pained shoulder was enough to make Catherine open her eyes. Groggily, she tried to make sense of what was happening. Where was she? What had happened? Why was she in so much pain?

"Catherine, you're awake. Thank God. You scared the shit out of me."

Squinting because of the pounding headache residing over her right eye, Catherine slowly turned her head. Holly stared at her with red puffy eyes, her face unnaturally pale and tear-stained, and her hair stood out in utter disarray.

"I thought you were in a coma or worse," Holly said. She added a forced nervous laugh.

Catherine tentatively lifted her fingertips to her forehead to explore the place where most of the throbbing pain was coming from. A large swollen lump now occupied the place where her forehead used to be.

"Yeah, it looks nasty," Holly said, grimacing. "You were out for a few minutes. How are you feeling? Any other injuries?"

Catherine went to shake her head, but let out an involuntary cry as her neck flared in pain. She tried to massage the pain away.

"Whiplash," Holly said quietly. "I've got it, too."

Everything came flooding back and a sense of urgency overtook Catherine's injuries. In a shaky voice she asked, "Are y-you okay?" Her gaze travelled over Holly's face and body looking for signs of trauma.

"I'm a bit battered and bruised, but other than that I'm fine."

Relieved, Catherine had to agree from her appearance Holly did seem okay. Turning her attention to the next priority, she took her time to look around the car. The power was back on, giving them essential light and heat but also suggesting the engine may not have suffered as badly as she originally feared.

The windscreen was covered in a thick layer of snow, so seeing what was on the other side of the glass wasn't possible. Catherine wasn't sure if this might be a blessing for the time being. There was a deep crevice in the glass on Holly's side of the windscreen where something had struck with force. An intricate design of tiny cracks crept out from the chipped centre, resembling a spider web.

Catherine's side window was covered in snow and so was Holly's, which also prevented them from seeing out. The car itself had come to a standstill in a slightly awkward position: the front was in a perpetual nosedive, while the back end remained raised. They were definitely stuck in some kind of ditch. She peered over the back of the seat only to find the back windscreen was as obstructed by snow as all of the others.

"What do we do now?" Holly asked. Her eyes remained puddled with unshed tears as she shrunk farther down into her hoodie.

Catherine unbuckled her seat belt and reached behind her to grab her handbag. She rooted inside and pulled out her phone. As she switched it on and watched it come to life, her stomach dropped. No signal. Not even half a bar.

Following suit, Holly fumbled in her pocket and produced her phone. Catherine watched the flicker of hope extinguish from Holly's face. "No signal," she said.

As the car creaked and groaned from the raging gale outside, Catherine considered their next option. No signal meant no help. Not that she would've been able to give the emergency services an exact pinpoint on their whereabouts anyway.

They would have to save themselves. They needed to get out of this ditch and back onto the road where someone might drive by and rescue them. It was a slim chance, but it was the only one they had.

"We need to g-get back up onto the road. B-buckle up and try reversing."

"I can't see a thing. I don't know how steep this ditch is. I don't know how far the road is. What if I hit something else while driving blind and damage the car or put us in worse danger? Shouldn't we stay here and wait to be rescued?"

There was an edge of growing hysteria to Holly's tone. Catherine reached out and took hold of her hands, giving them a fierce squeeze. "We're in this t-together. You and me." Startled, Holly held her gaze. "We have to b-be strong for one another. No one is g-going to rescue us. No one knows where we are and w-we can't tell them. We're going to have to r-rescue ourselves. Okay?" Catherine watched as a few tears leaked from Holly's eyes and her bottom lip quivered ever so slightly. "H-Holly, okay?"

Holly gave a weak nod.

Adrenaline coursed through Catherine's veins. She ground her teeth and fought against the throbbing pain from her forehead. "G-go on." Holly turned the key. The engine choked and the lights flickered as the power wavered.

Acid scorched the back of Catherine's throat causing another wave of nausea. Was she wrong? Should they stay put? If the engine died and they lost power there would be no chance of survival.

Holly tried again and this time the lights and power cut out completely. Plunged into darkness yet again, Catherine could only make out Holly's shape but no distinguishing features. Desperate terror radiated off her.

With only a few seconds without the heat, the temperature in the car had already dropped significantly. In a matter of minutes they would be at risk of the bitter cold seeping into the car. The prospect of freezing to death seemed horrendously possible. What had she done?

Holly turned the key again, but only a weak wheezing sounded from the engine.

"Come on, you bastard!" Holly said, her voice hoarse and full of frustration. Her hands pummelled the steering wheel and the car rocked slightly as she jumped up and down in her chair.

"Holly—" Catherine said, but was interrupted as Holly twisted the key again, this time rewarded with a heartier chug of the engine.

"Come on, baby. Come on," Holly said. She bowed her head as if almost in prayer. "Please."

The engine stuttered for a few milliseconds and then came to life with a tremendous revving. A stream of warm air began to circulate again, taking the edge off the chill. The windscreen wipers at the front and back of the car began swiping at the heavy snow. It took a while, but eventually, the snow started to clear and what lay on the other side became visible.

At first Catherine questioned if it was night because of the darkness, but glancing back at the rearview window showed the world outside remained greyish white. A few seconds later, the last of the compacted snow was swept away from Catherine's side and the cause of the darkness made sense. A large tree had stopped their descent.

"R-reverse," Catherine said. She clicked in the buckle to her seat belt and braced herself for whatever would happen next.

Holly moved the gearstick and applied pressure to the accelerator until she found the biting point. Turning to look over her shoulder, she released the handbrake. The car began to slowly reverse. An awful metallic screeching filled the air as the bonnet tried to rip itself from the bark of the tree. Holly accelerated, and the back of the car began to climb higher. They reversed maybe a foot up the slope before their progress came to a halt. Holly applied a little more power, but they moved nowhere.

"Come on!" Holly said. Her expression showed steely determination as she flatfooted the pedal. The revving and screech of the wheels was almost deafening, but the car remained static, apart from a bit of bobbing up and down and sliding slightly to the left.

Holly gradually took her foot off the accelerator and applied the handbrake. Once again, the brake lost out to snow and gravity. The car slid back down and bumped the tree again with an audible thud.

Something was blocking their ascent. There was no choice. Catherine would have to go investigate. She unbuckled herself, removed her trainers, and started the wearisome task of forcing her overlarge feet into the small wellies.

"You can't go out in the middle of a blizzard, Catherine," Holly said. She looked genuinely horrified by the idea.

"N-need to c-check wheels." Catherine made stabbing gestures as she pointed downward, trying to distract attention away from her stutter. A potent mixture of humiliation and frustration warmed her cheeks. The last thing she needed on top of all of this was not being able to speak properly. It made communication difficult and affected her self-confidence. Most likely, it made Holly feel the same.

"I'll go instead—"

"N-no." Catherine cut her off with an aggressive shaking of her head and thumbed her chest. Holly shrank back a little in her seat. She looked like she wanted to argue, but bit down on her bottom lip instead.

Catherine's feet felt like they'd been painfully bound, and she emitted a fleeting sympathetic thought for the poor Chinese women who had endured a permanent version of this torture. She pulled on her coat, followed by her new hat, and then fumbled for a little while inserting batteries into the new torch. Testing it proved it worked fine.

Holly silently presented Catherine with her own thick purple scarf. Catherine nodded her appreciation and wrapped it around her neck, mouth, and nose. It smelled of Holly—earthy with a hint of spicy sweetness. Glad the scarf hid the flush creeping up her neck, she zipped up her coat, pulled the hood over her hat-covered head, and tugged the drawstrings so only a slit for her glasses remained. Finally, she pulled on her new gloves, grateful they were thick and warm. With her torch in hand, she prepared herself for venturing outside.

"Wait a minute," Holly said urgently. She rummaged behind her seat and produced a roll of gold glittery ribbon. "Just in case you get disorientated or lose your way, we'll wrap this around one of your wrists and then you'll be able to follow it and find your way back to the car."

Catherine held out her left arm, and Holly found the loose end of the festive ribbon and began wrapping it around her wrist. Although her coat was thick and the gloves were big, she eventually began to feel a light restriction from the ribbon, enough to let her know it was there. After a few more loops, Holly tied a knot and unravelled a few meters in preparation.

"Be careful," Holly said. With a sniffle, she lunged forward, pulling Catherine into a tight embrace.

Padded by so many heavy layers, Catherine resented not being able to feel the press of Holly's body against hers. It seemed wholly unfair. Taking a deep breath, she tried to keep up the pretence of bravery. In reality she was crapping herself.

Her cowardice—she was under no illusions about what it was—had always been masked by her declaration of being overcautious. She'd never been moved to do anything overtly brave or truly altruistic, believing it wasn't in her nature and finding it best to leave it to others more capable than herself. Did that make her selfish? Yes, but it had also kept her relatively safe until now.

She'd also never taken a real interest in the big outdoors, preferring to be inside with her nose stuck between the dusty pages of one book or another. At school she'd always had an excuse ready so she could skive off PE, especially when it came to orienteering or cross-county running. While her peers had trundled through thick mud, usually while it was wet and cold, she'd happily taken herself off to the library.

There was a reassuring safety that accompanied books. They allowed her to explore an infinite number of places and possibilities without ever having to put herself in danger. And if things ever got a little too scary or wildly adventurous she could skip some pages or leave the book unfinished. It was a shame she'd never taken a keener interest in survival stories. And yet at this precise moment in time, an overwhelming desire to do everything in her power to keep Holly safe took precedence over everything else. Risking her own life wasn't exactly appealing, but it was a sacrifice she'd make without a second thought to protect Holly or die trying.

Spurred on, she pulled the handle and pushed the door. Nothing happened. Edging closer to the door, she pulled the handle again, and this time shoved with the full weight of her body. She met resistance. As a painful twinge stabbed her neck, a loud creaking came from the door before it gave way and flung open.

Bitter cold unlike anything she had ever known engulfed her. Fog clouding her lenses rendered her immediately blind. Stumbling forward in nearly knee-deep snow, she clambered out of the car and tried to mostly close the door for Holly's sake, leaving it slightly open to prevent the ribbon from getting trapped.

With limited dexterity from her gloved hands, she tried to clear the lenses of her glasses. Icy stings and talons descended, pricking the bare and lightly covered flesh on her face. An unrelenting coldness seeped into her body as if she were naked, despite the layers of clothing. Freezing breath caught in the back of her throat, and when she managed to draw another breath, it burned her chest and caused a coughing fit.

The strength of the storm's gale shoved her against the car; the snowflakes were so dense and remorseless, she feared she might suffocate. Turning away from the elements, she made out the tyre on her side. A large groove of ice cupped the tyre like a bowl. She trudged forward as the snow and wind battered her and found the back tyre was in the same state.

There was no way the car was going to make it back up the slope because the condensed snow had turned to thick ice, which wouldn't allow for grip of traction. They were completely and utterly stuck.

Shielding the right side of her face with her hand, she tried to look up and gauge how far from the road they'd travelled. Only managing to make out two feet in front of her gave no clues other than more of a slope and plenty more snow.

Unable to stand another second of the cold, she made her way back to the door by feeling along the side of the car. On her third attempt, the wind dropped off enough for her to pry the door open. She dove inside, and the door slammed behind her.

CHAPTER NINE

S he would never be warm again.

The cold had buried deep into her core, crystallising the marrow of her bones. After half an hour of trying to defrost inside the car, she was too far gone to even recall a memory of heat. Her body shivered uncontrollably, while her teeth rattled in her skull. On inspection, her hands were red raw and the tips of her fingers tinted with blue. She returned them to the protection of her insulated gloves and tucked them under her armpits.

On her request, Holly had raided her suitcase and Catherine was now wearing every item of clothing she'd packed, including the previously worn socks from the day before. She had never worn so many layers before, and yet if she had access to more clothes she would have donned those, too. Holly's suitcase was trapped in the car's boot but she claimed she was warm enough. Catherine didn't believe her and was keeping a close eye on her.

Since her return to the car, Holly had been nursing her. She'd helped pull off the wellies, retrieved the clothes, turned away when Catherine had needed privacy, and helped untangle some of the clothing that had gotten bunched up around her shoulders. She'd made a snowpack using a plastic bag and a large handful of snow and insisted Catherine keep it pressed against the lump on her forehead.

Secretly, Catherine thoroughly enjoyed having the attention showered upon her. Through disjointed sentences caused partly by her chattering teeth but also by her stutter, she finally managed to relay the disturbing news that they were going nowhere. They were stranded in the snowstorm from hell. But they had shelter and heat while in the car and two-thirds of the tank of petrol left. Holly had switched off the wipers to conserve energy.

They had to be careful they didn't get snowed in. Catherine was going to have to brave the elements for a couple of minutes every hour or so to clear her doorway, a prospect she loathed.

As for provisions, they had the water she'd purchased at the petrol station and, as Holly pointed out, an endless supply of snow should they run out. They briefly skirted around the uncomfortable subject of keeping hydrated while not overdoing it. Having to relieve oneself outside during a blizzard was a little too distressing to ponder. The lack of food was a concern as the large pack of crisps, sweets, and half pack of breath mints wouldn't keep their hunger at bay for long. But the biggest worry was the prospect of subzero temperatures they'd have to face during the night. For the time being, Catherine kept this fear to herself.

"I could eat a s-scabby horse," Catherine said. She wondered if hunger pains would eventually take over from all the other complaints sounding from her body.

"I'm so stupid," Holly said. She climbed into the back passenger compartment. After a lot of rustling she offered out a brown cardboard box.

Catherine dropped the dripping snowpack into the door's empty side compartment before taking hold of the box and studying the top. An elegant purple rectangle with the single word *Indulgence* printed across the centre in silver ink. Before she could open it up, Holly passed her another two boxes: one the same size as the first and another smaller in size but heavier in weight. Balancing the tower of boxes in her lap, she used both hands to try to prevent them falling. She'd no choice but to wait for Holly to return before she could peruse the contents of the boxes. The smells drifting up made her stomach growl.

"This is the last one," Holly said. She placed another box on top of the previous three.

Unable to see behind her, Catherine had to make do with listening to and trying to discern what Holly was up to now. Huffed, oddly sexual sounding groans stood out over familiar rustling and zipping noises, zapping Catherine with a wholly inappropriate twinge of arousal.

"Mustn't forget these," Holly said. She leant into the front compartment and dropped a bundle of what looked like knitted wool on her seat. For the next few minutes, she continued to rustle in the back stopping only to drop a few more items on her seat.

Hitting her head, Holly swore as she clambered back into the front of the car. She narrowly avoided knocking the boxes out of Catherine's hands while grabbing the items off her seat. Full arms made her movements cumbersome in the small space. Her backside honked the horn five times before she finally sat down.

"We need to put more layers on, and these will be perfect." Holly held up a thick green knitted woollen jumper large enough to quite possibly fit them both inside. "This one is for you." She grinned.

Catherine was too cold to bother thinking about a potential fashion faux pas. The jumper looked warm. It was only when Holly turned the jumper around that Catherine realised she'd been shown the plain back. Staring at her now with unblinking eyes was the cartoonish head of a huge knitted reindeer. Rudolph, if the bulbous red nose was anything to go by.

Before she could speak, Holly showed off the next knitted woollen jumper in her collection. This one was red and had a Christmas pudding on the front. The next one was blue with a lopsided Christmas tree and a large wonky star. But the last one was the worst of the bunch. The mustard-coloured jumper had an evil-looking snowman on the front.

Catherine folded her arms. "N-no way."

Holly's grin faltered and her eyebrows knitted together. "It's freezing and these are warm. Don't be ridiculous."

"They're horrendous," Catherine said without a hint of a stutter. Apparently, her subconscious agreed enough to not interrupt her. Holly's mouth formed a thin line and two pink spots coloured her cheeks.

"I'll have you know, I knitted these jumpers myself. They're not amazing by some people's standards, but I invested a lot of time and an awful lot of effort into knitting them."

Catherine was rendered speechless. The jumpers were truly awful, and wearing one would be embarrassing, but to relieve the hurt expression on Holly's face, she'd do just about anything. Keeping the boxes balanced in her lap without the aid of her hands, she reached out for the Rudolph jumper.

Holly's face lit up. "There are two each. Which other one do you want?"

Not daring to risk causing more offence, Catherine pointed

unenthusiastically at the red jumper with the Christmas pudding on the front.

A little while later she sat shrouded by both jumpers, feeling warmer. Holly pulled both of her jumpers on, too, choosing to hide the mustard one beneath the blue. In Catherine's opinion, she looked cute.

"I've found some painkillers. They might help with your head." Holly tossed the plastic strip over. "I also found a lighter and some crayons in case we end up without light."

Catherine swallowed two of the tablets, narrowly avoided choking. The lighter might be useful, but what were the crayons for? Writing a last will and testament on the dashboard? Drawing in the dark?

"I read somewhere a crayon can burn up to an hour, and these are jumbo so they'll probably last a bit longer." With the lighter resting on top of the pack, Holly placed them in the central compartment. "I'm sure Florence won't begrudge us using them."

Catherine felt suitably berated and a little in awe of Holly's resourcefulness. First the ribbon, then the jumpers, and now the crayons. Above anything, she was eager to discover the contents of the boxes. "Can we open the b-boxes?"

"Of course." Holly smiled shyly. "You do the honours. I'm afraid none of the contents are particularly healthy, though."

Catherine all but ripped the first lid open. Her gaze fell over an array of foil-lined individual pies. Some had a pastry apple on the top, while the others had a star.

"Apple and mince pies," Holly said.

Catherine passed her the box, and Holly replaced the lid before resting it in her lap.

The second box contained a large iced Christmas cake, decorated with festive ribbon, a little Santa, and a tree figurine. A strong smell of brandy pleasantly tickled Catherine's nose.

Catherine handed the second box to Holly so she could focus on the unopened ones. The next box had the most incredible looking and smelling brownies.

"Triple chocolate," Holly said. "I know they're not a festive staple, but they're too delicious to miss out."

Trying not to salivate unattractive pools of drool in front of Holly, Catherine opened the final box. The warming scent of ginger filled the air. Reasonably large and varying shapes of golden gingerbread were attractively displayed in sections.

"These have been a best seller. Build your own gingerbread house, with the parts all ready to assemble. There's icing in the tub to use as glue. I did consider supplying sweets and chocolate to decorate with, but it would've been too costly and everyone's tastes differ."

Catherine lifted out a folded sheet of paper. Instructions on how to assemble the house and suggestions on different ways to decorate it were listed.

"Florence gave me the idea. The last time I saw her she badgered me into helping her make a gingerbread house like the one in *Hansel and Gretel*. I figured leading up to Christmas it was worth a shot, and they've flown off the shelf."

They had water and enough naughty food to cause them to slip into a glucose-induced coma. But their real chance of survival depended on how long the storm lasted and the possibility of being rescued before night descended. In subzero temperatures the likelihood of them maintaining enough heat was wishful at best. They had a couple of hours until things started to get seriously dangerous.

Catherine felt a little queasy from the hit to her head, but her appetite was still very much alive and kicking. Not wanting to eat away the opportunity of Holly and Florence making the gingerbread house together, she succumbed instead to the temptation of a brownie.

The brownie was quite possibly the most deliciously decadent item of food ever to pass her lips. A loud groan of pleasure escaped her, but she was too caught up in the chocolate-fuelled orgasmic bliss to care.

Savouring the last mouthful, she sucked the tips of her fingers so as not to waste any. When she opened her eyes, Holly was watching her with an unreadable expression. A gentle flush coloured her cheeks and her eyebrows were arched high.

"That w-was incredible," Catherine said. Now suitably sated, a warm snugly feeling settled over her.

"No kidding," Holly said, sounding a little flustered. "Catherine, I want to apologise. This whole situation is my fault. I'm so sorry for dragging you into this mess."

"Holly—"

"If we'd continued driving last night or skipped breakfast this morning like you'd suggested, we wouldn't be in this mess. And using the coin to decide was childish. So, yeah, I'm sorry for not listening to you."

"There's no b-blame. We're in this together."

Holly gave a nod, but her shoulders sagged, as if still burdened by guilt. "You know what I regret—apart from everything?" She gave a weak laugh.

Catherine shrugged, reluctant to speak unless she had to.

"I regret not joining you for dinner last night in the restaurant. And I owe you another apology," Holly said quietly. She picked some nonexistent fluff off the jumper. "The excuse about being tired was a lie. Don't get me wrong, I was tired, but the real reason I didn't join you was because of my stupid pride."

Catherine was confused and wasn't sure if it was because of the whack to her head or because Holly's words were like riddles. She suffered a little sting of hurt, too, because she'd been looking forward to the meal and Holly had lied to her. But excitement wriggled in her belly because Holly had admitted she regretted the dinner that didn't happen.

"I didn't join you because I couldn't afford to. With the business still in its first year, cash is a real sore point for me. After I've paid my personal bills, the rest of my money goes straight back into the business. That's why I couldn't afford to go away with my family for Christmas and why I didn't join you for a meal last night."

"I would—"

"I know you would have offered to pay, Catherine." Holly gave a wan smile. "But I wouldn't have allowed myself to accept. I know from the outside it must seem silly, but honestly, I find it humiliating. I hate not being able to pay my own way. Especially when I'm trying to impress a gorgeous woman."

Gorgeous woman? Catherine's cheeks warmed at the compliment, and her stomach did a somersault.

"My regret is, I missed the perfect opportunity to get to know you. And I can't help but wonder what might have happened after the meal was over."

The car was getting hotter. Catherine might have to remove some layers. How was it possible for a few words to change the dynamic of their situation? One minute, she was contemplating their untimely demise, and a minute later, her senses were on fire and she was horny as hell.

"I want to get to know you better." Holly edged closer.

"O-okay," Catherine said in a rasp.

"Can I ask you some questions?"

Catherine's heart sank. Questions? That meant speaking, which in turn meant stuttering. Her demeanour went from hot and bothered to just plain bothered. Holly watched her with those eyes that seemed to see right into her soul, her focus intense as she waited for Catherine's response.

Catherine realised Holly was serious about wanting to get to know her, and although having her do so in the biblical sense would've been her first choice, getting to know her through talking was still more interest than anyone had showed in years. "O-okay," Catherine said. She moved around trying to find a comfortable position but failed. She was overly aware of how cramped her body was. Her lower back ached, her backside was numb, and her legs craved space to stretch.

"Why do you hate Christmas?"

There it was. Bam! The question she dreaded more than any other and it had to be the first one out of Holly's mouth. Talk about starting as you mean to go on. "It's a long s-story," Catherine said, hoping with every fibre of her being that Holly would drop the subject.

"Well, we have plenty of time."

"It's depressing."

Holly shrugged. "If you really don't want to tell me—"

"All right." Catherine gave up. Focusing on the snow-covered windscreen, she took a deep breath. "When I was nine, my parents went out for an evening. They died in a car crash on their way home. It was early December."

Holly gasped, but she remained silent.

"One m-minute they were there, and the next…" Catherine shrugged. "I wrote over twenty letters to Santa. I demanded Granny Birch take me to see all of the Santas at the different stores." Poor Granny Birch. She'd had so much on her shoulders, making all of the arrangements to bury her only son and his wife, taking care of Catherine, and still trying to keep the magic of Christmas alive—all while her heart was breaking.

"I'd wait my turn, s-sit on their laps, and when they asked me what I wanted, my answer was always the same. I wanted my mum and dad back." The memory of being quickly hurried along, given a cheap crappy toy and a pat on the head, and then being sent away remained fresh in her mind. As were the memories of Granny Birch's tears and the many times she'd sat Catherine down and tried to explain Santa couldn't give her what she wanted.

"Christmas Eve came, and I was certain my wish would be granted. I'd been a good girl all year, and Christmas was a time for miracles. I was convinced, come Christmas morning, I'd wake up and my parents would be home. I couldn't wait to hug and kiss them, smell my mum's perfume, and hear their voices. And I couldn't wait to see Granny Birch's face, knowing all of her sadness would be gone."

Holly wiped away tears as she tried to keep her sniffles quiet.

Catherine faltered. It was clear what had happened—hadn't happened. Normally, she'd say the words invoking no emotion to their meaning. And yet now, the pain she'd kept bottled up and buried deep inside for so many years was gushing out. "I went to bed at five in the afternoon and Granny Birch gave up trying to argue with me. I woke after seven on Christmas Day. I rushed downstairs—"

She couldn't do it.

She couldn't speak the words.

The memories were too painful and yet, in her mind's eye, she relived it all.

The sound of her feet as she bounded down the wooden stairs. Seeing the mince pie had been eaten and the milk had been drunk only added to her excitement. Santa had come. The green tree with vibrant flashing lights and the many colourful presents placed beneath its branches. The fragrance of pine mixed with the smell of the turkey cooking in the oven. The cold as it nipped at her bare feet. The crushing heartbreak as she ran from room to room calling excitedly for her parents. The agonising, gradual realisation that Christmas miracles and Santa were nothing more than childish lies.

The knowledge of her parents' deaths was the only stark truth remaining.

Granny Birch's strong arms wrapping around her waist, her voice trying to soothe through her own disjointed sobs. The horrendous animal-like sound filling the house, which turned out to be Catherine's own screams.

"I'm...so sorry, Catherine," Holly said. She pulled Catherine into her arms.

Unable to speak, Catherine allowed herself to be held. She didn't wipe her tears or try to silence her cries. The pain was as fresh as that Christmas morning long ago, and yet she needed to let it out. As she sobbed, she was aware Holly didn't speak or shush her. Instead, Holly wrapped her arms around Catherine and rested her chin on top of her head, her own tears flowing all the while.

CHAPTER TEN

Catherine ended their embrace not because she felt embarrassed but because her body was seizing up. Mentally cursing the limited legroom and claustrophobic confines of the car, she pulled away from Holly and immediately mourned the loss of warmth and comfort. She'd never allowed herself to be comforted by a stranger before, but then she'd never broken down either. Holly seemed to be the catalyst for a number of dramatic personal changes.

Exhausted but feeling as though a huge weight had been lifted, Catherine swallowed, trying to dislodge the hot lump of emotion stuck in her throat. "I'm sorry for—"

"Don't you dare apologise for what happened. You're one of the bravest people I've ever met," Holly said. She puffed out her chest as if preparing for an argument.

"Actually, I'm s-sorry for the snot and mascara stains on your jumper." Catherine watched as Holly looked down. There was a patch of tear-stained mascara on the left side of Holly's chest above the mound of her breast.

Holly examined the stain. "No worries. I'm sure it'll wash out." She looked up at Catherine and smiled. "You might want to glance in the mirror. You've got a little bit of mascara under your eye."

Catherine pulled down the mirror and scoffed at her reflection. "A bit of mascara? I look like a l-long lost member of Kiss." It was true. Black streaks beneath both eyes and cheeks stood out against the pale greenish hue of her complexion. She looked like crap.

"Well, I didn't want to be rude," Holly said. She stretched her arms above her head, letting the tips of her fingers brush the ceiling.

"I'm sorry for asking about the Christmas thing, but I'm glad you told me. It's no wonder you hate it."

Catherine was in the process of wiping her face with a wad of spit-covered tissue. She'd originally tried to perch her glasses on top of her head, but the monstrous lump on her forehead put an end to that plan. Her glasses now lay in her lap, and her poor eyesight made Holly look like an unflattering blob with no distinguishing features. "Ever since that year, Christmas is something I've gritted my teeth and tried to get through as quickly as possible. Like a trip to the gynaecologist." What the hell? Did that actually come out of her mouth? Yes. Yes, she mentioned a trip to the gynaecologist in front of a woman she was attracted to.

Holly laughed. "Catherine, you're so funny," she said, her tone musical and light. "But I'm getting to the point where my bladder is full, so you need to not make me laugh. Otherwise it's going to get messy in here. Okay?"

"Okay," Catherine said. She put on her glasses and glanced at her reflection. It was as good as it could be under the circumstances. She'd never been called funny before, well, maybe funny as in weird, but definitely not funny as in ha-ha. She'd never considered herself amusing, but if it meant she'd get to hear Holly's laugh again, she'd consider becoming a clown.

"So your birthday is on Christmas Day?" Catherine asked. Trying to simultaneously fill the silence and get out of the limelight.

"Yeah." Holly swept a curly strand behind her ear. "As a kid I hated it. It never seemed fair. I couldn't have a party because all my friends were celebrating with their families. I kept asking to change it. My parents eventually agreed to let me celebrate my eighth birthday on June fifteenth instead. For the next eight years, that's the date we used."

"Why that date?"

"It was a Saturday and the weather looked good. When I turned seventeen, I couldn't be bothered anymore and we started celebrating it on Christmas Day again. I love that the whole holiday is steeped in family tradition, and my family is huge. With the exception of occasions like weddings and funerals, Christmas is the one time we all make an effort to contact each other. I've always liked that aspect of it. The togetherness. This year Katie and I are going to Skype with my parents, sisters, and other family in Canada."

Catherine watched as Holly nibbled her bottom lip and tears welled. "What is it?"

"I'm scared. What if we don't…"

Get rescued? Catherine couldn't help but ask herself the same question. "Beth and Katie will report us m-missing."

"No one knows where we are," Holly said. "We're on a deserted road in the middle of nowhere. How can they find us if they don't have a clue where to look?"

"We've got provisions, shelter, and each other. We'll be okay."

Holly continued to cry and her voice sounded nasally. "I'm so scared. I can't bear the thought of not seeing my family again." She shook her head. "I'm sorry. You must think I'm a totally selfish cow, and you're right."

"I think nothing of the s-sort. Of course you're scared and upset. I am, too." Another thought occurred to Catherine, and before she had engaged her brain, she voiced it aloud. "Other than Beth and Katie, the only other person who'd probably realise I was missing is my personal assistant, Eve." Wow, that was depressing. At thirty-one years of age, she was alone now, more than ever before, and only had herself to blame.

"That can't be true."

"It is," Catherine said honestly. There was no one else. Even now, as she racked her brain, she could think of no one else who would miss her.

"What about the people you work with?"

"Yesterday when you asked me about my job I lied. I don't enjoy it. I'm good at it and it pays well, but I've no friends other than Eve. I was embarrassed."

"Embarrassed?"

"Yes. You're so confident in your abilities. You have this amazing passion for your career, and it made me realise how much I loathe my job."

Holly looked uncomfortable. "I'm sorry. I do love my job, but I went overboard yesterday a bit because I wanted to impress you."

"Impress me?"

A blush turned Holly's face beet red. "Yes. I wanted to impress you and assure you I wasn't some young foolish girl."

Catherine couldn't help but smile. "I think you're very impressive."

Holly's colour bordered on purple as she spluttered out her next question. "Why don't you change jobs?"

Catherine hesitated in replying. She could reel off all the usual reasons: decent money, she was good at it and was due a promotion anytime soon, but something stopped her. She knew Holly wouldn't accept her reasons, and for the first time in years, neither did she. She'd gotten the job straight out of university so she could support Paula in her ambition to become an artist. When Paula left, it had been the only thing she could focus on to distract her from the hurt.

"Catherine?"

"I wouldn't know what else to do." And that was the truth. Her job had been the constant rock to which she'd clung when everything had slipped out of her control. Paula leaving and then Granny Birch's death had both taken their toll. But now, trapped inside this car and facing an uncertain future, she gained a new insight. It was like an epiphany. She'd become complacent with living a monotonous life. It'd been easier to stick to a routine than consider taking risks and changing her life for the better. She had financial resources most people would be envious of. So what was holding her back? Fear of the unknown?

"You must have considered a different career at some point," Holly said.

"Not really."

"Well, what hobbies do you have?"

"I don't have any." She sounded pathetic to her own ears. When had she turned into such a loser?

"I don't believe that. What do you do to relax? Where do you go and what do you do outside of work?"

Catherine opened her mouth but hesitated. She enjoyed drinking wine, but sounding like a raging alcoholic wasn't helpful. She also liked to read—loved to read, in fact. That was what she did to take her mind off work. "I enjoy reading and I volunteer at the local library twice a week. I help out at the children's homework and reading clubs."

"I'm pretty sure the people there would miss you." Holly smiled. "What is it you do?"

"I help out. Sometimes I listen to them read and other times I help them with whatever homework they have. There are thirteen children who attend. Some of them need extra support with their literacy, while others come after school because it's a safe place to wait until their parents can pick them up."

"What are their ages?"

"The youngest is five, and I think the oldest recently turned thirteen." A little wave of vertigo assaulted her senses. "You seem surprised."

"Not surprised, impressed. It's awesome you give up your free time. If I had any spare time I'd love to do something similar, but for the foreseeable future it's not practical with the business. I knew there was more to you than meets the eye."

Catherine felt her pulse quicken. "So you think I should work in a library?" The words had sounded preposterous in her mind, but now she'd spoken them there was a certain kind of appeal.

"If that's what you want, then sure." Holly gave a shrug. "But there are other careers that would allow you to work with books and people. The publishing industry is one. Bookshops and charities are another two. You don't have to make a decision right now, Catherine. Think about it for a while."

Catherine gave a nod. "I suppose."

"Make it one of your New Year's resolutions. You know, to move on to a career you feel passionate about."

"Have you any resolutions?" Catherine asked, glad to turn the spotlight again. Her head was killing her and her vision kept swimming in and out of focus.

"Actually, this whole experience has made me think a lot about my future. There's so much I want to do and experience. As soon as I get back home I'm going to rent out the spare room in my apartment. The extra money will help me out, and I'll also have company. Then I'm going to make an effort to catch up with family and friends. Since opening the business I've been neglecting them."

Holly spoke with enthusiasm, smiling and gesturing animatedly. Catherine forced down the rising fear they wouldn't get rescued in case her thoughts somehow turned that fear into reality.

"And I'm going to make a real concerted effort to lose some weight. I've never been this big before." Holly patted the material over her stomach.

"You're perfect the way you are."

Holly met Catherine's eyes before her gaze darted away. "You think so?"

"Yes."

"Thank you," Holly said shyly. "I also want to get another tattoo and maybe another piercing."

"You have a tattoo?"

"I have two. This is the first." She pulled back the material on her right arm, bunching it up past her elbow. Tilting her arm slightly, she presented her forearm so Catherine could see.

Catherine took in the black outline of a butterfly; its wings were coloured with blue and green ink. It was beautiful and she had to almost restrain herself from reaching out to touch it. "It suits you."

"That bump to your head has made you cordial. But I'll take any compliments I can get," Holly said. "My other tattoo is a lot bigger."

"Can I see it?"

Holly blushed. "As much as I love showing it off, it isn't worth the risk of developing frostbite. Plus, there's not enough room in here for me to do a decent striptease. You'll have to wait until we get out of here."

"Oh," Catherine said lamely. Forget the heater and many layers. All Catherine needed was for Holly to keep talking like this and she was at risk of spontaneously combusting. Flirting was practically a different language to her and one subject she'd always flunked out of. She supposed, under the circumstances, she could give it a go and if she humiliated herself like she usually did, she could always blame the concussion. "Whereabouts on your body is it?"

"It starts from around here." Holly pointed to below her hip. She trailed her index finger slowly upward. "And it goes to here." Her finger stopped beneath her right breast.

Catherine gave an audible gulp. "Is it another butterfly?"

"Nope. A winding branch with pink cherry blossoms."

Catherine tried to imagine it, but had to quickly give up as a barrage of inappropriate thoughts filled her mind's eye. "Is there a meaning behind them?"

"My dad's always called me his little butterfly, so before I went to France I got it done. He wasn't overly impressed, though. As for the cherry blossoms, I totally fell in love with the design. It reminds me of Paris in springtime. What about you, any ink?"

"No. Tattoos aren't my thing. I'm not an exciting enough person to express myself in a creative outlandish way. No offence."

Holly laughed. "None taken. You have your ears pierced."

"Yes," Catherine said. She automatically felt the plain studs in her earlobes. "Beth encouraged me to get them done on a drunken night out when we were at university."

"You rebel," Holly said, teasing. "Do you regret having them done?"

"Not really." They were a reminder she'd once let her hair down and done something spontaneous. And also that Beth could be a bad influence. "It really hurt, though, and put me off ever getting another one. I don't have a strong pain threshold."

"Are those the original studs?"

"Yes." Catherine felt a little embarrassed. "I meant to take them out and try wearing earrings, but I never got around to it." The truth was she'd been too self-conscious about trying earrings and she was scared it'd hurt.

"How's your head feeling?" Holly asked. "You're a little green around the gills."

Before Catherine could reply, a huge gust rattled the car. The wind sounded like an eerie wailing, as if a banshee were right outside. It was enough to ruin their comforting pretence that everything was okay.

Catherine snuck a glance at the gauges; they had already used up over half the tank of petrol. The storm still raged and showed no signs of letting up any time soon. How much longer would they have heat and light? She couldn't bring herself to do the maths.

"Can I ask a favour?" Catherine asked. She closed her eyes and pinched the bridge of her nose. The inside of the car was spinning and exhaustion was settling in.

"Of course."

"Will you tell me about your family's Christmas traditions?"

"But you hate Christmas."

With her eyes still clenched shut, she removed her hand and felt as her glasses fell back into place. "I'm tired of hating it." And she was. She'd carried this huge chip on her shoulder and hole in her heart for years. She'd blamed Christmas and everything associated with it for the death of her parents. She'd allowed the bitterness to thrive, and every year she'd fed it with more pent-up anger and hurt. Christmas, as a concept, had become alien to her. She'd always convinced herself Granny Birch had felt the same way, but now she was plagued with doubt. While sorting through her house Catherine had discovered a loft full of decorations that had never been opened or unwrapped. Had Granny Birch secretly purchased the decorations in the hope that one year, Catherine might finally let go of her hatred and blame? That together they might have celebrated and enjoyed themselves like everyone else?

She could only speculate, but that was enough to stab her heart with guilt and regret. Yes. Granny Birch had been waiting for Catherine to come to terms with her grief so they could share a Christmas together. It had never happened, though, because Catherine had been blinded by pigheadedness and selfishness and now it was too late. She could never retrieve those lost years. But she could change her mindset. She could make this Christmas—providing they survived, of course—the best one ever, for Holly, Beth, Katie, Florence, and perhaps even herself.

Holly started talking and Catherine lay back against the headrest, listening intently. She imagined everything Holly described in vivid detail, and after a little while began picturing herself and Holly doing the things she spoke about.

Together they decorated the tree. They hung their stockings over the fireplace. Wearing new pyjamas, they snuggled on a sofa watching a film. It was called *A Wonderful Life*. Catherine had never heard of the film, but Holly described the gist of the plot. They prepared the ingredients for Christmas dinner and wore their woollen jumpers. Catherine felt contentment. The Christmas she visualized with Holly and herself was bliss. A fleeting thought resonated: if she were to die right now, she'd die happy. Then she succumbed to slumber.

CHAPTER ELEVEN

"Catherine?" Holly's voice spiked with stress. "Please wake up. Please."

Catherine's mind was groggy, and opening her eyes took real effort. Blearily, she looked across at Holly.

"You can't sleep. I think you've got concussion and it's dangerous. You've got to try and stay awake."

Catherine didn't want to stay awake. As nice as it was to be looking at the real Holly, she much preferred the dream she'd been having. They were safe and enjoying a romantic Christmas in her dream, not huddling together in a damaged car trying not to freeze to death.

"Say something, Catherine."

The more awake she became, the shittier she felt. Her body was stiff and sore. She craved a well-needed stretch, but the cramped space wouldn't permit it. The whole of her head throbbed painfully. Her stomach felt icky, as if she might retch at the slightest provocation.

"How long was I out?" she asked in a raspy voice.

"Maybe twenty minutes or a bit longer. You turned so pale and your breathing...I freaked out."

Catherine gave a dismissive wave of her hand. She slowly bent forward and picked up a bottle of water. She took a sip and her stomach lurched. Queasiness settled over her like a fog. The temperature had grown cooler, but the vents were still streaming hot air. A ghost of vapour accompanied each of their breaths.

"Will you tell me about your gran?" Holly asked. "From the snippets you've shared so far, she sounds like an incredible woman. I'd love to hear more."

Catherine screwed the top on the water bottle and returned it to the footwell. It would hurt to talk about Granny Birch, but that wasn't enough of a reason to not do it. She had been an incredible woman. The more people Catherine told about Granny Birch, the closer she felt to her. Plus it kept her memory alive and kicking, a sentiment Granny Birch would've appreciated.

"She was eighty-three when she died. She described herself as being as tough as old boots, and she was. She was obsessed with Elvis. She used to play his songs constantly. As a teenager, I begged her to turn them off, but she wouldn't hear of it. He was the King and the only man in her life after Granddad's death." The memory of the radio blaring out his songs and Granny Birch's voice singing along made Catherine smile. "She always said that to have no vices was a sign of a wasted life, and she had more vices than most. She smoked cigars like a chimney, drank whiskey like a fish, and swore like a sailor with Tourette's. She was always playing cards or bingo for money with her fellow old farts—that's how they referred to themselves," Catherine said. She didn't want Holly to think she was being disrespectful. "But her absolute favourite pastime was gardening. There wasn't anything she couldn't grow. Her garden was her pride and joy."

For a while, she kept on talking, saying the slightest little thing that popped into her head. She explained the little traditions they'd made over the years. Like having Chinese takeaway at Christmas and on all other special occasions. They'd then play a game or ten of poker for the grand prize of damp matches.

She mentioned their constant disagreement about the supposed medicinal properties of whiskey. Granny Birch insisted decent whiskey countered the symptoms of colds, flu, headaches, and basically any ailment. If it didn't work, it meant there hadn't been enough whiskey administered in the first place. In hindsight, Catherine couldn't recall a time when Granny Birch had been anything other than as strong as an ox, so maybe there was an element of truth in it.

There had also been many escapades, a few of which she'd been fortunate to share in, but most which she'd only heard about. Like the time a man tried to mug Granny Birch. She'd taken to calling him "the sonofabitch," and had beaten him within an inch of his life with her purse. She'd then chased him three blocks while he tried to run away. Her story had spread, and she'd been interviewed on the local TV, but her use of "the sonofabitch" cut her interview short. Catherine's heart ached, but it was a good pain. A pain showing she had loved Granny Birch very much. "She helped me with my stutter, too," Catherine said softly

"How long have you had your stutter?" Holly asked. She kept the eye contact, seemingly unfazed about asking such a personal question.

"After my parents' deaths it seemed to come on overnight. They think it was caused by the emotional and psychological stress, although they could never be certain. All I know is it made my life miserable. I got picked on relentlessly at school. I had no friends, and my confidence disappeared into nothing. I used to hide away in the library during lunch and at break times so I could read books and avoid people. For years, I barely spoke to anyone except Granny Birch and the speech therapist she hired. That's why I'm not good around people. I lack the skills and finesse needed for social interactions."

Why was she telling Holly this? She never mentioned her stutter, let alone divulged her inability to interact with others. It was something she kept locked up tight to avoid making herself vulnerable.

"You've been fine around me and you haven't stuttered for a while now."

Catherine realised Holly was right. "It only comes on when I'm stressed or nervous."

"Well, I don't know about you, but I've never been in a more stressful or nerve-wracking situation than the one we're in right now." Holly reached out and gently caressed one of Catherine's hands.

Catherine's breath hitched in her chest. Holly's thumb traced ticklish circles across the back of her hand. It made her skin break out in goose bumps, each tiny hair standing on end.

"I've a confession," Holly said.

"Okay."

"We've kind of met before. Twice, actually." Holly twiddled the stray curl with her spare hand. "We never spoke, but I watched you from afar. The first time was at Katie and Beth's wedding. I was eighteen. And then I saw you again at Florence's christening."

Well, that answered the previous night's questions. Holly had been at both occasions, but Catherine still had no recollection of seeing her.

"I noticed you. How could I not? There was something about you that captured my attention. Both times I wanted to go over and strike up a conversation, but then I saw you were with the redhead."

"Paula," Catherine said. Speaking the name invoked an unpleasant taste in her mouth.

"Anyway, I never did have the guts to try and speak to you. But I did ask Katie about you. When Beth mentioned it was you who'd be travelling with me, well, I was pretty stoked. God, that sounds so stalkerish."

Catherine forced a smile. "No, it doesn't." *That's nothing compared to what I got up to last night.*

"You don't remember me, do you?"

Was this a trick question? The last thing Catherine wanted to do was hurt Holly's feelings, but the idea of lying sent alarm bells ringing in her head—unless they were from the concussion. "I wasn't in a great place during either of those occasions, but especially not during the christening. Paula and I were having major problems, and I think I repressed a lot of memories. The ones I do have are tarnished."

"You could've said no. I wouldn't have been offended," Holly said. She gave Catherine's hand a gentle squeeze. "I remember thinking you looked tense. Sexy, smouldering too, but also tense. You don't have to answer if you don't want to, but I'm kind of curious about what happened with you and Paula?"

Catherine had been honest and over-shared all the other personal issues in her back catalogue. What was one more?

"I met Paula when I was twenty. We were together for eight years." She took a moment to consider how much she would tell Holly before deciding it was easier to say it all. "I came back from work one evening and her stuff was gone. After a week, I managed to track her down. She'd moved in with the owner of an art gallery. They'd been having an affair for eighteen months. When I asked how she could hurt me after everything I'd done for her, she told me I'd brought it on us, that it was my fault she'd sought the arms of another lover. She said I was a cold, boring workaholic—"

"Bitch!" Holly said hotly. "And what a steaming crock of bullshit. How dare she have the audacity to do and say those things to you? Jeez. I knew that conniving ginger bitch was trouble the first time I set eyes on her."

Catherine was so stunned by the ferocity of Holly's angry words, she burst out laughing. Holly frowned, and Catherine tried to explain. "I doubt Granny Birch could've described her better."

"I'll take that as a compliment." Holly grinned mischievously. "I am sorry, though."

"I was a mess for quite a while. I ended up on antidepressants and became a workaholic, but Granny Birch was having none of it. She gave me the kick I needed to pull myself together, and that's when I started volunteering. I've been off the tablets for over a year now."

Holly moved closer, her torso leaning over the gearstick and handbrake. "I think you're one of the most honest people I've ever met. I have a proposal for you."

Catherine couldn't speak. Her gaze was transfixed by Holly's gleaming lips. She wondered how they would feel pressed against her own. What would they taste of? She was desperate to bridge the remaining gap and find out.

"If we get out of here, I want to do something with you."

Catherine managed a high-pitched squeak as Holly moved closer, but still not as close as she would've liked. Holly's breathing matched hers in quickening short bursts. Her warm breath caressed Catherine's face and teased that her lips would taste sweet.

"I want us to make this a Christmas to remember. I want to see you experience all of the little things that make it so special for me." Holly squeezed Catherine's hands, her body rigid with urgency. "I want us to make it ours. What do you s—"

Catherine surged forward, pressing her mouth firmly against Holly's. She was acting on instinct once again and it felt foreign to her. Her brain went into overload, shocked by her behaviour, while her mouth sought more.

Holly's lips were softer than she could've imagined. With a tentative flick of her tongue, she tasted her and was proven correct. Holly did indeed taste sweet.

With a half groan, half growl, Holly pulled Catherine closer. She opened her mouth and deepened their kiss. Catherine felt drunk off the intimacy. It'd been so long. She closed her eyes and relinquished control. In the darkness her senses heightened and her lust became a fierce driving force.

Softness, hotness, and wetness enveloped her. The taste of Holly was exquisite, and she would never get enough of it. What had started as a nervous exploration turned into a battle for control. Tongue battling tongue and hands fumbling to uselessly caress over layers of material.

Blood rushed in Catherine's ears. Her heart pounded and her head swam with more than concussion. Her senses were alight.

Holly pulled away gasping for breath, and Catherine whimpered at the loss.

"Is that a yes?" Holly asked, her breathing laboured and her mouth wet from their kiss.

"Yes," Catherine said. She blew out a shaky breath.

Holly leaned toward her again. "That's gre—" but a tremendous pounding sounded on Catherine's door.

Jumping, Catherine screamed and dove over to Holly's side. The handbrake stabbed her side as she floundered with her legs sprawled helplessly in the air.

The pounding struck again, this time on the window, and the sound reverberated through the car. Before either of them could react, the door groaned as something repeatedly pulled on the handle from outside. After another few seconds of unhealthy metallic creaking, the door burst open and icy air blasted inside.

They both screamed as the wind and snow assaulted them, but their voices were quickly lost in the ruckus. A snowy figure appeared in the doorway and thrust its head inside the compartment, providing a slight respite from the elemental assault. The fur-lined hood covered the figure's head, the coat was fastened up past its nose, and only two blue eyes showed.

In a loud voice muffled by material, a voice boomed out, "Come on!" The gloved hand motioned dramatically for them to follow.

"Quickly, Catherine," Holly said from behind her. "We're being rescued."

Catherine didn't need to be told twice. She blindly grabbed her coat and a few other belongings and rushed out the doorway. As her feet crunched onto the snow, she heard the engine cut out. Covering her face from the vicious onslaught of cold and snow, she trudged a few steps, giving room for Holly to get out.

Sensing Holly behind her, she peered through squinting eyes and made out their rescuer a few feet ahead. Ignoring the intolerable cold, she led them forward, shielding her eyes. She'd no choice but to trust in her ability to blindly lead them up the embankment as the blizzard shrouded them.

CHAPTER TWELVE

Catherine had never been so grateful to meet a stranger in all her life. She, Holly, and their rescuer now huddled safely inside the snowplough. Her teeth violently chattered and her body felt as though it had turned to marble beneath her clothes. A quick glance at Holly showed she was in a similar state. The compartment was warm, though, and she hoped their bodies would follow suit soon.

Adrenaline coursed through Catherine's veins. She couldn't believe they'd actually been rescued. What were the chances? A thought troubled her: perhaps she was still in the car unconscious and this was nothing but a vivid and wonderful dream. She quickly dismissed it. She was far too cold, exhausted, and in pain to be asleep.

Their rescuer handed them some thick blankets, which they didn't hesitate to wrap around themselves. While trying to thaw out, they both peered sheepishly at the hooded person who, still a mystery, had saved their lives. Other than the one sentence shouted at them down inside their car, they hadn't spoken again.

Finally, the hood lowered and the buttons at the neck of the coat popped open, revealing a mass of ginger hair. The man shook his head and brushed off the snow from his shoulders and arms. The unkempt mop of bright red hair lay a little flat. He beamed a toothy smile through an equally red beard. "Hello. The name is Angus Boyd."

Embarrassingly, it took Catherine longer than usual to grasp what he said because of his thick Scottish accent.

"I'm Holly and this is Catherine," Holly said. "Thank you so much for saving us, Angus."

"It's nay bother. You're lucky I got held up a wee while back. You try and get warm. I'll have us back in Athegither in nay time at all." He gave another smile and revved the engine to life.

The seat beneath them trembled with vibrations and the cabin filled with a loud growling from the powerful engine. Catherine was relieved they wouldn't be able to converse over the sound. She was too exhausted to worry about her stutter making an unwelcome reappearance. Settling deeper into the thick blankets, she felt a nudging by her side. She looked down and saw Holly's hand. Hitching her blanket up, Holly's trembling hand sought hers and gripped tightly. She felt Holly give a squeeze and she returned it.

"I'll tell you, somebody up there must be looking after you," Angus said, half shouting so as to be heard over the noise. He nodded up to the sky and gave a wink. Turning his attention back to the road ahead, he pressed a button and music blared into the compartment.

Catherine snapped her gaze from the radio dial, to Holly, her own surprise mirrored on Holly's face.

The song was already halfway through, but the familiar melody formed a lump in her throat and sent a tingle down her spine. She mentally berated herself and enforced the mantra that she didn't believe in miracles, ghosts, or any spooky goings on.

Angus meanwhile, remained oblivious to their feelings and was happily tapping his fingers on the sturdy steering wheel in time. And Elvis's distinct voice continued to sing the lyrics to "Can't Help Falling in Love." It was a coincidence Elvis was on the radio. That was all. And the fact it also happened to be Granny Birch's favourite song? Well, that was nothing more than a coincidence, too.

The journey took around forty minutes, and the local radio station continued to play an eclectic range of tracks. A few cheesy Christmas songs were thrown into the mix, but Catherine was too preoccupied by the haunting memory of Elvis's song to care.

Angus drove them into the centre of a village, but other than glimpses of lights and a few buildings, the snow made everything undistinguishable.

"Okay, ladies. Welcome to Athegither," Angus said. He turned off the radio but left the engine running. He pulled up his hood up. "I'll show you in."

He opened the driver's door and leapt out. A few moments later, he appeared by the passenger window and tugged the door open, struggling against the wind. Clutching her few meagre belongings and tightening her grip on the blankets, Catherine jumped down from the unusually high height. Fresh snow broke her landing. Holly followed behind her and they waited for a few freezing seconds while Angus slammed the door shut, after which he motioned for them to follow again and led them into the whiteness.

Catherine stumbled when her foot struck the first step, but she gained her balance and rushed up the next three and in through the doorway. Warmth and light engulfed them in welcome. Holly came to Catherine's side and they both surveyed their surroundings. They were in a small cloak room. White walls and beams of wood painted black gave the sense of the building being old but well maintained. Red lettering and arrows gave directions. The door to the left led to the bar and restaurant. The door to the right led to the reception, hotel rooms, and study.

A smell of smoke mixed with the tantalising smells of food lingered in the air. Loud chattering and laughter emanated from behind the door leading to the bar. It sounded busy.

"I'll go and fetch my maw," Angus said. He disappeared through the door leading to the bar.

"I can't believe we've made it back to civilisation," Holly said. Her face looked haggard. Her usual vitality drained. It wasn't surprising considering everything they'd been through.

Before Catherine could reply, the door swung open and a tall blond woman marched in. She came to a halt and looked them up and down. "You poor things. Look at the sight of you. Angus?" she said in an equally strong accent but with a clipped tone. Angus appeared behind her in a flash but didn't get an opportunity to speak as his mum continued. "What were you thinking leaving them stood here freezing to death? I thought we raised you better than that. Go on, take them through to the study and watch out for wee Kimmy. I'll be through in a moment."

Angus blushed. "Aye, Maw. Sorry." He walked over to the

opposite door and held it open for them. "Sorry," he said sheepishly as they passed through. He led them past the reception desk, down a corridor away from the staircase, and in through a door with a bronze plaque with *Study* engraved on it.

The room was large but felt snug thanks to the furnishings. White walls and black beams continued. Three hefty-looking bookshelves, solidly packed, lined two walls. An elegant fireplace drew Holly and Catherine closer. A fire burned fiercely feeding off the blackened logs with popping and crackling sounds. Smoke danced up the chimney, but some of the smell still lingered. Catherine had never seen a more welcome sight.

"I've got to be on my way. I'll come over tomorrow after I've spoken to the mechanic and let you know what's happening with that car of yours."

"Thank you again, Angus. You're a lifesaver," Holly said. Catherine gave an appreciative nod.

With one last smile, he rushed from the room. Catherine suspected he didn't want to encounter his mum again.

Holly shrugged off her blankets and hung them over a comfortable-looking leather reading chair before edging closer to the stifling heat. Deciding she'd also rather risk third-degree burns than wait for the blankets to dry out, Catherine placed her blankets on top of Holly's.

Angus's mum entered the room, quickly closing the door behind her with her backside. She carried two cups of something steaming. She placed the cups on a coffee table, stood, and smiled.

She was thin and her hair was pulled back into a ponytail. Her eyes were the same blue as Angus's. She was dressed in a pair of jeans and a thin black jumper, with a blue and white striped apron covering her front. Her cheeks were rosy, her smile friendly, and the creases around her eyes and mouth suggested she smiled often. An undeniable air of matriarchy surrounded her.

"I'm Fiona, Angus's maw. I take it he's scarpered, then?" At their nods she gave a laugh. "He's a good lad, but sometimes I wonder what goes through that head of his. Anyway, welcome to the Dew Drop Inn. It's the only pub, restaurant, and hotel in Athegither. Most folks around here call it The Inn."

"Thank you, Fiona. I'm Holly and this is Catherine. We were driving up to Cairngorm National Park to spend Christmas with our family. The storm hit so suddenly and I lost control of the car. If it wasn't for Angus we'd still be stuck there," Holly said. Her voice was tight with emotion. "He saved us."

"Aye, he said something of the sort. It sounds like you've had a day from hell, but you're safe enough now. Shall I phone Dr. Maddock? That lump on your noggin looks pretty nasty."

"No, thank you," Catherine said. Her fingers automatically flew to the swelling.

Fiona's blue eyes lingered a moment longer, concern knitting her eyebrows. "Okay," she said in a tone suggesting it was anything but. "But if you change your mind, let me know. I think it's lovely you're in the festive spirit."

Catherine glanced down at the woollen jumper and decided it was best not to say anything.

"I'll leave you both to warm up and drink your drinks." Fiona headed toward the door.

"Um, can you point me in the direction of the restroom please?" Holly asked. She was squeezing her knees together and wringing her hands. "Also, would I be able to use a phone to call my cousin and let her know what's happened? She'll be worried sick. We were meant to arrive hours ago."

"Aye, of course you can. Come with me and I'll get you sorted," Fiona said cheerily.

"Will you be okay?" Holly asked Catherine.

"Sure. I'm going to drink whatever's in this cup and not move from this fire."

Holly smiled before quickly following Fiona out of the room.

Catherine wasted no time in scooping up one of the cups. Strong, hot coffee. She was officially in heaven. Cradling the cup with both hands, she blew the steam, took a tentative sip, and swallowed.

Turning slowly, she took in the room. The ambience appealed to her nature. Books, a fire, comfy seats, antique-looking coffee tables, one of which held an elegant chess set, and a large coat of arms hanging proudly on the wall. A sudden noise sounded. Catherine turned in the direction it came from but couldn't see anything. From the corner of her eye she saw something flash by. Heart pounding and palms sweating, she took a few steps forward, but the room remained still. Only the noises from the fire interrupted the silence.

Maybe she should ask Fiona to call the doctor? Something wasn't right. She was having auditory and visual hallucinations. Perhaps the concussion was more severe than she'd originally thought. Or maybe she was winding herself up? The Elvis song had spooked her, and after the ordeal she'd been through it was possible her overactive imagination had gone into overdrive. "Get a grip, Catherine," she whispered to herself.

A high-pitched sound emitted from seemingly nowhere. Catherine jumped. It sounded like an anxious or frightened cry.

"H-hello?" she asked the empty room. "Who's there?"

No one responded. She was losing her mind. Placing the cup down, she decided she'd go in search of Holly. The room had lost all of its charm. She managed one step before the harrowing sound cried out again, this time for longer. Catherine's temper flared. Someone was obviously trying to make a fool out of her. Well, she wasn't going to let them get away with it. "I know you're there. Come out right now." She looked around for a possible hiding place, but to her dismay, found no place that could conceal a person. It didn't make sense. Faltering slightly, she took a step nearer the back of the room and said, "I said c-come out. You're not funny."

Her eyes darted to a flash of movement on the floor. Something had disappeared beneath one of the chairs. Something grey. Was it a rat? A shudder tore down her body. She hated rats. But a rat didn't make sense. This place was spotless. And she was sure it'd been bigger than a rat. Plus, a rat wouldn't have made such a sorrowful sound, would it? She wasn't entirely sure of her logic and so it took a few more seconds of egging herself on before she closed in on the chair.

Leaving a few feet of distance between herself and the chair, she slowly got to her knees. Breathing heavily, she lowered her right shoulder and head until they hovered an inch off the ground. Pain flared in her neck, but she gritted her teeth and squinted, trying to make out anything untoward hiding beneath the shadowed gap. Not seeing anything, she dared to crawl a little closer. She made out two glints and took a moment to realise they were eyes, then gulped to calm herself. The eyes were too big to belong to a rat. The animal beneath the chair was bigger than she'd originally thought. Perhaps it was a cat.

A high-pitched whimper sounded again, and this time Catherine felt certain it was a fearful sound, a sound that wasn't feline in origin.

The sorrowfulness of it prickled her flesh with goose bumps. "Come here," she said, trying to make her tone gentle. "Come on. Let me see you." The cooing of her voice sounded strange to her, but she continued regardless and was rewarded with a shuffling sound. "That's it. Come on. Come out and see me, providing of course you're not a huge rat."

The two glints came closer, until a little black nose snuck out of the shadows. It shone and looked like the kind of nose you stitched onto a teddy or stuffed animal toy. The small amount of muzzle surrounding the nose was light grey and hairy. Catherine became quietly convinced this was a dog. "That's it. You're nearly here. Come on." One grey furry paw followed by another came out into the open. Slowly, the little dog crawled out of its hidey hole with its belly pressed low to the ground. Its little ears were flattened against its skull and the two coal-like eyes watched Catherine warily.

The dog was small and its body was covered in grey shaggy hair. Its muzzle was a darker colour than the rest of it. It looked like a grey version of a white Westie.

"Hi, there," Catherine said. She held out a hand. The little dog crawled closer and it looked to be trembling. Tentatively, it lifted its black nose and sniffed Catherine's fingers. A moment later, a warm pink tongue gave a gentle lick.

Normally, Catherine would've freaked out at the prospect of being covered in dog spit, but she didn't want to scare the little dog any more than it already was. "What's your name?" she asked. She smiled when the dog's ears pricked to the sound of her voice. Its tail brushed back and forth excitedly. Daring to be a bit braver, she slowly moved her hand to stroke the dog's head. With her slow, deliberate movement, the dog ducked a little.

"I'm not going to hurt you," Catherine whispered. She gently stroked the little head. She'd expected the fur to feel coarse, but it was soft. Her hand travelled down the little body until it reached the raggedy tail.

All the while, the two eyes watched her intently. Now she moved her hand away, the little dog sat up on its haunches. Its two front legs were stubby and the chest and face had more protruding hair. With deep, soulful eyes, possibly the most soulful eyes Catherine had ever seen, the dog kept eye contact. Its grey fringe stuck out in such a way it almost looked like bushy eyebrows. Both ears were now standing up. The little dog's attention was solely focused on Catherine. "What do you want?" she asked. Then felt incredibly self-conscious at the realisation she was talking to a dog.

The dog cocked its head to one side, which was cute, and lifted its nose a little closer, never breaking the eye contact. It gave a little huff of breath as if sighing.

Transfixed, Catherine moved her face closer until her own nose was only a wisp away from the dog's. The cold wet nose touched hers, and she was unprepared for the warm tongue that administered a perfectly placed doggy kiss across her lips. "Ugh!" she said, falling back on her backside while rubbing her mouth on the back of a hand. The little dog's ears twitched and its backside jiggled with the wagging of its erect tail. It actually looked like it was smiling at her. "That wasn't funny," she said, spluttering dramatically.

The dog dived into a sideways roly-poly, proudly presenting its tummy. With its stubby legs stuck up in the air, it wriggled happily from side to side. Catherine was surprised the dog's tummy wasn't as hairy as the rest of its body. A lot of the tummy was bare. The skin was light in colour, and tiny nipples symmetrically lined either side of the abdomen. The chest was hairy up until the ribs and then the skin looked soft with only a few light hairs.

"Not a chance," Catherine said. She still felt violated by the unexpected snog. "It's not going to happen."

The dog seemed undeterred. Its tongue happily lolled, paws prancing in the air. Unable to resist, Catherine touched the tummy and found it warm and soft. She moved her fingers upward through the coarse hair of the upper chest and gave a reluctant scratch. As she started to remove her hand, the little dog gave a high-pitched bark of protest.

"Just one more," Catherine said, trying to sound stern. A moment later, she was giving a double-handed tickly-tummy fest. The little dog seemed to be enjoying it immensely and was writhing in bliss. Catherine had to admit she was enjoying herself, too.

She found a particularly ticklish spot, and the harder she scratched the more one of the little hind legs danced up and down. "Aha. Does that feel good?"

"Catherine?" Holly's voice called from behind her.

Catherine spun around to find Holly and Fiona watching her. They were both smiling and she felt her cheeks warm. "How long have you been watching?"

"Long enough." Holly laughed. "I see you've made a new friend."

Catherine glanced down. The dog crept beside her and cowered next to her thigh. She placed a hand on its back and felt it relax a little. "Well, yeah. It kind of appeared."

"That's wee Kimmy. She's a cairn terrier," Fiona said. "She's a new lodger, too. She was orphaned three weeks back, and I promised her owner I'd find her a nice home. We did plan to keep her here. She's such a loving and funny wee thing. But she's not settling at all."

Catherine felt something like an affinity with Kimmy. Now when she looked, it was obvious she was a female. Everything about her from the fringe, the deep-set eyes, to the short legs and scraggly tail all seemed feminine. She was cute and beautiful.

"Let's sit down and we can have a chat about things," Fiona said. She indicated the table and chairs next to the fire. "I've left the old man in charge, so we've got at least half an hour until things go drastically wrong."

Reluctantly, Catherine stood. She felt inexplicably guilty at the thought of abandoning Kimmy, so she patted her thigh while walking over to the table. Kimmy followed loyally at her heels, and when Catherine sat, Kimmy crept beside her feet.

"She's certainly taken a liking to you. I've not seen her act that way around anyone other than Agnes," Fiona said. She reached for a glass of wine. "There's some stew and bread for you both. Tuck in."

Catherine reached for the steaming bowl and pulled it nearer. The stew looked hearty. Thick chunks of beef and vegetables were covered in a rich stock. With her mouth watering, Catherine needed no encouragement to get stuck in. It was every bit as delicious as it looked and smelt. Through steaming mouthfuls, she asked about Kimmy's owner.

Fiona's shoulders sank and she gave a small shake of her head. "Agnes was a lovely old dear. Eighty-seven years of age. She was a spinster, and her wee cairns were her life. I remember seeing her with them when I was a wee girl. She used to breed them and take them to shows." She glanced beneath the table. "Kimmy here is her last one."

"Poor Kimmy," Catherine said.

"Aye. Anyway, over a month ago, Agnes took a nasty fall in her cottage. She had to go to hospital, which is a good thirty miles away, but she outright refused to get in the ambulance until I agreed I'd take Kimmy and look after her until she came out. She had nay other family. I was reluctant, but she was so bloody stubborn I had nay choice. None of us expected her to be there for more than a few days." She tutted softly. "Trouble was she'd been ill for a while and not told anyone. It became clear early on she wouldn't be coming home at all. The doctors didn't tell her straight away, but I think she already knew. She made me promise I'd find Kimmy a good home. I did, and then she gave me the longest list of instructions you'd ever lay your eyes on." Fiona took another sip of wine, grimaced, and added, "The next day she passed away."

"Oh, how awful," Holly said, tears welling in her eyes.

Catherine lowered her spoon and tried to swallow a mouthful of stew over the lump of emotion lodged in her throat.

"Aye," Fiona said solemnly. "She was buried two weeks ago. We've kept Kimmy here with us, but she's not happy. For the first two years of her wee life, she lived with only Agnes in a thatched cottage. It's too busy and noisy here for her. She's escaped twice and that's why I've had to put her in here today, with strict instructions for nay body to come in."

"Where did she go?" Catherine asked, the comforting weight of Kimmy's head resting on her foot.

"Back to the cottage, both times. We found her in the outhouse the second time. She'd been there for nearly two days. It breaks my heart, so it does. After the holidays I'm going to have to take her to the shelter in the next town."

"No," Catherine said a little too forcefully. "I mean, surely there's someone in this town who'd adopt her? She's beautiful and friendly."

Fiona smiled sadly. "I know she is. And Lord knows I've asked around, but I've had nay response from the locals. I'll leave it until January. Maybe she'll settle down before then, or someone might come forward to take her."

Catherine was angry, but she knew it wasn't Fiona's fault. She was doing her best. She forced down another spoonful of stew, although her appetite was diminished. It was taking the edge off her exhaustion.

Holly filled Catherine in on her conversation with Katie and Beth. They'd been worried but were now relieved.

The bad news came in threes like it always does. Firstly, they were stuck in this village and wouldn't make it to Katie's for Christmas. The storm was due to last a while longer, and the roads leading to Katie's were impassable for the foreseeable future. When Holly had pushed her for a vague idea, she'd been told at least three days if not longer. The roads were treacherous, and so close to the holidays there was no way they'd be cleared in time.

The next bit of bad news was both Catherine's and Holly's purses with money and cards were back in the car. Catherine wasn't worried so much about them getting stolen—it was rather the fact they couldn't pay for anything, including the meal they'd eaten.

The last bit was delivered by Fiona. The hotel was at full occupancy thanks to all of the family and friends who'd returned for the holidays. "So, we're stuck in this village over Christmas. We don't have any means of paying for anything until tomorrow at the earliest. And there's no room for us."

"Basically, that's the gist of it," Holly said.

"We can't pay for this food or our drinks." Catherine rubbed her face with both hands. "Will our luck ever change?"

"Luck? You're the two luckiest women in this village right now. You could both be stuck in a car, but instead you're here. That's a wee miracle in itself," Fiona said. Her tone made Catherine feel like an ungrateful arse. "As for the money, it's nay bother. You're my guests and this food is free of charge. And anything else you need, you only have to ask."

"But—" Catherine said.

"No buts. You're not going anywhere fast. Now, I've another proposal for you both. As well as the hotel, restaurant, and bar, we also rent out a few log cabins. Those are fully booked too, but we had a cancellation earlier tonight due to the weather. It's a deluxe cabin, which is the most costly. The couple were coming to celebrate their honeymoon."

Catherine glanced at Holly and saw her frown. She looked stressed. Holly's eyes flickered to her, and for a second they held each other's gaze. Catherine sneakily pointed to her chest before looking away. She hoped the message was understood.

"The couple who cancelled insisted we keep half the money because of the late notice. So I can offer you the cabin for half the price. It's fully stocked and Christmas dinner on the big day, here in the restaurant, is also included. There's only one bed but it's a king-size. It's a lovely place, even if I do say so myself. Are you interested, ladies?"

Another glance at Holly showed that she was chomping at the bit, but the death stare Catherine shot her was enough to keep her quiet. "Fiona, we'd love to accept. Thank you so much."

"Excellent. I'll go get the old man to set things up for you. It'll take him a little while, so you may as well stay put. I'll come and get you when it's ready."

They watched as Fiona left the room, and only once the door was closed did Holly let rip.

"You didn't ask how much it would cost us. You just agreed."

"I don't care how much it costs. I have money and—"

"I don't! We've been through this, Catherine."

"Please listen to me," Catherine said. She held her hands up in placating gesture. "We agreed in the car if we escaped, we'd make this the best Christmas ever. There are no other choices except maybe sleeping in here. I have money," she said, cutting off Holly's interruption before she managed a word. "I'm not going to apologise for that. And I'm not going to let your issue with me paying ruin what could be a fantastic Christmas for us both. I want to spend the money. I'm not trying to buy your affection. I don't expect anything in return. I'm not trying to show off either." Catherine reached across the table and took hold of one of Holly's hands. "What's the harm with me paying for a nice place for us to spend Christmas?"

Holly pulled her hand away. "I told you why. It humiliates me. I want to be able to pay my own way."

"Your car is in a state. It's going to cost money to get it towed back into town and then more money to get it fixed."

"I have insurance which covers all of that."

"Okay, fine. But the cabin is non-negotiable. I'm going to be staying there and so I'm paying for it. I'd like very much, in fact I'd love for you to join me, but if your pride is going to stop you, there's not much I can do about it."

Holly folded her arms and kept quiet. Catherine had said all she could and had no choice but to leave it for Holly to decide. Wanting some distraction, she got up from the table and sat on the floor in front of the fire.

Kimmy groggily followed, her paws plodding, to sit beside Catherine. Smiling, Catherine fussed Kimmy's face and began scratching behind her ears. Kimmy grew particularly helpless when Catherine scratched beneath the leather collar. One paw tapped excessively on the carpet until she finally collapsed into a heap.

Catherine realised her eyes weren't black like she'd first thought; they were in fact a dark brown. "Kimmy, sit," she said.

Kimmy obediently sat up.

"Paw."

Kimmy presented one of her paws and wouldn't put it down until Catherine touched it.

Holly came over to the carpet and knelt down. Although initially shy, Kimmy soon showered her with attention, too. Catherine felt a little sting of jealousy, but it faded when she saw the delight in Holly's face and heard her laugh. Plus Kimmy kept glancing back at her as if to make sure she was still there.

"I'm sorry," Holly said. "It's my pride, and I need to get over it. I know you're only being kind, and I appreciate it. If it's still all right, I'd like to come and stay with you in the cabin."

"Of course it is." Catherine was trying her hardest to mask her excitement. The prospect of sharing days and nights alone with Holly in a romantic cabin stoked a burning ache of arousal between her thighs. Especially as there was only one bed.

"I have one condition," Holly said, her tone serious.

"Go on."

"Kimmy joins us. She'll be safer with us, and it'll give Fiona a break."

Feeling two pairs of eyes watching her, Catherine looked down and met Kimmy's gaze. She'd never experienced puppy dog eyes before. Now she was getting them from Kimmy *and* Holly. The tiny bit of reluctant resolve melted into soppy goo. She couldn't refuse them anything.

"I suppose that's okay."

"You're such a softie," Holly said. She leaned forward and planted a quick kiss on Catherine's lips. She pulled away a moment later and pulled a face. Sniffing loudly, she looked accusingly at Catherine. "Talk about killing the moment."

Confused, Catherine opened her mouth to ask what Holly meant, but then the stench hit her square in the face.

"That's vile," Catherine said. She jumped to her feet, gagging. She had never smelled anything as rancid in all her life. "And it wasn't me! What the hell is it?" She retched. "I can taste it."

Holly burst out laughing. She moved farther away from the fire and pointed down.

Catherine followed the finger and found herself looking at Kimmy, whose tail wagged twice before her eyes closed and she looked like she'd fallen asleep.

"How can she lie there?" Catherine asked. "Do you think she's ill? That smells like something died months ago."

"It obviously doesn't bother her." Holly pinched her nose. In a nasally tone she said, "She's letting you know she's relaxed."

Catherine took another step back and wafted the air around her face. "So that was a…"

"Dog fart. Yes."

Catherine couldn't believe something so pungent could come from such a little innocent thing.

"Think of it as a taster." Holly beamed a devilish grin. "If you think that was bad, wait until you have to pick up the real deal."

Chapter Thirteen

The cabin was a five-minute walk from The Inn, and they were escorted by Fiona's cordial husband, Alistair. Catherine had been tasked with the stressful job of carrying Kimmy. She held the grey body tightly in her arms. After some initial fidgeting, the little dog settled with her chin resting on Catherine's shoulder.

Holly carried a heavy-looking bag containing dog food, bowls, some toys, and Agnes's list of instructions on how to keep Kimmy alive. It was Alistair who had the heaviest burden. Even flat packed, Kimmy's crate was heavy and difficult to manoeuvre. Catherine had never seen a dog crate before. She thought dogs slept in kennels or on dog beds, but Fiona explained some owners used animal crates and Agnes was one of them.

Alistair dropped the crate off inside the doorway with the reassurance he or Fiona could be reached on the phone at any time, then bid them farewell. As soon as the door was securely closed and they were left to their own devices, they rushed around the cabin in excited exploration.

It far exceeded Catherine's expectations. A large spacious living room had a comfy-looking sofa and armchair positioned in front of their very own raging log fire. A sheepskin rug lay at the foot of the stone hearth. A large flat screen TV perched on top of a cabinet to the left of the room. A decorated real pine Christmas tree stood to the far left-hand side, its lights twinkling in the reflection of the large bay window. The fragrance of pine and smoke combined to give a smell of Christmas.

To the right of the living room, an archway led to an open-plan kitchen and dining area. On inspection, all of the cupboards were well stocked, as were the fridge and freezer. A spotless cooker with an inbuilt oven gleamed. On the dining table waited a bottle of champagne in an ice bucket, a pair of flute glasses, and a box of chocolates with a note saying, *Welcome, Catherine and Holly.*

The bedroom hosted a huge solid wooden bed. Catherine felt sure the size was bigger than king-size but there was no way she was going to argue with Fiona. The bedspread was red tartan. A matching wooden wardrobe and chest of drawers loomed nearby. Two large white towelled dressing gowns hung on the back of the door and two pairs of matching slippers nestled next to the bed.

The adjoining en suite lay through the door at the far end of the room. As well as the shower cubicle, toilet, and sink, there was also a Jacuzzi corner bath.

"I think we've died and gone to heaven," Holly said, her eyes as wide as saucers as she took in the bathroom.

Catherine nodded. "It's stunning."

Kimmy bounded into the room, stopped suddenly, and skidded across the tiled floor. Legs splayed, she gave a bark of protest and then ran away.

"Let's go read the instructions and set up her cage," Catherine said, resigning herself to the fact she would have to wait a little longer before she could take the shower she craved.

"It's a crate," Holly said, bemused.

"That's what I said."

"No, I'm pretty sure you said cage."

Back inside the living room, Catherine thrust the wad of instructions at Holly. "You read these and I'll set up the ca—crate."

Holly compliantly sat on the sofa, pulling her legs up and resting her head on the cushioned arm. Kimmy leapt up to join her, and after circling three times, she finally settled down, resting her head on Holly's lap, her beady gaze lazily watching Catherine.

The crate was relatively easy to assemble, but Catherine still managed to painfully catch a finger and bash one of her shins. She placed Kimmy's dog bed inside and stepped away with her hands on her hips. She felt a sense of butch pride, but neither Kimmy nor Holly paid much attention.

"Anything interesting?" she asked, trying to peer at the thick lines of text.

"Agnes was a stickler for routine. She's precise about everything."

Holly lowered the pages and rubbed her eyes. "I'm only about a quarter of the way through. So far I've learnt cairn terriers were originally used to hunt vermin. Toto, the dog in *The Wizard of Oz*, was a cairn. Kimmy needs to be walked at least once a day and played with. She has to be brushed twice a week. She has a double coat, which is why she's so hairy. Some human foods are poisonous to dogs, like chocolate, grapes, and raisins. That's as far as I've gotten, I'm afraid." Holly stifled a yawn.

Catching the yawn, Catherine asked, "So what do you want to do now? Shall I open the champagne?"

"You shouldn't drink if you have concussion. And I'm running on fumes. I think maybe a shower and bed. I need to sleep."

Catherine masked her disappointment. In her head she'd envisioned champagne, cuddling in front of the fire, and then, well, maybe cuddling without clothes. Those visions were now dashed, but she was reminded of how tired she felt. "Okay. Should I put Kimmy to bed?"

Holly gently moved Kimmy so she could get up. "She needs to be taken outside to do her business first. Can you manage or—"

"Sure," Catherine said. She was terrified at the prospect but didn't want to lose face. "What exactly does it entail?"

"Attach her lead, which is on the table. Then take her outside and she'll go to the toilet. She should be quick."

Catherine nodded and headed into the kitchen. She picked up the extendable lead and called Kimmy. Holly stood in the archway with an amused expression.

Kimmy trotted into the kitchen, looked up at Catherine, and then at the lead. Her backside jiggled as her tail thrashed.

Catherine attached the lead and headed to the back door, but before she turned the lock, Holly tapped her on the shoulder.

"Don't forget these," she said. She handed over some little black plastic bags. "If she does a number two you'll need them. This is how you use them." She gave a quick demonstration and then stepped away. "Then you tie the handles and throw it in the outside bin. Good luck. I'll head for a shower."

Catherine's hand felt contaminated from holding the bags and so she couldn't consider the prospect of actually picking up dog faeces.

Kimmy scratched at the door and Catherine had no choice but

to open it. In a flash Kimmy disappeared into the blizzard, and for a terrible second, Catherine panicked she'd not find her. The lead tugged forcefully and Catherine followed the cord.

Please don't need a number two. Please.

When she found Kimmy she was squatting. "Oh, God." She moved closer, a bag already covering her trembling right hand. She braced herself and bent forward, but there was only a little yellow patch.

"A number one!" Relief flooded through her. "Good girl, Kimmy."

She led Kimmy back into the cabin and dried her paws with the designated doggy towel. Once unclipped, Kimmy ran off, leaving Catherine alone to take off her shoes.

When she went in search of the little canine, she couldn't find her anywhere. Holly called for her to come into the bedroom. Hovering by the threshold, Catherine's breath caught in her throat. Holly dripped wet from the shower and only had a towel wrapped around her body. Her damp hair looked darker and was tied in a ponytail draping over her shoulder.

"Catherine?" Holly asked, as her hand flew to her chest. "Did you hear what I said?"

Catherine hadn't—she'd been too busy perving. "Sorry?"

Holly pointed to the bed. Catherine reluctantly removed her leer and followed the direction of Holly's index finger...to find Kimmy sprawled out in the middle of the bed. Her dark eyes were hooded and flickered idly between them.

"Get off the bed, Kimmy," Catherine said sternly. She was rewarded with a single wag of the grey tail.

"Agnes's instructions were very clear on the sleeping arrangements. Kimmy has always slept in her crate," Holly said. She moved to stand beside Catherine. "I think she's testing us."

"Testing us?"

"Yes. She's trying to assert her dominance. She wants to be top dog. And if we let her, she'll be a nightmare. Well, that's what Agnes's instructions said. Do you want me to try to get her off?"

Catherine felt something primal stir inside. She wanted to be top dog. "No, I'll do it." She marched forward and looked down at the little grey face. "Get out." She pointed to the open door and waited. Kimmy didn't move a muscle.

No way she was going to let this little ball of fluff show her up in front of Holly. Not a chance. Taking a deep breath, she prepared herself. She was known for being a bitch in the office, and now it was time to use her skills in this bedroom. Squaring her shoulders and raising her chin, she said, "Out now!"

Her tone had been sharp enough to cut glass. She sensed Holly's surprise from the quick intake of breath. But her eyes remained fixed on Kimmy, who flew from the bed and out of the room like lightning. Trying not to show her smugness, Catherine turned to Holly and said, "Sorry if I came across as harsh."

"Not at all." Holly returned to the bathroom door. She glanced over her shoulder. "I quite liked it." The door closed.

Striding purposely into the living room, Catherine wasn't surprised to find Kimmy in her crate. She gave her a quick fuss and then locked the door.

"Sleep well, Kimmy," she said, stepping away. The sad little eyes pierced her and the little whine that escaped was heart wrenching. Regardless of what Agnes's instructions said, the crate did look more like a cage. Feeling heartless, Catherine went into the kitchen and returned with a chewy treat and a toy bone. She sneaked the contraband through gaps in the bars as a peace offering. Kimmy pinned the chewy treat with one of her paws and chomped happily.

Catherine suspected she'd been manipulated once again. Leaving Kimmy, she checked the locks, put the fireguard in place, and switched off the lights before joining Holly in the bedroom.

"Do you want me to sleep on the sofa?" Holly asked. She was wearing one of the dressing gowns.

"No, of course not. This bed is more than big enough for the both of us."

"And I should probably stay close to keep my eye on how you're doing with your concussion." Holly pulled back the duvet and climbed beneath it.

"Yeah," Catherine said. She was wondering about what she was going to wear as pyjamas. "So, you're sleeping in the dressing gown tonight?"

Holly nodded. "It's the only thing I have."

"Me too." Catherine unhooked her dressing gown and headed into the bathroom.

She stripped, which took a considerable amount of time considering how many layers she was wearing. She kicked the garments into the corner behind the door. She was relieved to find a brand new toothbrush still in its wrapper was left on the side of the sink beside a little tube of toothpaste. She brushed her teeth and took great satisfaction in putting her toothbrush in the same pot as Holly's. The brushes crossed each other as if in an embrace.

Next she grabbed a fluffy towel and hung it outside the shower. She stepped inside the shower, closed the door, and removed her glasses. Blindly, she showered and slathered her body in the overly sweet-smelling floral body wash. She squirted shampoo from one of the tiny bottles on the shelf and massaged it deep into her scalp. The hot spray of water was almost too much to bear, but it soothed her skin and left her feeling toasty. Although her muscles ached and the lump on her forehead throbbed, there was no denying how amazing it felt to be clean. She fumbled her glasses back on, opened the door, and dried herself with the towel, soft as a cloud.

She found the plastic comb Holly had used and removed the strand of blond hair caught in the teeth. After combing her hair, she put it into a bun, pulled the dressing gown on, and tied the belt. She checked her reflection in the foggy mirror before returning to the bedroom. She switched off the light on the wall and felt her way around to the other side of the bed. Butterflies soared in her stomach. Excitement coursed through her veins.

She pulled back the duvet and slipped beneath it. The mattress was soft and welcoming, as were the pillows.

"Holly?" she asked quietly. Her heart missed one, two, three, beats while she waited for a reply. A soft snore sounded from Holly's side of the bed.

So much for keeping an eye on me. What a wasted opportunity.

Her disappointment quickly faded as her body relaxed. The important thing was they were safe now. They had plenty of time to get to know each other over the upcoming days. Plus it had been years since she'd shared a bed with someone. Just knowing Holly was next to her was a huge comfort. The soft snores and warmth radiating over from Holly's side of the bed were surprisingly welcome bedfellows.

"Good night, Holly," Catherine whispered. She knew her words wouldn't be heard, but she needed to say them all the same. She closed her eyes and let out a deep sigh of contentment.

CHAPTER FOURTEEN

Catherine was awake but found it impossible to move. Her body ached in various places and to various extents, but that wasn't what was keeping her in the bed. Warmth and comfort held her captive.

She couldn't remember the last time she'd slept so soundly. She'd woken briefly because Holly had snuggled up against her, spooning her from behind with an arm draped around her waist as if to keep her close. It had been divine and Catherine had fallen back to sleep with a huge smile plastered on her face.

Holly's side of the bed was empty, and muffled sounds of life resonated from behind the closed bedroom door. Stretching her entire body out like a starfish, she tried to rouse her get-up-and-go. She put her glasses on first, then finally managed to persuade her body to crawl out of the bed. She slipped her feet into the large but comfy slippers, made the bed, and tried to make the dressing gown look presentable by smoothing it and retying the belt.

As soon as she opened the door, a flash of grey appeared and assaulted her legs with scratchy paws and doggy kisses. Catherine had no choice but to stand still for a few minutes while Kimmy danced around her in tight circles. Catherine bent and tried to stroke Kimmy in the hope she might calm down. It didn't work.

"Okay. Enough now, Kimmy," she said. Secretly, the loving reception pleased her. The little dog ran a few feet ahead of Catherine, rolled onto her back, and wriggled excitedly. Unable to resist, Catherine gave her belly a scratch.

She looked around, but couldn't quite place what was different.

It took a few seconds to realise the Christmas tree was bare. All the decorations and ornaments were gone. Confused, Catherine's gaze moved to the front door. A lopsided sign hung, reading *Put Kimmy in crate before answering the door!*

Muffled Christmas music wafted out from the kitchen. She stepped carefully over Kimmy and snuck to the archway.

Holly wore yesterday's clothes, her attention focused on the cooker and totally oblivious to Catherine's presence. She danced, hips swaying, feet tapping, and one hand waving a spatula around in time to the tempo. She belted out the lyrics to the cheesy song, and her voice was good.

Catherine's heart buckled in her chest. This felt surreal and yet so right. As if she'd somehow slipped into a little piece of heaven. Mentally, she recorded everything to memory. The desire to walk over to Holly, wrap her arms tightly around her waist, and kiss her neck was almost too much to bear. Her knees turned weak thinking about it.

An incredible smell of freshly baked bread filled the kitchen and made Catherine's mouth water. She spotted the golden circular loaf resting on the work surface. Something brushed her leg. She glanced down and watched as Kimmy sat beside her. She too avidly watched Holly, her head cocking from one side to the other as Holly sang.

A moment later, Holly tried to reach a soprano note out of her range. Catherine grimaced at the out-of-key screeching. Kimmy's hackles raised as she barked loudly. Her stocky body charged toward Holly, ears pricked and tail stuck up in the air. Each bark was punctuated by a low, menacing growl. Her head swung from one direction to the other searching for the imminent danger.

Holly's whole body lurched with surprise and she dropped the spatula. Hissing a swear word and clutching her chest, she turned and looked down at Kimmy. When Kimmy barked her high-pitched bark again, Holly pointed a stern finger and said, "No more barking."

Kimmy's bark cut off midway and her whole demeanour changed in an instant. Her head lowered, her ears slumped, her backside dropped onto the tiled floor, and her tail gave a halfhearted wag. She looked guilt-ridden.

"Everybody's a critic these days," Holly said. She bent to pick up the spatula and gave Kimmy's head a quick fuss. "I thought I sounded pretty damn good."

Catherine tried to hide her laugh, but ended up snorting unattractively. Holly's head snapped to the side and her gaze pinned Catherine where she stood.

"You saw all of that, didn't you?" Holly asked. She stood upright.

Catherine nodded. "And I heard it all, too."

Holly pursed her lips, placed one hand on her hip, and used the other hand to point the spatula at Catherine. "If you're referring to my singing, it was supposed to be a private thing."

Catherine held her hands up in defence. "I'm on your side. I thought you sounded great, and the last note was ridiculously high."

Holly's gaze intensified before she broke out in a grin. "It was ridiculously high. Take a seat." She indicated to the table, which was already laid out. "Breakfast is almost served."

"Maybe I should go get changed," Catherine said. She was feeling underdressed.

"I'm afraid your clothes are still drying." Holly gave a little shrug. "They should be done by the time we've eaten."

"Oh," Catherine said lamely. "You washed all of them?"

Holly smiled. "Yeah. I was up early and figured I might as well be productive. Is that okay?"

"Yes, of course. Thank you." Catherine walked over to the table and sat. She watched Holly discard the spatula in the sink, switch off the radio, and miraculously manage to avoid tripping over Kimmy, who followed at her heels.

The table was set for two, with cutlery, a little jug of milk, and a dish of sugar. Two glasses of orange juice were already poured, so Catherine took a sip from hers.

Holly presented a plate in front of Catherine. Two poached eggs, crispy bacon, and sautéed mushrooms. It looked great. The only problem being Catherine's utter dislike of mushrooms.

"Everything okay?" Holly asked.

"It looks wonderful. Thank you." Catherine picked up her knife and fork.

Holly's shoulders relaxed and she smiled. She returned to the counter and began cutting some bread. "Would you like your bread toasted or as it is? It's not long out of the oven and is still warm."

"I'll take it as it is, please. It smells delicious."

Holly returned to the table with two side plates, both of which had two thick wedges of bread. "Go ahead, please. I'm going to get Kimmy her breakfast, otherwise she won't leave us in peace."

Catherine smothered the soft, warm bread with butter, which immediately melted and soaked in. Licking some excess from a finger, she watched as Holly filled Kimmy's doggy bowl. Kimmy eagerly glanced from the bowl, to Holly, and back to the bowl again. Her tail wagged and then she did a bizarre thing: her front legs drew out in front of her and she stretched her head and torso down to the floor, while her bottom stuck up in the air.

"Was that some kind of trick?" Catherine asked.

Holly placed the bowl down, washed her hands, and returned to the table. "It was a bow."

"A bow?"

"Yeah, she's bowing to me. My parents' old dog used to do it. I think it's a sign of respect or something," Holly said. She poured some freshly brewed rich black coffee into each of their cups. "She keeps doing it."

Catherine glared at Kimmy, who was happily oblivious because she was wolfing down her food. "She's not done it to me."

Holly's eyebrows arched. "Maybe you didn't realise."

"Maybe," Catherine said, hating the sulky tone of her voice. She took a bite of her bread and groaned happily. "That's so good."

"It is. Even if I do say so myself." Holly took another bite of her own slice.

They spent a few minutes in silence happily chowing down. Catherine did her best to eat the mushrooms. It was the squidgy texture and flavoured juice seeping out of them that put her off. In the end, she shovelled them into her mouth and washed them down with the coffee before enjoying the bacon and eggs.

"Wow. You really like mushrooms."

"Err, yeah," Catherine said weakly.

"Here, have some of mine." Holly picked up her plate and scraped more than half of her mushrooms onto Catherine's plate. "Happy Christmas Eve, by the way."

"Oh, yeah. You too." Catherine tried to prevent the yucky mushroom juice contaminating the other items on her plate.

"I've made a list of things to do today. Shall I read it to you?"

Catherine nodded, amused by Holly's organisation. Holly pulled out a neatly folded slip of paper from a pocket. She opened it up and started to read it.

"Once you're dressed we'll take Kimmy for a walk. It'll give us a chance to explore Athegither and get our bearings. At lunchtime, the car is being towed back and we can get our things. After that, Angus will take the car and me to the local mechanic."

Catherine nodded, wondering when Holly had spoken to Angus to arrange all of this.

"Then we're going to decorate the Christmas tree."

"I wondered what happened to the decorations."

Holly blushed. "Well, we said we'd make this the best Christmas ever, and part of it is doing the little traditions. I want to mix my traditions with yours. We'll decorate the tree and then build and decorate the gingerbread house."

Catherine bit back her retort. She knew Holly had wanted to build the gingerbread house with Florence, but this was her decision and Catherine wouldn't argue.

"This evening there are carols in the church. Afterward, Fiona is insisting we go and have a festive drink in The Inn. Then I thought maybe we'd collect a Chinese takeaway and come back here to celebrate the rest of Christmas Eve alone."

Catherine wiped her mouth on her napkin. Excitement bubbled in her stomach for the first time in years. "I can't wait. It all sounds wonderful."

Holly kissed a lingering peck on Catherine's cheek and whispered, "Me neither." She pulled away. "Oh yeah, we need to talk about the presents."

"Presents?" Catherine was surprised she'd managed to form the word. Her head was spinning from a potent mix of adrenaline and lust.

"Yes. We can't have Christmas Day without presents. I was thinking if we agree on an amount, say thirty pounds, and buy each other presents. That way we'll have some surprises to open tomorrow morning. What do you think?"

"Thirty pounds sounds fine," Catherine said. She forced an enthusiastic smile. Previous occasions which had included conversations regarding money had always been full of contention. But if Holly was happy to suggest that amount, Catherine would match it. A barrage of thoughts flooded her mind.

What the hell am I going to get her?
I've always been terrible at buying gifts.
Paula hated every single thing I ever got her.
Is there a shop in this ghost of a town?
Shit! It's her birthday tomorrow, too.
Do I get her a birthday present as well?
What if I do and she's offended?
What if I don't and she's disappointed?
She's gone to so much effort already to make this special.
I need to do something equally special.

"Excellent," Holly said, beaming with enthusiasm. "This is going to be the best Christmas ever. I just know it."

❖

Dressed in jeans, two pairs of thick socks, three tops, and her coat, Catherine joined Holly in the living room and noticed Kimmy sporting a bright red harness. Catherine pulled on her hat, grateful it covered the lump, and then her gloves. "Ready?"

Holly clipped the lead onto Kimmy's harness and nodded. "Let's go explore Athegither."

The sky outside was thick with clouds and snow continued to fall, but there was no wind to drive it. The air chilled, but nothing compared to what they'd experienced the previous day.

Someone had done the backbreaking job of clearing snow for them, from their door to the pavement leading up to the main road, and they didn't have a clue who to thank. She made a mental note to ask Fiona when she next saw her. They quickly found their bearings and made their way onto the high street. Snow covered the pavements, and they found it easier to walk on the deserted roads. Catherine hated that she only had her sneakers. While she kept slipping and struggling for grip, Holly's boots crunched along without a problem. She regretted not bringing the wellies from the car.

"I can't stop thinking about what would have happened if Angus hadn't rescued us," Holly said with a shudder.

"It's probably best we don't dwell on that. Let's just consider ourselves very lucky." Catherine's small steps were carefully placed, and she struggled to match Holly's and Kimmy's pace. "I didn't get a chance to ask you last night. How did Beth take the news that we aren't going to make it for Christmas?"

"It was obvious she was disappointed, but I think ultimately, she was just relieved we're okay." Holly slowed down. "So, you went to university with Beth?"

Catherine's feet skidded on a particularly slippery patch of black ice. She flung her arms out and managed to regain her balance. "Yeah. We were roommates in the first year and remained friends ever since." Warily, she started walking again.

"She talks about you often. Both Katie and she obviously think very highly of you."

"I think very highly of them, too. They're the closest I have to family." Catherine felt guilt weigh down on her shoulders. It was true. They were the closest to family, and that brought back with perfect clarity the promise she'd made to Beth during their first semester.

Beth had broken down one night and revealed the source of her distress. Her mum's best friend from childhood had married her mum's brother five years previously. The marriage had taken a turn for the worse and ended badly. Although everyone in the family was upset, Beth's mum bore the brunt of the hostility from both sides. The divorce was savage, and the horrendous battle for custody of their two small children was under way. The entire family was divided with animosity, and Beth's mum was caught up in the middle. Even now, years later, Beth's family remained split. After the family pressure had gotten too much, Beth's mum chose to support her brother's fight for custody. Her ex-best friend was awarded custody, and Beth's family hadn't had contact with the children in years. Beth's mum suffered a mental breakdown not long afterward, no doubt caused in part by the stress. Caring for her mum while completing her studies had taken its toll on Beth.

Beth had begged Catherine to make a pact: that neither of them would ever pursue a romantic relationship with a member of each other's family, or with a close friend. Catherine had agreed without hesitation—and why not? Up until the last few days, she'd never come close to considering breaking her promise. That was until she met Holly. Now she was torn between her promise to Beth and her growing attraction toward Holly.

"Have you ever met Beth's family?" Catherine asked.

"I met her mum, dad, and brother at their wedding and Florence's christening, but that's it. Beth doesn't really speak about them. I figured they're very quiet and like to keep to themselves. Have you met them?"

Catherine nodded. "The same times you have, and also at our graduation." She'd secretly hoped Holly might already know about Beth's family history. If she did, Catherine could have told her about the promise she'd made to Beth, but as it was, she couldn't divulge Beth's secrets. It wouldn't be fair.

"This must be where the carols are being held later," Holly said, leading them onto the pavement outside the church's graveyard. The church wasn't huge, but the pointed steeple and skilled masonry distinguished it from the surrounding buildings. On the opposite side of the road, a hairdresser's and dentist's practice were open for business.

Catherine's feet skidded from under her again. "Shit," she said, grabbing onto the iron railings to stop her fall.

"Do you want to hold on to me?" Holly asked.

It was tempting, but guilt weighed heavily on her conscience. She wanted to try to build some distance between herself and Holly. "I'll be okay," she said. They followed the curve of the road and came across a big convenience store, with a post office next door. A man exited the store, looked across the road, and waved cheerily to them. "Is that Alistair?" Catherine asked, struggling to make him out because her glasses were steamed up.

"Yes," Holly said, waving back. "That's a huge box of chocolates he's carrying. Fiona's a lucky lady." They watched as he disappeared in the direction they'd come. "Shall we turn back and go explore what's down the road from The Inn?" Holly asked. Her cheeks were rosy and her breath formed clouds of steam.

Catherine nodded. "Sure." She glanced at Kimmy and noticed clumps of snow clinging to her little legs. "Do you think those lumps of snow are hurting her?"

Holly bent and examined Kimmy's legs. "She seems okay, but we'll try to keep her off the thick patches to be safe." Kimmy jumped up and licked Holly's face. "Ugh."

Catherine laughed. "You were asking for that."

"You're just jealous," Holly playfully bumped shoulders with Catherine as they began walking. "Has Beth ever tried to set you up with anyone? You know, like a blind date?"

Catherine was surprised by the question, but answered honestly. "She's always trying to set me up. She created a Facebook account for me under the pretence of us keeping in touch when she moved up here. I kept getting messages from random lesbians who happened to be single. She claimed it was a coincidence."

Holly laughed. "She's not subtle. She keeps trying to set me up, too. I wondered if…"

"Go on," Catherine said.

"Well, do you think she's trying to set us up?"

"Oh. I don't know," Catherine said. Her mind raced with the possibility. Could Beth be trying to set them up? If that was the case, then she didn't need to feel guilty for breaking her promise. "What makes you think that?"

"For the last six months, she's been trying to set me up. Every time I visit, there's another single acquaintance who happens to be a lesbian that she wants me to meet. I wonder if arranging for us to travel together and then spend Christmas with them is just another attempt? It wouldn't surprise me."

"Me neither," Catherine said, unable to hide her grin. The more she thought about it, the more likely it seemed. Perhaps their long-ago pact had simply arisen out of passion and anguish. Perhaps it didn't matter to Beth anymore. Perhaps she'd forgotten about it?

"If it is another one of her matchmaking schemes, I'd say she's done very well this time." Holly shot Catherine a flirtatious wink. "Wouldn't you agree?"

"Ye—" before Catherine could finish her sentence, her feet flew out in front of her and she went up in the air. A second later, gravity came into play, and she crashed down to earth with a thud. Her backside took most of the brunt.

"Are you okay?" Holly asked. She rushed to Catherine's side.

Catherine wasn't sure what was more painful, the bump to her right bum cheek or the sting to her pride. To add insult to injury, cold and wetness seeped through the material of her jeans.

She accepted Holly's hand and slowly got to her feet. Her backside was definitely more painful, she decided. "I'm okay." She brushed herself off and winced at both the dampness and pain from her rear. Why was she such a klutz? Especially in front of Holly. It was beyond embarrassing.

"You went down with a proper thump." Holly was clearly trying not to laugh.

Kimmy climbed on her back legs and rested her front paws on Catherine's legs. She licked some of the snow from her knees. "Thanks, Kimmy," Catherine said. She ruffled her furry head. "I think we might have to cut this adventure short. I need to change."

"Okay." Holly enticed Kimmy away and offered Catherine her arm to link. "Do you want to hold on to me now?"

Catherine was going to say no, but then her feet skidded again and she changed her mind. "Yes, please." She linked her arm through Holly's and they started walking back. With each step, her backside throbbed. She appreciated Holly refraining from pointing out her gangster limp.

Fifteen minutes later, Catherine was inspecting her newly acquired bruise in the bathroom mirror. It was going to be a big one. Why she was so accident prone around Holly was beyond her. As much as she'd like to blame Holly for sweeping her off her feet, it definitely had more to do with lack of grip, ice, and gravity. Her thoughts were distracted when Holly knocked on the door.

"Catherine? Angus is here with the car."

"I'll be out in a minute," Catherine said, wincing as she pulled up her knickers.

❖

After unloading their belongings from the car, Holly left with Angus to go meet with the mechanic. Catherine insisted she take the spare key with her, because she reluctantly planned on biting the bullet and going Christmas shopping. While Catherine was unpacking her suitcase, Kimmy gave everything an inspective sniff before settling down in the middle of the bedroom floor and watching.

"What am I going to do?" Catherine said. She'd put everything away and tidied up, both of which had helped with her Christmas shopping procrastination. "She's gone to all this effort and I need to do something special for her in return. Any ideas?"

Kimmy wagged her tail, looked Catherine right in the eye, opened her mouth, and yawned.

"I'm actually talking to a dog. What would Eve say?" She'd no doubt tut loudly and proclaim Catherine had lost her mind. Putting off leaving for a little bit longer, she decided to count how much money she had with her. While she riffled through the notes, Kimmy stood on her hind legs, nudging Catherine's hand with her wet nose. "I'll fuss with you in a minute. Let me finish counting."

Undeterred, Kimmy nudged more forcefully.

"You're so demanding." Catherine shoved the money back into her purse, tossed it on the bed beside her, and ruffled Kimmy's face. "What's up? You can't need to go out again so soon." The little dog dropped back down onto all fours and strolled to the bottom of the bed. A moment later, she was back up on her hind legs, her front paws planted beside Catherine's tablet.

"Hey, get down from there." Catherine rushed over and scooped up the tablet before it was scratched or marinated in dog slobber.

Kimmy sat and once again looked Catherine in the eyes.

Raising her chin slightly, Catherine felt compelled to keep the eye contact. It was weird how Kimmy held her gaze like this—almost like she was trying to communicate. Perhaps all dogs did it? It wasn't as if Catherine was an expert.

"Or maybe I've lost my mind," Catherine said, relieved when Kimmy slumped down in the middle of the room. Catherine decided to put the tablet away. She wouldn't be reading for a while, and without Wi-Fi, she'd have no access to her email or social media. She started walking, but stopped abruptly when an idea struck. It was too good to resist. It was perfect. After a few minutes of thinking it through, she had a plan to make tomorrow extra special for Holly. She needed to talk to Fiona and find out if the components of her scheme were possible.

"You're a genius, Kimmy." She ruffled the mop of grey hair. "I've got to go out for a bit, so you need to go into your crate. Come on."

Catherine tossed her purse and the tablet into her bag and hurriedly pulled her coat on. She rushed into the living room and opened the door to the dog crate. Kimmy trundled unenthusiastically behind her.

"Come on," Catherine said. She pointed inside the crate. Kimmy gave a tiny huff but obediently climbed into her bed. "Good girl. I'll be back soon." She squeezed her feet into Holly's wellies, grabbed her bag, and left the cabin, locking the door behind her.

❖

"Is that everything?" Fiona asked from behind the reception counter.

Catherine handed back the phone. "Thank you." She watched as the final download completed on her tablet before switching it off. "I think that's everything. Are you sure you're okay with me using your Wi-Fi and messing up the dinner plans for tomorrow? If it's too much trouble—"

"It's nay bother," Fiona said cheerily. "I only wish I could see her expression. She's a very lucky lady."

Catherine blushed. "Well, hopefully she'll like them." She packed away the tablet and took out her purse. "Now, before you argue, please hear me out. You've been so generous and kind to Holly and me. We really appreciate everything you've done for us." Catherine braced herself for an argument. "Please let me pay the full price for the cabin? I've got more than enough money and it's worth every single penny."

Fiona glowered. "We've been through this, Catherine. You'll pay half price, as previously agreed. And if you ask again, I'll feel insulted."

Catherine accepted defeat. She made a mental note to ask Eve to come up with a way to repay Fiona and Alistair's generosity.

"Okay. Here you go." She handed over her bankcard and entered her PIN.

"It's a pleasure doing business with you," Fiona said. "Now, is there anything else I can help you with? Later on this evening, I may not get a chance. Madness tends to descend on this place as soon as dusk settles."

"Actually, there is something else." Catherine's anxiety spiked. "I need to buy Christmas presents, and I haven't got a clue what to get or where to go. Help me, please?"

Fiona laughed and slapped the counter. "You look like a woman condemned. It's the same expression the old man wore today before he decided to go out for a walk. He never goes for walks, unless it's the morning of our anniversary, my birthday, or Christmas. I bet you a hundred pounds I'll get a box of chocolates tomorrow. I don't even like chocolate, but it's the same every year. I swear he does it on purpose, so he can end up eating them. I suppose I should be grateful. He made the effort to go out today, even though we're so busy."

Catherine shoved her hands in her pockets, deciding to keep quiet about seeing Alistair earlier. Her own panic took priority. "I really don't want to disappoint her."

"Oh, you won't. The surprises you've organised are lovely." Fiona scribbled a map on a crumpled piece of paper. "Here are the directions to the convenience store, and there's a post office next door."

"Thanks. We passed them earlier today." Catherine accepted the slip of paper and tried to mask her disappointment.

"Why the long face?"

"I was hoping there might be somewhere else in the village. I want to buy something special," Catherine said, nibbling on a fingernail.

"I swear, I wouldn't remember my head if it wasn't screwed on." Fiona tapped her head dramatically. "There's a quaint boutique shop a little way down the road. It sells some nice jewellery and other knickknacks. The tourists in summer can't get enough of it. It's not cheap, though." Fiona looked at the clock and tutted. "And it's only open for another hour or so. She doesn't usually open during winter, but as today's Christmas Eve, there's bound to be some business from the male villagers. I'm not holding my breath that I'll be lucky enough to get anything from there, mind. Chance would be a fine thing."

Catherine's spirits rose. The boutique shop sounded exactly what she was after. "It sounds perfect."

"It's down the road a wee while and then you turn left." Fiona gestured with her hands.

"Thank you, Fiona. You're a lifesaver." Catherine turned to leave, but only managed three steps.

"Don't you forget about coming here after the carol service tonight and having a wee festive dram with us. I've already mentioned it to Holly. I'll be looking out for you."

Catherine gave a nod, trying to be uncommitted. "Thanks again."

"See you tonight."

Catherine passed the Chinese takeaway and glanced at the opening times. A card was stuck to the door saying they would open at 7:30 p.m., after the carol service. She made a mental note of its whereabouts so she could lead Holly back later that evening. Almost ready to give up on the shop and head to the convenience store instead, she spotted a man leave a building with a shopping bag in tow. It was worth a shot.

She entered through an old weathered door, and a bell overhead signalled her arrival. Warm air greeted her and the smell of lavender tickled her nostrils. From all appearances, the little shop was exactly what Catherine needed.

"Can I help you, m'dear?" a small ancient-looking woman asked. She had a broad Scottish accent and peered up through thick bottleneck glasses. Her grey hair was tied up in a plat and wrapped around her head, framing a face shrunken with wrinkles. Beneath a blue tartan shawl she wore a fuzzy-looking light blue jumper, a long, dark blue pleated skirt, a pair of thick socks, and some sturdy-looking laced boots. The smell of lavender intensified tenfold.

"I need to buy some Christmas gifts for a friend. I'm not entirely sure what I'm looking for, though," Catherine said. She discretely covered her nose with a finger and took to breathing through her mouth. "But I'd like at least one gift to be extra special."

The old woman gave a nod. "Tell me about this friend of yours."

Catherine explained Holly was young, beautiful, and intelligent. This was her first time in Athegither, she loved Christmas, and it was her birthday tomorrow.

"Come," the woman said. She began shuffling farther into the back of the shop. Catherine followed with tiny steps and nearly toppled into the back of the woman when she stopped abruptly. She unlocked a glass cabinet, reached inside, and withdrew something. She turned to Catherine and presented a box.

"Thanks," Catherine said. She took hold of the rectangular box, carefully removed the lid, gazed down, and felt her hope soar. The silver pendant was beautiful: a decent sized chain moulded flawlessly to a pretty silver decoration, and in the middle nestled a turquoise stone.

"This is the birthstone for December. It's set in sterling silver with a Celtic knot design. It's handmade."

"It's beautiful," Catherine said. She touched the cool metal with a fingertip. It was priced at ten pounds over their agreed budget. After a few seconds of deliberation she said, "I'll take it. Can I leave it with you while I look around?"

"Aye. Just ask if you need help, m'dear." The old woman took back the box and shuffled past Catherine.

Thrilled with the pendent, Catherine decided she would outright deny any allegations she'd spent over the budget. She felt certain Holly would like it, and she was already desperate to see her expression when she opened it.

With a spring in her step and money burning a hole in her purse, she began ransacking shelves. Within a matter of minutes, she had an armful of items which she carried over to the counter.

The old lady started to ring up each item and carefully wrapped the breakables before putting them inside the bag. Handmade Christmas and birthday cards. A tartan apron with a message splayed across the chest in white text reading "Kiss the Chef." A little white Scottie dog toy, dressed in a kilt, holding bagpipes. A pack of eight red berry candle tea lights, and a tea towel that said "Athegither" and had quaint little pictures on it. Finally, for Eve, she chose a Scottish shortbread selection presented in a smart-looking tin. The total flashed on the till's screen.

"Do you accept cards?" Catherine asked.

"Aye," the woman said. She took the card and managed to get it inside the machine on the fourth attempt.

Catherine graciously accepted the bag. "Thank you. Your shop is lovely, by the way."

The old woman beamed a smile, which showed more gum than teeth. "Merry Christmas. May it bring everything your heart desires, m'dear."

"Merry Christmas to you, too," Catherine said, unable to resist returning the smile.

❖

It'd taken a while to get to the convenience store because, although the wellies provided grip, each step was uncomfortable and bordering on downright painful. Once inside the store, she was surprised by the bizarre, eclectic array of products. There was food, drink, toiletries, and other essential household products, but there were also humongous sacks of cattle and horse feed, fishing gear, tubs of paints, and various other DIY paraphernalia. She supposed, as the village was situated in the middle of nowhere, they had to be prepared for every occasion.

In the end, she purchased three Christmas stockings, a bottle of luxury bubble bath, a large packet of microwavable popcorn, a cable to connect her tablet to the TV, a roll of festive wrapping paper, and tape.

She went in search of a small birthday cake and candles. The candles were fine, but the smallest cake was big enough to feed eight people. She popped it into her basket anyway, added a small packet of balloons and a tacky foil banner. She queued for a minute, but then had to forgo her place and rush back to the pet aisle. After throwing a couple of dog treats and toys into her basket, she returned to the checkout and got back in line.

Normally queuing was a pet peeve, but today she didn't mind one bit. She was not only tapping her feet to the Christmas music playing over the sound system, but humming along, too.

Walking back to the cabin, she decided to check the garage in case Holly was still there. A stocky man dressed in oily overalls, with a thick neck and dark hair sprouting from his nose and ears, told her she'd left half an hour ago. Catherine thanked him and took in the sorrowful sight of Holly's car. The bumper hung off one side, and scratches and dents tarnished the hood. A tiny shudder tore through her body at the memory of being trapped inside. They had been lucky to get rescued.

As she turned to leave, she spotted a sign for tyre chains. Turning back to the man, she pointed at the sign and asked, "Excuse me. Do you have any of these in stock?"

"Aye."

"Excellent. I'd like to buy four of them. Would it be possible for you to put them on the tyres of this car before we leave?"

The man gave a curt nod and wiped his hands across the stomach of the overalls. "Aye. But this here car's not going anywhere for at least three days."

Catherine grinned and clasped her hands together. "Great. I mean that's fine." The prospect of spending three days alone with Holly made her giddy.

Frowning, the man scratched his black beard and gave a shrug. "Office is this way."

CHAPTER FIFTEEN

Catherine lounged on the sofa with her feet resting on the footstool. The heat from the crackling fire warmed her toes, and she took great pleasure in wriggling them. Her stomach was full from the sandwich and brownie she'd eaten. Kimmy sprawled across her lap despite there being plenty of space free on the actual sofa. The weight and warmth of her little body reassured. Her ears and paws twitched while she slept, and little whimpers kept escaping.

She could hear sounds of Holly humming, unravelling tape, and scissors cutting through paper, from the kitchen. Catherine was under strict instructions not to enter the kitchen on threats of pain, death, and the prospect of ruining the surprises of all of her Christmas presents.

It was immature and unlike her, but she was curious and excited. What could Holly have gotten her? How many gifts? Had she struggled in thinking of things to buy too? She doubted it. Anyway, she'd no intention of venturing into the kitchen until invited. She was comfortable and so was Kimmy. As the saying went, it was best to let sleeping dogs and pigged-out humans lie.

Catherine had wrapped all of Holly's presents, written out the cards, and safely stowed the cake and decorations inside her suitcase. She'd written their names on the stockings in permanent marker and hung them on the fireplace mantel. Holly's and Kimmy's names had both fit perfectly across the white sleeve, but she'd had to shorten her name to Cath. It didn't bother her.

From where she sat, she had a perfect view of them. They made the fireplace look festive, and when Holly returned from her own shopping expedition, she seemed genuinely touched by the gesture.

"Close your eyes!" Holly said from the kitchen.

"They're closed." Catherine tightly shut her eyes. She heard the pitter-patter of Holly's feet scurrying across the floor, and a moment later, the bedroom door closed. Catherine couldn't help but smile. They were acting like children and she blamed Holly. Her Christmas cheer and excitement were contagious.

A few minutes later, the bedroom door opened. "So, what do you want to do now? We can decorate the tree or make the gingerbread house?" Holly asked. She perched on the far sofa arm.

Truthfully, Catherine was more than happy to stay exactly where she was. As Scrooge-like as it sounded, she didn't think decorating the tree or assembling the gingerbread house were her kinds of things. It was nice Holly had taken the decorations down so they could do it together, but did it really matter? Would their decorating the tree compared to Fiona's decorating it make some kind of difference? Probably not.

"Catherine?"

"Let's decorate the tree." She wasn't going to ruin Holly's plans, especially when she looked so eager.

"Okay. I'll be right back." Holly disappeared into the kitchen. She returned with a cardboard box and placed it on the floor beside the tree.

"What goes on first? Baubles?" Catherine asked, holding a shiny red bauble in each hand.

"Normally the lights go on first." Holly smiled and took the baubles from Catherine, put them in the box, and planted a light peck on her cheek. "Then the tinsel and finally the baubles. It's easier this way."

Catherine rummaged through the box and took out both sets of lights. "Do we start at the bottom or top?"

"It doesn't matter," Holly said. She moved to the opposite side of the tree, waiting for Catherine to decide.

Logic suggested start from the bottom and work their way up. Catherine passed the bundle of lights around the back of the tree into Holly's hands. Holly decorated her side and passed the bundle back. They continued until both sets of lights were wrapped around the tree.

Surprisingly, Catherine was enjoying this far more than she'd expected. It was fun, which didn't make sense. It helped that Holly and she were so good together, so in sync.

Catherine was bending down to the box when something caught her eye. A string of golden tinsel was disappearing around the back of the sofa inch by inch. A quick scan of the living room left no doubt in her mind.

"Kimmy!" Catherine rushed forward in time to see the final bit of tinsel vanish. She rounded the back of the sofa, but Kimmy and the tinsel were long gone.

"Drop it," Holly said, her tone authoritative. She stood with her legs shoulder width apart, knees bent slightly, hands ready to catch a ball. "Drop it right now."

Deciding to counter from the rear, Catherine circled the sofa. Kimmy glanced back and looked her square in the eyes with a glittery mass of gold strands protruding from her mouth. Her tail wagged.

"There's nowhere to run, Kimmy," Catherine said. She edged closer.

Kimmy turned her attention back to Holly, who was closing in.

"Good girl, Kimmy. Drop it." Holly was almost within reach.

Kimmy glanced back again and then burst into motion. In a flash, she raced through the gap between Holly's legs, the tinsel dragging after her.

"Shit!" Holly said. "She's so frigging quick."

"Don't worry. I've got this." Catherine jogged into the kitchen and spotted Kimmy hiding beneath the table. She crawled under the table. As she reached for the tinsel, Kimmy sped off again. Rushing to chase after her, Catherine misjudged the height of the table and cracked her head.

"Ow!" Rubbing the top of her head and hoping she wasn't going to have yet another lump, she crawled out to see Holly leaning casually against the archway wall, smirking.

"Have you still got this, or am I okay to step in?" Holly asked sweetly.

"I'm not going to be outsmarted by a dog." Catherine got up and went after her charge.

Five minutes later, bent double, with hands resting on her knees, Catherine struggled to catch her breath. The little shit was like the canine version of Speedy Gonzales on cocaine. The more Catherine chased after her, the more Kimmy's tail wagged and the faster she ran. She got through the smallest gaps and refused to be cornered.

Kimmy watched her, pink tongue lolling, eyes sparkling, tail wagging, and the tiny white teeth showing with each panting breath— resembling a victorious grin. The tinsel, what was left of it, was now nothing more than a slobbery mess. Clumps and stray strands littered the floor in the wake of destruction.

"Just say the word and I'll intervene," Holly said. She sat cross-legged on the sofa watching the whole spectacle.

"Fine. Go ahead." Catherine was happy to have a breather and let Holly see how difficult and tiring it was.

Holly went into the kitchen and appeared a moment later with something in her hand. She walked over to the crate, opened the door, and knelt. Holding something orange out in front of her, she waited.

"What's in your hand?"

"Carrot."

"Carrot?"

"Yes, carrot."

Catherine folded her arms and craned her neck. "You're bribing a dog with carrot?"

"Have you got a better idea?" Holly asked. She gave a pointed glare.

"Well, I think if you're going down the route of bribery, maybe try something a little tastier than a carrot." Catherine sat on the edge of the sofa.

"They're her favourite and carrots are perfectly tasty."

Catherine snorted. "Next you'll be trying to get her to eat her five a day and brush her teeth."

Holly clenched her jaws and held the carrot out a bit farther. Kimmy was lying down, but her attention was focused on Holly's hand.

"I'll go and get one of her dog treats." Catherine started to get up but stopped when Kimmy started to creep closer. Fascinated, she watched as Kimmy continued to make her way toward Holly. Apparently, the tinsel was now long forgotten.

Holly placed the carrot inside the crate and stood slightly to the side, hands resting on her hips.

Kimmy continued the belly crawl until she was close enough to rush into the crate. In she went, pouncing on the carrot, clearly excited. A moment later, she happily crunched away.

Holly locked the door then turned to Catherine and grinned. "Guess I'm right."

"You bribed her. That's basically rewarding her bad behaviour."

"You chased her around like a bellowing lunatic. It was probably the best game she's ever played. I think she enjoyed that more than the carrot." Holly moved closer. "How's your head?"

"Sore."

"Whereabouts is it?" Holly asked.

"Here." Catherine lamely pointed to the crown of her head.

Holly leant forward, gently cupped her face, and kissed the top of her head. "Better?"

"Yes, thank you."

"Good. Just don't expect me to kiss your bruised bottom."

Catherine's face burned with embarrassment. Before she could speak, Holly's lips pressed against hers. The kiss was powerful in its intensity, and Catherine let out an involuntary groan as Holly's tongue slipped inside her mouth.

It ended too soon. Holly pulled away, breathing hard. "We need to finish decorating this tree, otherwise we'll miss the carol serv—"

"Okay. Let's miss it." As soon as the words left Catherine's mouth, she regretted them. Holly's flushed face now looked disappointed or hurt—she wasn't sure which. "Scrap that. We'll make the service. Come on, I'm desperate to hang some baubles."

Frowning, Holly held out a hand to help Catherine up. "If you don't want to go this evening, I won't force y—"

"I want to go," Catherine said, forcing a smile to cover the blatant lie. If the service was important to Holly, she'd do her best to respect it. "I got a bit caught up in the moment."

❖

The newly decorated tree looked pretty. In Catherine's not so humble opinion, it looked far superior to when they'd arrived. The baubles were evenly scattered and the missing layer of tinsel seemed to only improve the overall appearance. Holly was a little disappointed because they wouldn't be able to leave their presents under the tree, not with their canine kleptomaniac fiend around. Now they'd moved on to building and decorating the gingerbread house. Again, it was more enjoyable than Catherine had anticipated. The radio played in the background, and an array of sweets and chocolates dotted the table. Holly had purchased them on her shopping trip.

The stickiness and lack of an organised plan of attack had initially stressed Catherine out more than she cared to admit. Gradually, with Holly's encouragement and light teasing, she loosened up—although she still systematically placed the tiles on her side of the roof in precise rows and all of the coloured sweets symmetrically. Holly was gracious enough not to mention it.

"You know what I get from this?" Holly asked. Her forehead creased with a frown and her tongue blobbed out in concentration as she fixed the roof in place.

"Diabetes?"

"You're hilarious." Holly shot a mock glare before returning her concentration to the roof. "I get a real sense of achievement. From starting with some simple ingredients we end up with this. I find it so rewarding."

"Thank you for sharing it with me."

"It's my pleasure. I've enjoyed today." Holly stood up, seemingly clueless to the large dollop of icing smeared on her forehead. "It means so much to me that you're willing to give all of this a go. It can't be easy for you. And I know I'm a bit full-on, what with organising a whole itinerary and all. I just…want to make it special for you."

Catherine bridged the gap between them. "You've already made it special. For the first time in years I'm enjoying myself. With the exception of picking up dog poo and being so accident prone, it's been great." She paused, lowered her tone to serious, almost grave. "I have to be honest with you, though."

"Sorry?"

"I need to tell you something you might not want to hear."

"Go on." Holly nibbled her bottom lip.

"If it was me I'd want to know."

"What is it?"

Managing to keep both a serious expression and tone, Catherine said, "You've got icing smeared on your forehead."

Holly's hands flew to her head and, upon finding the drying

icing, began rubbing it vigorously. "Jeez, you had me stressing it was something serious."

"You should've seen your face." Catherine wriggled her eyebrows and grinned.

"You think that was pretty funny, don't you?"

"Yes."

"Well, you're not exactly spotless yourself."

Catherine's grin faltered. "Oh. Where?"

Holly raised a hand and touched one of Catherine's cheeks and then the other. A cold, sticky residue clung to her skin. "There," Holly said. She jumped back and waved her fingers. They were covered in icing.

"You..." Catherine was speechless. She wiped her cheek and stared at the drying clots of paste.

Holly grinned, her eyes sparkling with mischief. "You should see your face." She blobbed her tongue out to add insult to injury. "And that was funny."

Catherine reached for the bowl of icing and submerged both hands. Holly gasped and watched with big eyes. With the thick goo covering her fingers, Catherine slowly withdrew her hands.

"Catherine," Holly said. She took a step backward. "It was a joke. Don't overreact."

Catherine had no intention whatsoever of backing down. She stepped closer. She'd exact her revenge on Holly and it would be sickly sweet, quite literally. The only problem was, she could feel the tightening of the substance on her skin. It was drying too quickly.

"Say you're sorry." Catherine eased closer.

"I'm sorry."

"I don't think you mean it."

"I do mean it."

"I don't think it's sincere. I think you're saying it because you're afraid I'm going to get you with my sticky fingers." *Damn it! It sounded so much better in my head.*

Holly stopped moving. One of her eyebrows arched, and a second later, she burst out laughing.

Using the momentary lack of defence, Catherine pounced, smearing her sticky fingers not only on Holly's face, but also parts of her neck and possibly even an ear. When she stepped away, she couldn't help but laugh. Holly was covered, and the pissed-off look made it all the more adorable.

"You should never start something you can't finish," Catherine said smugly. She walked over to the sink to wash her hands. As the hot soapy suds incapacitated her hands, she sensed movement behind her a fraction of a second too late—

An evil laugh filled her ears as a mound of icing plopped on top of her head. Holly rubbed it into her hair with light fingers. Holly's stealthy footsteps had been hidden by the radio and running faucet. How could she have been so foolish?

Holly's voice whispered in her ear, "You should never turn your back during a food fight. Big mistake. And you should know, I always finish what I start, Catherine."

❖

After washing her hair for the fifth time, the remaining granular traces of the icing finally washed away. Holly had graciously let her use the bathroom first, which Catherine took to be some kind of unspoken apology.

Today seemed to be full of firsts for her. Buying Christmas presents and wrapping them, decorating a tree, building a gingerbread house, and having a glucose-fuelled food fight. Was it possible for a person to change so quickly? Not only in her likes and dislikes but also her personality? There was no denying she felt happier than she had in years. Holly seemed to nourish the playful and adventurous side of her personality which had long been dormant. It was as if she was thinking and feeling from a completely new perspective—a colourful and cheerful one.

She picked up her icing-stained clothes and headed into the bedroom.

Holly stood waiting. "Are you done in there?" She scratched her neck and face.

Catherine nodded. "You okay?"

"It turns out the icing is seriously itchy and aggravating when it dries on skin," Holly said. She stripped mid-sprint as she rushed into the bathroom and closed the door.

After a few minutes of deciding what to wear, Catherine chose a pair of black trousers, a fitted white shirt with pink stripes, and a black jumper. She dressed so quickly, she could've given Superman a run for his money. The last thing she wanted was for Holly to walk out and see her in an unflattering compromising position. She need not have worried. By the time Holly eventually appeared, Catherine had had enough time to dry her hair and apply a little makeup.

"You look great." Holly's gaze slowly travelled over Catherine's body.

"Thanks. I'll go spend some time with Kimmy before we head out." It was true she felt bad for leaving Kimmy again, but her main reason for leaving the bedroom was her overzealous libido. Seeing Holly standing there, dripping wet with nothing more than a towel to cover her, gave a powerful jolt of arousal—which wasn't ideal, considering in less than an hour she'd be standing inside a church.

Kimmy greeted her in the usual rush of energy but still gave no bow. "We've twenty minutes to play, and then it's out to do your business and back into bed."

Kimmy seemed to grasp the gist of what she was saying because she picked up her squeaky bone and trotted over to Catherine. With a little growl, which sounded more like a purr, she dropped the bone and sat on her haunches. Choosing the less sodden end, Catherine flung the bone and waited for Kimmy to bring it back. It was a simple thing: her throwing it and Kimmy retrieving it, but it didn't diminish either of their enjoyment. Eventually, Kimmy surrendered herself— collapsing in a dramatic heap beside Catherine and nudging in close for a fuss.

"You can't be tired already," Catherine said disapprovingly. She tickled behind one of the furry ears. "Mind you, I suppose the tinsel escapade may have worn you out."

Kimmy closed her eyes and sprawled out in a most unusual fashion. Her back legs spread out behind her body like a frog's legs. It was quite comical. Catherine had never seen a dog lie like this before, but from all appearances, Kimmy was comfortable.

"What's going to happen to you?" Catherine asked quietly.

That question had been reverberating in her mind, refusing to be ignored. The relationship between the dog and her was developing no matter how much she tried to back away or put up barriers. And she *was* trying, because she sensed an immense amount of hurt on the horizon. She was getting too emotionally invested in Kimmy. In three days' time, Kimmy would return to Fiona's care and they would probably never see the little fluffball again. The realisation was deeply unsettling, but there was no other option. Catherine was not in a position to own a dog. She lived in an apartment with no garden and worked far too many hours a day. The guilt of selfishly inflicting that life on Kimmy, especially knowing it would do no good for her in the long run, made the decision slightly more bearable. A family out there somewhere would cherish Kimmy and shower her with the love and affection she deserved. To think otherwise was too upsetting.

"Penny for them," Holly said. She was stood behind the sofa.

Catherine jumped with surprise. "Pardon?"

"Penny for your thoughts. You look troubled."

Catherine ran a hand down Kimmy's back, tracing the natural parting of her fur. "I'm going to miss her when we leave."

"Try not to think about it yet. We've got a few more days left to enjoy our time together." Holly sat next to Kimmy and gave her a big fuss. Her expression mirrored Catherine's melancholy mood.

She wore jeans and a white, snug-fitting jumper. Her honey-coloured hair fell in heavy ringlets past her shoulders. Fresh faced with a healthy glow, she wore only mascara and lipstick.

"You look beautiful," Catherine said. "I think icing might make for a great exfoliation cream, because you're glowing. In a healthy way, I mean, not in a toxic or radioactive way. It suits you."

"Thanks, I think." Holly smiled. She stood and patted her thigh. "Come on, Kimmy. Time to go out and do your business." Kimmy leapt from the sofa, tail wagging vigorously as she trotted after Holly's heels.

Catherine watched as they disappeared into the kitchen and felt the bitter taste of melancholy again—only stronger, as if Holly and Kimmy hadn't simply left the room but were, in fact, gone. Never to return.

The assault of grief astounded her and served as a stark reminder that playing happy family was all well and good, but the familiar haunting loneliness waited in the wings, ready to swoop down and stake its claim on her as soon as the opportunity presented itself. If she had one wish, she'd choose to capture this break from her mundane life and treasure it forever. An endless supply of cosy fires, games of fetch, slobbery doggy kisses, festive cheer, laughter, and Holly's tactile flirtations would make for a content life indeed.

❖

Being an atheist didn't bode well for a carol service in a church. In fact, the last slightly religious building Catherine had entered was the crematorium for Granny Birch's funeral. As they made their way along the main street, an uncomfortable tension settled across her chest and shoulders. She felt like a fraud, deliberately infringing on an occasion precious to others.

Once again, she had no choice other than to wear Holly's wellies, which, unsurprisingly, didn't go with her outfit. She'd considered wearing something else on her feet, but the prospect of falling on her backside in front of the whole population of Athegither was enough to make her see sense. As they approached the iron gates, streams of people coming from different directions surrounded them. Everyone seemed to know everyone else, of course, but they were friendly enough to the outsiders, waving hello in greeting or wishing Catherine and Holly a Merry Christmas. When they reached the threshold, a young boy thrust a worn hymn book into Catherine's hands. He grinned at her and, a second later, brandished another book, and lunged for the person behind her. He obviously wanted to get his job, and possibly the service, over as quickly as possible. A slightly older girl with auburn ringlets falling to her shoulders shyly presented Holly with hers.

They continued to follow the queue of people and eventually shuffled inside the church. It was packed solid, and the heat from so many people already bordered on stifling. People of various ages filled rows upon rows of wooden benches to the brink. An aisle of worn, red carpet ran up the centre, splitting the benches into two sides. It led to the front where stone steps led to a raised area with a stone table.

Feeling self-conscious and totally out of her depth, Catherine looked to Holly for guidance. As if sensing her stress, Holly gave her hand a gentle squeeze and led her to the right-hand side. Eventually, they found a precious part of the exterior wall that hadn't already been claimed. They leant against it, looking out over the benches to the table, candles, and statues at the front. Catherine felt a little calmer and settled into a favourite pastime of people watching.

An excited buzz filled the room: quiet chatter and laughter, with the occasional cough or sneeze thrown in the mix. People smiled and seemed genuinely happy to be there. The children fell into two categories: the wide-eyed lot, brimming with excitement and bodily energy they were restraining—only just—so as not to slip up at the last minute in front of Santa. The other category of children seemed tired and grumpy, clinging to caregivers with heavy-lidded eyes and pouting bottom lips. Perhaps a few sleepless nights leading up to the big night itself had left them exhausted.

"Okay?" Holly whispered, giving a gentle nudge with her elbow.

Catherine nodded and turned to the front where some people were setting up seats. Seven people sat in a semicircle, took out varying musical instruments, and began fiddling with them to make sure they were in tune. A stir spread throughout the congregation. The man next to Holly opened his hymn book and ruffled through the pages.

The room darkened as some of the lights were turned off. Three large candle displays glowed at the front, and rows upon rows of lit tea lights danced inside red holders. Several large pillar candles stood next to the stone table, three purple, one pink, and the final one white.

A man—presumably the clergy—stepped up to the wooden lectern and spoke. "It's wonderful to see so many familiar, and unfamiliar, faces here this evening. In a wee moment we'll get started with the carols, but I want to remind you there's Mass straight after this service and again at midnight." He glanced around at the musicians. "Right. Without further ado, please turn to our first carol, which I believe is 'Silent Night.'" He stepped away from the microphone and everyone in the church stood.

Catherine turned toward Holly. Everyone seemed friendly, but she wasn't sure what was expected of her. Carols were one thing but Mass? Would Holly expect them to stay? Catherine wouldn't feel comfortable with that.

Music started up, and Holly smiled, warm and reassuring. Catherine felt some of her unease melt away. Glancing at the number in Holly's hymn book, Catherine quickly found the words in time to join in with the first verse. The voices from the congregation sang loud and mostly in tune. Sneaking a glance around, Catherine saw the closeness and love surrounding her. Families squeezed together sharing books, hands being held, shoulders leaning against shoulders, tapping of hands and feet—but more than anything else, she saw loving smiles. The tight quarters and uncomfortable heat didn't seem to dampen anyone's spirits. In fact, Catherine guessed most people here wouldn't rather be anywhere else.

It was a curious thing.

At the next verse, Catherine joined in once more. Her voice immediately disappeared into the ether, harmonising with everybody else's. It felt good, like she was a part of something big, something she couldn't put into words. She'd always believed Christmas was about receiving gifts, some of which you didn't want or like, and gorging yourself sick on vast piles of extravagant food and drink. This experience had proven her cynical beliefs wrong. There was definitely more to Christmas than she'd originally thought, and she was determined to experience as much of it as possible. As they started the next carol, she sang with genuine gusto.

❖

The Inn was full, so solidly packed with bodies Catherine nearly suggested they leave.

As if reading her thoughts, Holly said, "We have to show our faces. It'd be rude not to, especially after all Fiona and Alistair have done for us."

Feeling suitably berated, Catherine gave a nod and followed as closely behind Holly as humanly possible. After a few seconds of squeezing past people, Holly reached behind her and took hold of Catherine's hand tethering them together. They'd held hands a few times before, but this time Catherine noticed their hands fitted together perfectly, as if they were made for each other.

The raucous sound of laughter, good-natured shouting, and faint background music filled the room. Catherine hadn't been inside the bar area before, and she wouldn't get much of an opportunity to check it out this evening, either. It was far too busy to see anything other than the occasional bit of floor and a fleeting glance of a wall or the bar.

Unlike most bars Catherine had been in, there were no tables or seats provided, although she assumed this wasn't always the case.

Tonight was obviously one of the busiest, and therefore standing room only would accommodate as many patrons as possible. After the church service finished, there would probably be a further influx of customers. Catherine hoped they might be gone by then, not because the atmosphere wasn't friendly, but because she felt a little claustrophobic, rather guilty for leaving Kimmy alone, and desperate to spend some time alone with Holly.

Holly glanced back and said something, but Catherine couldn't hear. She pointed to her ear and moved closer.

"What drink?" Holly asked. She added the universal hand gesture for drinking.

"Red wine please," Catherine shouted.

Holly smiled and turned back to the bar. A gap opened up, and like lightning, Holly filled it. A few moments later, she relinquished her hold of Catherine's hand and presented a large glass of wine in one hand and a small glass tumbler with a generous shot of amber liquid in the other. Regaining her balance after someone accidentally shoved past her, Catherine held both glasses steady and changed her stance so she wouldn't be knocked so easily. When Holly moved away from the bar, she held a second glass of wine and an identically filled glass tumbler.

Catherine led them to the farthest end of the room hoping there might be more space. There wasn't, so they hovered by the door leading to the restaurant and fire exit.

"Thank you," Catherine said loudly. She raised both glasses.

"The whiskey's from Fiona. Everyone gets a wee festive dram, apparently."

Catherine gave a nod. That's probably why it was so bloody busy in here. She decided to forgo the whiskey for the moment and concentrate on the wine instead. Trying to hide her snobbery, she lifted the glass and breathed the wine's bouquet in through her nose before taking a sip. It exceeded her expectation, so she drank some more.

Conversation was limited because of the noise, which led to them both drinking their wine far more quickly than advisable. A familiar warmth surged through Catherine's body. Holly's cheeks were flushed pink, her eyes narrow, as she followed suit and drained her glass.

"Shall we drink this and go get some takeaway?" Holly asked.

She raised her tumbler a little haphazardly, managing to narrowly avoid spilling the contents.

"Okay." Catherine lifted the glass to her mouth, but stopped when Holly tugged her arm.

"Like this." Holly interlinked her arm through Catherine's like people do at weddings. "A toast. To the best Christmas ever!"

Catherine snorted a laugh. Wow. Holly was tipsy and her loud toast had drawn attention from the people surrounding them. They were all smiling and a few raised their glasses in cheers, too. Holly gave a frustrated nudge with her arm and Catherine laughed. Giddy, Catherine said, "To the best Christmas ever." Heads thrown back, they downed the contents of the tumblers. The whiskey was nice but strong. Catherine grimaced at the aftertaste as the fiery trail made its way down to her stomach. Granny Birch would be highly disappointed in her.

"Ugh," Holly said, spluttering. Her face screwed up tightly. "That's why I don't drink neat spirits."

They received a small round of applause from three people to the left of them. Catherine wasn't quite sure how to respond, but grinning with mischief, Holly dropped into a curtsy and received a wolf whistle too.

"Come on." Holly grabbed Catherine's hand and pulled her out through the double doors. "I'm starving."

❖

Catherine poured the wine into their glasses. Normally, she would've let the bottle breathe for a few hours, but she hadn't thought far enough in advance. Plus the whiskey they'd drunk had most likely destroyed a good few taste buds. Holly placed a plate in front of Catherine and one in front of herself. The food looked good.

"Here's to our Christmas Eve," Catherine said. She raised her glass and clinked it against Holly's.

"Our Christmas Eve," Holly said, her tone somewhat wistful.

Kimmy settled beneath the table chewing happily on one of her bones. Catherine suspected she was waiting to claim any dropped food.

The meal was wonderful. They talked about their day and Kimmy. They laughed and joked while eating the best Chinese takeaway

Catherine had ever had. They'd chosen their dishes together, so it wasn't quite the same as when she'd done it with Granny Birch, but it was special in its own right.

Before clearing up, Holly held out two golden foil wrappers. Each contained a fortune cookie. "You pick," she said.

Catherine hesitated for a moment and then pointed to the right hand. The golden packet flung in her direction, hit her chest, and fell into her lap.

"Here I go," Holly said. She snapped the cookie and picked out the thin strip of paper. "Now is the time to try something new."

"Slightly ambiguous."

"I like it." Holly flattened the curling paper with her fingers. "Come on. Stop keeping me in suspense. What does yours say?"

"I never bother to open them. It's a complete waste of time. It's some general mumbo-jumbo made to fit everyone on the planet. Like horoscopes and all that other crap."

"It's a little bit of fun, Catherine."

"Fine," Catherine said with a huff. She picked up the packet and ripped into the foil. She took out the crescent cookie and snapped it, feeling as it crumpled beneath her fingers. Talk about making a mess for no reason.

She could feel Holly's gaze watching her, so she riffled through the sticky crumbs and took out the slip of paper.

The font was tiny, but she finally read the words: *There is only one happiness in life: to love and be loved—George Sand.*

"What does it say?" Holly asked, leaning across the table.

Catherine pulled the slip closer to her chest, shielding it from Holly's prying eyes. No matter how many times she read it, the words seemed intricately personal. A small lump lodged in her throat, and her palms were sweaty. The smeared words on this cheap, tacky bit of paper had a tremendous impact on her. Hadn't she secretly considered the exact same thing recently? Either this was some cosmic joke at her expense, or it was a weird coincidence.

"Catherine?" Holly asked with obvious concern.

"It says…" She desperately tried to think of something. She couldn't bring herself to read the actual words. Holly might laugh and joke about them, which would be unintentionally hurtful. Or she might want to talk about the meaning in greater detail, and that created its own host of problems. For instance, why had she spent so long rereading it? It could tarnish their newly blossoming relationship with unreal expectations. Catherine was attracted to Holly, and hopefully the feelings were reciprocated, but in no way was she in love with her. This whole thing—whatever was happening between them—was nothing more than harmless fun and flirting. To read anything further into it was ludicrous.

"It says change is on the horizon."

Holly slapped the table and sat back in her chair. "I told you there's more to these than general mumbo-jumbo. Perhaps it means a new job, eh?"

"Perhaps. Shall we clean these up and go sit in front of the fire?"

"I was thinking the exact same thing." Holly carried her plate over to the sink.

Catherine carefully folded the slip of paper and placed it in an empty compartment of her purse for safekeeping.

❖

Kimmy lay sprawled on the sheepskin rug gnawing on her bone, her back legs spread out behind her in a frog-like fashion. They'd tried, on three separate occasions to deter her from lying so close to the fire, but within minutes, she'd sneakily crawled back. Even with her double coat, she was a heat-seeking fiend. She was cute and so clearly happy, they didn't have the heart to move her again. And it kept her away from the Christmas tree and tinsel, which was an added bonus.

Catherine sat on one side of the sofa and Holly on the other. Their wine glasses were almost empty, and as tempting as it was to open a new bottle, Catherine resisted. She didn't want a thick head in the morning.

Little waves of excitement randomly swept through her. She couldn't wait for Holly to open her presents and experience the other surprises she'd laid on for her. Although lethargic from wine and the fire, she knew sleep wouldn't come easily. She'd also reached an important decision with regards to breaking her promise to Beth. The alcohol had helped to quell her guilt and convince her wholeheartedly that Beth had indeed planned to set them up. That being the case, she wasn't really breaking the promise or Beth's trust. If that *wasn't* the case…well, she hadn't dared give that too much thought. Perhaps Beth might never find out? It was only a harmless festive fling. After years of being alone, didn't Catherine deserve some happiness, even for a short while? Couldn't she be forgiven for putting her needs above everyone else's, just this once? She'd nearly bloody died—surely that counted for something? The wine agreed with her on all accounts and conveniently drowned out any logic that her conscience tried to raise. Tonight, she would do what felt right, and hoped it might involve nakedness.

They'd been talking about various subjects and Holly had opened up. She hated being seen as young and foolish. She'd worked hard and sacrificed a lot for her business, money, and spending time with family and friends. "I do miss my friends, but I feel like we've been drifting apart for a while. Their lives revolve around going out and partying. I'm so over it. It holds absolutely no appeal for me anymore. I haven't the money to waste. And I haven't the time for hangovers and all of the incestuous lesbian drama that comes with it. I'm ready for something more meaningful. Does that make sense?" Holly asked, her words slurring slightly.

"Complete sense," Catherine said. "You have to do what's right for you."

"I feel guilty, though. We grew up together. I'd hate for them to think it's because I consider myself better than them."

"You can't live your life worrying about what others might think of you." Catherine cringed inwardly at the hypocrisy she was spouting.

Holly nodded. "Thank you."

"For what?"

"For everything." Holly gestured wide with both hands. "You saved us. You were so brave and caring." She crawled closer. "Shall I let you in on a little secret?"

Gulping, Catherine hoarsely said, "Yes."

"I wouldn't rather be anywhere else in the whole entire world than right here with you."

Catherine was speechless and could only watch as Holly closed the remaining distance. Her lips gleamed and shadows danced across her face and body, thanks to the flickering flames of the fire. Her eyes sparkled and her expression looked almost hungry.

"I've been attracted to you from the first moment I saw you all those years ago," Holly whispered. Her mouth less than an inch away from Catherine's. "I want you."

Excitement flamed in Catherine's body. An ache flared between her legs; she squirmed with its intensity. She'd never felt like this with Paula. Her body had an agenda of its own. A sexual agenda.

Holly's mouth was now only a hairsbreadth away, and Catherine smelled wine on her warm breath.

"Do you want me?" Holly asked. She straddled one of Catherine's legs in order to get closer.

Catherine wrapped her arms around Holly's waist and pulled her down on top of her, her mouth blindly seeking Holly's soft lips and forcing a searing kiss. Holly's mouth opened and their tongues met. Catherine groaned into the warm wetness they created. Hands battled against clothing while they tried to balance on the perilous ledge of the sofa. Catherine managed to partially raise Holly's white jumper, her fingers gripping the welcoming soft flesh of Holly's stomach.

Having already removed her own black jumper when they'd sat to eat, Holly's nimble fingers unfastened the shirt's buttons in super-quick time.

Their kiss was all consuming. Eyes closed, breathing laboured, hands caressing skin—something wet and cold prodded Catherine's foot. "Shit!" Catherine said, pulling away and narrowly avoiding head-butting Holly.

Gasping, Holly looked understandably startled. Her hair was a mess and her swollen lips looked ever-so-inviting. "What the hell?"

Catherine pointed. "I'm not great with an audience, let alone one who tries to participate."

Holly looked to where Catherine's finger pointed. Kimmy sat beside the sofa staring at them with her dark, accusing eyes. Her ears pricked and her head cocked from one side to the other as she studied them. Her little tail thump-thump-thumped against the floor.

"Oh, God. The poor thing," Holly said. She climbed off Catherine and pulled down her jumper bashfully.

"Poor thing? Little perv more like. She nearly gave me a bloody heart attack nudging me with her cold nose," Catherine said. She wrapped the loose shirt around her torso, pinning it in place by folding her arms.

Holly stood. "I'll take her out to do her business and then put her in her crate."

"But, what about…aren't we, what should I do?" Catherine asked, feeling hot and bothered.

"You can wait for me in the bedroom."

Catherine's desire soared in her chest. "Okay," she said. She rushed to the bedroom door. She glanced back in time to shoot Kimmy an evil look without Holly's knowledge before skipping inside the room.

Chapter Sixteen

After a few seconds of looking aimlessly around the bedroom, Catherine decided to quickly freshen up in the bathroom. Fortunately, she'd seen fit to prepare her body while in the shower earlier in case this exact situation happened to arise. Her pulse raced, blood rushed in her ears. Her stomach flipped with a mixture of excitement and nerves. She was lightheaded, giddy with arousal. It'd been so long since she'd been physically or sexually involved with someone, she'd almost forgotten how it felt. The only downside of their inopportune break was that her mind had time to inundate her with worries and self-doubt.

What if I disappoint her or leave her unfulfilled?

With the exception of one drunken night at uni—most of which she couldn't recall, and so had to go purely on hearsay, Paula had been her only sexual partner. It'd taken so long for her to open up enough and allow herself to finally trust someone. She'd always been awkward in her own body and struggled to understand her emotions. But Paula had persevered and gradually overcome all of her defences. Catherine had enjoyed their lovemaking, although it'd never been particularly earth-shattering. Paula had always claimed she'd enjoyed it, too, which, considering what a selfish lover she was, wasn't a complete surprise. Ultimately, it hadn't been enough for her, as she'd actively sought sex with someone else behind Catherine's back. The hurt still flared when Catherine allowed herself to remember it. Her inexperience and low self-esteem had always been an issue. Now they returned with a vengeance rocking what fragile confidence she had left.

What if I do something wrong?

Or, heaven forbid, cause discomfort or embarrassment for either of us?

It didn't bear thinking about.

What if Holly is into kinky sex?

Catherine didn't have a clue what it would entail. Sure, she'd read her fair share of sex scenes in books and had occasionally tried to read erotica, but always ended up skimming over the more intimate details. She regretted her prudishness now.

Surely the basics of sex couldn't have changed too much in recent years?

Could they?

"Why is she interested in me?" she asked herself in a whisper. All she'd successfully managed to do during their time together was be accident prone. That was hardly an aphrodisiac. A sudden realisation burst to the forefront of her mind, startling in its clarity: Holly was interested. Forget the reasons why. Why was she trying to talk herself out of it? It was all she'd been thinking about since meeting Holly. It was the frigging reason she'd gotten into the death trap car in the first place. Everything had been leading up to this moment.

Her body was primed and ready to go. Her mind could either get on board or shut the hell up. There was no way she was going to pass up the opportunity of spending the night with a beautiful, sexy, and charming woman. They were both consenting adults, and if weird kinky sex was on the cards, well, she'd cross the bridge when she came to it. Who knows? She might even like it.

Taking a deep breath and holding it, she finally opened the bathroom door and crossed the threshold into the bedroom. A bedside lamp was the only source of light in the room. Holly was waiting for her. Catherine's heart leapt to her throat, causing her breath to come out in a shaky stream. She froze, unable to move, as all messages from her brain had ceased.

"Hi," Holly said. She lay on top of the bed, her head propped on one hand, her golden hair loose and wild looking. She wore only a matching red bra and panty set.

Catherine's eyes roamed over the scantily clad body, feasting on the roundness of her curves and the freckled pale flesh. The winding tattoo of a branch with pink blossoms crept from below Holly's hip bone up to beneath her right breast. Even from this distance it was evocative. Catherine wanted to trace the snaking pattern.

"Are you coming to join me?" Holly asked, her tone seductive, but the twiddling of a curl of hair was a telltale sign she was a little nervous.

Without speaking, because there was no way she could form a coherent sentence, Catherine walked over to the bed and climbed on top. The pounding of her heart was deafening, and she felt certain Holly could hear it, too. Holly crawled closer and beamed such a bright smile, Catherine's inhabitations and worries seeped away.

"You're so b-beautiful," Catherine said. God, she meant it. Holly's body was as warm and inviting as her personality. Her sparkling eyes, the easy smile that lit up her face and revealed cute dimples. Her musical laugh, the colourful tattoos that were an extension of her personality, her quick wit and sharp intellect all complemented perfectly the shapely body. She was the epitome of femininity, and the swelling of her breasts against the red lace holding them captive stirred something primal inside Catherine.

"So are y—"

Catherine kissed her deeply, cutting off her sentence mid-flow. Their passion grew fever pitched once more, as if no time had passed. The caress of their tongues, the warmth and wetness of their kiss enveloped them. Her heightened sense of taste enabled Catherine to derive the most pleasure. The faint linger of wine was overshadowed by the exquisite taste of Holly. Sweetness, layered with an indescribable depth of flavour Catherine could happily spend years—perhaps the rest of her life—trying to decipher and depict it. Holly's essence, paired with the intense physical sensations of their kiss, exhilarated. Catherine craved more intimacy and deepened their kiss, her senses intoxicated.

She held Holly's waist, pulling her closer. The skin beneath her palms was hot and impossibly soft. Holly's hands were busy at work and had managed to pull Catherine's shirt over her shoulders, but her sleeves bunched up by her elbows. Not wanting to end their kiss, Catherine freed the shirt from her arms and flung it behind her.

The coolness from the room reacted with the heat from her body, and goose bumps broke out across her flesh. And as Holly's hands brushed her stomach, a shiver crawled across her body. Her sensitive nipples puckered.

Holly ended their kiss with laboured panting. Catherine's own breaths were short and shallow, her lips wonderfully swollen and sore. Holly's taste lingered on her lips and tongue, feeding her lust. Her head swam pleasantly; she felt high. She mourned the loss of their kiss acutely.

"These are coming off," Holly said, her tone seductively low. She unfastened the button and pulled down the zip on Catherine's trousers. With her legs sprawled in the air, Catherine lay back on her backside and winced from the bruised cheek. Holly wasted no time in tugging the trousers down, and Catherine obligingly kicked her legs to help. In a flash, the trousers were gone, leaving only her underwear.

Holly pounced on top of her, positioning one thigh between Catherine's legs and the other on the outside. Lowering herself, Holly kissed Catherine's mouth, sucking on her bottom lip before trailing a path of delicate, ticklish kisses over her jaw and throat.

Catherine whimpered. She hitched up on her elbows, raising her body toward Holly's for the slightest brush of contact. She wasn't fully aware of Holly's hands until her bra unclipped at the back.

Holly's eyes were dark pools and they captivated Catherine's gaze. She lowered the straps and carefully removed the bra. Only once her breasts were free did Holly's gaze drop. She subconsciously wet her bottom lip, making it gleam. The intensity of Holly's gaze set Catherine's body on fire and turned her nipples rock hard. As Holly's face lowered to her left breast, Catherine fought back a moan. The softness of Holly's hair brushing her chest tingled, followed by a tickle of warm breath teasing her nipple. The wait bordered on torture, but after a lifetime, the hot flick of Holly's tongue zinged her nerves. With a gasp, Catherine's whole body bucked. A shot of raw arousal fired from her nipple straight to her crotch. Holly's tongue continued to torment, giving a taste of what she had in store but always pulling back at the last moment.

"H-Holly—" Catherine said, hissing loudly as her hips jumped off the bed.

Holly looked up with a wicked grin as she tweaked the sensitive nipple between her forefinger and thumb.

Catherine cried out again, the throbbing in her crotch reaching an all-time high. She could feel the dampness of her panties. She lifted her backside off the bed and tried to press herself against Holly's thigh, but Holly moved her leg away, denying the contact Catherine so desperately craved. After another two sharp squeezes to the same nipple, Holly drew it into her mouth. She swirled her tongue in lazy circles, giving the occasional suck and rake with her teeth.

Catherine's throat was hoarse and tears brimmed her eyes. Every muscle in her body tightened. The throbbing ache flaring in her crotch walked the fine line between pleasure and pain. She couldn't take any more, yet couldn't form the words to warn Holly.

As if sensing her on the edge, Holly lowered a hand and with light dancing fingertips stroked the material between Catherine's thighs.

Choking a sob, Catherine thrust herself against Holly's hand, needing more. This time Holly granted her wish, and with harder strokes they formed a rhythm. Catherine teetered on the verge of orgasm—eyes clenched, head tilted back, breaths ragged, fingernails digging into Holly's waist.

Holly suddenly withdrew her hand. "Hold on, sweetheart," Holly whispered breathlessly as she changed position.

Peering up through watery eyes, Catherine watched as Holly's red panties went flying across the room. Before she'd fully registered what she'd seen, Holly straddled her thigh. She moaned involuntarily when Holly's wet centre burned against her thigh.

Holly's hand slipped inside Catherine's panties and her fingertips explored. Her body rocked in perfect time with the thrusting of her fingers.

Managing one last look, Catherine gasped as she watched Holly's body move above her…golden hair tousled, face flushed, eyes clenched, mouth open slightly as her moans grew louder and more fraught. Her breasts had a natural bounce, and although still covered by the bra, both nipples were erect and straining against the material. Holly increased their pace, rolling her hips and grinding herself harder.

As she writhed in agonising ecstasy, the powerful orgasm descended and tore through Catherine, making her body thrash and jump. The sound of her own voice reverberated in her ears, until Holly's cry took over.

Gasping, Holly slumped down on top of Catherine's body. She rested her head on Catherine's chest, her sweaty forehead sticking to her skin. She withdrew her hand from inside Catherine's panties and rested it across her stomach.

Catherine, too, was damp with perspiration. As her breathing returned to normal, she enjoyed a pleasant humming as it rolled through her body in waves. Grinning, she wrapped her arms tightly around Holly's body.

Her senses picked up on various things: the warm weight of Holly's body pressed against her own, the rise and fall of Holly's breasts, the sound as Holly's breathing started to calm, and the raised tempo of Catherine's own heartbeat. The heady, musky fragrance of sweat and sex filled her senses. Sweeping some of Holly's damp hair to the side, Catherine planted a gentle kiss on her forehead, enjoying the sting of salty sweetness on her lips.

"Hi," Holly said, timidly looking up and smiling.

"Hi there." Catherine wrapped her arms tightly around Holly. "That was...great." She cringed. Of all the words she could've come up with. Her brain was fuzzy and so she blamed it on that.

"That was just foreplay." Holly's expression was serious and her tone husky.

"Foreplay?" Catherine asked, shocked by another spike of arousal.

"Uh-huh. Are you feeling relaxed now?" Holly asked.

"Very much so."

"Good. Me too. And now that we've got the first sexual encounter over with, we can take our time to explore and enjoy." Holly sat up and unhooked her bra at the back. She removed it in one fluid motion and sent it sailing across the room.

Catherine's eyes were glued to the perfect pair of breasts in front of her, pale skin with rosy pink nipples. She'd never considered herself a breast woman, until now.

"Ready for round two?" Holly asked. She hiked an eyebrow, a ghost of a smile twitching in the right corner of her mouth.

"How many rounds are there?" Catherine asked hoarsely. Previously, after having sex with Paula and more often than not having to sort herself out, she'd want nothing more than to sleep. Now, though, her libido fired on all cylinders, apparently wanting to make up for lost time. The sight of Holly's breasts and the promise of more intimacy fuelled her insatiable desire.

"I was thinking as many as we can manage before we collapse in exhaustion. The night is young and there's all manner of things I intend to do to you."

"Oh," Catherine said, not entirely sure how she should respond.

"That sounds nice." *Nice? What the hell was wrong with her? She didn't want to talk anymore. What had happened to the vast vocabulary she'd accumulated throughout her life?*

"Promise, if you're not entirely comfortable with something, you'll say."

"Okay," Catherine said, her body and mind both reaching the same conclusion: kinky sex.

"Take those off." Holly pointed to the damp panties Catherine still wore.

With her stomach somersaulting and her mouth incredibly dry, Catherine attempted to remove her panties in a seductive manner. It didn't work. Blushing with embarrassment and finally managing to unhook them from between two toes, she flung them away. She reached for Holly, but Holly stopped her.

"Wait. Let me look at you," Holly said.

Catherine lay back, unable to raise her gaze to meet Holly's.

"You're so fucking sexy."

Catherine opened her mouth to reply and then thought better of it. Holly's dominance and tone wreaked havoc on her body; the aching returned and she was already wet.

"Get on all fours."

Catherine gasped. She struggled to give up control and do what Holly commanded. She wanted to…but it was different from what she was used to.

"Catherine?"

A deep breath and slow exhalation granted Catherine time to put things into perspective. She didn't want another regret to dwell on. Instinctively, she knew passing up this opportunity would haunt her. She'd made an affirmation to start opening herself up to new possibilities—although this wasn't entirely what she'd had in mind.

What the hell? She relinquished her absolute need for control, giving it up to Holly. It was unnerving but also incredibly liberating. She stretched forward and planted her hands and knees on the duvet.

Bring on the kinky sex!

CHAPTER SEVENTEEN

Catherine had been awake for a little while but was far too comfortable to consider moving. Holly was snuggled in close, her right leg and arm draped over Catherine's body. She was sound asleep, her tiny snores keeping a steady rhythm. Content didn't come close to describing how Catherine felt. Calmness unlike anything she'd ever experienced before had settled over her. Her body ached everywhere, and she'd potentially pulled a muscle in her side. One of her ankles felt a little tender, too, but it had been totally worth it.

She broke out in a big smile remembering their evening's escapades. She'd never known how diverse and fun sex could be. The human body was an incredible machine. Her stamina was pretty good and her body was far more flexible than she'd ever realised. She'd learnt so much about sex, herself, and Holly. It turned out kinky sex was definitely her kind of thing—a surprising development.

Her sexual experiences with Paula had been mundane and unfulfilling at best and paled significantly in comparison to last night. Holly had spent time, a great deal of time, exploring and learning Catherine's body. At first it'd been a little peculiar having someone show such intense interest in her with the clear aim of giving her pleasure. Holly had obviously enjoyed it, though, and in turn had allowed Catherine to loosen up. Catherine, of course, had her own opportunities to repay the favours—several times, in fact. It did go to show, giving could be as rewarding as receiving.

They'd finally both collapsed in a multi-orgasm-induced stupor at around three in the morning, exhausted but beyond sated. Sleep had come quickly. It was after seven in the morning, and Catherine had two hours before Holly's first surprise. Her heart skipped a beat in excitement.

Holly stirred. Her eyelashes fluttered and finally opened. Her eyes were clouded with sleep as she peered up through hooded lids. As soon as her eyes locked onto Catherine, they grew a little wider. "Morning," she said. She smiled sleepily, then stretched her entire body out and reached her arms above her head.

"Good morning," Catherine said. Her cheeks warmed. In the light of day, she felt a little shy. How was it possible for Holly to look so gorgeously cute and innocent after an evening of borderline dominatrix behaviour?

"I'm going to go use the bathroom and then shall we open our presents in here?" Holly asked.

"Sure." Catherine switched off the alarm on her phone while trying to remember where she'd unpacked her pyjamas.

"I'll be back in a minute." Holly surprised Catherine by giving her a kiss and then crawling out of bed.

Holly sauntered over to the bathroom door, bare naked. Her backside was pert and round. Catherine was transfixed. When the door shut, she released a pent-up breath. How could she still be turned on? Surely after umpteen orgasms her body should be exhausted? She was beginning to feel sex-crazed.

It'd been so long since she'd experienced a morning-after scenario, she wasn't entirely sure how to proceed. Should she get dressed or was that rude? Quick deliberation confirmed she'd feel more comfortable dressed and perhaps Holly would follow suit. Trying to concentrate on opening presents wasn't going to be an easy task if there were perfect, naked breasts distracting her. Mind made up, she leapt from the bed and grabbed her dressing gown. She tied the belt when Holly reappeared. Catherine waited to see if Holly would say anything, but Holly smiled and pulled her own dressing gown on.

Catherine took the Christmas card and presents out of her suitcase. A mixture of excitement and nerves gurgled in her stomach.

"Would you rather we eat breakfast first?" Holly asked teasingly.

"No, it's fine." Catherine dropped the armful of presents onto the duvet. In her mind she decided the order in which she'd give them.

Holly lined up her presents and sat. They both eyed up their presents.

"Here." Catherine practically chucked the Christmas card in Holly's face.

"Oh. I didn't get one for you. I'm sorry." Two red dots coloured Holly's cheeks.

"I didn't expect one." Catherine gave a nonchalant shrug. Holly carefully opened the envelope and read the message.

"You're so sweet." Holly lunged forward and kissed her once again. When she pulled away, she carefully put the card down and offered her first gift to Catherine. "I hope you like it."

It was a large present wrapped neatly with a bow on the top. Catherine tore into the wrapping paper with gusto and lifted the box lid. A pair of green wellies rested on a bed of blue tissue paper.

"They should fit you. I sneakily checked the size of your sneakers. At least now you don't have to wear mine and cripple your feet. And you shouldn't slip anymore. I thought they might come in handy especially with walking Kimmy—"

"Thank you," Catherine said. She easily pulled one on and then the other. They fit perfectly. "They're great." She got up and walked the length of the room and back.

Holly gave a wolf whistle and Catherine had to laugh. She must look like a right idiot dressed in green wellies and a dressing gown.

"Here you go." Catherine handed over the first present to Holly. She watched closely as Holly delicately opened the gift. The smile looked genuine.

"Bubble bath and candles. I can't wait to use them in the Jacuzzi. I'll need you to come and help scrub my back, of course." Holly gave a playful wink.

Catherine accepted her next present and couldn't resist giving the ambiguous shape a shake. A rattling came from inside, but she was still none the wiser. She opened the paper and was astounded by the thoughtfulness of the gift. A packet of Athegither themed playing cards and a small packet of matches. A lump of emotion lodged in her throat and caused her eyes to water.

"Oh, God. You hate them, don't you? I'm sorry, Catherine. I thought maybe you could teach me some of the games you and Granny Birch used to play. It was insensitive of me. I'm so—"

"They're wonderful," Catherine said hoarsely. She couldn't think of a more personal gift she could've received. Holly had listened and took to heart their conversation about the Christmases she'd spent with Granny Birch. She was speechless, and it took a few more moments before she lamely mustered a few words. "Thank you, Holly."

Holly still looked uncertain. She twiddled a strand of hair and nibbled on her bottom lip.

Sniffing while trying to smile no doubt made Catherine look like she was grimacing. She quickly passed two gifts over to Holly in the hope of distracting her, so she could use the time to compose herself.

"Fabulous," Holly said. She slipped the apron over her head and ruffled the head of the little stuffed Scottie dog. "I shall treasure them forever. And excuse me, but aren't you forgetting something?" Holly puckered her lips and pointed to the "Kiss the Chef" emblem across her chest.

Catherine didn't need to be told twice, and what started out as a little kiss turned into a passionate snog. When she finally moved away, they were both breathing hard.

"Last present. Shall we open them at the same time?" Holly asked, her breathing still rushed.

"Okay," Catherine said. She unceremoniously threw the small box, more haphazardly than she'd planned. Her stomach knotted and her palms sweat. She was most excited about giving this present to Holly, but it was also the one that terrified her. Giving it felt strangely intimate, and as much as she tried to deny it, she'd be hurt if Holly didn't like it. It'd feel like a personal rejection—which she fully recognised as nonsense. But she'd not purchased a present for someone in so long, and she'd invested time and thought into it. Her instincts told her Holly would love it. But did she know Holly as well as she thought she did?

With bated breath, she pretended to mess with her gift while secretly watching Holly.

"Oh my goodness. Wow," Holly said. She looked into the box. Her eyebrows kitted together as she carefully took the pendant out and studied it closely. "It's stunning."

"Do you really like it?" Catherine asked, trying to mask the desperation in her tone.

Holly's eyes shot up and held Catherine's gaze. "I love it. It's beautiful and my kind of thing. I'm a little surprised you know me so well."

Catherine cupped her neck and gave it a rub trying to mask her bashfulness. "As much as I'd like to take all the credit, a little Scottish woman helped me choose it."

Holly gave a dismissive gesture with her hand. "Nonsense. You did amazing. The colour of this stone is gorgeous."

"It's your birthstone," Catherine said. She was relieved Holly liked it but also that she hadn't mentioned the over expenditure.

Holly smiled and held the pendant out. "Will you do the honours, please?" She turned her head and tried to tame the curly mass of sleep-matted hair.

Catherine slipped the chain over Holly's head so it rested on her chest and with trembling hands finally managed to fasten it. Unable to resist, she kissed Holly's neck, pausing to feel the light beat of Holly's pulse against her lips.

Holly turned around and glanced down at her chest. The pendant did suit her.

"Right, come on. Now time for your last present," Holly said.

Catherine nodded and tore into the paper. A similar box. The same kind, in fact, only shorter and squarer in shape. Glancing at Holly, she noted her nervousness.

Carefully, Catherine opened the lid and peered down. A pair of white gold handmade earrings sparkled up at her. A Celtic design with purple teardrop stones embedded in them. They were simple, elegant, and not garish in the slightest.

Once again, Catherine was reminded of the conversation Holly and she'd shared in the car. The thought behind each gift, as well as the execution, was tremendous.

"If they're not your kind of thing, I've saved the receipt so you can take them back before we leave. I checked with the woman, and she said she'll open the shop the day after Boxing Day. I won't be offended—"

Catherine kissed Holly gently on the lips. When she pulled away, she took hold of her hands and gave them a gentle squeeze. "You're incredible. I don't know how you came up with these gifts, but they mean more to me than I could ever put into words." Catherine tried to swallow over the lump in her throat. More tears threatened; she blinked against them. "You're the most beautiful and thoughtful person I've ever met. Thank you so much."

Tears brimmed in Holly's eyes, too. She gave a little cough followed by a sniffle. "I wanted to make it special for you. I'm so grateful for everything you've done, and I've come to care for you an awful lot." She swiped at a few stray tears before continuing. "And my gifts are wonderful. Thank you. Just when I start to think I know you, you go ahead and surprise me all over again."

They kissed again. And again. Soon hands wandered and pulses raced…and a whimper sounded from behind the door in the living room. Kimmy.

"Come on, there's plenty of time for that later," Holly said. She stood and nodded toward Catherine's wellies. "As you're dressed for the occasion, you can take Kimmy outside and I'll start making breakfast. Are scrambled eggs and smoked salmon okay?"

The ravenous growl from Catherine's stomach was answer enough.

❖

The weather outside was bitterly cold but glorious. Blue sky without a cloud in sight and dazzling winter sun, which was almost blinding when reflected off the snow. Catherine crunched happily through the snow wearing her new wellies. A tug on the lead snapped her out of her daydreams, and she wandered over to where Kimmy was flicking snow with her hind paws to try to cover up her excrement.

When she was done, Catherine bent down with a bag on her hand. Before she picked it up, something caught her eye. The turd was glinting in the sunshine. On slightly closer inspection Catherine discerned the golden strands of glitter.

She called for Holly to come out and shoulder to shoulder they both looked down.

Holly tilted her head, a frown creasing her brow. "I suppose it's festive."

"Very festive." Catherine gave a nod. "It's not every day you get to pick up a steaming golden poo."

"Exactly. Tinsel really can decorate anything. Who'd have known it was so versatile?"

"Should we be concerned about her insides?" Catherine asked. "Surely, it's dangerous for dogs to ingest tinsel?" Her shoulders tensed with the burden of guilt. This was the very reason she couldn't take on the commitment of having a pet. Having full responsibility for an innocent living creature's health and life was terrifying. And worse still, no matter how well you treated and looked after them, one day they had to die. She wasn't equipped to cope with the heartbreak. "I should've kept more of an eye on her. Why didn't I listen to you yesterday, instead of trying to show off by chasing her? I'll never forgive myself if something bad happens to her. Maybe we should call a vet? At the very least, I should tell Fiona. I'll take full responsibility fo—"

"Stop. Don't be so hard on yourself," Holly said. "I think the main thing is, it's passed through with no problems. She seems perfectly fine. Don't you think?"

Catherine looked down at Kimmy who sat studying them, head cocked, ears pricked, and her mouth open, showing tiny white teeth and a pink tongue. It looked suspiciously like she was smiling. "She seems to be in great spirits. I'd even go as far as to say she seems amused by it all," Catherine said.

"Exactly. We'll keep a close eye on her today." Holly gently stroked Catherine's back. "We're in this together. Okay?"

"Okay." The weight partially lifted from Catherine's shoulders. She reached down to clear up the mess. She was anxious to get on to the next phase of celebration for Holly.

❖

Breakfast was delicious. Once again, Holly demonstrated what a domestic goddess she was. The smoked salmon and scrambled eggs were complemented perfectly by the cold glasses of champagne mixed with orange juice.

It had taken some serious negotiating skills to convince Holly to go shower by herself. As tempting as the offer was to join her, it took all of Catherine's resolve to resist. Holly finally stopped persisting and accepted the excuse Catherine offered up. Kimmy couldn't be left unsupervised, and it'd be cruel to return her to her crate so soon.

As soon as Holly disappeared, Catherine leapt into action. In no time at all she had blown up the balloons and tied them using ribbon, hung the foil banner, and stabbed the cake with several candles. Holly's birthday card rested on the table beside Catherine's tablet and earphones. Time ticked away far too quickly, and in fifteen minutes, Holly's first surprise was due to take place. Catherine wasn't sure how to hurry Holly up without giving the secret away. To make matters worse, Kimmy showed a tremendous amount of interest in the balloons and the items atop the table. Her incessant sniffing suggested the cake was almost beyond temptation.

In a desperate attempt to distract her, Catherine gave her one of the Christmas presents she'd bought her: a ball decorated to look like a Christmas pudding. She hastily removed the tags and sent it rolling across the kitchen floor.

Kimmy bounded after the ball in a fit of canine delight, batting it from side to side with her front paws. Catherine's relief was short-lived when the most irritating high-pitched shrill reverberated through the cabin. The ball's sounds were the squeaky equivalent of nails across a blackboard. Catherine gave chase, but once again Kimmy was too fast and saw the whole thing as a game. In desperation, Catherine resorted to grabbing a carrot from the fridge and crawling on her hands and knees. Kimmy showed little interest. Suitably full from breakfast and having the time of her life with her new squeak-tastic ball, the carrot held no appeal.

"That's possibly the most irritating sound I've ever heard."

Catherine and Kimmy looked up at the same time. Holly stood in the bedroom doorway. She wore jeans and the blue woollen jumper with the Christmas tree on the front. The pendant chain hung around her neck, which gave Catherine a warm, fuzzy feeling.

In a flash, Kimmy sprinted over to Holly and dived into a dramatic bow, dropping the ball at her feet. Holly picked up the slather-coated ball.

"She bowed for you again," Catherine said. "And I've been trying for five minutes to get her to drop that ball."

Holly threw the ball at Catherine, who only just managed to catch it. "I guess she knows who's boss." Holly strolled toward the archway leading to the kitchen.

"Wait!" Catherine said. She rushed to block her off. "There's something I want to do. Can you wait here a minute?"

One of Holly's eyebrows arched and she folded her arms. "What's going on?"

"It's a surprise," Catherine said. She edged backward into the kitchen. "Just a minute." She rushed around the table and fumbled with the lighter. After scorching her thumb twice on the metal tip, all the candles were lit. A glance at her watch showed she had under ten minutes before the real surprise. "You can come in now."

Holly entered the room cautiously. Her eyes widened, her face turned pink, and her mouth broke out in a gorgeous smile.

With a tentative cough and hands balled into fists at her sides, Catherine began singing. "Happy birthday to—"

Kimmy rushed in and planted her paws, hackles raised. She lifted her head high, and howled with conviction. Catherine glared but the howling continued. She shook her head in amused frustration and looked to Holly for support but found none. Tears of laughter streamed down her cheeks. She hugged her sides, shaking with each gasping chuckle.

Catherine motioned to the cake. "Oh, forget the song. If you don't hurry up and blow these bloody candles out, there's going to be more molten wax than cake."

Holly managed to dispel the lit candles with one big puff. Grinning, she wrapped her arms around Catherine's neck and pulled her in close. "Thank you. It's a lovely surprise."

Catherine gave a shrug. "It didn't go quite how I'd planned."

Holly laughed and gently lifted Catherine's chin with a finger. "It was perfect. It's the first surprise birthday party I've ever had. And having a singing collaboration from you and Kimmy, well, that's been the highlight of my day so far. You could make a fortune with doggy duet if you went on TV."

Catherine smiled. "I taught her everything she knows."

"Of course you did. I'll remember it for the rest of my life." Holly planted the lightest of kisses on the corner of Catherine's mouth.

Fighting against the desire to kiss her back, Catherine pulled away and offered out a knife. "I know we've only just eaten, but we ought to have a little slice of this humongous cake. Will you do the honours, birthday girl?"

"It'll be my pleasure." Holly took the knife and sliced into the cake. Catherine held the plates while Holly dished out a small slab on each. They'd barely made a dint in the beast of a cake; there was still enough cake to feed half of Athegither. "Cheers," she said, tapping Catherine's fork with her own.

"Cheers." The cake was nice, but wary of time, Catherine wolfed it down.

"You really like cake," Holly said with a smile. She still had most of hers left.

Catherine gave a nod and discarded the empty plate. She rounded the table, picked up the birthday card, and presented it to Holly.

Holly opened the envelope carefully and read the message. Before she could speak Catherine spoke first. "Your birthday gift's inside the envelope."

Holly searched the envelope and took out the thin piece of paper and unfolded it. She scanned the text and frowned. "Catherine—"

"I know what you're going to say. Please hear me out." Catherine held her hands up in surrender. She was aware time was almost up, and having Holly angry at her would ruin it. "The snow chains are a gift for your birthday, but they're also a selfish gift on my part. We'll both feel safer travelling to Beth's. More importantly, I'll feel an immense amount of relief knowing, for however many winters to come, that you'll be safer when you venture out. So please accept them, Holly. Don't think about the price, because they're a gift. Just like I'm not going to mention the earrings you got me are obviously well over the budget we agreed."

Holly's face hosted a whole range of emotions, but after a few seconds, she gave a nod. "I guess I'll feel a lot safer with them. I know I've already said it a million times today, but thank you."

"Glad you see sense." Catherine pulled out a chair from under the table. "I have another surprise."

"You do?"

"Yes. I need you to sit down here, plug these earphones in, and close your eyes."

Holly looked confused but sat as requested. Catherine removed Holly's plate to one side. When Catherine handed her the earphones, she hesitated and searched Catherine's face.

"Do you trust me?" Catherine asked, her heart beating a little bit faster.

"Totally," Holly said. She plugged her ears and clenched her eyes shut.

Catherine quickly set up her tablet. The screen flashed, and when faces appeared she plugged the earphones in.

Holly physically jumped from the sound. Her eyes flew open and she stared at the screen in disbelief. After three quick blinks, her hands shot to her mouth, and she let out a gasp.

Catherine's work was done for the time being, so she stepped away from the table. She watched Holly closely, storing everything to memory, especially the expressions and the few stray tears of what she hoped indicated joy.

"Mum? Dad? Shit! How's this even possible?" Holly asked. Listening to an answer Catherine couldn't hear, Holly nodded at the screen, and then looked over to her. Swallowing and clutching her chest, she mouthed the words, "thank you."

Catherine shot her a wink and left the kitchen, patting her thigh for Kimmy to follow her into the bedroom. Her plan for at least the next thirty minutes was to take Kimmy for a walk so Holly could have some privacy while talking with her family in Canada.

❖

Athegither was beautiful in the sunlight. The snow complemented the postcard scenery, and the rolling hillsides were the perfect backdrop. While Kimmy sniffed everything, Catherine took the opportunity to sightsee.

The aroma of home cooking wafted on the faintest of breezes throughout the quaint village. Trying to hide her nosiness, Catherine stole peeks into the windows of the houses she passed and saw children playing with various toys while adults joined in or looked on. Everyone seemed happy and it was contagious. Catherine returned the waves and greetings to the few strangers she passed, feeling a spring in her step and a transformation deep inside. She didn't believe in souls, but it was almost as if the essence of her being had changed. She felt like a different person. A happier person.

Seeing the families together, and the festive chaos ruling over them, struck a chord. Catherine found herself thinking of how wonderful it would be to have her own little family gathered around on Christmas Day, the noise, anarchy, good cheer, and laughter to treasure. She'd never allowed herself to contemplate such daydreams before, but now they wouldn't leave her mind or heart. She could easily picture their small son and daughter chasing after Kimmy, who would run circles around them with something in her mouth she shouldn't have. Holly rushing around in the kitchen, while Catherine, surrounded by boxes, tried to assemble some kind of complex children's toy. The vision was so vivid, an ache settled in her chest. A maternal desire, deep and primal, ignited inside of her.

"Come on, Kimmy." She looked down at the cute little grey face. "Let's head back. I think this Scottish air is making me go soft in the head." Although the previous night spent with Holly had been spectacular, the overzealous confidence administered by the alcohol had worn off. In the cold, sober light of day, her actions seemed like a betrayal of Beth's trust. Had Beth planned to set them up? She still wasn't sure, but there was an awful lot more doubt now than there had been the night before. She'd have to wait until they spoke later today, and then try to gauge Beth's intentions. She knew it was foolish, but she pinned all her hopes on it being true, as thinking otherwise was unbearable.

She'd let her body succumb to its carnal pleasures and in the aftermath now possibly faced losing Beth, Katie, and Florence. The trouble was, as much as she regretted putting her relationship with Beth and her little family in harm's way, she knew she'd do the same thing again in a heartbeat. She cared for Holly a great deal, far more than she was prepared to admit. She was like a moth, drawn helplessly to a flame. When she was with Holly, nothing else mattered. And that was what worried her. She was prepared to risk getting burned, but it wasn't fair to draw other people in. If she wasn't careful, her relationship with Beth might disintegrate into ash before her very eyes.

As she walked Kimmy down the path to their cabin, she met Alistair on his way back up.

"Hello there," he said cheerily.

"Merry Christmas, Alistair," Catherine said.

"Merry Christmas to you, too. Isn't it a perfect day? And how's my little wee girl doing, eh?" he asked, bending down to give Kimmy a fuss.

"It's a beautiful day." Catherine watched as Kimmy bowed to him. She bit her lip to mask her frustration. "Did you get anything nice for Christmas?"

"Oh, aye," he said, standing up straight. "I got some new golf clubs. The wife really spoilt me this year."

"I'm glad to hear it. And what did you get her?" Catherine asked, remembering the big box of chocolates and Fiona's prediction.

"I got her a box of her favourite chocolates."

Catherine tried to hide her grimace. "Oh. Lovely."

"It's a wee tradition we have. I also got her a snazzy necklace," he said with a chuckle. "Good job, or else I think she'd have had my guts for garters."

Catherine nodded. "I think you might be right."

"Anyway, I've dropped off the dining supplies for your Christmas dinner. I'm so sorry, I didn't realise Holly didn't know. I didn't mean to ruin the surprise." His cheeks flushed and he looked genuinely embarrassed. "I'll no doubt have a scolding when the wife finds out."

Catherine was a little disappointed she'd missed Holly's reaction, but could tell Alistair's apology was sincere. As was his fear of Fiona's reprimand. "It's fine. She'd have found out sooner rather than later anyway. Thank you for bringing the supplies."

"It's nay bother."

Catherine noticed a smudge of brown on his chin. "You have a little something just here," she said, pointing to the same spot on her own chin.

"Oh." He quickly wiped his face. "Holly was kind enough to offer me a slice of birthday cake. It would've been rude to decline. Although it might be best not to mention it to the wife. She's had me on a healthy diet for months." His face turned bright red. "I'm the laughingstock of Athegither. What I wouldn't give for a big hunk of meat and some greasy chips." He wet his lips wistfully.

"Well, your secret's safe with me."

"Thank you, darling. I appreciate it. I'd better head back before she wonders what I've been up to. I'll pop down later with the food. Cheerio."

"See you later." Catherine led Kimmy down to the cabin. Inside, she removed her wellies and dried Kimmy's paws. Holly had cleared the kitchen table of the cake and balloons. A crisp white tablecloth covered the surface. Two unlit red candles stood in the middle and fancy napkins in holders rested by the placemats. The table had been set for an intimate feast with expensive-looking china dishes.

Catherine unclipped Kimmy and went in search of Holly. She found her in the bedroom tying the balloons to the bottom of the bed frame.

"You're amazing." Holly jumped on her and covered her in kisses. "We get to share Christmas dinner by ourselves in our little cabin. Alistair said they'll deliver the food after one. When did you arrange all of this?"

"Yesterday while you were at the garage."

"How on earth did you get in touch with my parents? They're thirteen hours ahead."

"I spoke to Katie and we sorted it out together. I had to promise we'd speak to her and Beth at five this afternoon. Is that okay?"

Holly laughed. "Of course it is. My parents asked me to pass on their gratitude. They're impressed by all accounts."

Catherine shuffled her feet and shoved her hands in her pockets, uncomfortable with the gushing attention. "It was nothing."

"It was incredible. I have to ask, though. You don't have any more tricks up your sleeve, do you? I'm not sure I can cope. You've turned me into an emotional wreck."

Tapping the side of her nose with her index finger, Catherine attempted to appear secretive. She only had one small surprise left and it wouldn't cause anywhere near as big waves as the first two. She decided to keep quiet. "I need a shower."

Holly stepped back and smiled mischievously. "Actually, I've drawn us a bubble bath."

"What about Kimmy?" Catherine asked, in a noticeably higher pitch than normal. Her arousal rocketed.

"She's had breakfast and been for a walk. I'm pretty certain if given one of her Christmas treats, she'll happily settle in her crate."

"Shall I meet you in there?"

"Sounds like a plan, sexy." Holly planted a tap on Catherine's bottom.

"Ouch." Catherine glared in accusation while rubbing her bruised buttock tenderly.

"Shit!" Holly tried not to laugh. "I totally forgot about it. I'm sorry."

"Why am I always making an arse out of myself in front of you? I'm the butt of all your jokes." Catherine flashed a cheesy smile and pulled Holly close.

"I see what you did there." Holly smiled. "Smooth."

"Honestly, I'm not usually so accident prone. I think there's something about you that makes me lose concentration."

"And balance?" Holly shook her head. "Sorry, sweetheart. It's all your own doing."

"I think you might be a bad influence."

"Oh, I'm a very bad influence," Holly said, her tone low and seductive. "But it was only a gentle tap. You're being a wimp."

"So I get no sympathy whatsoever?" Catherine pouted. "My backside is black and blue."

"I know it is. I've seen it up close and personal." Holly leant in close and whispered in Catherine's ear, "You weren't complaining when I did the exact same thing last night. Were you?" She teasingly nibbled on Catherine's earlobe.

"That's…beside the point," Catherine said hoarsely.

"As I recall, that was one of the points you particularly enjoyed."

Face burning, Catherine accepted defeat. "My bruised backside and I will be waiting in the bath."

❖

By the time they'd finally left the bath, Catherine's skin had shrivelled like a prune. Holly left her to wait for the food delivery. She'd stuck her head back around the door and made Catherine promise she'd wear one of the Christmas jumpers. Apparently, they were going to take a Christmas portrait photo and email it to Holly's family. Still weak-kneed and fuzzy, Catherine was in no fit state to consider arguing.

The time had come to brave putting on the expensive earrings Holly had gotten her. After a bit of a struggle, she finally removed the plain studs. The silver earrings were undeniably pretty, but she wasn't sure they'd suit her. They slipped in easily with no discomfort.

Stepping back from the mirror, Catherine scrutinised her reflection carefully. After turning her head a few times and accepting it would take a while to get used to having something dangling from each lobe, she decided she liked the way they looked on her. They made her look more feminine, possibly a little bit more attractive. She doubted she'd be able to sleep in them, but she could always put the studs back in.

Dressed in everything but a top, she ended up choosing the green woollen jumper with the freaky-looking Rudolph on the front. As she went to pull it over her head she spotted something white and puzzling. On closer inspection the label revealed a whole host of information. The jumper was to be washed on a woollen setting, no tumble drying, and most importantly it was made in China for a clothing company. After quickly pulling the jumper on, she searched another jumper and found an identical label. "Handmade my arse," she said, bemused. She left in search of Holly and found her lighting the fire in the living room. After providing a few tummy tickles for Kimmy, Catherine sat on the sofa.

"I chose the green jumper," she said conversationally.

Holly smiled, and gave a nod. "Good choice. Those earrings look great. They suit you. Do you like them?"

"Yes, I really like them."

"Good." Holly turned back to the fire to add some more logs.

"How long did it take you to knit this jumper?"

Holly shrugged. "I honestly couldn't say."

"Do you know what I'm really impressed with?" Catherine asked and watched as Holly blew the embers. "Your dedication." She waited for Holly to respond, but she didn't. "I mean, going all the way to China to make it. That's true dedication to a craft."

Holly spun around and had the decency to blush. "You looked like you were getting hypothermia, and I could tell by your expression you were going to be too pigheaded to wear them. My only option was to guilt-trip you. I did it for your own good."

Catherine folded her arms and tutted loudly. "You admit you lied and tricked me into wearing this monstrosity."

"I did," Holly said. "But it was a tiny white lie for your own good."

"That's not the point."

"Come on. You've lied to me, too."

"No, I haven't." Catherine puffed out her chest and folded her arms. Holly looked suitably smug and so she asked, "When have I lied to you?"

"Yesterday at breakfast, I asked if you liked the mushrooms and you said yes." Holly flicked her hair from her eyes.

Shit! Okay, so she'd told a lie, but it was only so as not to insult Holly's cooking or hurt her feelings.

"You're not denying it, then?" Holly asked in an infuriating cheery tone.

How did Holly even know? She thought she'd masked her dislike of them pretty well. She'd even eaten the ones Holly had scraped onto her plate. "You knew and yet you deliberately gave me more of yours, too?" Catherine asked, both appalled and amused by the sly trickery.

"Of course I knew. I can read you like an open book, Catherine. You were practically holding your breath with every forkful and then grimacing after each swallow."

"Then why give me more?"

"Because you should've been honest with me."

"So you punished me?" Catherine asked.

"No. Well, maybe," Holly said, shrugging. "I honestly didn't think you'd eat them. I tried to call your bluff. I figured as soon as I gave you mine, you'd tell me the truth. Only you didn't."

Catherine pouted. "I didn't want to be rude or hurt your feelings."

Holly came over and knelt in front of her. "That's sweet, honey. But it's more important to me you're honest about things. You nearly ended up with them for breakfast today."

Catherine gasped. "You're evil."

Holly chuckled. "I suppose I am. Look, I'm sorry for telling the tiny white lie about the jumpers. I did have your best interests in mind. I also apologise for feeding you some of my mushrooms, even when I suspected you weren't keen."

"I detest them." Catherine gave a dramatic shudder.

"How about we make a pact to only tell the truth from now on?" Holly presented her hand to shake on the deal.

"Okay." Catherine shook her hand.

A loud knocking sounded on the front door and Kimmy erupted into a rampage of aggressive barks and growls.

"Do you forgive me, then?" Holly fluttered her eyelashes.

"Only if I don't have to wear this jumper."

"Nice try. That's not going to happen," Holly said. She got to her feet and smiled. "But I promise never to feed you mushrooms ever again."

CHAPTER EIGHTEEN

The meal was delicious and the portion sizes were overly generous. They only managed to eat the soup and main course. The pudding, cheese, and biscuits would make a perfect supper later on.

Holly washed and Catherine dried the dishes in domesticated bliss. It seemed so normal, as if they'd been doing it forever. After they'd cleaned up, Catherine insisted Holly sit on the sofa and then she revealed the third and final surprise. She connected her tablet to the TV, and in no time at all, the opening credits to the film *It's a Wonderful Life* rolled on the screen.

"You've literally thought of everything," Holly said in disbelief.

"I even got us popcorn, too, if you fancy it?"

"I'm filled to the brim, so I'll have to pass."

"Phew. Me too." Catherine dropped onto the sofa and wriggled around until she was comfortable. She ended up resting her head on Holly's lap.

"This has been the best Christmas ever." Holly placed a kiss on Catherine's forehead. "Thank you so much, darling."

Catherine forced a smile and kept her eyes on the screen. The entire day had been perfect, and she was already mourning its loss. The looming conversation with Beth and Katie in a little while filled her with dread. It was a reminder this little piece of heaven would soon be over.

❖

The film was good, in a way that makes you cry loads and re-evaluate your pathetic existence. Unfortunately, it only added to Catherine's growing melancholy. She didn't want to go to Beth's, and she didn't want to go back to London. She wanted to stay with Holly and Kimmy in their little cabin forever.

It took a few failed attempts to work out the camera's timer setting, but eventually they got a few decent Christmas photos of them together holding Kimmy while standing by the tree and fireplace. Catherine insisted they use her phone, claiming the camera was better. It was better, but the main reason for her insistence was, she wanted to keep the photos. She continued taking pictures and videos of Holly and Kimmy up until the point where Holly teasingly complained she felt like she was being hounded by the paparazzi. They chose the nicest three and emailed them to Holly's parents.

At five o'clock, the time came to speak to Beth and Katie. Before their conversation began, Holly and she agreed not to mention their relationship was anything other than platonic. In its own right, it raised the issue of what their relationship actually was, but the call came through, saving them by the bell. It'd be a conversation they'd have to face at some point soon, and Catherine wasn't sure how it would pan out.

Catherine had a long catch-up with a super-chatty Florence, which cheered her spirits. She showed Catherine all—as in every single one—of the toys Santa had gotten her. Then showed the presents from everyone else. Although she garbled on about the pirate ship, her favourite gift by far was a pair of SpongeBob SquarePants wellies, which she refused to take off. Catherine showed her own Christmas wellies, and they spent five minutes talking about why wellies were so good.

When Catherine pointed the camera at Kimmy, Florence became obsessed. It took seven attempts to get her to realise Kimmy was actually a girl dog and her name wasn't Bob.

"Is Kimmy coming to visit, Aunty Cat?" Florence asked.

Catherine opened her mouth to reply, but fortunately, Beth interrupted.

"Florence, go and help Mummy Katie in the kitchen." After an initial bout of sulking, the promise of chocolate was enough to pacify

Florence into leaving the room. "Right. How are you both getting on?" Beth asked, getting straight to the point as always.

"Great," Holly said.

"Fine," Catherine said.

"Good. I'm glad to hear it. Catherine, do you mind if I talk to Holly for a bit?"

"No." Catherine minded a lot. Her paranoia increased tenfold. She moved away from the tablet, but hovered within earshot.

"Holly, are you okay? Is there anything you want to tell us?" Beth asked, her tone serious.

Catherine struggled to breathe. Why would Beth ask that? Did she suspect something? The only miniscule positive was that Holly was taking the brunt of the questioning, not her.

Holly laughed easily. "Like what?"

"Anything. How did you sleep?"

Catherine gasped. That was a loaded question if ever she heard one. Beth was definitely up to something. She tried to gesture to Holly to warn her, but Holly paid no attention.

"I slept fine. How about you guys?" Holly made herself comfortable on the sofa. She looked cool, calm, and collected.

"Not great. It doesn't help that Katie is so hyperactive. It's like having two overly excited children on Christmas Eve. She barely slept, which meant I didn't sleep. Out of all of us, I think Florence got nearly the full eight hours."

"Katie's always been immature." Holly blobbed her tongue out when Katie shouted something in the background.

"Next year, I'm going to drug her—Katie I mean, not Florence. So, what have you been up to?" Beth asked, a little too casually for Catherine's liking.

"We've just taken the last few days easy. We had Christmas dinner here and then watched a film."

"How are you finding being alone with Cat?"

Catherine folded her arms and shot an evil glare into the back of the tablet. What was that question supposed to mean?

"I'm enjoying our time here. She's very funny."

"Funny? We are talking about Cat, right?" Beth asked.

"I heard that!" Catherine said, unable to refrain from responding.

"We're talking about you, not to you. Go away. I'll get to you in a minute. Holly?"

Holly shot Catherine an apologetic look before glancing back at the screen. "Yes, Beth."

"Ignore her for a minute. What I wanted to say is, if she comes across as rude or impersonal, she doesn't mean anything by it. It's just how she is."

"She's been friendly and ni—" Holly said before Catherine snatched the tablet out of her hands.

"I'm not impersonal or rude," Catherine said hotly. "Why are you asking her all of these stupid questions?"

Beth glared at her from the screen. "They're not stupid. I want to check she's okay. No offence, but you're hardly the easiest person to get along with."

Catherine glared back. "Offence very much taken. If I'm such a difficult person, why did you insist I join you for Christmas in the first place? Huh?"

Beth scowled. "Because you're my best friend. I'm used to your unique ways. Hell, I lived with them for a year. But inflicting them on someone who—"

Before Beth could finish or Catherine could verbally explode, Katie's face filled the whole screen. Loud shuffling could be heard as she fought for control. "Whoa. It's the season of good will and all that. Cat, what my darling wife is trying to say, but failing spectacularly at doing so because she has zero tact, is that we miss you. We wanted you to spend Christmas with us because we love you and your quirky ways. Please don't get offended. She means well."

Beth appeared back on the screen and had the decency to look somewhat guilty. "I'm sorry. Sometimes I don't say things in quite the right way. You of all people should appreciate that. Anyway, we do love you. You're as much a member of our family as Holly is. We wanted to celebrate today with both of you. I'm just snarky because I'm tired and my plans went to sh—rubbish."

Catherine sighed. "Okay. Should I pass you back?"

"No. I want to catch up with you. Have you explored the village?"

"Yeah," Catherine said. She sat on the sofa, wishing she'd never interrupted Beth and Holly's conversation. "It's nice. Everyone's friendly."

"Any single lesbians?"

Catherine's cheeks burned. "Seriously? We nearly died in a car crash, and you're only interested in whether there are single lesbians? Nice priorities."

"Methinks you doth protest too much." Beth arched an eyebrow. "Has someone caught your fancy? They have. I know that expression, Cat. Who is it? What does she look like? She's not ginger, is she? You know what happened with Paula."

"You're ridiculous." Catherine was dying a slow and painful death.

"Holly?" Beth said loudly. "Holly, come back a minute."

Holly appeared behind the sofa and rested her hands near Catherine's shoulders. The slightest touch from Holly's fingertips made Catherine flinch and scoot forward.

"Yes?" Holly asked.

"For the love of all that's good in the world, don't, under any circumstances, let her fall for anyone. Seriously. She has the most horrendous taste in women. The last one was a psychopath and Cat had a lucky escape. I remain convinced that if they'd stayed together, we'd have ended up finding Cat's body buried beneath the patio. I know you don't know her, but I expect you to keep her safe. Okay?"

"Sure," Holly said, her tone straining to remain light.

"Good. The same goes for you, too. Family looks after one another. I'll be relieved when you're finally up here so I can keep my eye on you," Beth said.

Catherine felt nauseous. Quite clearly, Beth didn't have a clue that anything was going on between Holly and her. The prying questions had been to uncover whether Catherine was being pleasant toward Holly, instead of her usual grumpy self. She got the distinct impression Beth felt sorry for Holly.

It was obvious that Beth had never intended to set them up as an item. She considered them both family. Catherine had broken her promise and there would no doubt be hell to pay.

After suffering another torturous twenty minutes of inquisition, they finally said good-bye, with the promise of seeing each other in two days' time. Guilt and dread burrowed deep into Catherine's heart. She had no idea what she was going to do.

"I don't think she tried to set us up after all," Holly said while stroking Kimmy. "She also doesn't think very highly of your taste in women. At least we'll be able to prove her wrong on this occasion. I can't wait to see their faces when we tell them. Do you want a cup of tea?"

Catherine shook her head. She didn't trust herself to speak.

❖

During supper and the many card games they played, Holly seemed to sense something wasn't quite right. She asked outright, twice, if Catherine was okay. Both times Catherine said yes and the awkwardness remained.

"Right, I give up. Thank you for showing me how to play and then repeatedly kicking my arse. I appreciate that you didn't feel the need to go gentle on me and let me win even once," Holly said, stifling a yawn.

"Granny Birch's ruthlessness obviously rubbed off on me. You nearly had me on the last few games though." Catherine fought back a yawn.

"We agreed to tell the truth." Holly smiled. "I was useless." She stood and stretched her arms above her head. "I'll sort Kimmy out. You may as well go ahead and get ready for bed."

Catherine looked down and met Kimmy's dark eyes. Her grey, furry face was rumpled from sleep, and she looked more dishevelled than usual. Catherine gave her an extra long fuss behind her ears and across her chest. She'd slept beside Catherine's feet all evening, as if she'd also sensed her sadness. "Good night, girl. Sleep well."

After one last lick of Catherine's hand, Kimmy toddled after Holly.

Catherine stood and headed to the bathroom. She was tired but doubted sleep would come easily. After brushing her teeth, she carefully removed the earrings and returned them to the box, then changed into pyjamas. Kinky sex, no matter how enjoyable, was not on the cards tonight. She got into bed and watched as Holly disappeared into the bathroom. Alone with her thoughts, she tried to pinpoint exactly what was getting her down. She'd had a wonderful day and enjoyed it. Perhaps that was the problem? She'd built herself up for this day, and although it'd gone above and beyond her expectations, it was now over. Was it possible to mourn the passing of a day? Because that's how it felt. She felt like she was grieving.

Holly emerged wearing a pair of baby blue linen shorts and a pink strap top. She climbed into bed, switched the bedside light off, and gently took hold of one of Catherine's hands. Although the room was dark, Catherine could make out Holly's outline from the corner of her eye. Her perfume lingered in the air, the sound of her breathing was light, and the warmth from her body was radiating across the gap between them.

Without speaking a word, Holly moved in closer until her body was pressed softly against Catherine's side. She placed the gentlest of kisses on Catherine's forehead and trailed them slowly down until she reached her mouth.

Catherine was turned on but in a completely different way from the previous night. She needed to be touched, held close, and…loved? Before the thought could fully register, she kissed Holly back.

This kiss was slow and tender. It invoked a torrent of emotion. As if sensing exactly what she needed, Holly wrapped her arms around Catherine, surrounding her with warmth, and drew her closer.

For the first time in years, Catherine felt safe enough to be emotionally vulnerable. Last night had been about sizzling passion and sexual fulfilment. This situation was entirely different. There was no bravado as she opened herself up, laying bare her thoughts, emotions, dreams, and aspirations. Each caress provided more than physical pleasure; there was emotion and meaning behind them. Their fingertips told intimate truths, skin upon skin, creating its own memory. Breath mixing with breath through each gasping kiss and moan.

Their connection deepened, tethering them together in body, mind, and soul. They shared an orgasm. It tore through Catherine's body, leaving her trembling in its wake. Hot, salty tears spilled down her cheeks, and with a shaky breath, she succumbed to relief. Holly had taken all of her broken pieces and miraculously fitted them back together. Each kiss and touch mended her, and now she felt whole.

Holly kissed the tears away and cuddled closer, providing the reassurance Catherine desperately craved. And there it was, as clear as day: the difference between having sex and making love. It had never been so startlingly clear.

There could be no denying it now. Catherine had fallen in love with Holly. She sensed Holly felt the same. No words had been spoken, but they didn't have to be.

Was she ready to commit to more than just a festive fling? What did Holly expect from her? Things were happening too quickly. And how the hell was she going to tell Beth she'd betrayed her trust and broke her promise?

Their situation had become a million times more complicated.

Chapter Nineteen

Boxing Day dawned gloriously sunny. After sharing a shower, getting ready, and eating breakfast, they headed out on a long walk with Kimmy. They intended to make the most of their last day. Neither Catherine nor Holly broached the subject of what had happened last night or what it meant in the great scheme of things. It hung over them all the same, but for the time being, ignorance was key. The need to touch was almost a compulsion, and it seemed they were always conjoined in some physical way, whether by holding hands, hugging, or brushing past each other.

They wandered aimlessly and it didn't take long for them to border on the outskirts of the village. They came to a closed fence that had a vast snowy field beyond it. A group of four boys climbed the fence and ran onto the field excitedly. They made their way to the farthest end and launched a snowball fight. Catherine and Holly watched with amusement.

"We should head back," Catherine said, gesturing to the dead end.

"It's such a beautiful day. It'd be a shame to go back already." Holly squeezed Catherine's arm and smiled brightly. "Let's go explore."

"I don't think we should trespass." Catherine pointed to the weathered sign that read *Private Property Keep Out*, in faded red paint.

"That sign looks ancient. It's Boxing Day, and other than those boys, there's no one else around. We're only going to have a walk around. We're not doing any harm. Where's your sense of adventure?"

"I don't have one," Catherine said honestly. "Rules are made for a reason."

"I thought rules were made to be broken?" Holly pointed to Kimmy. "Even Kimmy wants to go." Kimmy was stood on her hind legs, with her front paws rested on the lower bars of the fence, as she looked out at the boys playing. Her tail wagged and little excited whimpers escaped.

Catherine felt awkward. She didn't want to come across as boring or dull, but the thought of trespassing went against her better judgment. "I just don't think it's worth the risk."

"What risk? Catherine, we're talking about walking around a field, not doing a bank heist or a bungee jump. Don't you ever just act on impulse? Go with the flow?"

"Spontaneity isn't one of my strengths." Catherine looked away from Holly's disapproving gaze. It reminded her of the look Paula used to give—the "you're so boring and why am I even with you" look.

A young girl, perhaps seven or eight, trotted up to the fence, gave a shy smile, and didn't hesitate in climbing it. Once in the field, she made her way up to the boys. Although they weren't close enough to hear the exchange, Catherine gathered the gist. The boys didn't want the younger girl cramping their style. Her small shoulders slumped, the little girl turned back and made her way to the centre of the field. She bent down and scooped up a handful of snow.

"Forget it," Holly said. She turned away from the fence and gave a gentle tug to get Kimmy to heel. "Let's head back."

"Wait," Catherine said. She didn't want to be a spoilsport and ruin Holly's day. The children showed no sign of apprehension and the sign did look old. "We'll do it, but only once and around. Then we head back. Okay?"

With an exuberant laugh, Holly hugged Catherine. "Check you out, living life on the edge." She pulled away and handed the lead to Catherine. In one fluid motion, she leapt up and over the fence. She held her hands out and Catherine passed Kimmy's squirming body over.

Looking around self-consciously, Catherine climbed the fence and struggled to get her leg over. Swearing, she landed painfully on the frozen ground. She took hold of Kimmy's lead and they began walking around the perimeter, which was cordoned off with hedgerow. Catherine kept her eye on the young girl. She was trying to pat snow onto the snowball in her hand, but ended up dropping it. Next, she put half of the broken snowball onto the ground and started gathering snow around it.

"Do you want to go see what she's doing?" Holly asked, her expression all-knowing.

"Do you mind?"

"Not at all. I was the youngest and my sisters never let me join in with anything."

They made their way up to the little girl and the strange-shaped mound of snow she was cultivating.

"Hello," Catherine said. She passed the dog lead to Holly.

"Hello," the little girl said, looking up. Her face was rosy and a tuft of black hair stuck out of one side of her pink hood. She smiled when her eyes fell on Kimmy. "Is that your dog?"

"We're kind of looking after her for a little while," Catherine said.

"Like babysitting, but for a dog. What's her name?" the girl asked. She burst into a fit of giggles as Kimmy showered her in kisses.

"Kimmy. I'm Catherine and this is Holly." Catherine pointed to herself and then to Holly.

"I'm Lydia."

"It's nice to meet you, Lydia. What are you making?" Holly asked.

"It's supposed to be a snowman, but I'm not good at it. My mammy told Ben and Matty they had to help me, but they wanna throw snowballs instead." Lydia sniffed and shot a sad look in the direction of the boys.

"I can help you make one if you'd like?" Catherine asked, hoping Lydia might take her up on the offer.

"Oh, aye. Please." Lydia's face brightened instantly.

"How about making a snowwoman instead?" Holly suggested.

Lydia thought about it for a few seconds and nodded vigorously.

"Right, well first of all, we need to make a snowball." Catherine squatted down. She glanced at Holly and saw she was watching her intently.

Lydia presented the snowball.

"Excellent. Now we need to make it tight," Catherine said. She demonstrated how to compact the snow. After a minute or so Lydia handed the snowball back. "You're a natural at this. Now this is the important bit. We have to roll the snowball on the ground." Catherine rolled it along and Lydia followed enthusiastically at her side. The ball quickly grew bigger, and Catherine felt an ache settle in her lower back. She was too old for this. "Do you think you can take over for a while?"

"Aye," Lydia said, practically shoving Catherine out of the way.

Catherine watched as Lydia took on the job of rolling the snowball. Her pink tongue popped out of the side of her mouth and her expression was of steely determination. Kimmy followed at Lydia's side, giving the snowball an occasional wary sniff. As the snowball grew, Kimmy would pounce near it and then run away. A moment later, she'd go back.

"Do you have any kids?" Lydia asked, wiping her nose on her sleeve. She started rolling the snowball again.

"No," Catherine said, not entirely sure if the question was directed at her or both of them.

"Me neither," Holly said.

"Do you want kids?" Lydia asked, without looking up.

"In the future, yes," Catherine said, feeling uncomfortable with the topic.

"What about you?" Lydia asked Holly.

"I've never given it much thought, to be honest." Holly blushed. "I'm not sure I'm really cut out for being a parent. I think maybe I'm better as an aunty."

Catherine felt her stomach drop. Holly was looking at her, so she tried to mask the barrage of emotions. Holly's answer had been like a kick to the gut. She'd never considered asking Holly about whether she wanted children in the future. They'd only known each other for a few days, and the prospect of their newly formed relationship having a future remained uncertain. There wasn't really a way to broach the subject without sounding like a blatant bunny boiler.

"You've got to have a baby soon, or else you'll be too old," Lydia said to Catherine, her tone serious. "My mammy is too old now."

Catherine blanched.

Holly touched Catherine's arm. "Are you o—"

"Should I roll for a bit?" Catherine asked weakly, flinching away from Holly's hand. She felt nauseous.

"Aye," Lydia said, skipping to the side. She remained oblivious to the bombshell she'd dropped and the aftermath that would come.

The snowball was now as big as a bowling ball, and Catherine rolled it along the ground, glad she didn't have to face Holly. As her body worked hard physically, her mind raced at a million miles an hour. Holly didn't want children. She reeled from the shock. She was in no doubt, if she found the right person, that she definitely wanted to raise a family. Lydia was right; her biological clock was running out. The sense of déjà vu that had hounded Catherine since she'd met Holly now made sense. Although a seemingly much nicer person overall, Holly was similar to Paula in many ways. How had she not made the connection before? Holly was artistic, career driven, fun, passionate, and spontaneous, and didn't want children. Basically everything that Catherine wasn't. She'd never considered that she might be attracted to a specific type of partner before, but the similarities were too obvious to ignore. She was attracted to her opposite. But the issues from her relationship with Paula were already manifesting themselves again with Holly. It didn't bode well.

The ball was nearly up to Catherine's thigh in size and Holly insisted on taking over. Eventually, the ball was nearly too big and heavy to move.

"That's big enough for her body, now let's start on her head," Catherine said. They set to work on a new snowball.

As Lydia was rolling it, Catherine felt a nudge. Holly nodded to the side and Catherine turned to see the four boys walking over to them. They approached a little shyly and gave awkward smiles.

"Lydia, do you want us to help you make the snowman?" one of the boys asked.

Lydia stood and a host of emotions flickered across her face. Catherine imagined it was tempting to tell the boys they weren't allowed to join in, but her eagerness for them to actually play with her proved too strong to resist.

"Aye, but it's a snowwoman, not a snowman," she said, her tone matter-of-fact.

The boys grumbled but seemed to soon accept it. They began rolling the ball in turns and it quickly tripled in size.

"Lydia, do you think that's big enough?" Catherine asked. She hoped Lydia would agree. If it got much bigger there was no way they'd be able to lift it on top.

Lydia brushed her gloved hands together and nodded. "Aye."

In the end, Catherine and Holly had to lift it together in order to get it on top.

"That's too big for a head," one of the boys said.

"Aye, she'll look stupid," another boy added.

"Nay, it's not. It's her top half and now we do the head. Don't we, Catherine?" Lydia asked a little desperately.

"That's right. But the head has to be a lot smaller." Catherine had only ever used one ball for the body, but if it meant saving face for Lydia, then so be it.

Fifteen minutes later, the snowwoman's body and head were all assembled. The boys and Lydia searched around for things to decorate her with. She ended up with one short and stumpy branch arm, and another long and thin one. Her eyes were different coloured and shaped thanks to the different rocks. Her nose and mouth were made from sticks. Her eyebrows were bright green holly leaves. Apparently, she was happy to be bald, as none of them saw fit to find hair.

"I think she's great," Catherine said, trying to ward off a chill and wishing she'd worn more layers.

"Aye. Just one more thing," Lydia said. She made two big snowballs.

Confused, Catherine looked at Holly who shrugged. They watched as Lydia moulded the first snowball onto the snowwoman.

Holly grasped what was happening a few seconds before Catherine. Her eyebrows shot up and she muffled a laugh. The boys began to giggle and blush.

"Lydia, what exactly are those?" Catherine asked. The realisation dawned on her a moment later. She immediately regretted asking the question, as it was fairly obvious now.

"Boobies," Lydia said. "She can't be a snowwoman without boobies."

"Oh," Catherine said lamely. She tore her eyes away from the misshapen and wonky snow breasts and looked to Holly for some kind of guidance. Holly's shoulders shook as she tried to unsuccessfully muffle her laughter.

"Oh no!" One of the boys pointed up the field.

They turned in unison and saw a figure of a man at the other end walking toward them.

"Oh no, what?" Holly asked.

"That's Farmer Kerry. He doesn't like us on his land," Lydia said.

"Run!" She and the boys sped off in the opposite direction, running for the gate and the safety of the village.

"I told you we shouldn't have trespassed," Catherine said, panicked. She wasn't sure how she was going to explain the topless snowwoman to this Farmer Kerry person. The way he was purposely marching toward them was a little daunting. "Now what?"

"You heard the girl. We run," Holly said with a grin.

"Don't be daft. We're not childr—"

"Suit yourself." Holly ran off with Kimmy.

Catherine glanced back. Farmer Kerry had started to jog. "Shit," she said under her breath and bolted after Holly.

❖

They returned to the cabin, and while Catherine dried Kimmy's paws Holly brewed a fresh pot of coffee. She disappeared out of the room with her coat only to return a moment later holding a slip of paper.

"What's that?" Catherine asked, wobbling while stepping out of her wellies.

"It's a note from the garage. The car will be ready first thing tomorrow morning. There's nothing stopping us from making it to Katie's now. The weather forecast for tomorrow is great."

Catherine didn't know what to say, and so sat at the table. Since Lydia had asked the question, the atmosphere had changed between them. Awkwardness filled the air.

"Here you go," Holly said. She handed over a steaming mug of coffee and sat in her usual chair.

"Thanks."

They both blew steam and cradled their cups in silence. The ticking of the kitchen clock and Kimmy cleaning herself were the only sounds.

"I think we probably need to talk." Holly placed her cup down so she could hug herself.

Catherine's guts squirmed. This conversation had always been inevitable, but after thinking it through until her brain hurt, she still wasn't sure of her thoughts and feelings.

"I'll start," Holly said quietly. "I like you, Catherine. More than

I've liked anyone in a long time. You're sweet, thoughtful, and funny. You're also sexy as hell and great in bed."

Catherine swallowed down her desire to fist-pump the air and grin. As flattering as Holly's comments were, they didn't grant her any further insight on what her perspective was.

"We have awesome chemistry, well, I think we do anyway." Holly picked up her mug and took a slow, savouring sip.

Catherine wasn't sure if she should speak. The silence while Holly drank felt kind of purposeful. As if perhaps Holly was waiting for her to say something. But if that wasn't the case she'd come across as insensitive and rude. After another few tortuously long seconds, she decided to bite the bullet.

"I think we have good c-chemistry." It seemed to be the right thing to say because Holly's tense body seemed to visibly relax. "Um. I also like you."

Holly beamed a dazzling smile. "I'm glad to hear it. I suppose logically that leads on to talking about what happens next."

"Err, yeah," Catherine said. She gulped a sip of coffee, but it went down the wrong pipe and she ended up spluttering. Wiping her mouth, she shot Holly an apologetic look.

"There's no easy way of doing this, so I'll come straight out and ask it. Are you interested in maybe having a relationship with me?" Holly nervously twirled a strand of hair around a finger so tight the fingertip turned purple.

Catherine floundered. Her mind raced with too many thoughts to register. Was this what she wanted? Her heart said yes, but her mind was throwing out so many questions and scenarios, she couldn't give herself a definitive answer. What did Holly see in her anyway? Weren't they far too different for a relationship to stand a decent chance of working? Holly would surely get bored of her like Paula did. Was she ready to open herself up to the possibility of being hurt again? What would Beth and Katie say? She looked into Holly's eyes and saw the unmistakable fear of rejection.

"Yes," Catherine said weakly. She didn't want to run the risk of hurting Holly by delaying her answer further. Overwhelmed and panicked, the growing sense of claustrophobia made breathing difficult. "But I think we n-need to take things slowly." She spread her hands wide. "This has all happened so quickly. It's been a w-whirlwind. I need time to adjust."

Holly looked sceptical, which was understandable. She sat back in her chair and crossed her legs. "Catherine, if you're not interested please say so now. Sure, it'd hurt me, but nowhere near as much as it will in the long run. I really want you to be honest with me." Her tone sounded firm, but the edge of pleading was clear.

Shit! Catherine was terrified of committing, but equally petrified of losing Holly. "I w-want to. I'm just…" Catherine couldn't finish the sentence.

"Scared?" Holly asked.

Catherine nodded mutely.

"I understand. But it's not like I'm demanding we get married or you confess your undying love for me. I'd like to see how we get on outside of Athegither. With both of our schedules busy, I know meeting up isn't going to be easy, but I'd like to give us a chance."

"I want c-children." Catherine was as surprised as Holly that she'd blurted it out. "I don't mean r-right now, obviously. But in the future, I w-want to have children, and you don't."

Holly sighed softly. "I didn't say I definitely don't ever want children. At this moment in time, I'm so focused on the bakery, I can't think that far ahead." Holly shrugged. "In a year or two, I might want them. Or I might know for certain that I don't."

"Which would be a problem."

"I realise it's important to you, Catherine, but I can't give you a definite answer right here and now. To do so would be unfair to us both. It's a lot of commitment when we're not even officially together yet."

"I kn-know." Catherine resigned herself to the fact that Holly was right, but her heart ached all the same.

"I'd like to see how we get on together first. We don't want to start off with lots of pressure. If we're still together in a year or so, we'll both have a better idea of where our relationship is going and what we want. I promise I'll always be honest and upfront with you, but let's not try to make our relationship run before it can even stand."

"O-okay," Catherine said, hoping she sounded sincere.

"Any other important announcements or worries? Now's the time to tell me," Holly said.

Before she fully thought it through, she opened her mouth and said what was on her mind. "I'm not your type. I'm too boring for you."

Holly sat back in the chair and pinned Catherine with her stare. "How exactly have you come to those conclusions?"

Catherine bit painfully down on her tongue. She didn't want to voice her paranoia about Holly being similar to Paula. She knew it would hurt her.

"Catherine? Speak up. I want to know how you're suddenly a mind reader and have such expert insight on how I think and feel."

"I'm not spontaneous. It's not in my nature. I like routine and rules, and today with trespassing in the field, it showed how different we are."

"Seriously? You're basing those sweeping generalisations on this afternoon?" Holly asked testily. "We are different. But that doesn't mean we aren't suited. When I was young, I was very spontaneous, but since opening the bakery, I live an extremely boring life. Hermits have more of a social life than I do. I'm in bed by half eight most nights, and I work six days a week. Does that sound wild and exciting to you?"

Catherine fidgeted uneasily. "I guess not."

"That's because it's not." Holly drummed her fingernails on the table. "Look, I know Paula used the shitty excuse that she found you boring to end your relationship, but I hope you're not putting those words into my mouth. That's not fair."

"You're right. I'm sorry."

"We have the opportunity to give this our best shot. We just have to be honest and upfront. Is there anything else?"

Catherine wanted to mention that she'd broken her promise to Beth, but it wasn't her place to divulge Beth's secrets or drag Holly into the mess. She needed to think things through rationally and reach an informed decision on how to proceed. "No."

"Phew," Holly said with a bright smile. She planted a small kiss on Catherine's cheek. "Good. Now that the heavy stuff is out of the way, let's go spend some time with Kimmy."

Catherine followed her, but couldn't help wondering…was the heavy stuff really out of the way?

❖

Time sped up in the way it often does when you're trying to make something last. Every time Catherine glanced at the time, another hour had flashed by in the blink of an eye. The more she tried to preserve the memory and experience, the more quickly it disappeared. Depression settled over her. She played, fussed, groomed, and cuddled Kimmy, and the ache in her heart grew all the while. The little dog was so happy and totally oblivious to the fact that, the following morning, she'd be returned to The Inn and Fiona's care. They would never see each other again.

Guilt plagued Catherine, making her emotions raw and her mind frazzled. No matter how she tried to justify it, she was abandoning Kimmy to an unknown future. Shame weighed on her conscience like a millstone.

The sound of muffled sniffles drew her attention to Holly, who was crying but trying to mask the sounds by covering her mouth. Kimmy leapt onto her lap and nudged her face with doggy licks, which only made Holly cry harder.

"I can't bear it," Holly said. She hugged Kimmy close to her chest. "I love her, and the thought of giving her back is too awful."

"I know." It was a pathetic thing to say, but what else was there? Catherine's throat tightened with emotion. She knew what Holly was feeling because she felt it as acutely.

"I'd give anything to be able to take her home with me." Holly blew her nose on some tissue. "But it'd be cruel and selfish. My schedule means she'd be alone for most of the day. It also wouldn't be fair on a perspective lodger. Plus the cost of the vets bills and insurance, also her food." Holly rubbed her forehead as if massaging away a headache. Her tone was nasally and her complexion pale. Shaking her head, she stroked Kimmy's fur. "I just can't afford to keep her."

Catherine helplessly watched as Holly broke down again. She wished she could allow herself to cry, too. It would express her heartbreak but also release the emotions raging in a vicious tempest deep inside. "I've been thinking the same. I live in an apartment on the twentieth floor. There's no garden or outdoor space. Sometimes I have to work fifteen hours a day. It'd be cruel."

There was of course another reason, a darker reason, for why she couldn't adopt Kimmy. She couldn't face the responsibility. She'd never admit it to Holly or anyone else for that matter, but her conscience refused to let her ignore it. She was too selfish, too scared of commitment and responsibility, afraid in case she did something wrong and somehow let Kimmy down, unable to contemplate the day in the future when Kimmy's time on earth came to an end and she passed away. It was all too painful. She'd had enough of that kind of loss and pain to last her a lifetime.

"Do you think she'll find a family?" Holly asked, her tone begging for the answer she wanted to hear.

"Of course," Catherine said, as much for herself as for Holly. "She'll get snapped up. How could she not? She's gorgeous."

"It's late. We should go pack our things and think about going to bed."

"You go ahead. I'll sort Kimmy out and be through in a minute." Catherine watched Holly leave and turned her attention back to Kimmy. "Come here, girl," Catherine whispered. Kimmy obediently rose, walked across the sofa cushions, and climbed onto Catherine's lap. She bordered on being too big to fit but didn't seem to care. Keeping her balance as all four paws dug painfully into Catherine's thighs, she finally settled and lay down. She gave a huff and rested her head on her front paws.

"What am I going to do, Kimmy?" Catherine asked. She watched as the little ears pricked to her voice. "Tomorrow, everything changes. I've never been good with change. I'm so scared about what's going to happen in the future. Being here with you and Holly made me feel like I'd changed, like I'd become a better person. It's been so long since I've been this happy."

The heavy weight and warmth of Kimmy's body soothed some of Catherine's troubles away. Never one for talking things out, the compulsion to continue surprised her. Perhaps it was to prolong their time together. Or maybe it was because Kimmy was such an excellent listener. "I'm going to miss everything about you." Kimmy fidgeted and Catherine smiled. She scratched behind Kimmy's ears in her most ticklish spot.

"You're going to go to a great home where you'll be loved and taken care of by someone who knows what they're doing. I bet there'll be treats galore and as many tummy rubs as you want. Doesn't that sound good?"

She kissed the top of Kimmy's head. The soft fur tickled her nose and the smell of dog, which she'd first found musty, now smelled comfortingly familiar.

"I'm so sorry," Catherine said in a hoarse whisper, her throat on fire with emotion.

Kimmy looked up and licked Catherine's chin with her warm pink tongue.

"Come on. Out to do your business and then bedtime," Catherine said. After a bit of encouragement, Kimmy finally got up and stretched, shoving her backside in Catherine's face. She jumped down onto the floor and waited expectedly for Catherine to stand.

"All right, bossy," Catherine said. She got to her feet, but before she could take a step, Kimmy dropped into an elegant bow. Forepaws stretched out in front and backside high in the air, her two dark eyes pinned Catherine with their intense gaze.

"Are you bowing to me?" Catherine asked in disbelief. She turned to the closed bedroom door and was almost tempted to shout for Holly. When she looked back down, Kimmy stood normally, with her tail wagging and a doggy smile on her face.

"Thank you," Catherine said, genuinely touched by the gesture.

CHAPTER TWENTY

Catherine couldn't bear to be the one who led Kimmy into The Inn. Holly accepted her cowardly plea and held the lead, while Catherine carried the crate and bags filled with Kimmy's belongings. As soon as they stepped inside The Inn, Kimmy became skittish. Her tail, which was normally stuck up high, disappeared between her hind legs. After only a few sheepish steps, she planted her paws and refused to move another inch. Holly tried to encourage her, and when that failed, she tried to tug on the lead, which was attached to the harness, but Kimmy fought to stand her ground. Kimmy's heartbreakingly sorrowful whimpering made the situation a million times worse. Her little body trembled, and her innocent eyes flitted between Catherine and Holly, as if questioning what terrible crime she'd committed.

"Don't you both worry your heads. I'll take her from here. Leave her things against the wall and I'll come back for them," Fiona said.

Holly reluctantly handed over the lead, tears welling in her eyes. Biting her bottom lip seemed to be the only thing holding them at bay.

"You did a grand thing taking this wee little beggar in for as long as you did. She'll be okay. It's been a pleasure to meet you both, and I wish you a safe onward journey. And if you ever happen to be passing by Athegither again, be sure to come in and say hello," Fiona said.

"I'm sorry, but please excuse me, Fiona." Holly burst into floods of tears and rushed out the door.

Catherine watched her go and turned back to Fiona with an apologetic grimace. "We've enjoyed it. Your cabin is wonderful and your hospitality is second to none. Thank you for everything."

Kimmy squirmed and flailed, trying to drag herself over to Catherine. The lead was taut, which lifted the harness, its straps cutting into her skin.

"It's nay bother." Fiona fought to hold Kimmy back. She changed her stance and held the lead with both hands.

Catherine met Kimmy's gaze one last time, and it proved to be too much. She saw accusation and abandonment—but Kimmy was a dog. Surely what she saw was merely a reflection of her own conscience. The little terrier's distress, however, was very real. Not wanting to prolong the horrendous situation, Catherine turned and started toward the door. A high-pitched bark and whimpering chased after her, and as the door closed behind her, it hardly muffled the sounds.

With heavy legs, she walked away from The Inn and found Holly waiting for her in the car. Their stuff was already packed, and as she buckled herself in Holly started the engine. They didn't speak as the car pulled away from the pavement and made its way into the flow of traffic.

The sun hung low in the blue sky, dazzling in its intensity. They both lowered their visors. Catherine looked out her window but was too preoccupied to appreciate the passing hedgerow and stone walls. A myriad of thoughts and emotions fought for space in her head and heart. The only thing they both seemed to agree on was, this situation was all wrong.

"I need to go back," Catherine said with urgency.

"Have you forgotten something?" Holly asked, a frown creasing her brow. Her eyes, puffy from crying, remained focused on the road ahead.

"No."

Holly shot her a glance before returning her gaze back to the road. "The road's too narrow for me to turn around. I'll have to keep going and turn at the first opportunity."

Catherine nodded, but her anxiety spiked. She needed to go back now. She needed to make things right.

"Are you sure about this, Catherine?" Holly asked in a serious, almost challenging tone. "You listed all of the reasons why you couldn't keep her. What's changed?"

"I love her."

"So do I. But that doesn't change anything."

"If you love something enough you can make it work," Catherine said.

Holly pulled the car into a ditch area and turned it around. She applied the handbrake and turned to Catherine. "What about her being alone all day?"

"I'll walk her in the mornings and evenings. There's a park down the road. Plus I'll hire a dog walker to take her out during the day."

"What about the hours you work? Even with a dog walker she's going to be alone for long periods of time."

"I'm not sure about work," Catherine said. "I can demand to do my contracted hours only, but honestly, I think it's time I started looking for something new. I'm not going into this lightly, Holly. I know it won't be easy, but I'll make it work."

Holly asked the million-pound question. "Why didn't you suggest these things earlier?"

"I was being a selfish coward, but I want to make it right." Admitting she was weak and selfish wasn't easy, but she did feel better for it.

"I'm in love with her myself. Do you think maybe I can come over and visit her occasionally? Maybe take her for walks on Sundays?" Holly asked.

"Of course," Catherine said. Her pulse quickened. She was actually doing this and it felt good. Kimmy was going to be her companion for life. The responsibility didn't seem anywhere near as daunting as it previously had.

"Let's go get our baby back," Holly said. She revved the engine.

❖

Kimmy was still trembling and so Catherine hugged her closer. She'd received the brunt of doggy sulking but had accepted it graciously. Now Kimmy lay cuddled in her lap.

Fiona had been surprised when they'd burst through the doors, but she agreed to letting Kimmy go with them in a heartbeat. The journey gave an opportunity for Catherine to consider her future. Adopting Kimmy was a given, but her relationship with Holly remained uncertain. The prospect of telling Beth and Katie she'd gotten to know Holly in the biblical sense worried her. She wasn't sure how they'd react. Would Beth feel betrayed? Would Katie feel awkward? The upset it might cause wasn't appealing.

She needed time to assess her feelings for Holly, to be sure what had occurred between them wasn't down to a peculiar strain of cabin fever, heightened emotions caused by their near-death experience, or the overly romantic setting they'd found themselves in.

After an hour of intense deliberation, she was certain of one thing: it would be best for everyone if their relationship wasn't made public to Katie and Beth just yet. They didn't need the additional pressure that would come with revealing their relationship to Beth and Katie. It would buy Catherine some much needed time, too. When Holly and she returned to London they could see how things worked out. If they got on well and it looked like there was a future, it might be worth telling Beth. But potentially losing Beth, Katie, and Florence wasn't something she was going to risk on a whim. It might seem selfish, but it made perfect sense.

They pulled onto a singularly narrow road.

"I think the house is at the top of here," Holly said. "Let's hope nobody decides to come down while we're going up."

Now was the time. Catherine took a deep breath and prepared what she was going to say in her head. "So, I've been thinking it'd be for the best if we continue not to mention what's happening between us. You k-know, keep it between ourselves for now. That way nobody gets upset."

Holly slowed the speed of the car, but the house came into view at the top of the road. "Who'd get upset?"

"Well, Beth and Katie might not approve."

"I seriously doubt it. But what's it got to do with them anyway?"

This wasn't going the way she'd envisioned it. Changing tack, Catherine tried again. "We don't want to p-put unnecessary pressure on ourselves, do we?"

"Catherine, what are you saying?" Holly asked, her tone testy.

Catherine swallowed and dropped her gaze to Kimmy's fur. "I'd feel more comfortable if we didn't tell anyone about what's happening with us. It's a private thing, between the two of us. I think it should stay that way, for the time being anyway. Telling Beth will bring us a whole host of drama, even with her good intentions. You know what she's like.

To give us the best shot, we don't need unnecessary pressure. We can take our time and evaluate how we feel when we're back in London."

The tyres crunched on snow-covered gravel as the car came to a standstill outside the house. Holly switched the engine off and turned to face her. "You're asking me to keep our relationship a secret?"

"Yes, I suppose I am."

"I'm confused, Catherine. We talked about this yesterday and we both agreed we were going to give this a fighting chance."

"I know—"

"Then why the secrecy? Are you embarrassed to be in a relationship with me?" Holly asked, angrily, her cheeks pink and her eyes flashing with emotion.

Catherine hesitated a moment too long. "No."

"I don't believe you." Holly turned away. "There's no other reason for keeping it a secret. And doing so makes it feel sordid."

The front door to the house opened. Katie, Beth, and Florence all appeared on the steps with big smiles and waves.

"Holly, please let's keep it between ourselves for now. I'm not embarrassed. I swear I'm not. I need a little bit of time, that's all." Catherine reached across and took hold of one of her hands. "Please?" she begged. Time was almost out.

"It's not like I have a choice, is it?" Holly spat the words as if they were venomous.

Catherine dropped Holly's hand like it was hot when Katie appeared at her window. The hurt on Holly's face would be seared in her mind forever. Swallowing down the self-disgust, she forced a big smile and opened the door.

CHAPTER TWENTY-ONE

Hugging Beth, Katie, and Florence was far more emotionally bittersweet than Catherine had envisioned. It didn't help that she felt shitty about how she'd treated Holly. She vowed to make amends as soon as they left to return to London.

"Come on, Aunty Cat," Florence said excitedly. She tugged on Catherine's free hand, trying to lead her into the house. Kimmy didn't hesitate in following Florence, and soon Catherine was being dragged by both of them.

Florence was the five-year-old version of Beth. Her dark hair was a mass of unruly curls, her eyelashes and eyebrows were dark. Her eyes were the same colour blue and a generous sprinkling of freckles covered her face. Her personality was definitely a mixture of Beth's and Katie's traits. She was a tomboy who loved getting mucky and playing sports, which was Katie's influence. Beth hated anything remotely sporty, claiming she had no natural ability, interest, or stamina. Catherine could affirm the first two, but the third was an ongoing bone of contention, as Beth could walk in stilettos for hours if there was a sale. Florence had inherited Beth's stubbornness, but Katie's quick wit and sense of adventure. Catherine's heart swelled with pride and love.

The house was huge. Catherine stumbled out of her wellies and Florence took them straight into the kitchen. Beth and Holly followed close behind.

"What do dogs eat?" Florence asked. Shyly, she watched Kimmy, while leaning in close to Catherine's side.

"Dog food," Catherine said. She unclipped the lead and harness.

Kimmy wasted no time in sniffing everything. Florence hid behind Catherine's legs, peeking out, to keep her eye on Kimmy's exploration.

"She also likes carrots." Holly brushed past Catherine coolly and stood by the fridge. "May I?" she asked Beth.

"Sure."

Holly took out a knobbly carrot, knelt down, and motioned for Florence to come over. Florence ran over. "Here you go," Holly said. She wrapped a reassuring arm around Florence's waist and helped her offer out the carrot. "Come on, Kimmy."

Kimmy took the carrot with the gentlest of touches and then rushed under the table to happily munch away. Florence's nerves were long gone, as she lay on her tummy on the wooden floor, chin resting in her hands, watching Kimmy from a distance. She was clearly besotted, and Catherine could identify.

"So let me get this straight. You've actually adopted a dog?" Beth asked. She leant on the kitchen counter. Her black curly hair fell to her shoulders, bright blue eyes pinned Catherine with their intelligence. She stood only five feet in height—the only attribute Catherine could ever tease her about. Beth's body was curvaceous, and although she'd always been lots bigger in the chest department, since having Florence, her breasts were huge. She was naturally beautiful, and the makeup she wore only enhanced the naturally dark eyelashes, red lips, and blushed cheeks.

"Yes," Catherine said. She shrugged off her coat and hung it on the back of one of the chairs.

"And you think you're equipped to own a dog?" Beth's tone clearly revealed she didn't think so.

"Yes, I do." Catherine's annoyance prickled beneath the surface.

"After three days," Beth said—a statement not a question. "I'm sorry, but I think you've rushed into this without thinking it through. You've never had a dog. Do you even know the first thing about looking after one?" The room loomed silent, apart from the crunching from beneath the table. Florence remained oblivious to the awkwardness, kicking her cartoon wellies back and forth. Holly silently rested against the fridge. Beth's intense gaze didn't waver.

"I'll manage," Catherine said.

"For both your sakes, I hope so."

"She's been incredible with Kimmy," Holly said. "They've got a great bond, and Catherine's proven herself to be more than capable of looking after her." She folded her arms and her gaze darted everywhere except in Catherine's direction.

Beth looked flabbergasted and it took her a moment to recover. When she finally looked away from Holly and back at Catherine, she seemed suitably chastised. "Holly's right. I'm sure you've thought about this in your special in-depth way. And it's good you'll have company."

Catherine tried to portray her gratitude to Holly, but after a brief meeting of eyes, Holly looked away.

"As soon as you get to know her, you'll love her," Catherine said to Beth.

"I never had you pegged as a dog lover." Beth filled the silver kettle with water from the tap.

"I wasn't," Catherine said. "There's something about her. You'll see."

The door opened and Katie slipped inside. She wore loose-fitting jeans and a baggy jumper. She'd always worn her blond hair short, as far back as Catherine could remember, the sides and back cut close. Her skin was naturally sun-kissed in winter, thanks to the amount of time she spent working outside on the ski slopes. Catherine stood an inch taller than Katie, but it never felt like it. There was something about her confidence, her muscular body always in the peak of fitness, and the way she held herself that made her seem larger than life.

Katie gave Catherine a hug before going to Holly. "How's it going, baby cuz?"

Holly laughed and pulled Katie into a hug. "Glad to have finally made it here in one piece."

"How come things are never easy with you, huh?" Katie asked, playfully bumping shoulders. "Fancy a trip out on the slopes? The conditions couldn't be better."

"They've only just got here," Beth said, clearly not happy by the proposal.

Holly glanced at Catherine, her expression darkened, and she gave a nod. "I'd love to. Go easy on me, though. It's been a few years."

"It'll all come flooding back. Come upstairs and I'll get you kitted out. I've missed you, baby cuz. I can't wait to catch up on what you've been up to. I want to hear all the juicy details." Katie beamed a cheesy grin. She kissed Beth on the cheek and ruffled Florence's hair before heading to the door. "See you later, family."

"Be safe," Beth said. She stirred a spoon in one of the cups.

Holly walked past Catherine without speaking or looking at her. It hurt far more than Catherine expected.

"Here you go." Beth handed Catherine a cup. "Let's go to the living room. We can have a proper catch-up."

"Thanks," Catherine said unenthusiastically. A catch-up in Beth's world meant a lengthy interrogation, which she didn't need.

❖

As predicted, within the space of five minutes, Beth had become smitten with Kimmy's cuteness and charm. It took less than half that time for Kimmy to make herself completely at home in front of the raging fire. Florence sat beside her, stroking Kimmy's belly and happily chattering gibberish. From the tired whooshing of Kimmy's tail, she appeared to be in heaven.

"I'm glad you're here." Beth stretched her socked feet across Catherine's lap. She knew it bugged Catherine but always did it anyway.

"Me too."

"I never thought you'd genuinely consider driving up here. Eve was beside herself when you agreed. It means a lot, Cat."

Catherine shrugged. "I've missed you all."

Beth playfully swatted her shoulder. "Jeez! What's happened to you? How come you've turned into an emotional wreck since the last time I saw you? Bring back the old, miserable, workaholic Cat. You know the one—she always avoids my calls."

Catherine smiled. "You never were good at taking a hint."

"Touché." Beth laughed. "So what do you think of the house?"

"Well, I've only seen the kitchen and this room so far, but I think it's beautiful. I almost understand why you moved to the middle of nowhere."

"It's everything we ever wanted." Beth smiled. "But I do miss the hustle and bustle of The Big Smoke. Oh, and the shops. I miss shopping so much. You have no idea how dire the shops are up here."

"I'm glad to see being up here hasn't changed you. You're still as superficial as ever," Catherine said.

"And you remain about as funny as a wet fart in white trousers." Beth wriggled her feet. "Speaking of funny, you seemed to get on well with Holly."

"Yeah. She's okay." Catherine begged her body not to give her guilt away. She drastically needed to change the subject. "Did you decorate this room? It's surprisingly tasteful."

Beth gave a pointed look. "My taste is impeccable. I've done the whole house. It took a lot of time and even more money, but it's exactly how I wanted it. Thanks."

"What made you go for cream carpets?" Catherine asked, glad to have chosen a safe, if somewhat boring, topic of conversation. Anything was preferable to talking about Holly.

They spent the next few hours chatting away and poking fun at one another. Catherine realised how much she'd missed it. It reaffirmed how important their relationship was, and the prospect of losing them was crushing. But all the while, Holly hijacked her thoughts. Unanswered questions repeated on a loop in Catherine's mind. She'd convinced herself that her actions had been justified, but doubt and regret were closing in. Her teeth were set on edge, trying to prevent hidden truths from being carelessly blurted out. She missed Holly desperately. Without the presence of her encompassing warmth and light, Catherine felt thrown into cold darkness. Holly was like a bruise that Catherine couldn't leave alone, no matter how much it hurt.

"Mummy Katie and Aunty Holly are back," Florence said. She rushed to the bay window.

Panic stirred in Catherine's mind.

What if Holly told Katie the truth? She wouldn't, would she?

"I need to start preparing dinner," Beth said, getting to her feet.

"I can help if you want?" Catherine asked, hoping if she was in the kitchen, she might keep out of Holly's way. At the very least, she'd be preoccupied.

"Aunty Cat, will you come and play with me? Please?" Florence asked, dragging out the please for a few seconds in a whiney tone. Her head slumped to one shoulder and her bottom lip began to wobble.

"Err, okay," Catherine said. Resistance was futile.

"Yay!" Florence bounced up and down on the spot. "Kimmy's coming to play, too."

"Florence Louise Locke-Collins," Beth said sternly. "Calm down. Kimmy might not be allowed to play."

"Why?" Florence asked in a surly tone.

"She might try and eat some of your toys—"

"No, she won't. Me and Aunty Cat will watch her."

Beth and Florence both turned their attention on Catherine. She looked from one to the other uneasily. She'd feel better having Kimmy with her. If she did misbehave, there was always the option of taking her downstairs. "She can come up. But if she's naughty she'll have to go downstairs."

Grinning in triumph, Florence rushed from the room, with Kimmy following at her heels.

"You spoil her rotten, Cat."

"No, I don't. I just want to play with the toys."

Beth smiled. "She's got you wrapped around her little finger and she knows it."

"Let's be honest. I never stood a chance. She knows how to play me. She's obviously learnt from the best."

"Damn straight," Beth said.

CHAPTER TWENTY-TWO

Santa got me this too," Florence said. She proudly pointed to another stuffed toy.

Catherine nodded. "I like it." She'd been shown umpteen toys and her brain was starting to hurt a little.

Kimmy sniffed a few toys before settling on the pink rug.

"Do you wanna play pirates with me?"

Catherine nodded and sat crossed-legged on the floor. The pirate ship Eve had purchased on her behalf was awesome. They split the plastic toys and started playing. For a five-year-old, Florence's imagination was impressive, but Catherine had to tune out of the verbal diarrhoea that accompanied it.

A timid knock on the open door made them look up. Holly stood in the doorway and Catherine suspected she'd been there a while.

"Aunty Holly, do you wanna play pirates, too?" Florence asked eagerly.

"I'd love to, but dinner's ready. Definitely another time, Flo," Holly said.

"I don't wanna have dinner," Florence said. She folded her small arms and huffed.

"Oh dear. That's a shame. I suppose I'll have to decorate the chocolate cake for pudding all by myself." Holly turned slowly to leave.

In a flash, Florence wrapped herself around Holly's legs. "I wanna do it. Please, Aunty Holly? Please?"

"I don't know, Flo. What's the rule about decorating puddings?" Holly asked. She stroked Florence's back.

"People's got to eat dinner and then decorate pudding," Florence said, clearly rehearsed with the rule. Giggling, she squirmed away from Holly's tickling fingers.

"That's right. Shall we go eat dinner?" Holly whispered conspiratorially.

"Yeah." Florence looked back at Catherine and Kimmy. "Come on, Aunty Cat and Kimmy, we're gonna go eat dinner now." She raced from the bedroom with Kimmy hot on her tracks.

"See you down there," Holly said, seeming to hesitate.

"You're great with her," Catherine said. It'd been lovely to see how Florence and Holly got on. She ignored the tiny sting of jealousy caused from their familiar closeness.

"I was thinking the same thing," Holly said. She shoved her hands into her pockets. "You're a natural with children." Holly left the room before Catherine could reply.

Catherine wondered if it would be possible to make things up to Holly when they left. Their interactions were cooler, and they'd only been here for half a day. If things continued to deteriorate at this rate, there might not be a relationship to keep secret.

❖

Catherine entered the dining room and her stomach dropped. Her place had been set opposite Holly. In all fairness, Holly didn't look particularly enthused by the seating arrangements either.

They passed the dishes around. The chicken casserole smelled good and was served with creamy mash and plenty of veg. Florence sat on a booster cushion between Holly and Beth. She looked bored and lazily watched the dishes move over her head. She squeezed her cheeks together with her palms and blew a raspberry.

"Florence, don't do that please," Beth said. She dished out a small spoonful of mash onto Florence's plate.

"What?" Florence asked, her lips puckered like a fish.

"You know exactly what." Beth gave her a stern look, and Catherine was glad she wasn't on the receiving end. "Now what veg are you having tonight?"

"Peas."

"And what else?" Beth asked, as she scooped some peas on to the plate.

Florence frowned and mumbled something incoherent.

"Kiddo, you know the rules. Three types of veg with dinner. Come on," Katie said.

Florence pouted and covered her face with her hands.

Beth shot an apologetic glance at Catherine and Holly. "She's recently decided to be a fussy eater. Although in a peculiar twist of fate, it seems to be only vegetables and fruit she doesn't like." Beth turned back to Florence. "You have exactly until the count of three and then I'm choosing for you. One. Two. Thr—"

"Carrots and broccolis," Florence said. "Please."

Beth and Katie both looked surprised. Beth dished out the veg and presented the plate to Florence. She started serving herself. "I think Kimmy's set a good example for a certain person. She's refused to eat carrots for months now."

"Don't suppose you can teach Kimmy to stay in bed until after seven every morning, can you?" Katie asked with a grin. "Sure would be nice to have a lie in."

"She's a dog, not a miracle worker, darling," Beth said.

"It was worth a shot." Katie chuckled. "Kimmy's a real beauty though, Cat. She reminds me of the dog we had when I was a kid. Maybe we should think about getting a—"

"Don't even think about finishing that sentence, unless you want a world of pain," Beth said through gritted teeth. With violent nods of her head in Florence's direction, she added, "Walls have little ears and understand more than we think."

"Walls don't have ears, Mummy Beth," Florence said, proving Beth's point without looking up from the plate, where she was chasing a pea around with a mini fork. In the end, she squished the pea with a finger, inspected it, and put it in her mouth.

"The mash is great, wifey," Katie said with a smirk.

"Creep," Beth said.

Catherine could feel Holly watching her, and it took all of her resolve not to look up.

"I love your necklace, Holly," Beth said, clearly trying to fill the awkward silence. "Where did you get it from?"

Catherine raised her gaze. Holly looked flustered.

"It was a gift."

"How lovely. Who from?" Beth asked, taking a sip of wine.

Holly took a sip from her own glass before replying. "A friend. This wine is lovely. Is it expensive?"

Beth went into great detail about how she got the crates of wine shipped here, and Catherine slowly released a breath.

Conversation was stilted throughout the rest of the meal, and it was a relief when it came to an end. Catherine helped Katie clear the table while Florence and Holly decorated the chocolate sponge.

They had dessert in the living room with the comfort of the log fire and Christmas tree. The atmosphere remained frosty. Florence rubbed her eyes, notably grumpy.

"Right, kiddo. Time to head up the wooden hills," Katie said, getting up.

"Aunty Cat, will you tuck me in and read me a story?" Florence asked. "Please?"

"Of course." Catherine was grateful for the excuse to leave the room and Holly. "I think I'll probably call it a night after."

"Cat, don't be a lightweight," Beth said. She topped up her own wine glass. "Stay up a bit longer."

"Honestly, I'm shattered."

"Don't let my tipsy wife bully you. Your room is the last one down the corridor on the left. I put your suitcase and stuff on the bed earlier," Katie said.

"What about Kimmy?" Beth asked. "Is she okay to stay in here with us? How does the cage thingy work?"

Kimmy was sprawled by the fire and showed no intention of moving.

"I'll put her to bed when we all go up," Holly said. She avoided looking at Catherine. "The crate is easy to assemble."

"Err, thanks." Catherine quickly exerted all her attention into giving Kimmy a fuss good night.

They were about to leave when Florence decided to give everyone a good night hug. Catherine wasn't quite sure if she was supposed to do the same thing. The decision was made for her when Katie pulled her into a bear hug. As she hugged Beth, her heart started to race and butterflies thrashed in her stomach.

Turning to face Holly's direction, her heart missed a beat. Her mind warned her to try to act natural, otherwise she'd give something away. But her body was behaving of its own accord. Awkwardly, she stepped forward and refused to look Holly in the eye. Their bodies were drawn to each other as if magnetised. They fit together perfectly. Holly's smell engulfed her in a comforting haze. The warmth of her body was wonderfully familiar. It felt like home and she didn't want to ever let go. Holly's arms tightened and her hair lightly tickled Catherine's neck. A tiny moan escaped Catherine's mouth.

How long had they been hugging? Would friends hug for this long?

Catherine forced herself to step away. Her body jilted from the loss. Not daring to look at Beth or Katie, Catherine took hold of Florence's little hand, and together they left the room.

❖

The one bedtime story turned into four, but Catherine didn't mind. She helped Florence to read the first book, but after a barrage of yawns and eye rubbing, she read the rest.

As soon as Florence had drifted off, Catherine planted a gentle kiss on her forehead and crept out of the room like a ninja. She found her own room easily. It was huge and had its own en suite. After taking a shower, dressing in pyjamas, and brushing her teeth, she settled beneath the soft duvet with her tablet and began reading.

A while later, she heard everyone else come upstairs. Eventually, the house fell silent. Sleep was a luxury Catherine expected to be granted, but she was too tense and her mind refused to switch off.

"Argh," she whispered. She'd read the same sentence at least twenty times. And although the bed was comfortable, it was also massive. The empty space beside her added to her depressing loneliness. She pined for Holly.

A timid knock sounded on her door, and Catherine didn't doubt for a second it was Holly. Panicked, she tried to assess her options. She either opened the door or she didn't.

The knock sounded again.

Speaking to Holly would be a mistake, but she couldn't fight the desire to see her. Excitement made her a little giddy, as she tiptoed over to the door and opened it. Holly stood on the threshold, her hair scruffily tied up. She wore the same pyjamas from the cabin.

"Can I come in?" Holly whispered.

"Yeah, okay." Catherine stepped aside, holding the door open. As soon as Holly was safely inside, she sneakily glanced down the hallway. They were alone. She closed the door and turned to find Holly watching her from the bed. Her expression looked sombre.

"This situation is shitty," Holly said. She spread her hands wide. "I'm sorry, but I can't keep lying to them, Catherine. They know something's going on."

"With us?" Catherine asked. Bile scorched the back of her throat.

"No. They know something's not right with me." Holly crossed her legs and folded her arms. "I've always been honest about my life. I don't keep secrets from them. Lying is killing me."

Catherine sat, ensuring a decent-sized gap between them. "I'm sorry."

Holly studied her carefully. "I believe you are. But that doesn't help me. What is the big deal with them knowing? I don't think they'd batter an eyelid. They love us. They want us to be happy."

Catherine dropped her gaze to the floor. "It's not necessarily about them. I'm the one who needs time."

"Time for what?" Holly asked. When Catherine didn't answer, she pounded the duvet with her fists. "Was it all a lie? Was I just a plaything to occupy you while we were snowed in?"

"Of course not."

"Really? Because that's how you're making it seem. I feel used, Catherine. I don't know if you care about me, or if you're stringing me along, or if you're trying to let me down gently. But if it's the latter, it's not working."

"Sorry—"

"Stop apologising," Holly said with a snap. "Talk to me. Explain what's going on."

"I care about you. I do," Catherine said. She rubbed her face with her hands. "I need time to sort my head out. Telling Beth and Katie will bring a whole host of pressure and expectations down on us. I can't deal with that right now. Why can't we keep it to ourselves for a couple of days and see how we get on in London? I don't think that's asking too much. I get this isn't a big deal for you, but it is for me."

"This is a huge deal for me. I swear to God, if you were anyone else, I'd have ended this in the car when we arrived. And I'm furious at myself for not doing exactly that," Holly said loudly. Anger radiated off her in waves. "And I hate that you can make me feel so cheap and hurt. It's not just about what you want and feel. Don't you care about me at all?"

"I do. And I'm going to make it up to you." Catherine's chest constricted and breathing became painfully difficult. "It's another five days, and then we'll leave. That's all."

"That's all?" Holly asked. Her eyebrows arched, her mouth formed a thin line, and two red spots coloured her cheeks "Do you know what's happening tomorrow?"

"What?" Catherine asked, dread surfacing.

"Beth's organised a meal and invited two blind dates, one for each of us. Katie let it slip while we were out."

Catherine didn't know what to say. How could Beth do this to her? Why was she always interfering and scheming?

"Are you actually going to say something?" Holly asked. "You can't seriously expect us not to tell them about us now?" When Catherine didn't respond Holly raised her voice. "Catherine?"

"I…" Catherine faltered. Holly was too loud. If they weren't careful, they'd wake everyone. "Shush."

Holly stormed to the door. When she looked back, her eyes were fierce with anger and brimming with tears. "It's over." She tore open the door and left.

The door slammed and Catherine flinched. She daren't go after Holly in case Beth or Katie came out to investigate all the noise. She didn't know what to say anyway.

"She'll calm down by tomorrow," she whispered to herself. "And then when we leave I'll do everything I can to make it up to her. It'll be okay."

She didn't believe a word of it.

CHAPTER TWENTY-THREE

Catherine had barely slept. Her mind and emotions refused to grant her a reprieve. When she finally made her way downstairs, she was relieved to find Holly and Katie had gone out.

The day dragged and the situation wasn't improved by Beth's smugness. She merrily cleaned and cooked, content in the knowledge that she'd arranged the secret blind dates. That Beth was so excited about her betrayal galled Catherine.

She couldn't bear feeling like a prized idiot any longer. "You can shove your smugness up your arse. I know about the blind date," Catherine blurted. She got some satisfaction from Beth's astonishment, but as always, she recovered quickly.

"It's for your own good. You can't blame me for trying to help you find someone. I care about you. I hate seeing you so lonely."

"That's bullshit. You're a nosey busybody who derives pleasure from interfering in other people's lives. You should mind your own bloody business." Catherine grimaced. It had come out a little harsher than she'd intended.

Beth glared and folded her arms. "I know you don't always appreciate it when I spring surprises, so I'm going to forgive your little outburst. I get you're not keen, but tough titty, because it's happening." She looked up at the kitchen clock. "In less than an hour and a half. So, go and make yourself presentable."

"Sometimes I hate you," Catherine said. She felt like a petulant child.

"I can live with that."

❖

It was a strange situation. Dressing for a blind date was always difficult, but when it was one you didn't want to encourage in any way, shape, or form, that only made it all the more stressful. There was the added pressure of having to look like she'd made an effort, otherwise people would question why. She'd heard Holly and Katie return a little while ago. At least being stowed away in her room meant she didn't have to face Holly.

"This is ridiculous," she said to herself. And it was. Perhaps Holly was right? After sleepless hours of replaying their argument and considering Holly's points, she was beginning to think maybe she was in the wrong. If they'd been honest and upfront from the start, like Holly had suggested, they wouldn't have to endure this stupid blind date dinner. Holly would be talking to her, and perhaps they'd be able to kiss and cuddle. At this point Catherine would give anything to be able to hug and kiss Holly. The realisation that she might never get to do either again was far too painful to consider.

"Our guests are here!" Beth shouted up the stairs.

Catherine glanced at her reflection. The dark trousers and green jumper would have to do. She'd considered wearing the earrings Holly had gotten her, but decided against it.

"Catherine!" Beth shouted up the stairs. "Don't make me come up there."

Catherine walked to the door. "Shoot me now."

❖

She was ambushed as soon as she descended the stairs.

"Catherine, this is Amanda Doyle," Beth said in an infuriatingly sickly sweet tone.

Catherine turned her attention to the woman beside Beth. Her straight bright red hair—which could only have come from a dye, was cut in a slanted bob. Her tanned skin was bordering on orange. The chunky gold jewellery looked heavy and garish. The makeup wasn't too bad when compared to everything else. The large tangerine breasts practically popped out of her white top, which was at least two sizes too small.

Amanda presented her hand. Catherine did a double take when she saw the long nails. They were painted the same colour red as her hair and showcased little glittering stones. Nearly every finger had a gold ring, although the designs were different.

"It's wonderful to meet you, Catherine," Amanda said, her voice loud and her Scottish accent prominent. "I've heard so much about you."

"I can't say the same," Catherine said. She weakly shook the tip of Amanda's hand and couldn't help but sneakily glance, to make sure none of the orange had transferred to her own skin.

"What Catherine means is, I kept your identity a surprise." Beth forced a smile.

"I'm sure we're going to get to know each other well." Amanda gave Catherine a slow wink that looked more like a physical tic.

The way Amanda was looking at her made Catherine uncomfortable. The directness of her gaze was intense. She seemed overly keen.

"Follow me and I'll introduce you to everyone else," Beth said, leading Amanda into the living room.

Catherine followed and dabbed her sweaty palms on her trousers. She wasn't looking forward to seeing Holly or her blind date. At least if the date was anything like Amanda, Catherine wouldn't have to worry.

"Amanda, this is Holly and Sky." Beth stepped aside.

Catherine's ears pricked at the name. Sky? What kind of a name was that? She brushed past Amanda and looked around the door. Holly sat on the sofa, wearing a low-cut top and the skintight jeans that drove Catherine crazy. Her hair flowed freely around her shoulders, and she wore makeup. She hadn't worn the pendant—a sucker punch of grief struck Catherine's gut.

"Hi, Amanda," Holly said and then laughed at something the person sitting next to her said. Craning her neck farther, Catherine finally laid eyes on Sky. She felt the blood drain from her body.

Sky was young and attractive, in a handsome kind of way. Her blond hair was shorter than Katie's. She had chiselled good looks and great bone definition. She wore no makeup, but her bottom lip was pierced and had a ring through it. The shirt she wore clung to her muscular frame. The jeans were stylish, as were the boots. The way Sky was sitting suggested she was comfortable and confident. Her eyes focused only on Holly.

Fiery anger scorched Catherine's chest, surging its way to the back of her throat. Sky's foot brushed against Holly's. Worse still, Holly didn't appear to mind. She was turned toward Sky, and her attention rapt by whatever funny antidote Sky was reeling off so effortlessly.

Catherine didn't like Sky. Not one bit.

Sky couldn't be more blatantly flirtatious if she tried. It was a disgusting show, especially when surrounded by a room full of people.

"Here you go," Katie said. She offered out a wine glass to Amanda, but Catherine snatched it. Frowning, Katie presented Amanda with the second wine glass. Catherine drained the maroon liquid in one go. She didn't taste the wine or enjoy it.

"Let's go and sit down, shall we?" Amanda asked.

Catherine wiped her mouth and gave an unenthusiastic nod. She needed another drink. As they passed by the coffee table, she poured herself a large refill.

"Beth told me about your career. Very impressive," Amanda said. She tapped the cushion beside her in what Catherine could only presume was supposed to be a seductive manner.

"Thanks."

"I work in financial investment. I'm very good at making money, amongst other things."

"Mm," Catherine said, watching Holly and Sky from the corner of her eye.

"I think we could do some good business together." Amanda reached out and pinched Catherine's leg with her Freddy Krueger nails.

Catherine flinched and stared at the trespassing hand in disbelief. What on earth was wrong with this woman? She was about to say something to Amanda when she noticed Holly looking over. Biting her tongue, Catherine forced a weak smile.

"We'd have some pleasure as well, of course," Amanda said and erupted into a loud, shrill cackle.

Catherine wasn't sure what she was doing. She knew it wasn't wise to let Amanda think she stood a chance. The problem was Sky. As much as she disliked Amanda, she disliked Sky and the way Holly was acting around her a lot more. Trying to make Holly jealous was childish, but she couldn't resist. She wanted Holly to feel how she felt. Taking a hearty chug from her glass, she felt the warmth of tipsiness seep through her body.

Her spirits rose when Kimmy bounded into the room. She looked around, spotted Catherine, and rushed over. She leapt up on Catherine's lap and covered her face in doggy kisses. It meant so much that she'd come straight over to Catherine and ignored Holly. Again, it was immature and petty, but it made her feel better.

"Could you put it down?" Amanda said coldly.

Catherine looked over Kimmy's head and saw Amanda bunched near the end of the sofa. Her expression was difficult to read, but from the unattractively scrunched-up face, Catherine determined Amanda wasn't a fan of dogs.

"Her name's Kimmy and she's my dog," Catherine said. She ruffled the grey fur affectionately.

"I'm highly allergic to dogs," Amanda said in a nasally tone. She shivered dramatically, covered her chest with her arms, and began to hiss loud breaths.

"Come here, Kimmy," Holly said. She clicked her fingers. "Come and meet Sky."

"I love dogs," Sky said in a velvety voice.

Of course she does! Catherine held on to Kimmy, but after a lot of squirming, she had to let go. She watched with dismay as Kimmy went to Holly. Sky actually got down onto her knees to fuss Kimmy, and when she stood, her shirt hitched, revealing a toned stomach.

"Excuse me," Catherine said. She left the room with her glass. She hovered in the hallway outside the kitchen. She could hear the clattering of pans and Florence's chattering. After finishing the wine, she entered the kitchen.

"What are you doing in here?" Beth asked.

"I've come for a refill." Catherine held up her empty glass as proof. Common sense told her to drink some water, so she poured another glass of wine.

"So, what do you think of Amanda?" Beth asked. She stirred a steaming saucepan on the stove.

"She's allergic to dogs."

"Oh, well there are tablets for that," Beth said dismissively.

"She's got bright red hair," Catherine said.

"You like redheads. They're your type. I thought you'd be happy."

"Happy?" Catherine asked in disbelief. She was astounded by Beth's faulty judgment. "Just because Paula was ginger doesn't mean red-headed women are my type. Amanda's isn't even natural."

"The first course is about ready," Beth said cheerily. "Please ask everyone to take their places."

Catherine went to storm from the room, but a wave of vertigo assaulted her senses, making her grab the counter and wait for it to pass. She returned to the living room and gave the announcement in a slightly slurry tone. She also shot Sky a dirty look, but as she was too busy looking at Holly, it was wasted.

What kind of a name was Sky anyway? It was a stupid name. She doubted it was her Christian name—more likely an attempt at quirkiness, by naming herself after an inanimate object.

Holly and Sky. It sounded like a hippy folk group. What did Holly see in Sky? Apart from her sexy body, her youth, her outgoing personality, her affinity of piercings and probably love of tattoos, too.

A hell of a lot more than Catherine could offer.

The thought was so sobering, she drank more wine.

❖

Catherine was well on her way to being drunk but didn't care. She sat opposite Amanda, and as rude as it was, the leering looks and Amanda's overall appearance ruined Catherine's appetite. Beth sat next to Catherine and aimed disapproving looks and jabs to her ribs, both of which Catherine ignored.

Holly sat between Amanda and Sky. Florence sat at the head of the table next to Katie. She was unashamedly gawping at Amanda in the innocent way children can do. Her eyes were wide, as if studying something completely alien. Katie tried to encourage Florence to eat her soup, but she sat transfixed. Catherine hadn't seen her blink in a while. Her mouth hung open and her hand limply held the small spoon.

"Florence, eat your soup, please," Beth said. She looked uncomfortable at Florence's behaviour.

"Mummy Beth, why she looks so funny?" Florence asked with a deep-set frown.

Catherine nearly choked on her wine while trying to stifle her laugh. *From the mouth of babes!*

"What did she say?" Amanda asked, directing the question at Beth. She mustn't have heard what Florence said, or she was an excellent actress who was hell-bent on making Beth squirm.

"She said you look so sunny," Beth said, clearly flustered. "I think she means your disposition."

Sunny my ass! Catherine thought to herself. If anything, you've had too much of the fake sun.

"Aw. Aren't you a sweetie-pie? I could eat you all up," Amanda said in a condescending way, waving her claw like fingers at Florence.

Florence's eyes bulged. Her bottom lip stuck out and began to wobble.

"Florence, come and help me clean up." Beth hastily scraped her chair backward. Florence, on the verge of crying, ran from the room.

"Cute kid," Amanda said, seemingly oblivious to the terror she'd caused.

"Do you have any children, Amanda?" Holly asked.

"God, no. I'm not giving up this figure for anything." Amanda chortled her loud atrocious laugh again.

"Do you have any pets?" Holly asked, persevering for a reason Catherine couldn't fathom.

"I'm allergic to most animals, so no. Although I suppose in your case I might make an exception, Cat." Amanda turned the limelight onto Catherine. "I have it on good authority that I'm excellent with pussies." Her laugh filled the stunned silence.

Catherine covered her mouth with a napkin, trying to mask her retch and swallow down her nausea. This woman was vulgar and terrifying. The only small mercy was Florence hadn't been in the room to be subjected to the comment. For the umpteenth time, Catherine questioned what the hell Beth had been thinking. She risked a glance at Holly, noting she looked equally appalled, as she pushed her half-filled soup bowl away from her. The rest of the meal was torturously slow, but at least Amanda refrained from making any further inappropriate comments. Katie excused herself to keep an eye on Florence, who for some unknown reason wouldn't step back inside the room.

Holly and Sky continued to giggle and talk in whispered voices. It struck at the core of Catherine. She wanted to valiantly demand that Sky back off and then kiss Holly in front of everyone. She'd claim her as her own. Screw what Beth, Katie, or anyone else thought. The only thing prohibiting her from doing exactly that was her cowardice. Even copious amounts of wine didn't seem to provide enough Dutch courage.

"Beth, the meal was divine, darling. How about Catherine and I clear up?" Amanda asked.

Beth shook her head. "No, you're guests."

"Nonsense. It'll be our pleasure, won't it, Catherine?"Amanda asked, grinning manically.

"Whatever," Catherine said. If it meant she didn't have to watch Holly and Sky canoodling, she'd do it.

Once inside the kitchen, it turned out Amanda had no desire to help clear anything up.

"I don't want to risk breaking one of my nails. You don't mind emptying the dishes and putting them in the dishwasher do you, baby?"

Catherine didn't bother replying. She scraped the plates and rinsed them, while Amanda watched from her seat at the kitchen table like Lady Muck.

"I like a woman who isn't afraid to get her hands dirty," Amanda said.

Catherine could feel her temper rising. She was fed up with Amanda's comments. All interest in making Holly jealous had lost its appeal. She wanted to clear the kitchen and go to bed. "Seeing as I'm doing all the frigging work, you might as well go and be with the others."

"And miss watching you bending and stretching. Not a chance."

Catherine shoved the cutlery into the plastic tray and turned to face Amanda. The time had come to be honest and put an end to this absurd pairing. "Amanda, you seem nice."

"If by nice, you mean gorgeous, I know. But thank you anyway."

Catherine was almost speechless at the gall of the woman. She was seriously deluded. "I'm sorry, but I'm not looking for a relationship at the moment."

Amanda sauntered over to her. "Poor baby. Beth told me all about what happened with your ex."

"It's got nothing to do with that," Catherine said. Anger settled in the pit of her stomach. Beth and she were going to have a big conversation about respect.

"Shush, baby," Amanda said as she closed the distance. "You have to let yourself love and be loved again. You're cute, and I can see in your eyes that you want me. You and I are going to have some fun."

Catherine stumbled backward, her backside meeting with the wooden counter, effectively cornering her. She held her hands up to ward Amanda off. "I'm not interested in having fun with you. Ever."

"You're scared of getting hurt again," Amanda said, her tone infuriatingly sympathetic. She interlocked her fingers with Catherine's, her strength surprising and the tips of her nails clawing into the back of Catherine's hands. "I'll fix you, baby."

"You really aren't listening to what I'm—"

Catherine was cut off as Amanda's mouth assaulted hers. Shocked, it took a few seconds to fully register what was happening. Amanda's breath was sickly sweet, and her tongue felt invasively foreign as it stuck in her mouth. Forcing her face away and tearing her hands out of Amanda's vice grip, Catherine pushed Amanda away. She gulped down fresh air, trying to cleanse herself.

A smashing sound made them turn in unison.

Holly stood in the doorway and shard remains of her wine glass were scattered on the floor. Her gaze bored into Catherine. Harrowed hurt flashed across her face.

"We didn't realise we had company," Amanda said, her shrill laugh filling the silence.

"Holly—" Catherine started toward her.

Holly turned and fled without saying a word.

"You're not going anywhere, bab—"

"Move," Catherine said. She shoved past Amanda's body and rushed to the door.

"Hey! Who's going to clean up this glass?" Amanda asked.

Catherine raced down the corridor and bumped into Beth.

"What did you break?" Beth asked.

"Nothing." Catherine tried to get around Beth, but failed.

"I heard something smash. It wasn't the decanter, was it? It's an heirloom."

Catherine heard a door slam from somewhere in the house. "Holly dropped her glass. Move, Beth."

Frowning, Beth finally stood aside. Catherine rushed past her into the living room. Sky was helping Florence to teach Kimmy to sit and give a paw.

"Where's Holly?" Catherine asked. Her panic was spiralling out of control.

"She's sick. Katie's taken her upstairs," Sky said in a brusque tone. She looked at Catherine strangely, as if she knew what had transpired in the kitchen.

Catherine ran up the stairs, taking two at a time. She knocked on Holly's door, wanting to burst inside, but knowing it would only make the situation worse. Getting no response, she knocked again, this time louder. The door swung open.

"Catherine?" Katie said, sticking her head out. She blocked the doorway with her body. "Are you okay?"

Catherine tried to peak into the room but couldn't see Holly. She wet her lips. "I…wanted to check on Holly."

"She's not feeling well."

"Can I talk to her?"

Katie smiled weakly. "That's kind of you, but she's in a bit of a mess. I'm going to stay with her. Hopefully, after a good night's sleep she'll be okay. I'm praying it isn't the food, otherwise we're all going to get it."

Catherine rubbed her face. "Is there anything I can do?"

"Afraid not," Katie said. She studied Catherine. "How are you feeling? You look a little green around the gills yourself."

"Actually, I'm not feeling too great. I think I'm going to lie down."

Katie nodded sympathetically and took half a step back. "Shit. I said the meat smelled funky."

"Can you let Beth know for me?"

"Yeah, no problem. Feel better, Catherine."

Catherine turned and stumbled up the hallway to her room. What had she done? She'd ruined everything. She'd hurt Holly and this time it was irreparable.

"Shit," she whispered. She cupped her mouth with her hands. "What am I going to do?"

She tried to think up a plan of action. She needed to speak to Holly and explain, but it was impossible with Katie guarding her. Her only choice was to wait it out, and as soon as Katie left, which she'd have to do at some point, Catherine would sneak into Holly's room and beg her to listen.

She piled up the pillows on top of one another and leaned against them, propping her torso up. She would wait it out and then explain everything to Holly and apologise. She'd make everything right. They could tell Beth and Katie the truth if that's what Holly wanted. This madness would stop and things would go back to being fine.

Holly couldn't genuinely think she was interested in the monstrosity that was Amanda, could she? It was ludicrous, so absurd it was almost funny. She hoped they might laugh about it one day.

CHAPTER TWENTY-FOUR

Catherine woke, and pain flared in her neck. She wore the previous evening's clothes and lay on top of the duvet. She glanced at the bedside clock and did a double take. It was after one—in the afternoon.

"Shit!" She rushed to get up, but the urge to be violently sick nearly became more than an urge. Her head was killing her and her mouth tasted like crap. She didn't have time for the hangover from hell. Not today.

Taking a slower approach, she made her way to Holly's room. It was unlikely Holly would be in there at this time of day, but it was the best place to start. Catherine knocked timidly and waited. No response. She knocked again, and having wasted enough time already, ventured inside.

The room stood empty, the bed neatly made.

"I knew it," she said in frustration. She wasn't sure how she was going to convince Holly to speak to her alone. Maybe she'd want to talk? It wasn't likely, but a little bit of hope went a long way.

The house was eerily quiet. Normally, Florence or Kimmy would have appeared in noisy greeting. Not today. What the hell was going on? She found Beth in the living room and recognised the sulky expression straight away.

"You finally decided to come and face me, then?" Beth asked.

"Where's everyone?" Catherine chose not to reply to Beth's loaded question. She winced at the stabbing pain behind her right eye.

"Katie and Florence have taken Kimmy out for a long walk."

Catherine perched on the arm of the sofa. "Where's Holly?"

"Well, let me see," Beth said, glancing at her watch and frowning in fake concentration. "I'd say she's probably an hour or so away from arriving home."

"Home?" Catherine's voice raised several octaves. "What do you mean home?"

Beth sat back in the chair. "Home, as in London."

Catherine hurried over to the window and looked outside. Holly's car was gone. Turning back to Beth, she tried to mask her hysteria. "When? Why?"

"A little after six this morning. Apparently, there's a problem at the bakery. Which is total bullshit. She wouldn't say anything else, though. Do you know what's going on with her?"

"What do you mean?"

"Since you both arrived here she's been acting strangely. Has she mentioned anything to you?" Beth asked. Catherine shook her head. "Katie's worried sick about her. I had to insist she take Florence and Kimmy for a walk to try to take her mind off being so upset."

Catherine sat on the sofa. She felt numb.

"Don't worry. Katie's going to drive you home on the second of January," Beth said. Her annoyance was palpable. "Holly's the least selfish person I know. It doesn't make sense she'd just up and leave. Especially when she knows we've got the Hogmanay party in two days' time. I was relying on her baking skills. I'll doubt I'll be able to find something else at this late notice. Two days is not enough time."

"Hogmanay?" Catherine asked just to fill the silence. She couldn't give a shit what it was.

"It's huge in Scotland, bigger than Christmas. It's a big celebration of New Year's Eve, and after midnight we do the first-footing. We go visit neighbours and take them gifts and they return the favour. We've got loads of guests invited. Oh and here." Beth reached beside the sofa and took out a plastic bag. "Holly left these for you."

With trembling hands, Catherine accepted the bag but refused to look inside—knowing if she did, she'd start to cry and perhaps never stop.

"I'll hope you'll be better behaved for the Hogmanay party. Last night was a total disaster. What a complete waste of time and effort. You were exceptionally rude to both Sky and Amanda."

Catherine hugged the bag close to her chest. "I can't believe you honestly thought I'd be interested in that sex-crazed lunatic. And how dare you tell her about Paula."

Beth blushed. "She wanted to know about you, and it came out. It wasn't intentional."

"Don't ever try and set me up again," Catherine said angrily. "I mean it, Beth. It was one of the worst nights of my life. Thinking about it makes me feel sick."

"Are you sure that's not your hangover? You nearly drank us out of wine."

Catherine bristled. "It's probably the aftereffects of food poisoning."

Beth floundered. "I stand by the belief the meat was fine. Everyone except you and Holly are perfectly well today. You probably picked something up from that village."

Catherine wasn't in a fit state to argue further. She got up, holding the bag protectively in her arms. "I'm going to lie down."

❖

Time elapsed. The bag of Holly's things lay on the bed within hand's reach, but Catherine couldn't bring herself to open it.

Holly was gone.

It wasn't something she'd foreseen happening. In her mind, she'd convinced herself she'd be able to make things up to Holly. It would never happen now. Hurt washed over her in waves. Emotions crashed inside her as if searching for some way to spill out. They were filling her to the brink, and keeping them bottled up was near impossible.

It hadn't felt this bad when Paula left.

After a lot of consideration, she decided it was because she'd done everything she possibly could to make Paula happy. She'd busted a gut trying to fight for their relationship to work. The regrets she'd had at the end were about letting Paula walk all over her and being too naive to realise she was being cheated on. All of that was easier to manage than the oppressive regret she felt now.

She hadn't fought for Holly. She hadn't listened or took on board her thoughts and feelings. Ignorance in her self-righteousness had ruled over everything. *She'd* known what was best. Only...she hadn't.

"Stupid idiot." She regretted it all and was disgusted by the way she'd treated Holly. No wonder Holly left. She'd probably look back and think she'd had a lucky escape. Catherine wouldn't blame her.

The only positive thing to come out of the whole experience was Kimmy.

She began to think about their future together. Change was on the horizon; she'd reached a decision. She was going to quit her job and find a new career. Money wasn't an issue. She had more than enough to comfortably tide her over for a few years if need be. She couldn't imagine herself sitting around at home doing nothing, but there was no rush to move straight on to something else. In time, she'd find a new career that made her happy and also allowed her to spend time with Kimmy.

Something in her mindset had changed. Her future wasn't something to fear or dread anymore, it was something to treasure and make the most of. A huge weight lifted from her body, giving her a sense of freedom. Like a butterfly spreading its wings for the first time after emerging from its cocoon.

In her mind's eye she pictured the blue butterfly of Holly's tattoo.

"It could never have worked out," she said, trying to force herself to believe the words. But she didn't believe them, no matter how many times she told herself.

The bedroom door creaked open and a tiny head popped around.

"Hello, Florence," Catherine said, rushing to hide the bag of things in the bedside drawer.

"Hello, Aunty Cat." Florence skipped into the room and Kimmy followed. They both jumped up on the bed. Catherine fussed Kimmy while Florence watched.

"Are you sad?" Florence asked.

She's must've learnt the directness from Beth. Catherine gave a shrug and said, "I'm okay."

Florence sprawled out, her head resting on Catherine's lap. Personal space was something Florence wasn't accustomed to. "I miss Aunty Holly real bad."

Catherine stroked the mop of hair. "Me too."

"Do you have a photo of her?"

Catherine was going to lie, but thought better of it. "Yeah, hold on." She took out her tablet and brought up the photos from Christmas Day. Florence looked through them all, giggling loudly. When she reached the end, she went straight back to the beginning and started the slideshow again.

"Them tops are funny," she said, talking about the Christmas jumpers. Her pudgy fingers swiped the next photo. "You look like a family. Mummy Holly, Mummy Cat, and baby Kimmy." Florence pointed to each of their smiling faces, her fingerprints leaving smudges on the screen.

Catherine stared at the photo in shock. Florence's childish words resonated, granting startling clarity. They did look like a little family, a happy family. It was crystal clear. How hadn't she seen it before?

Oblivious to the revelation she'd uncovered, Florence tossed the tablet onto the duvet, her interest waning. "You're a cat, Kimmy's a dog, and I'm a monkey." She stood on the bed and began bouncing.

Kimmy circled Florence's feet with her tail wagging and playful barks.

Catherine was struggling to recover from Florence's description of the photo. Something monumental had shifted inside her.

"Play pirates with me?" Florence asked. "Please, Aunty Cat? Please?"

"Okay," Catherine said weakly. Preoccupied by her thoughts, she followed Florence out of the room. In her mind she studied the photo she knew by heart.

❖

After witnessing a five-year-old having a tantrum about bath time, Catherine was relieved to return to her room with Kimmy. She removed the plastic bag and tipped the contents onto the duvet. Her heart sank as she inspected the items before her.

The pendant, apron, and dog toy sent a clear message. Holly didn't want anything from her, especially not reminders of the time they'd shared. She slipped the pendant over her neck feeling as the cool stone rested against her chest. It was weirdly comforting.

Kimmy sniffed the contents of the bag and a little whimper escaped.

"I know, Kimmy," Catherine said. She watched as Kimmy lay down on top of the apron and buried her muzzle into the creases of the material. "I miss her, too."

The thought of Holly driving back to London all alone whilst angry and upset freaked Catherine out. What if there was an accident? What if she crashed again? At least the snow chains were on the tyres. Knowing the car had an extra bit of safety made Catherine grateful for small mercies.

She spotted something beneath the apron and tugged some of the material out from under Kimmy's body, finding the Christmas and Birthday cards she'd given.

Kimmy looked up with sorrowful eyes. Something small and white stuck to her wet nose.

"What's this?" Catherine asked. She peeled the white thing off. It took a moment to recognise it was the slip of paper from Holly's fortune cookie. She fumbled around until she found her purse. She tore through the compartments and nearly gave up on the search, when she found her own crumpled slip. She flattened it out and read the words out loud. "There is only one happiness in life, to love and be loved."

"Are you trying to tell me something?" Catherine asked Kimmy. A little wag of the tail and a chuff sounded suspiciously like a yes. "It's too late. She's gone and couldn't have made it any more obvious she doesn't care."

That wasn't strictly true. If Holly didn't care, she wouldn't have been hurt or upset. Her speedy departure and the bag of belongings suggested she cared an awful lot.

"What am I going to do?"

Kimmy didn't offer up any answers.

The thought of never seeing Holly again left a gaping hole in Catherine's chest. But the thought of seeing Holly again in the arms of someone else, well, that was unbearable. She considered the advice Granny Birch might offer. Firstly, she would let rip with her disappointment of Catherine being cowardly enough to let Holly get away. Then she'd suggest Catherine think carefully and weigh up the pros and cons.

Holly cared for her, and Catherine reciprocated the feelings. They always seemed to be laughing. The sex was phenomenal. Being with Holly eradicated the loneliness that had consumed her for so long. They could have a future together and maybe go on to have children one day if Holly decided it felt right.

The cons were she'd risk losing Beth, Katie, and Florence. That was a scary prospect. She'd be completely alone.

In her head, she heard Granny Birch's voice. "Do the pros outweigh the cons, Catherine?"

"I think so," Catherine said, overly aware she was talking to herself and feeling uncomfortable. *I've actually lost my mind.*

"Don't be dramatic. I didn't raise a fool," Granny Birch's voice snapped in the familiar cantankerous way. "As the King said, you can't help falling in love. You know what you have to do. Hold your nerve and go all in, darling. There's no bigger jackpot than a future full of happiness and love."

Catherine smeared the salty tears rolling down her cheeks. "I'm scared," she said. But Granny Birch didn't reply. She was on her own.

CHAPTER TWENTY-FIVE

Catherine took a deep breath before walking into the living room. She would tell Beth and Katie the truth. Taking responsibility was the right thing to do. After that, she'd head back to London and hope with all her heart Holly would forgive her.

They looked up from the sofa in unison. Beth's eyes narrowed, and a frown creased her brow. "What have you done, Cat? You're wearing the same guilty expression you used to wear at uni. The same one you wore the morning after you raided the fridge and ate the rest of my cheese."

Catherine was rendered speechless. Sometimes Beth's ability to read her was unnerving. *If only eating cheese was my crime this time. And if she remembers cheese, she's definitely going to remember the promise.*

"There's something I need to tell you." She sat and wrung her hands. "I'm not sure how to say it."

"Just spit it out," Beth said, her gaze as unrelenting as her briskness.

"If you give me a chance I will," Catherine said, and after a big breath added, "I've fallen in love wi—"

"I knew it!" Beth said, grinning triumphantly. "I promised I wouldn't say anything, but Amanda likes you, too. Which is miraculous after the way you behaved."

"I can't stand Amanda."

"Excuse me?" Beth asked.

"She's quite possibly the most vulgar person I've ever had the misfortune of encountering."

Beth opened her mouth to retaliate, but Katie spoke first. "Forget Amanda. Cat, who is it you're in love with?"

Beth pursed her lips and bunched her jaws, clearly trying to refrain from speaking. It appeared curiosity got the better of her. She also wanted to hear.

Exhaling slowly, Catherine forced herself to keep eye contact. It was now or never. "I love Holly."

Beth's and Katie's expressions deadpanned.

"I've been a coward and I'm sorry. I asked her to keep our relationship a secret because I was scared you'd hate me and I'd lose you. But it meant she had to lie, which she hated doing. Then last night, she walked in when Amanda forced a kiss on me."

"Holly?" Beth asked in disbelief. "As in, baby cousin Holly?"

Catherine nodded and turned her attention to Katie. "I know she's family. It happened gradually—"

"I'd hardly call a few days gradually," Beth said.

"So, she left because she was upset?" Katie asked, seeming to take the news relatively well. "Not because something happened at the bakery."

Catherine gulped. "Yes. I wanted to talk to her and explain about Amanda, but in my drunken state I fell asleep. When I woke up she was gone. I never meant to upset or hurt her."

"I can't believe you've done this." Beth said, shaking her head in disbelief. Her expression was unreadable. "You promised me you'd never do this."

"I'm so sorry—"

"How could you, Cat?" Beth demanded. "You're supposed to be my best friend. Do the promises we've made to one another mean nothing? I thought they did. Obviously you don't."

"It just happened. I didn't set out with the intention of breaking our promise or falling in love. It's been a whirlwind. But I swear, I'm sorry."

"You've ruined everything." Beth swiped harshly as tears spilled.

"What exactly am I missing?" Katie asked. She looked from Beth to Catherine, clearly confused. "What promise?"

"It's already gone to shit. I'm going to end up losing you or Holly. When Florence graduates or gets married, it's going to be so fucking awkward. Holly's family, and we see her a hell of a lot more than we see you. She makes an effort. Do you expect me to not invite her to any gatherings or important events now? And what about you?" Beth asked accusingly. "Is this going to be more of an excuse for you to cut ties and shun responsibility? You were my best friend."

Were.

That single word broke Catherine's heart.

She opened her mouth, but there were no words that could make amends.

"What's going on?" Katie demanded.

Catherine explained the pact. She felt guilt-ridden. "So, you see? I broke my promise and ruined everything."

"What?" Katie asked, turning her attention to Beth. "You made her promise that?" Beth nodded and wiped her nose. Katie looked furious. "That was really shitty of you, Beth. You had no right to demand that of anyone, especially not your best friend."

Beth gaped. "After everything I've been through with my mum, you're actually saying that to me? You've seen how things turned out. I don't think it was much to ask."

"Listen to yourself. You're dictating who Cat can and can't fall in love with. That's none of your bloody business." Katie held Beth's stare.

"I…" Beth said, seemingly stuck for words.

"What happened between your mum and Gina was shit. I get that. But you can't control your loved ones because of your fear and insecurities."

Catherine didn't know what to do. The absolute last thing she wanted was for Katie and Beth to argue because of her. She'd never witnessed them have an actual argument. The usual bickering was commonplace, but Katie always backed down or pacified the situation. Right now she was angry.

"Look, you've been trying to set them both up with other people for ages. Why?" Katie asked.

Beth shrugged, and when Katie refused to speak, she said, "I wanted them to be happy."

"Exactly. I watched you go to all the effort. Some people might say it's because you're a busybody, but I know differently. You're a romantic through and through. It's one of the reasons I love you. You want them to be happy," Katie said calmly. "They've got a chance for that to happen, sweetheart. With each other. Don't begrudge them that."

"But what about if it ends badly?" Beth asked. She looked vulnerable.

"What if it doesn't?" Katie took hold of Beth's hands. "It's not got anything to do with us anyway. If it goes tits up, we'll help pick up the pieces. But I honestly think it could really work for them."

Beth turned to Catherine, her eyes red and puffy. "I'm sorry, Cat. Do you forgive me?"

"Don't be soft. There's nothing to forgive. You're the closest to family I have. I never intended to hurt you." Catherine hugged Beth tightly. The relief was incredible. She hugged Katie, too.

"You have our blessing," Katie said with a grin, patting Catherine's back. "We love you guys. What happens now?"

Catherine braced herself. She suspected this next bombshell wasn't going to be well received. "I need to try to make it up to her. I'm going back to London tomorrow."

"You're not serious?" Beth asked with significantly less uproar than Catherine expected. "How are you planning to get there?"

"Taxi. Kimmy can't go on a plane, and there's too much stuff to take on a train."

"Are you mad? Do you know how much that'll cost?" Beth asked, sniffing loudly.

"I don't care. Money is the least of my problems. I need to talk to her."

"Why can't you phone her like a rational person—"

"I'll drive you," Katie said.

Beth's head snapped to the side and her eyes bored into Katie. "What?"

"I'm going to drive them back."

"It's over eight hours there and another eight hours back."

"I'll sleep over at Catherine's tomorrow night and then come back the next day," Katie said, giving a nonchalant shrug.

"What about the Hogmanay party?" Beth asked. "Do you expect me to arrange everything by myself?"

"I'll leave early and be back in time to help set up."

Catherine couldn't bear to cause any more strife. "I'll get a taxi.

It's not a problem. Honestly." Beth and Katie ignored her, as if she wasn't in the room.

Beth's expression softened. "Promise me you'll be back in time for New Year's Eve. I can't stand the thought of not spending it with you."

"I promise. I wouldn't miss it for the world." Katie kissed Beth's mouth tenderly.

Blushing, Catherine's eyes darted around the room. *Awkward!*

"You better be back," Beth said firmly. "Because I don't fancy explaining this to Amanda by myself. She scares the crap out of me."

❖

Everyone was up bright and early. Catherine helped Katie load the car while Florence said a long, emotional good-bye to Kimmy. "I—don't want them to—go," Florence said in a howling tone, her face tear-stained as she hiccupped sniffles. She had her arms wrapped a little too tightly around Kimmy's neck.

Catherine knelt down to intervene. "Come here, Florence," she said. She opened her arms wide for a hug. Florence reluctantly let go of Kimmy, who hid behind a chair. Catherine wrapped Florence up in a big hug. "We have to go, but I promise we'll come back soon."

"Tomorrow?" Florence asked. A trail of tears leaked from her nose.

"Not quite that soon, I'm afraid."

"I's gonna miss you."

"We're going to miss you, too. But don't forget the big present waiting for you in the office. Only two more sleeps and you can open it," Catherine said. It seemed to do the trick. Florence perked up and smiled. Catherine was relieved she wouldn't be here to see Beth's expression.

"Right, family. We're all packed up and ready to go," Katie said. She picked Florence up and spun her around. Without the slightest hesitation, she covered the small, wet face in kisses.

"You're going to look after Mummy Beth, aren't you?" Katie asked. She carefully put Florence down.

"Yeah," Florence said, giggling as she wobbled around like a short drunk person.

"I expect a phone call as soon as you've made up with her. I want to hear all of the juicy details," Beth said. She hugged Catherine tightly. "I mean it. Don't make me come down there."

"That's if she forgives me," Catherine said. Butterflies swirled in her stomach.

"Grovel, a lot. Admit you were an idiot and apologise profusely," Beth said. She gave a painful prod in Catherine's chest. "Then grovel some more."

Rubbing the spot where she'd been poked, Catherine gave a nod and left Katie and Beth to say their good-byes in private. As soon as Kimmy was in her harness they could get on their way.

CHAPTER TWENTY-SIX

K atie left a little after four in the morning. Her parting words wished Catherine good luck with the subtle underlying threat that she better look after Holly or else.

Catherine wandered around her apartment in disbelief. How had she ended up living like this? The apartment was sparse, cold, and emotionless. No wonder she'd ended up depressed and on tablets. Even Kimmy wasn't overly keen.

"Come on," Catherine said. She opened the crate door and scooped a rumpled Kimmy into her arms. "You can share the bed with me tonight."

She carried Kimmy into the bedroom and put her on top of the duvet, while she climbed beneath it. Kimmy crawled up the bed and snuggled in beside her. In a matter of minutes, she was asleep. Her snorting doggy snores filled the oppressive silence.

Catherine had pretty much decided on what she was going to say to Holly. Nerves gripped her stomach in an iron fist. Adrenaline coursed through her veins in short, sharp bursts, priming her body for fight or flight. When she wasn't wired, she felt exhausted. She wanted it over and done with. All this waiting around was unbearable. If it wasn't for Katie suggesting midday as the earliest reasonable time to go over, Catherine would be there now.

The unknown scared her. Rejection and heartbreak were real possibilities. But she hoped a future with Holly was also possible. "All in," she whispered, her voice echoing off the bare, white walls. She hoped with every fibre of her being this gamble would pay off.

❖

Catherine began to panic as she awaited the taxi's arrival. Should she take a conciliatory gift? Flowers or chocolates, perhaps? That's what they did on films when they needed to grovel. She didn't want to turn up empty-handed and look like she didn't care. But she also didn't want to look like she was trying to bribe Holly's affections and forgiveness.

As a last resort, she phoned Beth, who pulled no punches in her reply. She was told not to take a gift on this occasion because she'd look like a creep. However, after they'd made up, she should buy Holly lots of gifts. Catherine thanked her and hung up as the taxi pulled up outside.

With Kimmy snugly in the footwell, Catherine gave the driver the address of the bakery. It took less than twenty minutes for them to reach their destination, the purple sign familiar from Holly's photos. She paid the driver and got out of the car; he drove off almost immediately.

She crossed the road and peeked through the window. The bakery was larger than she'd imagined, spotless and spruce inside. The building next door was deserted and looked like it hadn't been occupied for quite some time. Feeling watched, she looked up to the windows of the second floor, where Holly's apartment was situated. She couldn't see anyone, but the hairs on her body stood on end. With her heart bucking in her chest, she went in search of the front door and found it down an alley. An ancient-looking intercom protruded from the wall.

As Kimmy sniffed around, Catherine summoned what little courage she had left and pressed the button. She didn't hear anything and wasn't sure if it was working. After no initial response, she pressed it again this time keeping her finger on it for a few seconds longer.

Should she knock instead? What if Holly wasn't in? The more she thought about it, the more likely it was for Holly not to be in. Who was at home on New Year's Eve at lunch time?

"Shit," she said. Knocking on the dense wood with her knuckles produced a dull thudding. Still nothing. She tried to think up a plan of action. Why hadn't she thought to ask the taxi to wait a couple of minutes? Should she call for a new one, or wait here for when Holly returned?

"What do you want, Catherine?" Holly asked coldly, as her voice burst through the speaker.

Catherine wet her lips and said, "Please may I talk to you?"

After a long silence Holly said, "I'm busy."

"Holly, please, hear me out?" Catherine glanced at Kimmy. She sat with her head cocked to one side, looking at the door in confusion.

Long moments of silence stretched on.

"You get five minutes," Holly said, finally.

The door buzzed open and Catherine took solace from the fact Holly was letting her in and giving her the opportunity to talk at all. She carried Kimmy up the steep stairs, but halfway up she wriggled and squirmed for freedom.

"Kimmy, stop," Catherine said. She tried to keep her balance while simultaneously preventing Kimmy from falling. The excited whimpers made her look up. Holly waited at the top of the stairs, wearing a large blue fluffy dressing gown and green slippers.

"Through here," Holly said, holding the door open.

Catherine managed to get over the threshold before Kimmy's fight for freedom prevailed. In a flash, Kimmy scampered to Holly. The lead yanked from Catherine's hand and trailed after Kimmy's furry backside.

"Hey, Kimmy," Holly said. She knelt and unclipped the lead. Kimmy pranced and butt wriggled her way around Holly in circles. Her little body shook as if she couldn't quite contain her excitement.

Catherine struggled to swallow. Kimmy had missed Holly as much as she had. She watched Holly smiling as she tickled Kimmy's belly and hoped the smile was a good sign.

As if reading her mind, Holly looked up at Catherine, smile gone and gaze fierce. "Why are you here?" Holly asked.

"I need to explain w-what happened the other n-night."

"I saw what happened."

"No, you really didn't," Catherine said. "It's not what you t-think."

"Really? Because it looked like Amanda's tongue was in your mouth," Holly said angrily. She walked past Catherine into a different room.

After a moment of deliberation, Catherine followed. "It was, but not because I wanted it there. She kissed me. Forcefully. And I didn't kiss her back. I promise, Holly. One minute I was standing t-there, and then next she'd latched onto my mouth like a demented succubus."

They'd reached a spacious living room full of eclectic knickknacks, photo frames, ornaments, and two vases full of colourful tulips. A red sofa stretched along the back wall, and a large black rug spanned the floor. It was cosy.

"Do you expect me to believe that?" Holly asked. She folded her arms and glared.

"Yes," Catherine said. She spread her hands in a placating gesture. "You saw Amanda. You heard the drivel coming out of her mouth. You can't seriously b-believe I was interested in her?"

"I don't know you, Catherine. I thought I did, but I was wrong."

Stung by the words, Catherine took a step forward. "You do know me. You know me better than anyone, even better than I know myself. I never meant to hurt you. I'm so sorry."

"Apologising doesn't change anything."

"I told Beth and Katie about us," Catherine said. She blurted it out hoping it might make an impression.

"What? Why the hell would you do that now?" Holly asked vehemently.

Shit. That wasn't the kind of reaction she'd hoped for. "I thought it's what you wanted."

Holly threw her hands up. "I wanted it when we were together. We're not together anymore. So all you've done is air our dirty laundry in public. Jeez. All of my family will know by now."

"Holly, p-plea—"

"You should go," Holly said. Her gaze dropped to the floor. "You've apologised and I accept it. There's nothing more to say."

This was wrong. This wasn't going how she'd planned. It was all slipping out of her grasp and she was helpless to stop it. Had things gone too far to ever be recovered? Was this the end?

"I came all the way back here to make it up to you."

"I never asked you to."

"But I did anyway. Do you know how h-hard it was for me to come here? I've been scared shitless."

Holly looked up, her expression softening ever so slightly. "I don't know what you want me to say, Catherine. You really hurt me. I can't get over it because you turn up with Kimmy and say you're sorry."

"So, my coming here m-means nothing to you? It's an i-inconvenience?" Catherine asked, her frustration seeping out. When Holly didn't respond she knew she'd lost. Turning away, she called for Kimmy, and started toward the door.

"Why did you come here?" Holly asked quietly.

"Because..." Catherine clenched her fists and revealed her very last card. "I love you."

Those three words hadn't been included in Catherine's rehearsed speech. They'd forced themselves from her, spontaneous and true. The admission revealed her greatest fear. She'd tried to bury it because the ramifications were huge. But she loved Holly. She felt it with every beat of her heart and breath she took. She slowly turned around.

Holly's eyes were wide with surprise.

Catherine sensed this was her final chance to make Holly understand. She needed to reveal everything, strip herself bare to the point of absolute vulnerability and offer it all up to Holly. It was make or break time.

"The reason I asked you to keep our relationship a secret wasn't just because of Beth and Katie. I'd broken a promise I made to Beth years ago, but I'll explain that later. The truth is, realising how I felt about you terrified me," Catherine said. All of the pent-up emotions poured from her. "You turned my neat, depressed little w-world completely upside down and inside out. You made me feel alive. Because of you, I felt happy and actually started to like myself again. You made me question everything about my beliefs, life, dreams, and ambitions. More than anything, you made me question myself."

Holly stumbled back and managed to sit on the sofa. Her eyes followed Catherine intensely.

"To go from being alone and unhappy to suddenly having the p-prospect of a future with you blew my mind." Catherine shoved her hands in her pockets. "And now I know what being without you feels like. A future without you would be my own p-personal hell. Without you, it's like there's no sun. My world is cold and dark." Catherine lifted her glasses slightly and wiped away tears. "I don't know how you did it, but you fixed something inside of me that's been broken for so long."

"Why are you doing this?" Holly whispered, as her own tears began to trickle.

"I'm doing it to fight for us, like I should have done from the beginning." Catherine knelt in front of Holly. "I love you, Holly. Whether you let me back in or turn me away, I love you. I love you."

Holly snorted a half sob and laugh. "You've already said it."

"I want to keep saying it for the rest of my life. If you'll let me?"

"Say it again."

"I love you," Catherine said.

"Again."

Catherine took hold of Holly's hands. "I love you, Holly Daniels. More than I've ever loved anyone or anything in my entire life. You complete me. You're my reason for living. I love you."

"Good," Holly said. She squeezed their hands together. "Because I love you, too."

❖

After the tears subsided and the tension faded away, Holly gave Catherine and Kimmy a tour. The apartment was huge. It spanned the length and width of both the bakery and the empty neighbouring shop. Outside at the back, there was a small garden complete with a grassy lawn and a few trees, which was impressive considering the building was in a commercial area.

"It's wonderful," Catherine said. She graciously accepted the mug of coffee and sat on the sofa. "I can see why you fell in love with this place."

Holly smiled. "It's home. I just hope a new lodger will feel the same way."

"You still want to find one then?" Catherine asked, trying to be casual.

"It's more a matter of need, as opposed to want."

"I might know someone." Catherine took a sip from the mug.

"Really?" Holly placed her mug down on the coffee table. "That's great."

"Well, there are two of them actually."

Holly frowned. "There's only one spare room. I don't know how I'd feel about living with a couple. It sounds a bit weird."

Catherine fought back a smile. "They're not a couple. Well, not in the traditional sense."

Holly's expression changed to confusion. "Are you talking in riddles, or has all that crying messed up my brain?"

"I was hoping maybe you'd consider letting Kimmy and me move in."

Holly's eyebrows shot up. "You?" she asked in a gasp.

Catherine forced a weak smile. "Yeah." She was trying to play it cool, but inside she was dying a slow and painful death. She'd thought about it during the journey back from Scotland and all last night. She, Kimmy, and Holly were a family. Sure it was a big step suggesting moving in so quickly, but it made perfect sense and felt right. She hated her apartment, she wanted to be with Holly, and Holly needed a lodger.

"Catherine, I'm sorry, I…" Holly shook her head. "It's so soon."

"It is soon, I agree. But it makes total sense. You need a lodger, so why not have Kimmy and me? I can vouch for her."

"You have an apartment."

"It's not suitable for Kimmy. Plus, there are so many unhappy memories haunting the place, I'm ready to move on."

Holly nibbled her bottom lip. She didn't look convinced.

"If it puts your mind at ease, I'll keep the apartment for a while. If we give this a go and things go tits up, I can move back. There's no pressure. Wouldn't you rather have us here than some random stranger?"

"Yes," Holly said with a sigh. "But that's not the point. I feel like you're doing this to make things up to me."

"I'm doing this because I can't bear to spend another night without you. We could've died in that car, but we didn't. Life's too short to put things off and be overly cautious. Sometimes you have to take risks."

"So much for not being spontaneous." Holly's eyes searched her face. "This is crazy."

"Yes."

"We've only known each other two weeks."

"Not even that long."

"People will say we've rushed into it without thinking."

"So?"

Holly hesitated. "If we actually do this, we split everything right down the middle."

Catherine took hold of Holly's hands. "If that makes you happy, fine. But I need you to know I'm not trying to steal your independence or buy your affection. I hope in the future you'll let me share what's mine with you, and vice versa. Isn't that what a relationship is about?"

Holly nodded with blushed cheeks. "It might take some getting used to, but I'll try."

"It's agreed then? Kimmy and I are moving in here with you?" Catherine asked, needing to hear the confirmation from Holly's lips.

"Yes."

"Great." Catherine grinned like the Cheshire Cat. "Beth said not to give you a gift today because it would look like I was trying to bribe you. I don't think returning a gift counts, though." She unhooked the pendant from around her neck and offered it out to Holly.

"On this occasion I agree with you," Holly said. She turned so Catherine could put it on for her.

"Are you busy tonight?"

"Yes," Holly said. She turned to face Catherine, her expression serious. "I'm going to a party."

"Oh, okay." Catherine was disappointed, but she shouldn't have presumed Holly would be free.

"It's a housewarming party. Right here, in this apartment, with my beautiful girlfriend and our dog." Holly caressed Catherine's face tenderly. "I'll go get changed and then drive us to your place. We'll pick up the essentials and grab some food supplies on the way back."

"Sounds good." Catherine started to get up, but Holly held on to her arm.

"This will work, won't it?" Holly asked shyly, her vulnerability showing.

"Yes," Catherine said. She pulled Holly close and kissed her deeply. She made a silent promise she'd do everything in her power to make it work. She'd lost Holly once and would never let it happen again.

This was for keeps.

EPILOGUE

Two years and six months later.

Catherine entered and the tinkling of the overhead bell signalled her arrival. Cool air welcomed her in from the uncomfortable heat. A queue of people stood in line waiting to be served, so she squeezed past them and carried on into the adjoining room. Nearly all twenty tables in the tea room were filled with customers eating and drinking, the constant stream of chatter comforting. Gripping the handrail, she slowly climbed the four wooden steps, her swollen feet and ankles making the ascent more difficult. At the top she took a moment to look around. High, inbuilt bookcases filled every wall. Rows upon rows of books lined each shelf. Looking at them filled her with a sense of accomplishment.

"What on earth are you doing in here?" Eve asked. She jumped up from behind the counter and pointed to the vacant chair. "Get yourself over here and sit down this minute."

"I'm fine," Catherine said. She was too hot and uncomfortable for an argument. She wobbled over to the chair and sat anyway. Her feet were sore, her back was killing, and the weather was playing havoc with her internal thermostat.

"What would Holly say if she knew you were gallivanting around in your condition?" Eve asked with a loud tut.

Catherine sunk down into the plush seat and immediately felt better. "I'd hardly call walking down a flight of stairs and coming in here gallivanting."

"What's the point of hiring me if you're going to keep coming down here and bothering me all the time? You're worse now than you were at the old office."

"I'm fed up of being in the flat by myself. God knows I love her, but Kimmy's conversational repertoire leaves a lot to be desired." Catherine fanned herself with a sheet of paper she found close at hand. "Ow!" She winced and held her stomach.

"Ow? What's wrong?" Eve asked, swarming around her and making a huge fuss.

"Relax, it was a kick." Catherine stroked her humongous belly protectively. She tried to peer down, but her boobs—which were now massive—got in the way.

"What are you doing in here?" Holly asked, as she rushed up the stairs. "I nearly had a heart attack when I went home and you weren't there."

"I told her," Eve said. She crossed her arms and pursed her lips.

"It's cooler down here," Catherine said in a whining tone. She sat up so Holly could kiss her.

"You take being a workaholic to a whole other level." Holly smiled and perched on the counter. Her chef whites were splattered with dried stains of varying colours. "What are we going to do with you?"

"You could be the best wife in the whole wide world and go fetch me an icy glass of water."

"I'm due a break. I'll bring one back," Eve said. She wasted no time in leaving them alone.

"How are you and our little boy doing?" Holly asked. She tenderly caressed the bump.

"We're hot and bothered," Catherine said. She put the makeshift fan down. "I'm peeing every ten minutes and his rendition of Riverdance on my bladder isn't helping." Another kick confirmed her moaning was justified. Holly's eyes lit up, same as they did every time she felt the baby kick.

"Can I do anything?" Holly asked. She planted a kiss on Catherine's sweaty forehead and then one on the bump.

"Not unless you can magically induce my labour?"

"I'm afraid that's not my area of expertise, darling. He'll come out when he's ready."

"He's stubborn."

"He takes after his mum."

Catherine playfully swiped at Holly, but she jumped out of the way.

"I'd better head back. If you or our little boy need me, shout and I'll come running."

Catherine looked into her eyes, and the love she saw there was almost overwhelming. Unable to speak for fear of bursting into tears, she gave a nod.

"Hey, what's up?" Holly asked, kissing her again. "Why are you crying?"

Catherine swiped at a few stray tears and tried to get a handle on her hormones. Never in her wildest dreams did she ever believe she could be so happy. Each day the love she felt for Holly seemed to grow tenfold. It was a remarkable thing to feel truly content. Six months after moving in together, they celebrated their wedding day. It was supposed to be a quiet affair, but with Holly's family that was never going to happen. She couldn't complain; the Daniels clan had welcomed her with open arms.

A few months later, she made a new proposal to Holly, only this time suggesting they become business partners, too. As well as extending the bakery, they knocked through, creating an adjoining tea room and book shop. The business was going from strength to strength.

Her world revolved around Holly, Kimmy, and—as soon as he decided to make an appearance—their son. She couldn't stop herself from obsessing about their future. In only six months they'd be celebrating their son's first Christmas. When he grew old enough, they'd tell him the adventurous story of their first Christmas together: the accident, their rescue, the cabin, Kimmy's love affair with the tinsel, the fortune cookie, and the miraculous festive transformation that changed her.

"Please don't cry, darling. I hate to see you upset."

"I'm not upset. I'm just so…happy," Catherine said hoarsely, as more tears spilled down her cheeks.

"So, these are happy tears, then?" Holly gently wiped the tears away.

Catherine nodded vigorously.

"I suppose happy tears are okay," Holly said with a smile. "There's only one happiness in this life…"

Catherine snorted a laugh. Holly always knew how to make her feel better. The words from her fortune cookie had become their family motto, and had even been included in their vows.

"You've got to join in," Holly said with a mock pout. She caressed the bump fondly. "There's only one happiness in this life…"

"To love and be loved," Catherine finished, her fingers interlocking with Holly's and resting on her bump. "And I couldn't love you," she whispered to her bump, "or your mum and Kimmy, any more, even if I tried."

"Ditto," Holly said with a smile.

About the Author

Amy was raised in Derbyshire, England. She attended Keele University and graduated in 2007 with a BSc in philosophy and psychology. Amy's debut novel, *Secret Lies*, won a Golden Crown Literary Award in 2014 for the Young Adult category. She's married to her best friend and lovely wife, Lou. They share a love of Dolly Parton and live with their two gorgeous cats and naughty dog.

Amy loves to hear from readers and can be contacted at:

Email: authoramydunne@hotmail.com
Blog: http://authoramydunne.wordpress.com/
Facebook: https://www.facebook.com/amy.dunne.165

Books Available From Bold Strokes Books

Venus in Love by Tina Michele. Morgan Blake can't afford any distractions and Ainsley Dencourt can't afford to lose control—but the beauty of life and art usually lies in the unpredictable strokes of the artist's brush. (978-1-62639-220-5)

Rules of Revenge by AJ Quinn. When a lethal operative on a collision course with her past agrees to help a CIA analyst on a critical assignment, the encounter proves explosive in ways neither woman anticipated. (978-1-62639-221-2)

The Romance Vote by Ali Vali. Chili Alexander is a sought-after campaign consultant who isn't prepared when her boss's daughter, Samantha Pellegrin, comes to work at the firm and shakes up Chili's life from the first day. (978-1-62639-222-9)

The Muse by Meghan O'Brien. Erotica author Kate McMannis struggles with writer's block until a gorgeous muse entices her into a world of fantasy sex and inadvertent romance. (978-1-62639-223-6)

Advance by Gun Brooke. Admiral Dael Caydoc's mission to find a new homeworld for the Oconodian people is hazardous, but working with the infuriating Commander Aniwyn "Spinner" Seclan endangers her heart and soul. (978-1-62639-224-3)

UnCatholic Conduct by Stevie Mikayne. Jil Kidd goes undercover to investigate fraud at St. Marguerite's Catholic School, but life gets complicated when her student is killed—and she begins to fall for her prime target. (978-1-62639-304-2)

Season's Meetings by Amy Dunne. Catherine Birch reluctantly ventures on the festive road trip from hell with beautiful stranger Holly Daniels only to discover the road to true love has its own obstacles to maneuver. (978-1-62639-227-4)

Courtship by Carsen Taite. Love and Justice—a lethal mix or a perfect match? (978-1-62639-210-6)